THE
ENGINE'S
CHILD

JAN 2009

BALLANTINE BOOKS NEW YORK

THE ENGINE'S CHILD

HOLLY PHILLIPS

A Del Rey Trade Paperback Original

Published in the United States by Del Rey Books, an imprint of The Random House Publishing Group, a division of Random House, Inc., New York.

DEL REY is a registered trademark and the Del Rey colophon is a trademark of Random House, Inc.

ISBN 978-0-345-49965-3

Printed in the United States of America

www.delreybooks.com

987654321

Text design by Karin Batten

To Lynne, Gyllie, and Thea, for doing it right.

ACKNOWLEDGMENTS

Thanks to Liz Scheier and Jim Minz, not least for managing the midstream horse change without drowning anyone. Thanks to the beautiful Sally Harding, who works so hard with such enthusiasm and grace. And finally, thanks, as always, to Steven Mills, for the reading, the writing, and the soothing phone calls.

CONTENTS

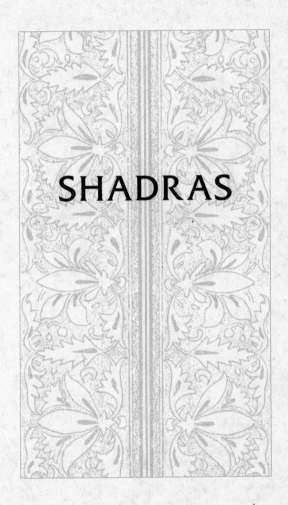

SHADRAS

THE BASTION

Moth slipped out the dormitory door and into the darkness of the porch. A small escape, a smaller victory, and not a certain one until she was well away, but still she paused to savor the pleasure of being alone. The rain beyond the porch roof sang and pattered and sighed. Electric lamps on the dam blazed all night, every night, but here, with the temple and half of the scholarium buildings between, the rain stole all the light. Passageways and cloistered yards were filled with falling sparks, while the buildings were only an absence, a darkness where nothing fell. Moth left the porch's shelter and suffered one sharp moment of misery before she grew resigned to the chill. The endless rain, the monsoon rain that refused to die. At least it smelled of clean stone and ferns, and not of the farts and borrowed breaths of her dorm mates. A few hours' escape was worth a soaking, and—Moth drew a quick, happy breath—

escape was only the beginning. The night was full of purpose, Moth's purpose, her lady's purpose, teeming through the darkness like the rain.

Tonight the priests were keeping vigil in the meditation hall beside the temple. Moth had taken her turn in the hours between noon and sundown, kneeling with the other dedicants while the damp ringed their prayer candles with halos. *Kistnu, absent mother, stretch out your hand. Kistnaran, mother of absence, turn your terrible face aside.* So they prayed for the holy breath of lost gods to snuff the candle flames, and so they prayed for an end to the rains, as if the two graces, the two miracles, were of equal weight. Moth, passing along the back side of the hall, felt the moss-slimed stones throb with three hundred murmured prayers and had to unclench her jaw. Why should it be harder to listen to all those souls begging for the absent Mother's notice than it had been to do the begging? Ah, but unlike the priests, she did not want or expect an answer to her prayers.

Her path took her behind the temple, where the new priests' dorm had swallowed up most of the old dancing yard, and where rainwater ran like a meandering stream across the foot-worn stones of what remained. Moth had lived all her life among the buildings of the *shadras* and knew nothing about the *hadaras,* the countryside. She had never heard the rush of a real stream over its rocks or the supple racket of wind-tossed bamboo, but she knew the gurgle of an overflowing gutter and the *tick-tack-tonk* of the consecrated bamboo chimes that hung from every eave. *Bless us, spirits of air, against the dark-shrouded evils of night,* the wind chimes said. A more cogent prayer, perhaps, but still, not one of Moth's. She grinned in private delight. Definitely not one of Moth's.

On the far side of the temple, close to the road that divided the bastion between the priestly scholarium and the fortress of the engineers, lay the scholars' hall, its angled roofs limned with electric gold from the lights on the dam. A bright roof raised by walls of bloody murder, themselves built on a foundation of secrets and lies: of course Moth came here first. She had hours yet before she was late, and the scholars' hall, where her daylight aspirations were aimed, was a perennial object of curiosity. Shining rain fell from invisible clouds, gurgled through gutters, spattered around brimming drains, so one slight Moth flitting across the scholars' yard would hardly be noticed, even if—especially if—she was not the only shadow abroad in the rain. Moth hurriedly tucked herself into the dark gap between two wings of the hall, where a choked gutter's overspill spattered her with frog slime and crumbs of moss. A quiet stream of people, a veritable furtive crowd, was jostling its way out of the high priest's dwelling and losing itself in the rain. *Aras* Baradam had been entertaining.

Oh, now *this* was interesting. *Aras* Baradam, new-minted high priest and scion of the wave-footed towers in the bay, was a son of privilege who could not speak a tidal orphan's name without a sneer. Moth. He said it as if he had just found one drowning in his soup, and he said it too often for Moth's liking. Why did he take notice of her when she tried so hard to be unremarkable? She could not fathom it. Perhaps it was simply that he had recognized, as she had with a single glance, a natural enemy. She suspected him of everything on principle, and by watching him closely had teased from his semblance of piety fuel for her suspicions.

And thinking this, she recognized one of the men ducking from that lighted doorway into the night. What was *he* doing *here*?

This went beyond the merely interesting. Startled, Moth eased herself out of the overflow and ran around one wing, through a covered passage where she left footprints on the flagstones, across a porch where more chimes clacked a counterpoint to the rain, and under a cloister, where she hung against a carved pillar, screened by living vines while she spied on the broad court fronting the temple and the scholars' hall. None of the figures slipping away from the hall bore a light, but *that* form she would have known if even the lights on the dam had died and the whole world had gone dark. She would have known him by the shape traced out by the falling rain. He paused. She held her breath. And instead of coming past her hiding place, as he should have done to make his way back to where he belonged, he walked away from her, climbed the broad temple steps, and disappeared within.

Very, very quietly Moth swore.

Once more around the hall and behind the temple. Time was not yet running out, but it was running, and so was Moth. As silent and unregarded as her namesake, she ghosted along the front of the meditation hall, where the carved screens between the pillars stung her with bees of light and a burr of sound. *Kistnu, absent mother, stretch out your hand.* Moth clung to the temple's front corner where the steps made a spidery niche, waiting for two more of *aras* Baradam's guests to vanish into the scholarium, and in that moment the massed murmur of prayers behind her softened into the long breathless *ssshhhooohhh* of the summoning, like the rumble of a wave dying with a last hiss of foam. Was it as late as that? Her heart beating quickly and lightly from the run and from more than the run, Moth hitched herself up onto the portico without bothering with the steps and padded around the corner of the eternally open door.

The immense bronze figures of the gods sat in shadowed splendor along the walls. Kistnu with the dreadful face of Kistnaran held like a mask half-hidden in her hand, beautiful Rohad-Haru ambiguously smiling at the nameless god with his ivory tusks and enameled claws, and wise Prosepurn with his golden key guarding the prayer-hung screen at the end of the nave, all of them flanked by their attendant saints, their

memorial stelae, their fonts and offering bowls. The priests
were at vigil, the scholars at whatever they were at (what *were*
they at?), the novices and dedicants in their beds—but with
such a crowd the temple would never be empty. Only Moth,
stalking her unwary quarry from behind the left-hand saints
and gods, knew those huge, somber, brooding images were all
hollow and full of spiderwebs behind.

He paced, reverent or thoughtful, down the open floor of
the nave; she scurried crablike between the gods and the wall.
Her bare feet were silent, but the air stirred by her passage
whispered against the hollow bronzes, making the faintest
imaginable hum. The candles left by absent worshipers made
more noise, their flames teased by damp and burning insect
wings, but still he slowed and looked about him, as if he had
been startled out of his thoughts. This hesitation gave Moth
the chance to achieve her place. By the time he had bowed and
lit a cone of incense at the oil lamp burning by Prosepurn's feet,
she was standing among the ranked saints at the god's right
knee, her shirt off and her wet breasts gleaming like polished
bronze. She breathed as lightly as she could to keep from giving the game away too soon, and she was giddy from lack of
air, from stifled laughter, from the freedom of the dangerous
night. He prayed.

"Aramis."

She breathed out his name and breathed in the drifting perfume of the incense smoke. He turned a slow circle, studying
the many shadows of the empty temple, dignified even as he
sought the source of this half-imagined sound.

"Aramis Tapurnashen."

He turned back and, deliciously, darted a suspicious look at
Prosepurn's face smiling high overhead. Moth made no sound,
but the laughter would not be denied and escaped her through
an involuntary wriggle of her spine. Aramis Tapurnashen
glanced down as if he had caught the movement in the corner

of his eye, and frowned at the clustered saints. The saints, wood and brass, copper and bronze, smiled or brooded or meditated on holy things behind demurely lowered lids. A sound fluttered up above the wreathing smoke, a word cut off just as it was begun, and then given a second chance at life with a sigh.

"Moth."

Saint Moth raised her eyes, drew one finger across her brooding smile, and drifted backward into the god's shadow. Aramis, his mouth taut and his dark eyes wide, wormed after her through the saints' close ranks.

"Moth?"

She breathed as softly as she could through parted lips. To find her, Aramis would have to put out his hands—and he did, reaching and finding with one motion, his touch warm and dry on skin still damp with rain.

"Moth," he whispered again, "this can't be right."

So he said, but his hands caressed her naked back as she stepped into his arms.

"It must be right," she whispered back. "It's love."

"But here?"

"Oh, everywhere."

Even whispers throbbed with muted echoes in the hollowed-out breast of the god.

"Do you have no scruples?"

"Shhh." Always so serious, her Aramis. Moth loosened the buttons of his sober coat and worked her hands through layers of cloth to his skin.

"Do you want to be found?" he said with real anxiety.

"No. So shush."

Which he had to do, as another late-night petitioner, walking with loud, honest footsteps, came into the temple. Shod feet spattered echoes across every stone and metal surface, and Aramis, deprived of argument, let his mouth be stopped by a kiss, and shortly thereafter let himself be pulled to the dust-carpeted floor. He always did warm eventually, hearth to Moth's flame. It was what drew him to her, she suspected, her reckless heat that lit a fire in his dutiful engineer's life, and sometimes that secret fire burned all the hotter for their silence.

A silence maintained, tonight, by dint of his palm against her mouth at the crucial moment. And even so, the bronze gods moaned in sympathy.

"Moth, my Moth."

They lay naked and dust-caked, as alone as two people could be beneath that roof, and traded words from mouth to ear.

"Aramis, my Aramis."

"In the temple, yet!" he said, though his dismay was tainted by smugness. "You lead me further astray every time I see you."

"Innocent boy. Did your mother never warn you about wandering abroad on such a night as this?"

"I know it is not safe for you to venture out at all. How many times can you be caught before you lose your position here?"

"I've never been caught."

"But—"

"But caught like this?" Her foot stroked his bare leg from buttock to heel, streaking it with dust. "I'd lose—"

"Everything."

"—more than my position. But not everything." No, not everything. "Would I lose you?"

"We'd both lose . . . You can't lose me, Moth. You could only cast me aside."

"Wicked Moth," Moth said, stung in her pride. "Leading you astray only to cast you aside. Poor helpless man! As if you weren't the one—"

"Sh!" His fingers brushed her mouth. "I know. My blame is no less, and your risk is far greater. And surely you know I would marry you if only—"

"Shhh, I know. The laws and my vows." *And me,* thought wicked Moth, who loved being a lover, but who had no great desire to be a wife.

"You know, and yet these reckless fits come over you and you forget."

"Or forget to care. But who's to see? Who will ever know?"

"Moth, Moth. I should have been back in the fort an hour past, and you should never have left the dorm." He paused, and though his whispered voice did not change, the pause itself was telling. "Whatever possessed you to come out tonight at all?"

"I knew you were coming," she said, twining her arms more firmly about his neck. "The rain told me."

"Moth."

"No, truly, I'll tell you. There is a little stream all hung about with ferns that creeps under the wall of the fort, across the inland road, through all the back ways of the scholarium, and into the secret lake that lies hidden within the mists of the dedicants' unconfessed dreams in the low place outside the dormitory door."

"Moth . . . ," Aramis sighed.

"And down that little stream today swam a poor bewildered frog, a froglet so young and new it still had its tail a-wagging between its tender thighs."

"Moth." This half-resigned and laughing.

"And this poor lost and lonely froglet, out in the terrible world alone for the very first time, told me a wondrous tale. Did I mention this frog had a tail?"

"You did."

"A most wondrous tail—I mean the tale he told, of a striding hero and his mysterious quest—"

"Moth! Mad girl, amaze me: speak one word of sense."

Her turn to sigh. "I came out tonight to gaze in humble awe at my betters. And this will amaze you—it certainly amazed me—for among the so very quiet, the *so* very discreet guests of the high priest and scholar, the lordly *aras* Baradam, was none other than that engineer of modest birth, that secret hero to frogs and other tender creatures, Aramis Tapurnashen himself."

He was silent for two breaths. Three. "Gods," he said at last. "And I thought you risked too much with *this*. What are you thinking, to spy on *aras* Baradam!"

"I can't be curious about the new lord of my own demesne? What are you risking, Aramis, sneaking off to secret meetings on the wrong side of Vashmarna's walls?" Where, it abruptly occurred to her, he had never sneaked to attend a secret meeting with her. Suddenly she was more than curious.

"Nothing," he said shortly.

"Ah," she said, an aside to the eavesdropping saints: "He was an invited guest, and with permission from his superiors."

"Moth—Oh, it's hopeless! But please, don't speak of it. Please. Not even to me."

"Who else could I . . . Oh . . . except *aras* Baradam, of course."

"Better he find you like this. That's plain truth if only you could recognize it."

"And you scold me for the risks I take! What are you involved in that has to be so dangerously defended?"

"Nothing! Oh, gods, you'll never let it go, will you? I can't tell you, Moth. I've given my oath."

"*Your* vows, is it now?"

"Moth." It was an anguished sigh.

"No, no. Keep them. Don't tell me. I'll tell you." Moth had only half-guessed before, but she felt the smooth cool exhilaration of that guess flowering into fact. "You and the noble *aras* both belong to the Society of Doors."

*   *   *

Moth waited in the temple's dark portico while Aramis made his way across the courtyard and started up the crooked street toward the scholarium gate and the other half of the divided bastion, the fort where he, like all the engineers of Vashmarna's limited demesne, belonged. With his halfhearted denial hanging between them, he had not parted from her kindly. He was no good with lies, her honest lover, and resented her for trapping him with the truth. Well, she had resentments of her own tonight. To think he'd had the temerity to scold her! But it was less a grudge than a smudge on the shining delight of her knowledge. *Aras* Baradam, Baradam Ghar, lord of the scholarium and son of the lord of the bay, was a member of the outlawed Society of Doors, dreaming of forbidden worlds. A fascinating, a delicious secret, worth a lovers' quarrel.

The lover in question disappeared into the black cleft of the street, and Moth slipped down the stairs and padded after him. Not to follow him—she knew where he was going—but because the first part of her way followed the same path as his. She was late by this time, the hour had to be approaching midnight, and she could not run without overtaking Aramis, who thought she was bound for her bed. How many secrets did this night hold? One more than Moth knew. Always at least one more than that.

And was this it here? The rain still pelted down, as steady and invasive as the night, and the form hovering in the narrow passage between the scholars' hall and the library was barely a glimmer in the corner of her eye. A curve of darkness traced by the rain's stolen light, a rounded edge etched against the shadow of other edges, a sliding gleam of water caught and diverted by something too large and clean-lined to be human. Squinting through the water trickling across her face, Moth could only guess at a shape. Wheels tangled within wheels? Whorls of glassy obsidian, dark coiled shells. She was shocked by the strangeness of the thing in such familiar surroundings. She stopped and stared, but the greater shock came treading on the first one's heels. Not that she did not know what it was, but that she did not know *whose* it was. This secret touched on hers, but was not hers, and when the thing, the ungainly manifestation of power, withdrew into the lightless passage, she darted after as if she could tear answers out of it with her bare hands.

It rolled away from her down the passage with a smooth, complex, yet awkward motion, a concatenation of too many gears spinning one within the next, dimly illuminated by the rain-caught reflection of the generating station's distant lights. The manifest rolled like a boatload of barrels tumbling in the surf, yet it was fast enough that Moth had to run to keep it in view. Down the back side of the library, from corner to corner across the junior priests' cloister, into the covered passage beside the copyists' hall. There was a small fish-oil lamp burning there, sheltered from the rain, and as the manifest rushed by, the yellow light splashed across the wet convolution of wheels, as lively as a blinking eye. It seemed impossible that the thing should be so real, so huge, and so silent. It should have thundered like the wind-driven surf. Moth hesitated between step and step. But it rolled quietly into the black night of the senior priests' cloister at the far end of the passage, and Moth's hesitation became a skip in her running as she held to her pursuit. Down the passage, back into the rain. Where? It was half a guess, a flick of movement in the corner of one eye, that turned her to the left, where another, narrower passage lay between the copyists' hall and the dedicants' dormitory, where her own bed awaited her. This was dangerous territory if her empty cot had been noticed. Moth flew across the cloister's sand, and with the rain streaking warm and salty into her mouth, sea-soned by sweat, she reached for the latch of the passage door and—

And flung herself back into the rain, for that particular pas-sage had no latch and no door; and that narrow opening, as black as the inside of a living skull, was no doorway. It was the manifest's mouth, its eye, its open arms: the lightless center of its innermost wheel. Moth stepped back and back, hollow with horror and the need for air. The rain was silent on the sand. Sad, hungry, and terrible, the manifest blinked, or turned, and fell away into the dark.

Moth, profoundly disconcerted, bent over with her hands on her knees, gasping and queasy from the run. Her mind relived that instant, that step she had not taken into the door that was not there, and veered away. She had never seen, never imagined the possibility of a manifest she had not herself raised up out of nothing. As the shock of that touch—that almost-step into the manifest's heart—receded, a deeper tremor made itself felt, questions beating within her like a second, alien heart. Whose working had cast that shadow? Whose power, wielded to what end? Whose trespass on her most secret and private realm? But then it occurred to her that in fact she prob-ably did know whose, and with a hot rush of anger she headed for the scholarium gate at a grim and purposeful jog.

THE TIDAL

She exited the scholarium gate and, despite the press of time, covered the tail end of the inland road at a walk. Her gut was still queasy after her exertions, probably a memento of unsavory haunts, but more than that, a running figure would attract undue attention at this time of night. The road that divided the bastion in two was deserted, but Vashmarna's fort, lit up by a badly hung string of dripping bulbs, was not. The rounded archers' windows above the lights were black, as was the deeply overshadowed gate, but Moth knew there were watchers. Men with guns. And who among them would connect Aramis Tapurnashen's late return with the weary dedicant in her creased and dirty shirt plodding off on some late errand of her own? Moth could not think why anyone should, but she found herself worrying for her lover's sake. He took a lot of chances for a man who hated risk, and she owed him better, or at any rate, loved him too well to add her chances to his. So while Aramis presumably took himself to his virtuous bed behind that drearily bedizened wall, she plodded on, insignificant Moth half-invisible in the rain, down to the end of the street.

The street that divided the bastion was also the end of the great inland road that strung together the city and the countryside, the *shadras* and the *hadaras,* the two halves that made up the *rasnan* that was both *island* and *world.* And like an electric cable plugged into its source, the road's end became a bridge, and the bridge, with its white stone and its polished lamps, sprang away from the shore and arced—electric ribbon, stony spark—across the water to the towers in the bay. The towers that both generated and consumed all the wealth and power in the *rasnan.* The towers that rose up ghostly and shining in the rain from the foam-toothed reef far out at the seaward edge of the bay. A world of halves, Moth thought. It should be the first lesson every novice learned. Scholarium and fort make the bastion. Bastion and bay make the *shadras. Shadras* and *hadaras* make the *rasnan. Rasnan,* the known human world of the island, and *mundab,* the vast unknown world of the uncharted ocean, make . . . what? But there the catechism had to end, for to the priests and the common people—to all the people of the *rasnan*—the *mundab* made nothing. It was the forbidden, the unknowable, the unknown.

Except, perhaps, to the slum dwellers of the tidal. But the tidal, crouched in the muck between low and high tide, stranded in the unlivable margin between *mundab* and *rasnan,* was left out of everyone's calculations. A fundamental truth that suited Moth, and Moth's lady, well.

Which was why, while the road ran to the bridge, and the bridge to the shining towers, Moth slipped aside to the steep zigzag stairs that crept down into the bridge's shadow. The tidal. Moth bared her teeth in an ugly grin, but she thought it: home.

"Who's there?" A demand from the deep shadow at the foot of the stairs.

Moth squeaked in surprise, then gathered herself to say hotly, "Where?"

"Oh, it's you," said the voice disgustedly.

"I cannot begin to imagine what you could possibly mean by that remark," said Moth.

"Shut up and get in," said the voice. "You're dead late, you know."

"I'm not *late*," Moth said. "I'm *delayed*."

"Black, bloody gods, will you hurry up and—"

"Get into what? I can't see you!"

"I'm right at the foot of the steps. And go ahead and shout about it, I'm sure the bridge guards don't care."

"They're guarding the inside of the guardroom tonight," Moth grumbled, but by groping down the last few steps she found the weed-slimed landing and the wooden deck of the little tidal scull. A hand belonging to the voice gripped her sleeve and hauled her inboard.

"Gah, you're soaked."

"It. Is. Raining." Moth paused for thought, and added, "Again."

"I hear they're making coats for that nowadays."

The scull was pushed off and, propelled by its single oar, skidded as if oiled over the water that drowned the mud streets of the slum.

"Coats," Moth muttered. "I'm lucky they give me a shirt." She was shivering now that she was still.

The oar paused, the boat drifted, a lump of fabric, damp and warm with body heat, was dumped into her lap, and the oar resumed its work.

"Now you'll be cold," Moth said, but she put the canvas jacket on.

"Least I won't complain about it," said her benefactor.

"Anyway, what do you mean, you were delayed? Delayed by what?"

Moth, reminded of Aramis, felt a sneaky grin tug at her mouth, but she was still angry about the manifest, and said shortly, "Ask Istvan."

"Oh, here we go again. Another mystery, another argument, another *something*."

"See? Did I or did I not tell you you wouldn't be bored?"

Finally, the voice in the darkness laughed.

The tidal's night was black; only the lamp-lined bridge shed enough light to distinguish buildings from rain, and it was not always enough to distinguish water from rock. All the inundated streets were studded with foot-stone paths, and Silk—for it was Moth's sister-orphan Silk who captained the scull—swore as she thumped the fragile hull against a stone that did not quite raise its head above the oil-calm, rain-pocked tide. The tenements that were scattered across the tidal plain wherever solid bedrock could be found were dark, their shutters latched and paper screens drawn against the night.

"The night," Moth intoned, "of the shadow gods."

"What are you on about now?"

"I was just thinking . . ." How afraid people were of what they did not understand. But had she not been afraid when the manifest in the scholarium had turned on her, or offered itself to her, or whatever it had done?

"It had better be the night of the shadow gods," Silk said, "or there will be trouble to pay. And by pay, I mean you and me. I've never seen such a crowd, and *they*"—Silk gave the oar a hard dig—"have been *waiting*."

Silk was good at ominous. When they were small, a pair of orphan children hunting mud snakes in the tidal weeds, Moth and Silk had played games of master and servant, dock bully and victim, pimp and whore—all the roles available to such as them. Only games, but while Moth had had her lessons, her sponsor, her place in the bastion when she survived to a novice's age, Silk had had nothing *but* their games. There was always something of the bully about her, and something of the slave.

She had a point, though, about the shadow gods. It could be deadly to frustrate a tidal crowd.

The fire shrine was as dark as its neighbors, barely visible against the cliff that footed the bastion wall, but it was audible. Even before Silk grounded the scull on a submerged step, Moth felt the buried rhythm, as if the shrine were trembling hard enough to shake the air. She was reminded of holding Aramis tight enough to feel his heartbeat, and felt a warming excitement. But that vibrant pulse was nothing to the explosion of sound when Silk hauled open the door.

BADAKADABADAN.

A rumbling storm of sound, a rhythm so thunderous in its unity it threatened to shake down the walls of the shrine.

Like the streets, the foundering shrine was awash with seawater reeking of brine and the tidal ooze. Fish-oil lamps, their red flames dazzling after the darkness outside, were doubled in the oily mirror of the wet floor, like each of the dozen saints that sat marooned on their weed-draped pedestals. Their cast and carven faces mingled with all the living faces staring down.

"How many?" Moth shouted into Silk's ear. "How many tonight?"

Silk shrugged. "Four hundred, five?"

Moth stared, awed in spite of herself. Men, women, children were crammed onto the swaying galleries built from driftwood and stolen bamboo, the smoke-veiled firelight sketching their features against the dark. A lip, a cheekbone, a liquid eye: Was this a saint cast in bronze or was it a man? Expressionless as a statue, wearing a mask of hunger and avid prayer. Hands pounded a complex rhythm against the banisters, a demand for appeasement, a summoning, a voiceless prayer—no quiet meditation here, no whispered holy breaths. Just rude, loud, restless, risky life. Just a hunger for change.

BADAKADABADAN. The tidal drumbeat like the racing heartbeat of a god, a thunderous wave great enough to drown the entire seaside slum.

Moth had to catch her breath, as if she had run the whole way here. Her heart pounded in time with the pounding hands; her stomach threatened to climb up into her throat. Silk dragged the shrine's door shut, closing in the noise and the light, and the two of them stepped down into the water and waded through the reflected faces and the flooded saints to the other door. Even when it was shut with them on the far side, the rhythm still shook the air.

Badakadabadan.

"You found her." A plain statement loaded with a wealth of delayed retribution.

"Hamana," Moth said.

"Dedicant," Hamana said just as distinctly.

The greenguard captain stood aside, and her crew pressed themselves to the walls of the staircase that led to the priest's room above. Moth edged upward through the sweat-smelling ranks with Silk behind her, knowing that if the impatient celebrants in the shrine tried to force an entry into the inner mysteries, some of them would be killed. Maybe quite a lot of them. And who outside the tidal would notice, or care?

Istvan Soos was waiting at the top of the stairs.

"You're late," he growled.

"I was delayed," Moth snarled back.

"And away we go," muttered Silk.

"Delayed by what?"

"By—"

"Why do I ask? We don't have time. The tide's already on the turn."

"It—"

"Do you want to be here at sunrise?"

"Listen to me!"

Istvan Soos, a narrow little man with gray hair framing a seamed and bitter face, folded his arms across his chest. "Unless it has something to do with tonight's work, I don't want to hear."

"It has everything—" This time Moth cut herself off.

"Well?"

But logic had finally caught up with Moth, and she realized that the manifest in the scholarium could not have originated here. Not only was it farther than any manifest could travel, by all she knew of them, but if the manifest had been sourced here in the shrine, then why were her colleagues so impatient? Why was the crowd still demanding its spectacle, unappeased?

But then—Moth's jaw sagged—did that mean the manifest was raised by someone inside the scholarium? Who? Her skin sizzled as if she had come too close to a raw electrical field, her body quivering between shock and incipient fury. It almost didn't matter *who*, only that there *was* a who, a trespasser in Moth's most precious, most secret, most intimate space.

"Well?" Istvan said again.

Bright with unfocused anger, Moth smiled and moved lightly to the inner door. "Nothing. Did you know the Society of Doors is active in the scholarium?"

"Yes." Istvan let her pass him, staring narrowly at her face.

Of course he did. Moth's guess to Aramis had been pieced together from fragments of Istvan's conversation, as much as from her own spying on *aras* Baradam. *Aras* Baradam and the Society. The Society . . . and manifests outside the scholars' hall?

Oh, stupid Moth. Listen to yourself. The *scholars'* hall!

"When we have time," Moth murmured to her old teacher, "you really must tell me what you know about Baradam Ghar."

"He's the Ghar's only son and he took priestly vows," Istvan said, his voice as tense as his eyes were wary. "After him there will be no more of his blood. That's all you need to know."

Moth wanted to shake it out of him. Her first and oldest teacher, and *still* he would not tell her outright the things she needed to know. But now was not the time. Still smiling, she opened the door and stood aside for him to enter the inner shrine before her. He sidled past her without looking away from her face, and when Silk followed him through the door, she murmured to Moth, "*That* was your delay?"

Moth made a face and stepped in after them, closing the door behind her.

(*Ba*daka*da*badan, the rhythm still trembling from the front of the shrine.)

The rest of the *mundabi* were waiting for her there, Nindi and Tarun and *aras* Crab, but Moth's attention was captured, as it was every time, by the engine.

My engine, was Moth's private thought, in defiance of the *mundabi* and her lady both. But it was hers. If it was anyone's, it was hers, like the power that made it. But her skin shivered again—the repeating shock like the lingering chill of the rain—when she remembered the manifest behind the scholars' hall. The sense of trespass grew every time she thought of it.

The *mundabi* had taken out all but a gallery rim of the upper floor to accommodate the engine's great size, and it rested now, only half-complete but still enormous, with its base in the tidewater and its upper portion rising within arm's reach of the gallery, close enough to touch if anyone dared. It glowed with the sheen of oiled metals; it captured the lamplight and cast everything else into gloom. Forgetting the frenzied congregation, her colleagues, her queasy and distracted self, Moth rattled down the access ladder and splashed onto the floor.

Istvan Soos followed her down. "Have you studied the plans for the next phase?" he asked, a bad-tempered teacher holding his pant legs out of the brine. He had skinny calves.

"I don't have to study it. It's mine."

"You are arrogant."

"No," Moth said, believing herself. "Honest."

Istvan trailed behind her, scowling, as she circled the engine. Lit from above, it was a dark, inhuman pattern, a half-realized design, as if the shadows of its underside were drawn in ink, the gleam slipping down the curve of the great wheel, a spill of brassy paint. Moth laid her palm against a shaft to feel the cold, frictionless slide of the unreal metal and was reminded of the touch of the manifest in the scholarium passageway. How had she not recognized that aching, bitter cold? She took her hand away with a shiver. For an instant, the engine had stirred, a deep internal quiver, as if it too were impossibly alive. Feeling a rare desire to be out from under the engine's shadow, she splashed back to the ladder and climbed up, following Istvan's callused heels.

The ceremony belonged to the *mundabi;* the power belonged to Moth. Usually she was patient with them, needing their involvement, but tonight she had to grit her teeth to keep herself in her role. She lived in the temple by day. She had no need for yet more rituals adapted by Istvan to call upon the *mundab*'s "gods."

"They are not gods!" she had said to Silk once, exasperated by Istvan's dogma.

"How do you know?" Silk had replied. "How do you know what the old gods once were?"

"I know what they are now," Moth had said, but Silk had not pursued the argument. She was not interested in philosophy, only rebellion.

Now Moth, dutiful dedicant, followed the *mundabi* with clenched jaw through the Gathering, the Un-naming, the Five

Silences, the Call, all the while listening to the throb from the fevered shrine, the groan of old foundations, the lick of water against the engine's base. Born for the water, Moth thought of her creation, a half-grown fish straining for the open sea. Her impatience became the engine's need. She was certain she could feel its desire for motion, for power, for release. The *mundab*—unknown ocean, ocean of the unknown—was calling.

How does the nameless world speak to her, this outlaw Moth? It does not. It washes through her and about her with currents and tides that bear her up, that move her and let her move. It is an ocean she was born into like a fish who hatches knowing how to swim, and she has never understood those who cling to their tiny isle and pray for the breath of absent gods. It is her home, this current, this tide, this unknown, uncharted, and forbidden world. She breathes it, she swims it, and with an act of will like a flex of youthful muscle, she bends it, or it bends her. The fish becomes the current, the current is the fish. The others drag the illicit electrical cables into position, the others pray, but it is Moth, the only real *mundabi*, who spins Vashmarna's stolen power into steel and brass and gold. Electricity flares, dancing in lightning arcs across the midnight waters. Shadows school and dart about the confines of the room, fleeing the actinic whips, but the current captures them, orders them, molds them into the new part bound to the solid world.

For a thrilling moment the engine quickens as if it were alive, complete, ready to achieve its purpose. The great wheel whirs in a near-silent rush; the drive shafts churn the flame-lit steam. Beyond the door to the shrine there sounds a triumphant roar and the thunder of feet dropping down ladders to splash across the inundated shrine. The shadows that escape the making, the manifests of Moth's work, flee half-formed into the tidal night, drawing the rhythm-mad celebrants after them, a holy hunt chasing down their shadow gods.

The shrine emptied. The engine slowed. Silence fell.

Then Silk stirred, wrapping her arms around Moth's shoulders and kissing her sweaty forehead. "Next time," she breathed. "Maybe next time it will be done."

That was the message Moth had to send to her lady sponsor before she returned to the bastion, the temple precinct, and home. Maybe next time the engine would be done. Maybe next time they would have their living generator impelled by the force of the *mundab* itself, giving them power as vital and as freely flowing as blood driven by the heart of the world. Maybe next time. Exhausted and filthy, Moth dragged herself back to her place in the scholarium just in time to run into *aras* Baradam, most pious of priests, on his way to the temple for a private prayer in the cold gray fog of dawn.

THE BAY

Maybe next time.

The message had come hard on the heels of Vashmarna demesne's latest crisis, and Lady Vashmarna had transcribed it and forgotten it in the same late-night moment. Now, even with her hasty scrawl hidden facedown on her breakfast table, Lady Vashmarna found herself staring at the rice paper as if she could force it to produce more words. *Explain yourself!* she wanted to say. More and more she regretted this line of communication, which, however secret, could run only one way—the wrong way, with Lady Vashmarna unable to give instructions or chastisements. Too much was being left to her agent's discretion; too much was happening outside of Lady Vashmarna's view. And she, lady of the demesne of power and light, had too much else demanding her attention, but it was only the unexpected flash of sunlight through parted clouds—

sunlight that strewed diamonds across the bay and glared white as lightning from the blank side of the paper—that forced her gaze away. She looked up, ignoring the dark silhouette of her latest petitioner, and rested her tired eyes on the northern view.

As *the* Vashmarna, she could have taken residence in any tower in the bay, but she had chosen the landward side of Shaudarand, the tower that footed the inland bridge and housed the bureaucrats, legalists, and fighting men who were sworn, as she was, to the shaudah's service. Here there was nothing but water between her and the terraced hills of the *hadaras,* the many-roofed bastion, the cankerous mass of the slum at the water's edge. To those who accused her of eccentricity, Lady Vashmarna extolled the virtues of the island view, speaking of the peaks far inland, raw black shapes rising above the green of the fields, and the conversations they had with the oceanborne clouds. But the secret truth, the central truth, was that Lady Vashmarna kept the rooms and the view as a penance. A penance, and a reminder that while her policies might yearn toward the open sea, it was here, here on this fragile fragment of land, that the world would be lost or gained.

Maybe next time, oh merciful gods.

The clouds rolled over the sun; the light faded back to gray; the vivid greens and ruddy browns of the flood-scarred fields blurred behind the veil of rain; and Lady Vashmarna sighed and touched her fingers delicately to her eyes.

"Master Tapurnashen, please, sit. You loom."

"*Jinnu.*" The fort's liaison bowed and settled himself carefully into the offered chair.

"Are you aware that the shaudah has summoned me to a private audience this morning?"

"No, *jinnu.*" The engineer was wearing a formal jacket of the kind that buttoned closely from knee to chin, and he had the look, familiar to Lady Vashmarna, of a young man half-strangled by his own collar.

She did not intend to put him at ease.

"We suffered a blackout on the bridge, Tapurnashen-*andas*. We suffered stalled elevators and malfunctioning water pumps. We suffered dark corridors, stopped fans, and a gallery opening wherein two sculptures were damaged and one defaced in the sudden loss of light. I mention this last, Tapurnashen-*andas,* because the artist had been sponsored by the Ghar and the three damaged pieces were all from his private collection. My demesne is a shambles, Tapurnashen-*andas,* and this—" Lady Vashmarna tapped the written report on her breakfast table. "*This,* Tapurnashen-*andas,* is simply not sufficient to my needs."

"No, *jinnu,*" the engineer said into the lengthening pause.

"Shall I take you with me into the shaudah's presence? Would you like to be the one to tell our gods-blessed overlord, 'O mighty shaudah, most gracious lord, we do not know what happened'?"

Tapurnashen's skin was too dark to show a blush, but he had a sturdy jaw. When he clenched it, it became even sturdier. "I am at *jinnuju*'s service."

Lady Vashmarna's finger went on tapping the inadequate report. After another silence, which he did not give in to, she said softly, "They chose you as liaison because they think I am easier on young men. Do you trust your superiors' wisdom?"

His jaw still tight, Tapurnashen met her gaze. His eyes were not so dark as his skin, which gave them an animal brightness, but he was not a man to be stampeded. Lady Vashmarna sighed.

"Aramis, I do value you, but can you give me *nothing*?"

"*Jinnu,* I give you what the investigators give me." Reading her shift in mood, he pulled at his collar and settled himself more comfortably into his seat. "Truthfully, I was up with the chief engineer until dawn. We have not sat idle while we waited for the next event, *jin'*. We have been contriving new meters, assigning doubled watches, replacing cables even when they test clean. As soon as the bridge lights started to fade, the whole of the daytime shift was out of bed and looking for the problem. The turbines are fine, the transformers, the fuses, the cables: they're all fine. We simply . . ."

"Lose power from time to time."

Tapurnashen gestured, helpless, tired, frustrated, and with a slow anger building somewhere beneath that ill-made coat. It was curiously reassuring, Lady Vashmarna thought, that honest men were so easy to read.

"But my staff here tells me there is more to the matter than a simple power drain," Lady Vashmarna said. "We have localized surges, freakish events. My maid swore she was chased by a demon that leapt from lightbulb to lightbulb in the corridor last night, flaring and bursting the bulbs just in front of her as she walked. The towers are full of such stories, and while one might deplore the superstition, the fear is real. What does one say?"

"Demons in the wires."

"That is not an answer!"

Tapurnashen shrugged. "*Jinnu,* it threatens to be the only answer we have. Things have been seen that . . ." He groped for a word.

"Very well. Engineers are not exempt from the common run of human fears."

"No, we are not," he said with an attempt at wry humor, "but at what point do superstition and fear become evidence?"

"Evidence of what?"

Keeping his eyes on hers with a visible effort, the liaison said, "There is a rumor that a shadow god was seen in the scholarium last night."

That silenced her for a moment. "Prosepurn the Wise. Is

that the explanation you would have me take to the shaudah? The drunken imaginings of some addled novice with the mud still wet between his toes? There is no such thing!"

"Perhaps not, *jin'*, but the shadow cult is real enough." Tapurnashen shifted forward in his chair. "What if the shadow cult is at large in the scholarium? And even if it is not the cult itself . . . *Jin'*, have you considered the temper of so many celibates crowded together in too small a space? Especially the many who are, as you say, from the *hadaras* and the tidal. With the scholarium so near the generating station—"

Lady Vashmarna cut him off with a lifted hand. "One does follow the direction of your thoughts." She gazed at the window without, for once, taking in the view. "Sabotage" was the word he carefully did not say, the word—grant the man his due—she did not want to hear. "I notice, merely as a remark, that you did not include any of this in your written report."

"No, *jinnu*. As you say, superstitions, rumors, fears . . ."

Lady Vashmarna gave him a grave look. "Politics is a fell disease, young man, easy to catch and impossible to cure. Take care."

He stood and bowed with a shuttered gaze. *"Jinnuju."*

She waved him away.

The tea had gone cold. Lady Vashmarna started to ring for a fresh pot, then stopped. Was there any comfort left in the world? Sabotage and shadow gods in the bastion, forbidden cults at work in the scholarium, even her own tame rebels in the tidal with the world itself bending its ear to their schemes— though they were Lady Vashmarna's schemes, and of course that was not what her agent meant by the *mundab*. The *mundab* was a philosophy as well as a world. The philosophy of the unknowable, the philosophy of the unknown. How many times could one say that before one began to hear a definition for madness? Lady Vashmarna stood before the breakfast room window, rubbing her arms against the internal chill, and for once wished she could look out on the ocean, the great, blank wilderness that surrounded them. She could feel the threat of it on her back like the rotten wind from a tidal wave that was about to drown them all, towers and scholars and farmers alike. The unknown world. This world.

Our world, she thought, but even the island denied her the possessive this morning. Clouds drowned the inland peaks, rain shrouded the flooded fields. The land was a vague and threatening darkness beyond the fragile ribbon of the bridge, a massive shadow without definition or boundaries. Lady Vashmarna could imagine the clouds lifting to reveal not roofs and fields but the jungle that had met their ancestors like a defending army and had nearly crowded the invaders into the sea.

Now we crowd ourselves.

A swirl of wind gusted around Shaudarand's peak and slapped rain against Lady Vashmarna's window. She started, and for a heartbeat felt the intimate chill of fear. "Bless us, spirits of air, against the dark-shrouded evils . . ." *Nonsense,* she told herself sharply. She was not as old as she pretended when she spoke with young men like Aramis Tapurnashen, but neither was she a child to be spooked by terrors of her own invention. The only part of the *mundab* she had to concern herself with was that ragbag collection of would-be scholars in the tidal who called themselves *mundabi,* and they were thoroughly under her direction and control. It was the shaudah she should be worrying about, and Lord Ghar's broken statuary.

The shaudah's private apartment was under the dome at the top of Magarand, the central jewel in a crown of roofs, and to get there from Lady Vashmarna's apartment in stubby Shaudarand at the head of the inland bridge, she had to take either a short, wet, windy boat ride or a dry walk through the tower ways: the low walkway to Itteranarand, the long glass-windowed bridge

to Sidirand, and the sole defensible passage to Magarand itself.
A long walk that would take time away from other crucial
chores, but it was better not to arrive at a critical audience with
sodden clothes and tangled hair—and better, too, to be seen,
however galling the stares and whispers would be. Vashmarna
had nothing to be ashamed of, and the people of the bay needed
to be shown as much.

The lady of the demesne donned a formal robe of gold and
brassy green, decked her hands, still slender in spite of the
spread of her figure, with three fine emeralds and one golden
topaz, and gathered up her secretary and her chief clerk as she
left her apartment. Although she was convinced that the engineers in the fort and all the other Vashmarna enterprises
spread across the face of the *rasnan* should be able to cope
with this emergency on their own, experience had taught her
that a few orders and a schedule of priorities kept them steady
and coping with necessities. "Sending out the lists" was how
she thought of it, and they all had to be sent out by messenger,
youngsters running the *hadaras* roads to the rubber plantations, the copper foundries, the glass forges and ceramic manufactories and Vashmarna's own farms: the entire demesne.
And if the shaudah were not so stubborn—so infuriatingly,
callously, traditionally stubborn—in his interpretation of the
ancestors' decrees, one year of running cables into the countryside would result in those messages passing in a matter of min-
utes. Vashmarna had the technical plans and the codes. Lady
Vashmarna's father had even developed a detailed budget for
the expenditure of resources and time . . . and there the project
foundered, like every other project Vashmarna proposed.

And yet here she stood, dictating her orders while the elevator operator pretended not to listen and her secretary angled
her writing board to get the best of the light from the electric
sconces on the beaten-copper walls. Vashmarna had helped
build the towers, Vashmarna kept them running with water

pumps and ventilation fans and power in the walls, and that, it seemed, was all the good Vashmarna was permitted to do.

She still had the word "permission" in her mind when the operator worked the lever that eased the elevator to a stop. He folded the accordion door open to reveal the busy concourse at Shaudarand's bridge level, the cluster of passengers waiting to ascend, and the anxious face of *aras* Chaiduur, the priest assigned by the temple to oversee Vashmarna's compliance with the ancestors' laws.

"*Aras.*" Lady Vashmarna made no attempt to conceal her impatience, and the priest's bow was an anxious bob.

"*Jinnu.* I was waiting—I came to see—"

Lady Vashmarna took several steps away from the elevator, clearing the way for the waiting passengers and forcing the priest to maneuver his rotund self aside. In a season of high prices and emptying stores, Chaiduur was looking rounder than ever.

"*Jinnu,*" he said, collecting himself. "We must speak before your audience with the shaudah."

Lady Vashmarna took this to mean he wanted to be reassured, but even as compromised as he had become over the years, Vashmarna's overseer had to be given his due—at least in public, which went far to explain this ambush. Lady Vashmarna sighed and waved her clerks back onto the elevator. They would have to carry on with what they had.

"Speak then," she said as she joined the river of pedestrians flowing through the high white-walled concourse. The light was white as well, rain-filtered daylight pouring in through the great arch opening onto the landward bridge, and it was pitiless in revealing the worried, questioning, angry looks directed Lady Vashmarna's way. Even the baysiders' clothes were cheerless, the colors flat and artificial in the blank light, and the decorative carvings above the shop doors, the goods on display, the woven grass awnings and door curtains that harkened back to the *hadaras*—it all seemed shabby, as if the disturbances in the night had extracted a toll on every aspect of life in the bay. But that, no doubt, was only a product of Lady Vashmarna's fatigue.

"I am told," *aras* Chaiduur said under cover of the foot traffic, "that the shaudah has only now sent for you."

"Yes."

"I can't help but wonder, *jinnu,* if you would not have been wiser to go at once to the shaudah before he summoned you, pressed for an audience, made a public display of your—that is, Vashmarna's—contrition and zeal."

A question Lady Vashmarna had already asked herself, and she did not appreciate having it put to her again. Her tone was sharp. "There is no advantage to being seen scurrying about in a panic, and less than no advantage to throwing myself at the shaudah's feet without all the facts at my command."

"And now you do? Have facts, I mean. What facts? If I may ask."

It took all Lady Vashmarna's long training in piety to keep from cursing the priest, even silently behind the pleasant mask of her face. It was well within his purview as the temple's overseer to ask, but it was his anxiety for himself that had Chaiduur puffing as he walked at her side; her pace was nicely calculated to express dignity and calm. However, she had to concede that although his distress arose from his own ambiguous position, strung up between Vashmarna's patronage and the temple's hostility, that fact did nothing to lessen the discomfort of his finger pressed firmly on that particular point. What facts, indeed? But it did occur to her, as they stepped out onto the covered walkway between Shaudarand and Itteranarand, that here was a good audience on whom to try her explanations—explanations, she insisted, rather than excuses. Never that.

"We have had a most disturbing report of these so-called

'shadow gods' appearing within the bastion walls, perhaps within the scholarium itself."

Chaiduur sucked in a wheezing breath, his black eyes glittering with light. The passage between the two towers was low and not long, but even in the rain, daylight shone up from the water and down from Itteranarand's glassy walls.

"Is it true, *jinnu*?" said the man who had once been, and was in some ways still, a credulous tidal priest.

"It is better than a rumor," Lady Vashmarna said, and inwardly noted that "better," in this case, meant more useful to her. But although it was clever of the fort's liaison to bring her the rumor of shadow gods within the bastion walls—too clever? Had it been the young man's idea, or someone else's?—the shaudah would not be as easily distracted as her present audience. But one made do with what came to hand. "And it is a report that raises some uncomfortable possibilities."

"Shadow gods in the scholarium," the *aras* said as if he could not get beyond that dreadful idea.

"Within the bastion," Lady Vashmarna prompted, "near to the fort itself."

"Shadow gods." Chaiduur wiped sweat off his upper lip with the tip of his skinny priest's braid. "*Jinnu,* are you thinking . . . ?"

Let him come up with it: if he could find it, so could others. "What do *you* think, *aras*?"

"A . . . curse?" His plump eyelids were creased and blinking. "A curse, *jinnu*, in these latter days? Forgive me, but the scholars teach us such powers were cast off, left behind in the ancestors' crossing from the *ramhadras.*"

"If the shadow cult can perform their blasphemies outside of the temple's control or understanding," Lady Vashmarna said carefully, "then I would be hard-pressed to say what else they might do once they got inside the bastion walls."

"Ah," said Chaiduur, enlightened at last. "Sabotage.

Sabotage! Inside the fort, do you think, *jinnu*? Perhaps even in the generating station itself? But this is dreadful! Who? What evidence have you to present to shaudah-*janaras*?"

Not an intelligent man, but he did have a knack for asking the difficult questions. What evidence *did* she have to present to the shaudah?

"That," she said, "is precisely the difficulty. We have, as you know, inspected the dam, the generating station, the transformers, the fort itself—everything, in short, within Vashmarna's own lawful province—and we have found nothing suspicious, nothing, in fact, that does not work precisely as it should. We have even replaced working units in the hope of correcting the fault by happenstance, but to no avail; and of course our personnel have been closely investigated and absolved, by you no less than by ourselves. The only thing that remains is interference from outside the fort's walls."

"Well, I . . . yes. Of course I did. As you say. But how . . . ?" The priest panted and took another swipe with his braid. "Oh. The shadow cult. Forbidden acts. Summoning demons. Blasphemous intervention. Yes. But, *jinnu,* if such things are as the temple understands them to be, as they were (saints bless us and keep us) in the First World, in the Days Before, then they are . . . Well . . . They are—gods forgive me, I don't know how else to say it—they are essentially a matter of prayer. How can you find evidence of, of a meditation, a, a, a . . . well, a prayer?"

"But *aras,*" said Lady Vashmarna, innocently, earnestly, with a respectful bow of her head and no hint of irony in her tone, "*aras,* if such a terrible and unholy act were performed inside the fort, surely you—you, a priest, living among us— surely you would have discovered it by now?"

Which gave her the double satisfaction of silencing the priest, and of laying a deadly weight of responsibility onto another's shoulders.

It did not, however, lighten the responsibilities that already rested with her, and she was aware that political finesse could take her only so far in the face of an arbitrary, fallible, and hostile power.

Prosepurn guide my steps, I pray you. Father of wisdom, guide my words.

The long arching bridge between Itteranarand and Sidirand, glass-windowed and streaked with salt spray and rain, gave out onto an open-sided plaza like an angular bite taken out of great Sidirand's side. Huge columns, the bare bones of the tower, were overgrown with vines and flanked by potted trees, so that the chill damp wind off the water was moderated and made musical by the leaves. The sea smell was strong here, though, and the waves beat with a deep and urgent sound, impossible to ignore. The passage that became the walkway to Magarand lay to Lady Vashmarna's left, flanked by guards in the dark blue coats and fringed turbans of the bay police, but Lady Vashmarna, after only a slight hesitation, continued straight ahead to where a tall triple arch opened onto the fluid light and echoing peace of the Temple of the Waves.

The temple was a haven of cool in the hot season, but now, after months of rain with no end in sight, all of the glass and icy quartz gave it an unaccustomed coldness, an edge as if the ocean wind could reach here, too. In fact, there was a draft, a murmuring eddy of air that muttered and hummed beneath the exquisite vault, as if the very light, reflected at a thousand watery angles by the waves, had a voice of its own. The whole temple was glass and quartz, even the floor in parts, above the tidewaters that foamed around Sidirand's knees. The only darkness here was of the dull human flesh of supplicants, and the shadows cast by the glass-jeweled statues of the gods.

Holy Prosepurn, I am in your hands.

Perhaps it was the press of time, perhaps it was merely the unusual chill in the air, but Lady Vashmarna was not comforted as she usually was. She lit a cone of incense to burn at the feet of the god, bowed, touched the immense hand that held a key on its palm, and turned away.

"Vashmarna-*jin'*." It was *aras* Chaiduur, who had lit his incense and made his bow without taking his eyes off the rest of the temple. His warning was more squeak than whisper, and unnecessary. She had already seen and recognized the tall dark figure crossing the light-spangled floor.

Divaram Ghar, lord of the bay. Ghar's demesne encompassed the towers that *her* demesne, Vashmarna, power and light, had been created to serve—or, depending on one's point of view, the demesne that could not possibly exist without Vashmarna. So much depended on one's point of view, including the question of whether this was an enemy or a friend.

Lord Ghar bowed. Lady Vashmarna bowed.

"Good morning, Vashmarna-*jin'*. I hope you have recovered from our night of disturbances."

"Ghar-*jandas*! This is an unexpected pleasure. May I offer my deep regrets over the disruption of your exhibit?"

"A minor tribulation, I assure you. If there must be blame, let them carry it who allow themselves to be overset by a moment of darkness."

"Ghar-*jan'*, you measure everyone by your own courage. Would you permit them their dismay if the floor gave way beneath their feet?"

"We are all dismayed when the illusion of certainty is withdrawn, *jinnu*, but we do not all give rein to our fears. I would never expect that of you, and you have more reason than most."

Lady Vashmarna laughed. "But I am too busy, *jan'*. Shake the foundations when I have a moment of idleness and then we shall see."

Lord Ghar indicated the temple's great arch. "I wish I had

such a moment to offer you. I think you are also called into the presence this morning. Shall we walk together?"

"Indeed we shall." Lady Vashmarna smiled at the lord of the bay, and then turned to give Chaiduur a frowning look. The priest, looking, if possible, even more anxious than before, dropped several paces behind.

Meanwhile, Lord Ghar was saying, "One does not dare be late, of course, but I am told there are worthies of the *hadaras* already claiming the shaudah's attention. I am just as glad to have your company while I wait."

"And so am I, of course." Lady Vashmarna was quite sincere, but she thought even as she spoke, *While you wait for what?* Perhaps nothing more than the shaudah's attention for a report on the night's disturbances in the bay. "Though even alone one can take great pleasure in Magarand's view."

"Can you, still? That same view one has seen so many times before?" Lord Ghar pondered this, as if it were a question worthy of deliberation. "Yes, there is something to be said for that, to watch the change of seasons and years. One comes to the understanding that so much of change is illusion, just as so much of certainty is."

"I have read the book of the *rasnan,* and I have found the *ramhadras* quoted there," Lady Vashmarna said softly. It was a line from the Book of Exile: *I have read the book of this world, and I have found heaven quoted there.*

Lord Ghar let that lie in an easy silence as they followed the inner passage to Magarand's bridge. He was an old friend and Vashmarna's bitterest rival, and she found his company more restful than anyone else's except her own. She knew the shape of his intelligence and his pride, his arrogance and his fear; she knew his face better than she knew her own. A good face, craggy and obdurate as the island's basalt coast. She sometimes thought of him that way, as the island, stubborn and inward-turning, and she had been tempted at times to lean on him, she with nothing but the ocean and the wild world at her back. She did lean on him, if one could speak so of an opposition that kept them balanced. That kept, she wondered now, the shaudah too well balanced between them? *Something has to give way,* she thought to her friend, *and, forgive me, I must hope that that something is not me.*

She said as they stepped onto the narrow walk between Sidirand and Magarand, "Now that the *ramhadras* is in my mind . . . I have heard disturbing reports from my engineers in the fort. I fear Baradam has not been granted an easy demesne to rule."

"Ah, my son." Divaram Ghar sighed and said with a rueful smile, "I'm afraid no demesne would be easy for him that was not in the bay. He was born here, with water beneath his feet. He always expected to serve in the Sidirand temple, and I suspect he is uncomfortable on solid earth. Perhaps he must make his ground uncertain before he can be certain as to where he stands. But he will find his balance. He must, or find himself recalled to greater shame than that which lost him the temple here."

"One prays that he will find it soon, Ghar-*jan'*. I would hesitate to speak of rumors, for there are always rumors, but these have been dashing themselves against the fort's walls as if the scholarium were running at high tide."

Lord Ghar's face lost its confiding hint of softness. "You speak of this tidal muck that is being tracked through the temple precincts, this 'shadow god.' "

"A troubling report, don't you agree?" She added, knowing Lord Ghar was not nearly so credulous as *aras* Chaiduur, "If only for the suggestion that the sponsored novices have not left their origins behind. It is disturbing to think that slum cults and the secret societies of the countryside might be finding a foothold in the scholarium."

"Engineers are not immune to gossip," he said, the mask of his face carved with stern lines.

"So they are not," she said gently, "but when gossip is the only answer they have to the difficulties with the power supply, what can one do but listen? The generating station is operating normally, the transformers and cables are sound. If the troubles do not lie within the fort, as my engineers and even the temple's overseer assure me they do not, then where can I look but beyond the walls? And what is beyond the walls but the scholarium?"

"Do you accuse—?"

"Oh, no." She held up her hand with a sad smile. "No, my friend, I do not accuse. On the contrary, I offer my help. This is part of the matter that brings me here: that if Baradam-*aras* cannot order the subversive elements in the scholarium with the resources he has at hand—and who can blame him if he cannot, given the numbers of tidal and *hadaras* postulants swelling the priesthood's ranks?—then Vashmarna is willing to provide men to help your son with an investigation into those elements that trouble both our demesnes."

There. It was said, and just as they reached the guarded elevators to the shaudah's aerie. Lady Vashmarna disguised a deep breath with a regretful sigh, but it might have been a sigh of relief. Having taken her stand here with the Ghar, she could be serene in the shaudah's presence.

"You surprise me, *jinnu*," the Ghar said, pausing just out of earshot of the elevator guards. One car stood with an open door, its attendant waiting with his hand on the lever, but the Ghar seemed oblivious. "And you reassure me, for I had feared your own resources were already stretched beyond their limits. Indeed, the purpose that brings *me* here this morning is to offer you a complement of my own men to help guard the sensitive points in the fort and elsewhere in your demesne." He smiled. She smiled. He added with dry humor, "But now I begin to wonder if we should not be formulating a joint petition to ask the shaudah to reconsider his marriage laws."

"His marriage laws?"

"If it is his restrictions on marriage that flood the scholarium with a superstitious, uneducable rabble forced into an unwilling celibacy . . ."

"Ah," said Lady Vashmarna, who had pledged herself to a willing celibacy when still a young woman, "but the shaudah would only say that it is the lack of such laws in earlier days that caused the flood."

"And I might say that it is this endless season of rain that causes that flood, along with many others. As if the literal floods were not doing enough damage!"

Responding to the Ghar's change of tone, Lady Vashmarna let him lead her onto the elevator car, waving the forgotten Chaiduur onto the car with them as the operator was about to slide the folding door closed. He continued to be ignored. Lady Vashmarna said to the Ghar, "What news from your *hadaras* estates?" and he was still telling her when the door opened high in the top of the tower.

Magarand's elevator debouched onto the reception area under the peak of the dome. The high ceiling arched up in wide bands of quartz and bronze, tapered rays that met at the pillar of the elevator shaft. It could be lovely at night when the electrics were alive and the quartz shone like starlit mist, but sometimes, particularly during the rains, Lady Vashmarna could not help but be reminded of a parasol's spokes. *Thus the shaudah shelters us,* she thought with an irony she did not often express aloud. What use was a rice paper parasol against the monsoon? Its dyes ran, it dissolved, leaving one holding a bamboo skeleton and nothing else. But a skeleton, Lady Vashmarna reminded herself, with the blessing of the gods.

Liveried servitors bowed them through the inner door, and

the window in the shaudah's anteroom greeted her with a view past Unarand's wind-tossed roof garden and up the island's rocky coast. A fine view, as she had said, but Lady Vashmarna spared it only a glance. Guards in the red tunics and yellow turbans of the shaudah's personal troops were bowing them into the audience hall.

Magarand's roof spread its sheltering rays here, too, a fan-like arc of them shining white and gold between the daylight without and the electric lights within. The shaudah's household bought thousands of bulbs in a year, and there were times when the Vashmarna took a secret satisfaction in these blazing chandeliers, for they represented no small part of Vashmarna's revenue. But today it was the scene beneath those swags and dangling chains of lights that held her attention.

The shaudah's couch was raised high enough that he could gaze over the heads of petitioners standing, and on more perilous occasions, kneeling, before him, and he—with his rugs and cushions and spangled awning, his jewel-starred raiment, his goblets and finger bowls and perfume bottles of colored glass and gold—was the most gorgeous object in the room. It was hard for the uninitiated to see the man through all that glittering display, but Lady Vashmarna and Lord Ghar had been in the presence countless times, and it was the man, however he camouflaged himself—however, she increasingly thought, he outright hid—with whom they had to deal.

Today the audience was already in session, and the space before the gaudy couch was occupied by a small cluster of men and women, most of them gray-haired, all of them in the stiff old-fashioned finery that marked them as noble landowners from the *hadaras,* each defending a rural demesne. Vashmarna had had ties with all of them in the past, contracts for mining rights and the like that had often evolved into more personal attachments. Lady Vashmarna's own mother had been raised on a *hadaras* estate. But in more recent times those contracts had been growing fewer as mines wore out and plantations decreased in yield, and Vashmarna's relations with the *hadaras* had been growing strained. Lady Vashmarna gazed with mixed emotions at faces she had not seen in several years.

Lady Meggarin of the Megra Bhasra estate on the north coast was speaking. "We are well aware of the shaudah's levy. In past years, as *janarasan* well knows, we have paid without question, indeed, with all due reverence. And with all due reverence, *janaras,* in past years that levy has returned to the *hadaras* in rebuilt roads and bridges, in the shaudah's grain stores, in the law courts . . ."

Lady Meggarin, who was not a young woman, paused to catch her breath, and the shaudah waited her out, his gaze so distant and his body so still it was impossible to tell if he were patient or angry or thinking about his midday meal. Lady Vashmarna had known him for most of his life, and she still found herself unable to guess. Lady Meggarin cleared her throat and forged on into the shaudah's silence.

"This year, *janaras,* the grain stores are full of vermin and all but empty of grain. Bridges are washed away by the floods, roads are gullied and overgrown—"

"And," interrupted one of the younger *hadaras* lords, "the shaudah's own troops are looting our personal stores!"

Lady Meggarin pursed her mouth, and Lady Vashmarna guessed she was just as glad to have someone else make that particular point. The shaudah stirred, giving the *hadri* nobles a reptilian glance and smoothing the gold braid on his sleeve.

"The grain stores, as Meggarin-*jinnu* points out, are nearly empty," he said, "and *hadaras* taxes are long overdue. If the rains continue to delay the planting season, the *rasnan* will feel the pinch of hunger, the *hadaras* no less than the *shadras*. Private hoards will not be tolerated."

"Forgive me, *janaras*," said Lord Ubatteran, an elderly man with skin weathered black and a shock of white curly hair. "Forgive me if I speak too bluntly. But when soldiers confiscated my foresters' grain, they were not liberating a black-marketer's hoard, nor were they laying claim to grain withheld from the shaudah's levy. They were stealing food from my foresters' kitchen pantry, and the children had nothing to eat in the three days it took for word to reach me. And even were such a small quantity worth transporting to the shaudah's keeping, the soldiers cannot have done so, for the bridge on the Kadjuran road was washed away sixty-eight days ago and never replaced. So I have no choice but to ask, shaudah-*janaras*, with a humble spirit: Is it the shaudah's intention that his soldiers should feed themselves by stealing food from our children's mouths?"

Lady Vashmarna gave a half-conscious nod at this telling question. Lord Ghar glanced at her and away. The shaudah went on toying with his cuffs.

"What do you suggest we feed our soldiers," he said after an uncomfortable pause, "when you deny us our rightful levies?"

"*Janaras*," said Lord Ubatteran, "we would pay your levies if we had any grain."

"And we *do* pay your levies," said Lady Meggarin. "In stone that repairs the towers, in paper for the scholarium, in silk for the shaudah's own household, in copper for Vashmarna's wires . . ."

Lady Vashmarna cleared her throat, and when the shaudah glanced her way, she bowed. "If I may speak for Vashmarna, *janaras*? Megra Bhasra has never supplied Vashmarna with mineral goods, so perhaps Meggarin-*jinnu* is not aware that Vashmarna pays for all goods received. The shaudah's levies do not supply Vashmarna's workshops, nor do they fill Vashmarna's stores. As to the towers and stone for their repair, I cannot speak."

Though in fact she knew very well that the shaudah's levies did support the towers, maintenance and repair having been decreed equivalent to the care of the *hadaras* roads or the bastion walls. But let Lord Ghar speak to that, if he chose. If he dared, with feeling running as high as it was.

But he was not given the chance. Lady Meggarin had turned at Lady Vashmarna's voice, and risking the shaudah's displeasure, she spoke directly to Lady Vashmarna.

"Do we not pay in other ways? Are we not paying now with this endless rain? I promise you, Vashmarna-*jin'*, no *hadaras* demesne has earned the displeasure of the gods and our ancestors by flouting the ancient laws. It is Vashmarna's unholy work, the trespass on the ancestors' own fort, the towers that are not even founded on good *rasnan* earth . . ."

Once more the elderly woman's breath failed her. Lady Vashmarna, who heard in the older woman's disapproval a whole world of resistance to her demesne and to the expansionist cause, hid her frustration behind another bow.

"Again, *janaras,* I fear Meggarin-*jin'* speaks from an ignorance of how matters stand in the *shadras.* The towers are not Vashmarna's province."

The shaudah made a thoughtful noise and the *hadaras* nobles turned back to face his couch, most of them bowing, Lady Meggarin biting her lip to keep her retort unsaid.

"I know where Vashmarna's province lies," the shaudah said. "And I know what laws it is founded upon. But," the shaudah went on, not surprising Lady Vashmarna, who knew how little the shaudah desired an open debate on the probity of the towers, "there is still the matter of the *hadaras* levy before us."

More than one of the *hadaras* lords looked as though they would speak; the shaudah quelled them with a lifted hand. "That the grain stores are low we do recognize, and we are prepared to grant a further delay in payment until such a time as this season's harvest has been assured. Moreover, we will relieve the *hadaras* of the burden of the support of our troops, but with the understanding that to be relieved of the duty is also to be relieved of the benefit. And since the burden now falls upon us, we will withdraw the troops into the *shadras,* where they can perform such duties as may be required of them."

There was a small moment of silence as the audience absorbed a major development. Troops withdrawn into the *shadras*? Lady Vashmarna glanced at Lord Ghar beside her and saw shock written on his face. The lord of the bay had not been prepared for this announcement, and as his mouth tightened and his dark eyes began to flicker in accordance with his thoughts, she could see the question forming before he spoke.

"*Janaras,* if I may speak? Where in the *shadras* are the troops to be housed? And where will they be deployed?"

Vashmarna's fort, with its vital systems and spiritual pitfalls, would remain inviolate, and Lady Vashmarna listened with an interested detachment to Lord Ghar's unvoiced concern: Would the shaudah's troops, a contingent of almost four hundred men, be housed in the towers—where such barrack space as there was was already devoted to the Ghar's overstaffed police force? Would they be deployed in the towers— where the Ghar's police jealously guarded every scrap of authority they dared to claim?

"They will be housed," said the shaudah, "in the empty warehouses on the docks, and they will be deployed, Ghar-*jandas,* in the tidal. If this rain is a punishment visited upon us for our sins, I cannot think of a more likely lot of sinners than the shadow cult and the demons they most blasphemously call their gods. It is time and past time they were rooted out once and for all. Do you not agree?"

There were murmurs of approbation and relief. The *hadri* bowed. Lord Ghar bowed and spoke a blessing. And Lady Vashmarna, with half her secret enterprises suddenly threatened with discovery and with no way to protest without risking immediate exposure, had no choice but to bow with all the rest.

THE BASTION

The drop of water clung to the cracked ceiling for an instant, glittering like an eye in the light creeping in through the filigree of the shrine's outer wall. Touched by the penitents' murmured prayers, it quivered like a frog's egg stirred by interior life, and like a frog's egg it swelled, grew fecund, and dropped, felled by its own abundance, to the floor. The splash of its destruction was swallowed by the soft voices, the sighs that presaged yawns, the small-winged flutter of insects drawn to candles that themselves fluttered as flames devoured wax. But the droplet's passing raised a tiny breeze in the still, damp, heat-laden air of the shrine, and that tiny breeze stirred a candle flame, and Moth's eye was snagged by the reflection in the growing puddle by her knee. As she watched, another droplet fell, and another, raising sparks of reflected candlelight, and by that token she knew it was raining again.

Kistnu, absent mother, stretch out your hand. Kistnaran, mother of absence, turn your terrible face aside.

Moth's mouth tightened momentarily before she let the prayers roll on without her. She was not the only orphaned dedicant paying for some slight sin with the pain in her knees; she wondered if motherless Snake and Eeling felt the same stab of impatience at that line. Mouthing the words, she could hear behind the human sounds the soft chorus of the rain. It was a silence that had grown loud as the wet season dragged on beyond its time. She slid her gaze toward the outer wall. At first all she could see was the screen's black silhouette against the white daylight, the stone filigree tangled by living green tendrils that visited a slow destruction on the work of the past. But as drop after drop fell from the ceiling and the puddle crept toward the base of Moth's candlestick, she began to make out the twisting strands of water spinning out from moss-choked gutters, and beyond that liquid curtain, the steadier fall of the rain.

Small bells rang, a sweet shock of golden sound that marked the end of the prayer and began the drone of the meditation note, the drawn-out *shoh* that was supposed to bind them into one breathing entity, one mind to summon the weak shadow of a goddess from the memories of another world—a mind utterly deaf to the call of the *mundab* that ran like an ocean current beneath the skin of *this* world. Moth rang her bell, just a touch behind the rest, and flexed her calves until her feet began to tingle with fresh blood.

The priest in charge of the dedicants' contrition looked her way with a frown. When he had turned his back, bowing again to the mask of Kistnaran and softly clapping his hands, Eeling tucked her chin on her shoulder and gave Moth a look of exaggerated and comical sourness: Moth, in trouble again.

With no change in her expression but a slight widening of her eyes, Moth returned her gaze to the front of the room and rounded her mouth to mimic the *ssshhhooohhh* that filled the penitents' shrine like the sigh of a rising tide. Her skin was prickling beneath her clothes, her heart beating to the rhythm of all the mysteries, possibilities, certainties that lay anywhere and everywhere but here. Her hand stirred as if moved by nothing but the wash of sound. Her fingers touched her candlestick's base. The candle slid on damp tiles the distance of a breath. A drop fell from the broken ceiling and doused the candle's flame with a *tsk* of disapproving steam. Moth's hand rested on her knee. She glanced down. Oh, look! Her candle was out before the ceremony's end. She picked it up and padded between the rows, her bare soles alternately warm on dry tiles and cool on damp. The master lamp sat with its three flames burning in a niche beside the rear door of the hall. Moth lit her candle there for the sake of any watchers—*aras* Stai knelt and bowed his face to the floor at Kistnaran's taloned feet—and then, once she was sure the holy breath had drowned attention, she slipped outside, where the flame could be doused again by the rain.

After a moment Eeling came out to join her in the shrine's shallow porch.

"*Aras* Baradam himself," Eeling whispered, meaning the author of Moth's punishment. She sounded impressed. "How long this time?"

"Ten days. And three already served."

Eeling *tsked*, a perfect mimicry of Moth's doused flame. "Me, I've only got today, and poor old Stai's too occupied with his own sins to worry too much about ours."

"What sins?"

"His or mine? Me, I only cheeked the copyist who blamed me for runny ink. Can I help it if the rain damps the brushes? But if you mean Stai, well, it's all through the novices about him and that north coast boy."

"Well, if it's only a boy," Moth said. Eeling, tidal orphan

like herself, would know what she meant: boys don't get pregnant. "Or do you mean a *boy*?"

"Old enough to apprentice himself," which meant about fourteen—though it meant other things in the tenements of the slum. "Old enough to know how to keep his mouth shut, but he didn't, more fool him, and now he's talking about running back to his chickens, even if he can't hope to marry his girl back home."

"And all *aras* Stai gets is a day on his knees? When I got ten? *Aras* Baradam doesn't risk being called an egalitarian, does he?"

"Stai only favored the boy in a class, or that's what they're saying. I mean, that's all he got caught doing. And what did you do? Get caught out after curfew again? They'll be looking for your lover next, and then look out. Ten days' vigil will seem like a sweet and momentary dream."

"They can look forever," Moth said, wincing over the thought of Aramis, whom she had not seen since the night of their temple tryst. "I'll tell you what they should be looking for—"

"Whoops! I'm gone." Eeling nudged Moth's elbow and then vanished into the shrine.

Moth looked out beyond the spiraling gutter spill, expecting and dreading to see *aras* Baradam bearing down on her with another load of outrage and scorn, but no. She drew a breath in moderate relief. It was only *aras* Chaiduur, Vashmarna's pet priest and sometime mentor of Moth.

"Dedicant. I've been looking all over. Of course you would be here. What is it this time? Should you not be within?"

Moth prodded the soft wax at the edge of her candle's flame. "I heard you wanted me. Will you excuse me with *aras* Stai? Or should I find you when the sitting is done?"

"No, no. Now I have you. Come, we can find somewhere, er, somewhere out of the rain."

Moth raised her eyebrows. No question as to how she had heard he was looking? No pious scolding that she had left her prayers before she was called? Another glance at the *aras*'s face showed her a surprising depth of worry. She reached her arm around the door frame to fumble the candlestick onto the shelf below the master lamp, and then followed the priest into the rain. The hem of his robe twitched to an entirely different rhythm from his skinny braid's.

He led her to the dedicants' dormitory, which seemed a peculiar choice for a priest who loved his comforts. But all the dedicants were at their studies, and the dormitory was a good place to be private if one did not have to fear the senior priests' prudery and everyone else's love of gossip. *Aras* Chaiduur, showing a surprising degree of good sense, went no farther than the sheltered porch. He sat on the narrow plank bench there, and Moth propped herself against a roof support where bamboo chimes ticked softly behind her ear and the dirty spill from a mossy gutter spattered her sleeve.

"In trouble again," he said, his soft voice as heavy as it could get. For all his physical weight, Chaiduur's voice had always reminded Moth of a lacefly, floating on calm days and inclined to quiver in a breeze. "Dedicant Moth, when, *when* are you going to come to grips with the exigencies of your position? Do you know that *aras* Baradam himself has spoken of you to me?"

Moth worried at the wax still clinging to her fingers. "What did he say, *aras*?"

"He has grave doubts, very grave doubts, about the sincerity of your vocation, both as a priest and as a scholar. Of course, no one can doubt your ability, and so I said to the high priest, just as I have said to your sponsor time and again. No, your intelligence, your quickness, your capacity to learn: I have defended them all. But I wonder myself about the strength of your dedication, and when *aras* Baradam wonders if it is too great a stretch, if it is simply to much to ask of you, to come from the tidal, from the very mud, and make of yourself not merely a priest but a scholar-priest, a gatherer and defender of our history, our people's very soul . . . Well, dedicant, what can I say? What can I say to the *aras* when he tells me of your nighttime wanderings? What can I say to these rumors of demons in the scholarium that the *aras* lays at your feet? What"—and here the priest's light voice rose almost to a wail—"what can I say to your lady sponsor?"

Moth realized she was still scraping at wax that was no longer on her fingers and forced her hands to be still. "I don't know, *aras*."

"Do you *want* to be sent back to the tidal for once and for all?"

Chaiduur's voice was thin with horror: he, too, had worked his way out of the slum. But he had risen, whether he knew it or not, because he was the proxy through which Lady Vashmarna could elevate her protégée out of the muck, the glove that let the Vashmarna keep her delicate fingers clean. Chaiduur, protected by his ignorance, had been buried up to his neck in one of the *rasnan*'s deepest conspiracies since the day he first began to teach Moth how to read. And where had it gotten him? Where had it gotten them both? Moth turned away to look out on the rain.

"No, *aras*, I don't want to be sent back to the tidal."

"And I," he said with commendable honesty, "do not want to be smirched by your disgrace. So I think it is time for you to think very carefully about what it is you *do* want. Are you still determined to be a scholar?"

"What else is there?"

"A priest's place in the *hadaras*," Chaiduur said promptly. Too promptly. "You have been long enough in the scholarium to take the lesser vows, and if you ask to serve in a *hadaras* shrine, the elders will be reassured that you mean to leave your unfortunate origins behind. And in only a few years, if you work hard and with a true, pious humility, you can hope for a posting here, in the scholarium, or even a place in the bay. In the towers, Moth, with most of your life still ahead of you! How is that second-best to a scholar's place here, to never leaving, never passing through the bastion gates, with the whole world going on unseen beyond the walls?"

Moth's breath caught on the pinprick to her pride. Doubt her dedication, her vocation? Promise her the towers, oh yes, in only a few years? She had been promised that before. With a sharp edge of anger hidden within her amusement, she said ingenuously, "But there are other vocations, *aras*. I wonder . . . can I ask your advice? . . . I have been thinking about asking you to ask my sponsor if it would be possible, if she would consider giving me an apprenticeship within Vashmarna's demesne."

Chaiduur looked nonplussed, but he was already shaking his head, even before he spoke. "Not Vashmarna, Moth, not in these days. Don't you know how close Vashmarna's industry comes to heresy? Itteran might have granted the demesne amnesty from the ancestors' laws in order to build the towers, but the temple has never retracted the laws themselves. The border between Vashmarna's legal undertakings and anathema is very thin, very thin. No, you'd be much better off to take a place in the *hadaras*, far from controversy. Ambition is safest within the orthodoxy. For you must know, Moth, that to be forgiven your dedicant's vow and to take an apprenticeship oath both require the blessing of the temple, and if you were to go to Vashmarna . . . Oh dear, and with your tidal background . . . No, it really wouldn't be wise."

Moth did know all of that, and she took less pleasure in her teasing than she had hoped. Still, she said, "You say this, *aras*? Vashmarna's own priest?"

Chaiduur drew himself up as best he could. "I am the temple's priest, Moth, chosen by the high priest to provide oversight and protect the spirit of the ancestors' law. And," he added, letting his hard-won dignity slip away, "I have already put in my request for leave to one of the mountain retreats. I am not old, Moth, but I am weary. I am ready to retire. To give the last of my days to meditation and contemplation . . ." Chaiduur tried to make it sound like his heart's dream, but the look in his eyes was one of desperation. If Vashmarna's conspiracies and machinations were the mud they both were wading in, he, at least, was obviously afraid of getting in over his head.

THE TIDAL

It rained, and it rained, and fresh water pooled in the muck of the low-tide streets, drowning the creatures of the salt mud. Small reeking corpses drew *tirindi* down from their nests in the cliff, and the streets were alive with the scavengers' bone-shadowed wings. The human inhabitants were no more civilized, Moth thought, their manners drowned like the crawlers by the rain. A woman blinkered by her conical straw hat and a man bent over by a sling of fish tried to occupy the same foot stone above the mud. The woman, being smaller, was knocked into the street.

"Mucker!" She had a hen's voice, the accents of a *hadri* fresh in from the countryside. "Shit-eater! Tidal trash!"

The man, *shadri* and tidal to his bones, spat on her, drawing the hostile attention of other *hadri* among the passersby. The woman threw a handful of muck and, missing her aim, hit one of the uninvolved. The ensuing mud battle grew ugly when the fishmonger's sling was thrown to the ground. *Tirindi*, overfed and fearless, quarreled over the feast in perfect counterpart to the squelching scuffle, the breathless cursing, the thump of connecting fists.

"—tidal shits—"

"—fucking *hadri*—"

"—scum—"

"—back to your chickens where you're wanted!"

Moth, observing from a safely distant doorstep, discovered that if she unfocused her eyes, the knot of combat became strangely fluid, like the rough swirl of water into a rock pool at the rise of tide. Was this what the view from the towers was like? So distant that one saw not desperate people but merely movement, pattern, hue. The brassy green of tidal weeds; black mud, silver scales, red blood; the scarlet-and-saffron tunics of the shaudah's guard blazing out like freshly ignited flames. Moth hugged herself as that pretty fire came too close and was doused by a sudden wave of mud. The battle tide receded just as suddenly, spilling away into the tenements and the streets, leaving behind four men who were a little older, a little wiser, and in desperate need of a bath.

Moth clicked her tongue in sympathy and minced on cold bare feet across the foot stones to where the guardsmen were heaving one another out of the muck. She hunkered down, neatly balanced on one stone, to put herself at eye level with the officer whose badge of rank still dimly shone on his rakishly tilted shako.

"May I be of assistance, *purdar*?" asked the saintly dedicant Moth.

The *purdar* snarled, a flash of white teeth in a mud-black face.

" 'Blessed also are the earth-born,' " she said in mild reproof, " 'for they who have no eyes yet see what even the spirits of air cannot.' Be patient, good sirs, for your service does not go unseen, and I am sure it will not go unrewarded, not in this world, nor the next. Remember that patience and humility are virtues of great worth, more loved by the gods than pride. And do be careful," she added as she moved lightly away, for she had noticed the unraveled sashes and missing pistols, "do be careful with your things. This mud will swallow anything. Even, so they say, the dead."

"You mad thing," Silk said admiringly when she heard the tale. "Just as well the mudrats stole their shooters. You'd have got a lead fly in the back quick as thinking."

"Not with their gun barrels all plugged up with muck. Besides, a dedicant's tunic is still worth something to some people, even if it isn't to you."

Silk made a *chuh* of disgust. "Say the same in the dark and see what it's worth to them, or anyone."

"Hmm." Moth nipped a tender leaf off the top of a green shoot and nibbled at the tip.

"Prune your own plants, Useless!" Silk said with a slap at her knee.

They were sitting toe to toe among the struggling plants of Silk's roof garden, being steadily soaked by the pale rain. The Red House was one of the taller tenements, and Silk's garden had a fine view of the tidal spread in its haphazard misery all around. Moth tried the same trick of the unfocused eye and discovered that it rendered the slum almost pretty. One saw the green of roof gardens and balconies rather than the crumbling plaster of the walls. Pumps and weathervanes whirled like pinwheels and the noon waters crept in like a silver mirage, untainted by the usual sewer sheen. But at this close remove one could not unfocus the nose offended by the tidal stinks, nor the ear buffeted by too many voices. Moth sighed and let her gaze drift out to the edge of the deep water, the floating docks, the boats, and beyond them the towers of the bay.

Silk shied a bit of broken roof tile at a *tirindi* hovering too close to her half-drowned sprouts. "Why don't you go, you? Instead of dreaming. They've temples and shrines same as us. Go, sleep in a clean bed above the waves, forget what it's like to have your feet in shitty muck up to your knee. I would if I was you. I've never seen why you don't."

Moth eased the fresh leaf into her mouth one nibbled fragment at a time. "You think one slum-born dedicant among hundreds gets a choice? If I didn't have a talent for scholarship, I wouldn't even be in the bastion, I'd be squatting in some dirt shrine in the *hadaras* picking seeds out of my hair."

"It'd be more use to me," Silk said, shying another bit of roof tile at nothing. "Seeds."

"Huh." Moth nibbled.

"You've got a sponsor," Silk said carefully.

She was right to take care. Moth's sponsor did not want Moth anywhere but where she was, and even if Moth obeyed, she did not have to love her lady for it.

"I'm in the bastion." On the "bas—" Moth inadvertently spat out her bit of leaf. She picked it off her knee, flicked a grain of sand away, and put it back into her mouth. "Aren't I?"

"And wishing you were there." Silk nodded at the bay. "And don't say you aren't when I know different."

"Why should I? Do you know anyone who isn't?"

"Me, for one," Silk said defiantly.

Moth drew in the last of the leaf with a curl of her tongue. "Liar," she said. "What do you look at when you're up here alone all day?"

"You think I sigh over those tombstones, those white bits of bone?" Silk looked scornful, and then laughed. "As for that, I wish I had been watching when all the lights went mad. To think of them running around in a blind panic like lizards turned out of their nest, when it's us who've drained their spark for our engine, and them never guessing. Oh, if Vash-marna only knew where their power was gone! If only I could be the one to tell them!"

She laughed again. Moth said nothing, feeling an uneasiness that had nothing to do with her still-troubled gut. Somehow, she did not think her sponsor would share Silk's amusement. On the other hand . . . well . . . it was a good joke, wasn't it? And all the better, really, for all the things Silk couldn't know. Secrets on either hand, and Moth doing the juggling! Moth laughed after all.

A peaceful silence fell.

"It's noon," Silk said when the Red House quivered to the nudge of the first wave. "Kiss me and go."

Moth dutifully kissed her, and marveled at how much more tender her mouth was, her skin, even her breath, compared to Aramis. Aramis, Aramis. Moth had not seen him since that night in the temple.

She went, and was not surprised when a thrown bit of tile stung her back.

"Liar yourself," Silk said.

◆

The *mundabi* were in a fret and had dragged Moth down from the scholarium to tell her all about it. What did they want her to do? She doubted even they knew.

For secrecy's sake they met in a different place each time; today's meeting was on one of the tidal rafts under a dripping roof of matted weeds, and although Moth had slept half the nights of her childhood on a raft just like it, today the bumping heave of the half-floated deck woke the nausea that the stolen leaf had allayed. She tried to listen past the complaints of her stomach and the ache in her back: after nine days of imposed vigil courtesy of *aras* Baradam, the base of her spine felt gripped by a vise. And yet here she was, soaked and provoked, instead of practicing meditational dance in the shelter of the dedicants' cloister.

"Yes," she said with some pretense of patience, "thank you, Tarun, I understand the shaudah's guards are here. I have seen them with these very eyes. What I fail to understand is why they have anything to do with me. I mean, with us."

"They are here," said Tarun through his teeth, "to root out the shadow cult. The shaudah's very words. Root out! That is us! In case it has escaped your notice, *we* are the shadow cult!"

He was hushed, most sternly by Istvan Soos.

"We," said Moth before the older man could speak, "are the *mundabi,* of whom the shaudah has never heard. The shadow cult is no one, it is the shadow of a shadow, it is a phantasm, a nothing, a dream. Let them chase it, I say, and get their pretty uniforms muddy in the meantime. If they're hunting a shadow cult, what can they possibly find but shadows?"

There were murmurs of defiant support, but Istvan accused her of being disingenuous.

"You are not as naïve as that, dedicant. They are not looking for shadows. They are looking for a secret society. They are looking for people with moral authority in the tidal secretly plotting against the shaudah's rule. When they find us, what do you suggest? Do we tell them politely, 'Begging your pardon, sirs, we are not the shadow cult; we are the *mundabi,*' and expect them to go peaceably on their way?"

"We are not the only secret society," Moth said sullenly. She did not mind if the shaudah had been stirred to action at last, but she did hate being lectured. "In the tidal alone there are dozens. Even in the bastion—"

"But they aren't looking in the bastion," someone said. "They're looking here."

"They aren't looking," someone else said scornfully. "They're standing around waiting for a shadow god to come strolling by."

"They've been asking," a greenguard said ominously. This was Nindi, a sometime pirate whose authority in the tidal was anything but moral. "They went through Little Dock House yesterday. Should've seen the 'stillers hopping out the windows like sandfleas." He grinned.

No one else smiled.

"Well, what *are* they looking for?" Moth demanded. "If it isn't shadows?"

"What does it matter what they're looking for," Istvan said hotly, "if while they're looking for it they find the engine?"

A chorus of hisses silenced him. The *mundabi* sat under their dripping shelter listening to the slap of the tide, the gurgle of a pole boat, the monotonous *ree-nee-nee* whine of a *tirindi*. The rain and a play-reading on the balcony overhead curtained everything. Moth sighed.

"Istvan is right," she said.

"Of course I'm right," Istvan snarled.

"Never mind that," Tarun said. "What are we going to do?"

"Hide it, move it, dismantle it, disguise it, abandon it," Moth rattled off. She looked around the circle of blank stares. "We discussed this at the beginning. If the thing is to be made, it has to be made—and used—here. It's the tidal's engine. Either we abandon it or we go on."

A silence.

"I hardly care which today."

Further silence.

"Please just decide so I can go somewhere to be privately ill."

Nindi shifted, as if she had threatened to vomit on his feet. "It's not my decision," he said.

"There is no decision," Istvan said in a quiet extremity of bad temper. "Of course we go on."

"It is partly Nindi's decision," a woman said hesitantly. "It's his people who are guarding the . . . the thing. Are they guarding it against the shaudah's guards, too?"

More silence. Nindi smoothed the tips of his mustache, his black eyes flickering from face to face.

Tarun, the failed engineer, said, "If we're clever, it shouldn't come to a battle at the shrine."

"Right," someone else said. "If they're looking for something, then we give them something to find."

"Something anywhere but at the shrine."

"Why would they look at the shrine at all? It's under the temple's authority, and no one has ever looked twice at *aras* Crab."

"Thank you," said *aras* Crab. "I would prefer to keep it that way."

"Yes, but let's get back to this question of a decoy . . ."

Moth slid backward out of the circle, crawled through the low door, and was quietly sick over the end of the raft. Rain dripping off the balcony's greenery patted her head and back. She hardly noticed the additional pat of a cold human hand.

"So, so," said Istvan. "So, so."

Moth gave a shuddering cough, and spat, and watched the remains of her breakfast swirl with the sluggish current. It wasn't the nastiest pollution in the water. She closed her eyes and rested her head on her arm.

"Well," Istvan said with a final pat, "that got them moving."

"Explain why—"

"I can't hear you," he interrupted testily.

Moth lifted her head. "Explain why I needed to be here for that?"

"You didn't need to be here. They needed to call you here. There's a difference."

"A meaningful one?"

"The day you don't come is the day they think you will never come again."

Moth worked her mouth and spat again, thoughtfully. "But what if they call me down for something like this and I can't come?"

"What if they call you down for something really important and you can't come?"

"I would, for something really important."

Istvan sighed. "And of that promise they have just been re-assured."

So I come, thought Moth, *like a well-trained servant— where my lady would never stir herself,* she might have added, but her pride was too well-schooled to permit the comparison. She tipped her head back to catch leaf-dribbled rain in her mouth.

"Don't do that," Istvan said. "No wonder you're ill, with habits like that. Come with me, I'll give you some proper tea."

Tea with Istvan, even when he was feeling kindly, was not a prospect to be reveled in, but she could hardly refuse with his lesson so fresh in both their minds. And besides, she still had questions he could answer, if only he would.

"Thank you, scholar," she said meekly. And added even more meekly, "If it won't put you to any risk."

Istvan shot her a look and a growl. Whatever else he was, he was not a fool.

Istvan shared a room with Tarun in one of the tenements near the docks, if one could call it a room: it had once been the corner landing of a flight of stairs. The stairs themselves were inhabited, and Istvan and Moth had to pick their way up through the homely clutter of bed mats and children. Istvan's private room, walled off by screens of tindery bamboo, was a luxury and a refuge, even if it did echo with the voices that rang up and down the stairwell. It even had a window, screened by the sickly pea vines growing from the box on the sill.

Tarun had rigged shelves from floor to ceiling, and they mimicked the viny windowsill, spilling over with the pipes, fittings, and cables that Tarun begged, bartered, or outright stole. Tarun, like Istvan, had once had a place in the bastion, and like many of the fallen, he had abandoned himself to his obsessions rather than face up to his decline. He built little machines and tiny engines, exquisite and strange. What were they for? Tarun could only explain what they might be for, one day, if only. If only the tidal had power. If only the gods smiled. If only. But as they were, they were useless except as models for Tarun's dreams.

While Moth perched on a folded bedroll, Istvan took down a can stove and set it on the worn stone of the floor. He laid a fire of shredded rice paper and compressed weed pellets, and crouched over it with his hands shielding his face. He looked like a man in pain, and indeed, Moth found him painful to contemplate, but in fact he was praying. So much effort for so small a thing! A match would have done just as well.

Moth, looking tactfully away, spied a stack of folded broadsheets on a shelf by the door. She teased out the latest edition and unfolded it on the floor at her feet, bending over her rebellious stomach to read it with her chin on her knees. It carried the shaudah's proclamation on the front page, along with a tongue-in-cheek biographical note of the officer in charge of the new tidal detachment. "This heroic veteran almost single-handedly kept the Pilisi District safe from the chicken thefts that were the scourge of the east six years ago, although regrettably the identity of the thieves was never uncovered . . ." Moth snorted softly and turned the page. The shadow cult had apparently been quiet of late, although there were still alleged sightings of the shadow gods in the nighttime streets. Sirijin Naresh claimed to have accumulated an "inarguable preponderance of proof" of occupation of the island *before* the ancestors ever made their way from the ruined *ramhadras* to permanent exile in the *rasnan*. Natives! It was better than a play. Then, finally, Moth found the brief announcement she was looking for: the *Eelgrass* was still missing, having left the *shadras* bay for a deepwater fishing expedition fifty-six days before.

Fifty-six days. Long enough for some to despair, and for Moth to begin to hope.

A flicker caught the corner of Moth's eye. Istvan had woken a flame in the little stove, but it was not that. While the old man still bent self-blinded over his prayers, a lick of shadow teased the cluttered walls. Like the shiver of leaves against the absent sun, the shadow danced across the shelves and in its wake Tarun's inventions came briefly, evanescently, to life. Miniature cogs turned, wheels spun, balance arms lifted and fell with a whispered ticking, a flame-like flutter and sigh. In this private corner, the *mundab* breathed the merest breath, and the inanimate, useless things seemed to scuttle across the walls like rock crabs startled by a flash of light. Moth's skin prickled, for she had never seen a manifest answer to such a trivial working, even so insubstantial a manifest as this. Tiny shapes of polished brass and copper sparkled in the leaf-filtered rain-light, and to Moth sitting on the floor, the walls became tall beings that rose ceiling-high—more than that. They were the flanks of vast creatures with twitching infested skins, who would in the next moment rise and shake themselves, scattering Tarun's insectile inventions, tearing apart the tenement's walls. In the next moment . . .

In the next moment Istvan raised his head. The shadow passed away like a wisp of cloud across the sun, if there had been a sun, and that one fleeting, trembling instant was forgotten as if it had never been.

The tea was weak and hot and kind to her stomach. Moth said, "Thank you, *andas*."

"Have you spoken to a physician?"

Moth suppressed a shudder. "There's no need for that. It's just a touch of tidal belly. It will pass; it always does."

"And what of the ire of *aras* Baradam? Will that, too, pass?"

Caught off guard, Moth winced. That early morning meeting with the scholarium's high priest was not a memory she cared to revisit. "The *aras* has not given me a moment's notice since."

"He should not have had reason to notice you at all. How did you explain—"

"Never mind how I explained," said Moth hastily. "I only wish I had asked *him* to explain how his famous piety reconciles itself to his involvement with the Society of Doors."

Istvan was diverted, though not in the direction she would have chosen. He gave her an incredulous look and said, "His famous piety? It wasn't piety that got him driven out from under his father's wing. The Temple of the Waves should have been his for the asking, instead of this exile onto solid land."

"Is it an exile?" Moth asked curiously.

Istvan gave her a narrow look and said sarcastically, "You don't imagine the good and honorable Divaram Ghar would deliberately smirch his only son's reputation solely in order to put him in charge of the scholars' hall!"

Moth, who had indeed not imagined it, made thoughtful marks on her chin with the rim of her empty cup. "The Ghars and the Society? What does the Society want with the scholars' hall?"

"What did Mahogan ever want with it?" said Istvan, invoking his own personal martyred saint. Mahogan had been, in a manner of speaking, the first *mundabi,* and he, like Istvan, had been a scholar once. And like Moth, a dedicant before he was a scholar.

"Are you saying Mahogan had something to do with the Society?"

"He did not!" Istvan said, as if she had accused his hero of unspeakable things.

Moth groped after connections. There had to be some somewhere. Mahogan and the Society, Baradam Ghar and the scholars' hall, and a manifest straying in the midnight rain. Istvan did not give her a chance to formulate her questions, however.

"I didn't ask you here to revisit ancient history," he said scathingly, as if he had not bored her to tears a hundred times recounting his scholarly career. "Take out Tarun's plans. I want you to study them with me."

"I don't need to study them," she said with little patience. There was no use pressing him, but she did not have to be gracious about it.

"Tarun says that the engine is beginning to diverge from the models—"

"That's because it's real and the models aren't." Moth, struggling to spin an explanation that sounded true, refused to let Istvan interrupt. "If Tarun knew how to build the engine himself, he would do it without you or me or the *mundab*. He gave us the idea, the shell, the seed. It is the *mundab* that makes it real. It is real," she added, more honestly, if less practically, "only in the *mundab*. We might give it its shape, its outline, but . . ."

There she stalled, unable to put into words that sense she had of the *mundab*'s flow, the world's current that might be deftly turned, but never frozen in place. But while she groped, as she always did, for the right words, Istvan took up his own line.

"Mahogan tells us that the *mundab* is neutral," he began, Istvan-the-lecturer.

"Well," said Moth, who had never come to grips with the idea of neutrality, "it is itself."

"It is the passive force," Istvan said sternly. "Ours is the active. We determine its shape, for shape is an attribute of the physical . . ."

Moth let her attention lapse. Istvan had been quoting Mahogan to her since she was a child; Mahogan, the forgotten martyr of the Lamplighters Rebellion, killed the year before Moth was born. Mahogan's rescued notes had been her primer, Mahogan her first true teacher in her approach to the *mundab*. She had learned to read with her finger tracing out his smudged and faded characters, and as she would with any other beginner's text, she had long since put Mahogan's philosophical musings aside.

But those notes salvaged from the wreck of the murdered man's study, rescued or stolen by Istvan in the teeth of the riots that had marked the year of Moth's birth—those notes were Istvan's holy writ, and Moth had given up trying to suggest that her understanding of the *mundab* had by this time gone beyond Mahogan's. Saint Mahogan, in Istvan's mind, was as heroic and as holy as the ancestors who had found the island in the midst of the endless sea and called it *rasnan,* the world, as if the great ocean with its creatures and its currents and its tides were a nothing, a vague and chilling abstraction, the vast wilderness of the Unknowable: the *mundab,* which Mahogan had declared more than water and wind. Not only was the *mundab* the physical world beyond the human world, the boundless sea that surrounded and cradled the *rasnan;* it was the spiritual world as well. It was the divine. Mahogan, the heretical genius, had been silenced by a conspiracy that had reached from the tidal to the towers in the bay and had sparked a year of violence that shaped, still, more than twenty years later, the policies of the powerful and the lives of the powerless, Istvan no less than anyone else who had lived through those times. Within his own imagination Istvan had frozen himself in the shape of Mahogan's disciple; he had frozen Moth in the shape of *his* disciple, and he refused to countenance it when she climbed out of the mold. Not that he did not notice; he was neither stupid nor deluded. He simply, massively, and stubbornly disapproved.

Moth was not immune to irritation.

"What you want," she said into a pause for breath, "is for the *mundab* to birth itself in the shape of your gods. You want the shadow gods to be real. You want a mother and a father, human gods that will stand between you and the frightening world."

"Child, do you think you can provoke me after all these years?"

Moth was willing to try. "The *mundab* can't stand between you and itself. It *is* the world—not some passive abstraction, some ideal thought—it's the *world*—" But Istvan was looking saintly and she could see there was no point. He would always prefer Mahogan's theory to Moth's reality. She sighed. "The engine is taking shape. Maybe Tarun should redraw his plans taking into account the changes and see if he can extrapolate the parts we will need to finish. It's no use scolding me about what we've already done," she added when Istvan opened his mouth. "It can't be changed. Let's just see if we can come to grips with what we still need to do."

And let's hope, she added to herself, *that Tarun doesn't notice what kind of engine we're building for a while longer.* Safer to hope that than to try to move her lady's schemes on apace.

Though Moth was willing to risk the attempt. "Tonight is my last vigil for *aras* Baradam," she said. "I can come down again tomorrow night."

"Tomorrow night!" Istvan exclaimed. "With the tidal crawling with soldiers, you want to raise the shadow gods?"

"I want to finish the engine."

"We would be giving them exactly what they are looking for!"

"You'd rather wait for them to leave? Or die of old age, maybe? We have to finish it! Finish it, move it, dismantle it, abandon it—"

Istvan threw up his hands in surrender. "Gods watch over us. Tomorrow night it is."

Which is the message Moth sent to her lady. *Like it or not,* she wanted to add, but she refrained.

THE BASTION

The scholarium during the rains was the nearest thing to a forest that a tidal-bred Moth could imagine. There was life everywhere, too much life. White-flowered vines bannered the walls and roof ferns sparkled with dew, but the moss-choked gutters hatched flies that bit as hard as bullets, and with them hatched the poison-bright frogs and the lizards with gem-colored scales. They ate the flies, but they scuttled across the bed at night. Cats hunted the lizards across the roofs, and *tirindi* harassed the cats from the air. And then there were the people. They debated in the passages, gossiped on the porches, prayed in the shrines; they splashed in the gutters, raked sand in the cloisters, scraped moss and the occasional roof tile onto passersby. People, people, people. In all the *rasnan*, was there any escape? *Hadaras* farmers lived piled up like chickens in stacked baskets to make room for the fields, while tidal-dwellers scrambled onto one another's backs to escape the mud. Only in the bay—perhaps in the bay—

But what use was that to Moth? Dedicant Moth, tidal-scum Moth, who stepped through the scholarium gate only to blink tear-stung eyes at the sunlight glaring off the quartz-roofed towers and the water of the bay. She could admire that view, but the other view, the view from the other side, she could only imagine. One day, said her sponsor.

One day soon, thought Moth.

Even the fort's wall was shaggy with leaves. A few engineers leaned out of the archers' windows for a glimpse of the sun, and someone had hung a shirt on a sill to dry. An optimistic soul, for though sunlight spilled between the wind-driven clouds, it was tempered by gusts of rain. The shirt dangled its arms in mock defeat, forgotten perhaps, a pitiful object, abandoned, lost. Moth, seeing it, felt a rush of anticipation. At last! Aramis's punishment seemed to have the same term as *aras* Baradam's: today she was relieved of both. She scampered across the busy road, dodging two-wheeled handcarts and laden bearers, to the forbidding black cave of the fort's only door.

Moth, in her plain dedicant's tunic and fraying trousers, made herself dull as she mumbled, "Message for 'geneering liaison," to the guards and plodded under the arcade and up the corner stairs. To the left lay the archers' walk with its windows and its arcade open to the courtyard below. To the right lay the overbuilt mass of the fort itself, with its offices and workshops, bunk rooms and manufactories and stores. Moth made a slight detour to collect the rain-wet shirt off the windowsill, and then, because she had to spend some of the excitement inside her, she ran, ran, ran, bare feet slapping the floor, braid tapping the base of her spine, down a corridor, up a short flight of stairs, into the mazy depths of the Vashmarna's demesne, where she opened a door and flew into her lover's arms.

Or rather, she would have if he had been there. Aramis's cubbyhole of an office, lined with ledgers and smelling of ink, was empty.

Should she wait for him? She should. At least, Aramis would be furious if she did not. But what did he mean by hanging out their signal and then not waiting for her to come? And how did he expect her to resist the natural desire to rummage through the papers left lying so innocently in view? That he would never forgive, if he caught her at it, and yet he was the one who tempted her. It was very unfair of him. She would take herself away, leaving the sodden shirt behind to show that she, the faithful lover, had been and gone. Let him search her out if he would.

So thought Moth, cold and proud. But Aramis would never find her if she left the fort, so she made her way into one of her favorite places, the hollow interior of the generating station's dam. Standing on the catwalk above the bellowing turbines, bathed in an electrical mist, shivered to her heart by the bass whirl of the enormous drums, she could not imagine anything more powerful, more dangerous, more arrogant and foolish and deliciously daring than this harnessing of a river in flood, unless it was her own relationship with the *mundab*.

Istvan had never understood why they must steal the fort's electricity to create their engine when the *mundab* was the source of the engine's substance and power. If Moth could have brought him here, she would have said simply, "This is why," but he still would not have understood. Silk, knowing Moth so well, might have caught a glimmer. The engineer Tarun might have, though he barely perceived the *mundab* at all. But none of them had swum as Moth did in the *mundab*'s tides, and none of them would have recognized this sustained, muscular, and exquisite roar. What Silk would grasp, if she could only come here, was the wordless metaphor of the river in chains. Here the world was tamed and set in the service of the *shadras* rich. There, in the tidal, it was going to be set free. Freer than even the *mundabi* knew.

And on the other hand, if Lady Vashmarna wanted the tidal to build her her engine, it was only fair that she should pay *something* for it, and not leave Moth and the *mundabi* to foot the bill alone. But that was something else the *mundabi* did not need to understand.

Moth leaned on the catwalk railing and let the turbines' thunder numb the ache in her back, her belly, her breasts. The engineers down below circled around their growling beasts, reading their gauges and dials. Their movements made a complex pattern, and Moth fell into a waking dream that incorporated Tarun's models and the *mundab,* the struggle of the tidal, and her own great engine brooding half-born in the womb of the fire shrine. The engineer's hard voice shattered her trance like a hammer on an egg.

"Dedicant, do you have business here?"

She stared at him, blinking, caught with nothing to say. He grimaced and gestured her to follow him out of the noise. She did, trailing meekly at his heels as he led her to an airless niche of a storeroom.

Or rather, the storeroom itself was vast, but the only space left to stand was an aisle as narrow as a coffin. The rest was shelves filled two and three items deep, bins overflowing onto the floor, hulking carcasses rearing up against the lightbulbs that hung, dim with dust or burnt out altogether, from the cobwebbed ceiling. A store of dead things shaped in copper, iron, brass, and gold, their wires hanging like intestines outside a butcher's stall, their cogwheels toothed like beached sharks, their once-polished armatures as delicate and ungainly as limbs from a disjointed crab. A junk room to the uninformed eye. Moth, who had made a point of informing herself, saw the failed and disallowed experiments, Vashmarna's restless—or ambitious—challenges to the religious strictures that kept Vashmarna's technology, and Vashmarna's demesne, within its limited bounds. The engineer, knowing it was too late to protect this particular secret from this particular intruder, locked the two of them into this room that no outsider should ever have seen. The turbines rumbled on through the stones.

"You can't just wander around the fort at will!" he said, Aramis appearing through the engineer's hard mask. Moth's instinctive move toward him was repelled by his tone. She pressed herself against the hard round belly of a rusty boiler, mortified by how like, and how bitterly unlike, their first meeting this was. He had looked more kindly on her trespasses when they were strangers.

"Good gods!" Aramis went on. "How many times can you traipse past the guards before someone thinks to stop you and ask why the hell you're here?"

"The more often they see me, the less likely they are to question my presence. It's true," she added at his exasperated look. "No one notices the things they see every day."

Aramis rubbed his hands across his face and into his hair, visibly trying to let his anger go. "You are hard not to notice."

"That's only because you love me," she said wistfully. "I'm not much of anything to anyone else."

"What does that mean?"

"Oh . . ." She made a slight gesture. One could not be expansive in such a small space. "*Aras* Baradam sets me vigils, as if by disciplining me he has discharged his duty toward the entire scholarium. The place is rife with rumor and rebellion, but I am apparently the only disruptive element worth troubling himself with. Most of the other dedicants wouldn't even recognize him out of his ceremonial robes, yet here am I, called up one day after the next. He only hates me because I am a scholar with a tidal name."

"Only that?" Aramis said. "Why didn't you tell me you were the one who saw the shadow god?"

Moth was astonished. Was this her Aramis? What did he know? More on her guard, she said carefully, "When would I have told you? I haven't seen you since it happened."

"I thought it was that night . . ." Aramis trailed off with an anxious look.

Gathering herself, Moth said more forcefully, "How did you know it was me?"

His gaze flicked away and he grimaced, as if he would have dismissed the question without an answer. Moth did not need an answer.

"So he is a member," she said. She did not have to say *Baradam Ghar,* nor *the Society of Doors.*

Aramis's hands twitched, as if he would have flung them in the air if he had had more room. "You knew that already. Why do you put yourself in his path the way you do?"

As if she had meant to! But Moth had to wince, not for the first time, over the tale she had blurted out that foggy dawn, caught by the *aras* and too tired to think of a better lie. *The shadow god!* she had gasped. *I have been running . . . hiding . . . Oh,* aras. *I'm so afraid!* And had *aras* Baradam comforted her, this poor credulous dedicant cowering at his feet, frightened out of her wits? Gods forefend! He had torn a strip off her for spreading superstitious, blasphemous, slum-born rumors and had set her ten nights of vigil at Kistnaran's knee. And if she had lightened some of those wearisome hours by remembering the ecstatic moments she had spent with her lover behind the goddess's back, well, it seemed she was to pay for that as well.

She said coolly, "How fortunate for me that the *aras* was kind enough to relay the news to you, since I have not seen you to tell you myself."

"The *aras* did not tell just me. Don't you realize the whole Society knows your name?"

"Well? And what do they mean to do with it?"

"Nothing! Gods, Moth, what do you think they would do? I only mean that you're known. And known for spreading rumors about shadow gods in the bastion. Do you think that's something to take lightly after the shaudah's proclamation? Do you know how much trouble the Society could cause you?"

"The Society of Doors was outlawed before the shadow cult was ever dreamed of!"

"And what good does that do you when a well-placed member—someone who isn't known to *be* a member—drops a word in the shaudah's ear?"

"Why in the known world would anyone bother? Does the shaudah mean to arrest every person who's ever seen something lurking in the shadows? Half the *hadaras* and most of the tidal!"

"But you're the only dedicant, the only person in the scholarium—"

" 'Nothing,' he says. 'What do you think they would do?' he says. Is your Society innocent or isn't it?"

Aramis clasped his head in his hands, rocked by frustration. "I am only trying to suggest," he said in a muffled voice, "that you might consider comporting yourself with a little more care instead of traipsing about the fort where you have no business to be."

"*Is* that what you're trying to suggest?" Moth said, still hot. He dropped his hands. "Very well. Spread *this* rumor and they'll take my head. There have been power outages in the bay, and the Vashmarna has spoken to the shaudah about the possibility of sabotage. Sabotage and the shadow cult in the same breath! Do you understand what I'm saying? Do you see why it might not be wise to be the dedicant who sees shadow gods and wanders in and out of the fort at will? Even if the Society has nothing to do with any of this—especially if they don't!—surely you can see why an honest member might feel obliged to mention your name. Moth, Moth. Dear Kistnu, you'll wind up in the shaudah's courts if you don't take more care!"

Moth leaned against the boiler, her stomach sinking under the weight of a situation growing out of control. She had only mentioned the manifest to *aras* Baradam because . . . Well, to be honest, she had meant to stir them up, the *aras* and his Society both. But now her lady was involved—her lady, who was complaining of the shadow cult to the shaudah without knowing the cult and the *mundabi* were essentially one and the same. How many secrets could one juggle before they began to collide? Moth never prayed, but she found herself thinking, *Dear gods!*

Aramis mirrored her pose, his hands hanging in defeat. "Gods witness, Moth, you are clever, but you have no *sense*."

Moth said in a hard little voice, "And if the Society is not innocent? Where is your sense, Aramis? What are you involved with?"

"What are you?"

"Nothing!"

"Nothing? Truly nothing?" Aramis waited, as if she might have a different answer, before he added, his voice thin with restraint, "Then why does my lady ask me to bear a message to the scholarium addressed to the dedicant-scholar Moth?"

Moth's jaw sagged, and then she giggled. She outright laughed.

"I can't help it!" she cried at Aramis's glare. "What are you going to tell me next, that the shaudah himself wants to invite me up to Magarand for tea? Come on, Aramis, don't dole out your surprises like they're beggar's alms. Be generous. Give them to me all at once."

But he would not be lightened. Speechless, he undid two buttons in the breast of his coat and pulled out a flimsy sheet of rice paper, elegantly folded and sealed, and so fine Moth could see the dark brush strokes of the message inside. She took it, wanting to hold it up to the electric bulb that dangled from a cord overhead, to see how much he could have read. She did not, of course, with him watching, but her fingers hesitated on the seal. The quarters were just too close.

"Shall I leave you?" Aramis said bleakly. "Or would it suffice if I just turned my back and closed my eyes?"

"Oh, Aramis, Aramis." Moth crumpled the sealed letter in her fist and wrapped her arms around his waist, ignoring the stiffness of his back. "The Vashmarna sponsored me to the scholarium when I was a child, that's all. She is conscientious in her duties; she sends me a message every year. Why she chose you to carry this one I don't know, but it's no more than the usual admonitions to be good and study hard. Aramis, if you don't put your arms around me I'm going to think you are jealous of *her*."

Aramis the lied-to, Aramis the loved. She leaned her head against his breast so that she could hear his heartbeat. It was a faint pulse within the greater throb of the turbines. Slow to rouse, Aramis, and, she was beginning to fear, slow to forgive. But he did eventually lay his hand against her head. He did eventually stroke her back, and tease her brass-streaked hair from its braid. Their lovemaking was awkward, wordless, tender, and painfully exquisite. Moth was as sensitive to his touch as if she had a fever, her breasts hot and full, her womb heavy and ripe. And although for once she did not make a sound as desire peaked in a voluptuous release, a rare honest voice inside her cried out, *Moth! Who are you trying to deceive? You're pregnant!*

"Moth: You are *not* to make another attempt on our project until the occupation is at an end. This is an order. I will be obeyed."

THE BAY

Dear lady—ziiimmm—*do not be*—zzweezzwee—*distrac*—ktktk—*ted*—

The message hummed from all the wires in Lady Vashmarna's study.

Do not be distracted by rumors of the shadow cult within the bastion walls. Shadows have no substance. Look past them to the Society of Doors.

Each word sizzling from the desk lamp, the ceiling fan, the chandelier, was like a wasp; the whole message was like a swarm of insects defending their nest.

Szszsocietktkteezzweez of Doorszszs.

Lady Vashmarna sat still, her finger keeping her place in her book of meditations, and suffered the assault with what fortitude she had. To be herself, in this room she had known and loved for most of her adult life, and yet to have this strangeness inflicted upon her! How had this come to pass? The narrow windows, black glass framed by delicate scrolls, reflected her polished desk, her beloved treasures on their shelves. It seemed impossible that that reflection showed nothing of the voice that spat its wasp-words at her from every side. What stillness, what repose there was in that silent night-backed world! And then, as her heart quickened in her breast, Lady Vashmarna saw a shadow move between the window and the night, a shape sketched out by the streaks of moisture on the glass. It was only more rain borne on a swirl of wind, a wisp of the louring clouds. Do such things have eyes? Do they grin with a mouth full of electric teeth? But it was only a shadow, a nothing, a squall. It was gone. It had never been.

Bless us, spirits of air, against the dark-shrouded evils of night.

When the spark-wrought voice died away, Lady Vashmarna laid a worn silk cord between the pages and set her book neatly aside before she took out paper, ink, and brush. She noted down the message—and noted, too, that it did not acknowledge her order—and whence came this connection between the shadow cult and the Society of Doors? But while Lady Vashmarna's hand was steady, her characters elegantly formed, that shadow, imagined, dreaded, stirred again behind her heart. The room was so quiet she heard the pat of rain against the glass, the whir of the fan, the sizzle of current across the filaments in the lamp. . . . Surely not? But the voice lingered like an infestation brooding behind the paneled walls. Despite herself, Lady Vashmarna shivered, trying to cast off that instinctive unease. These messages, regardless of their content, grew harder and harder to bear.

But perhaps she suffered only the contrast between her present and the past that Divaram Ghar had woken from its sleep. They had shared a meal that day, a simple dinner between two old friends, and he had spoken as he often did about the passage of time.

"We are blinded by the threat of death," he said. "We are consumed by the fear of ignorance—not the ignorance of what we do not know in the here and now, but the ignorance of what lives have been lived before us, and especially of the lives that will be lived after us. That is where the greatest fear lies. In our bodies we know we will end, and it is as though life will end with us. But they are only bodies, and it is in our spirits that we continue, in the spirit of what we do, what values we hold to—just as it is in their legacies that our ancestors live on, with us, and in us."

And he had spoken of his ancestors, who had come through the door from the *ramhadras* and laid the foundations for a future they would see only through their descendants' eyes. Lord Ghar did not recount anecdotes like a lonely old man; he had constructed a philosophy of the past. And he did conjure up a sense of peace, of order, when he spoke of the days, as he said, "when there was only the human and the divine in the known world, and the divine was confined to the holy temples, its power trained upon the structure of ritual like a vine trained upon a garden wall. The gods' wall that shelters us all from the unknown."

Bless us, spirits of air, against the dark-shrouded evils of night.

"But isn't there a danger here?" she had said to him. "Isn't there a kind of blindness, a failure of perspective, that lets us look back and back until we find a day so far off that the troubles of that time seem insignificant compared to the tribulations of today?"

She did not say, but it was perhaps implied, *Already you forget the problems that led to the Lamplighters Rebellion, as you forget the tempest that exiled humankind from the first world*, the *ramhadras* that had become synonymous with heaven even in Lady Vashmarna's mind. In this the Ghar and his ilk were like the outlawed Society of Doors, who pursued one shining ideal, or one bitterly intransigent lie: that there was a home that humanity could return to without walking back into the hell from which their ancestors had fled so long ago.

Divaram Ghar; the Society of Doors. There was an unlikely connection! Yet Lady Vashmarna's agent was chasing equally absurd fancies in the bastion. *What are you doing tonight, my girl? Are you doing what you were told?* Handled properly, *aras* Baradam might unwittingly give her a handle on his slippery father, and yet all she got were vague missives about the shadow cult. And as for Lord Ghar giving her a handle on his priestly son . . .

"My son," Lord Ghar had said more times than she could count, his voice rich with pain and frustration, interest and pride. "My son."

"Do you ever regret your celibacy?" he had asked Lady Vashmarna once. She had replied with a deflection: "Do you ever regret your son?" For what can one answer to such a question? One wants to cry out in pain, *Yes, yes!* But it is impossible. The moment that truth was spoken it would become a lie. Lord Ghar had apologized for intruding on her privacy, but they had known each other for an instant, a pure meeting of heart and heart. "Yes" so often becomes translated into "No" by the alchemy of time.

And "No" into "Yes."

Restless now, Lady Vashmarna locked the message away with the others in the desk's hidden drawer and went to stand at the window. She had to cup her hands about her face to see through the reflected light of the room. The bridge reached out like a ribbon of pearls, its lights haloed by the rain. The fort sent up its few stars, the dam cast out its electric glare of pride. Too proud, Lady Vashmarna felt, as she often did, an arrogant display. The generating station framed a bright section of riverbank and fortress walls, its own dam's clean arc, the river foaming in its last descent to the sea. The scholarium, stubbornly unelectrified, was a dark mass barely visible against the black void of the island.

The tidal, to whom no one had ever offered—nor would ever offer—power, was invisible at the edge of the glimmering waters of the bay.

As invisible, Lady Vashmarna thought, *as those sins of the past that Divaram Ghar is so eager to drown.* She could sympathize. She did sympathize, which made it harder to make an enemy out of her most treasured friend. The tidal was like a cancer, a rotten sore that threatened the survival of the whole. But it was too easy to speak, as her peers often did, of its wholesale destruction.

"When the storm comes," people said. "When the waves finally claim their own."

How much easier life would be if one's conscience did not have to deafen itself to those cries of hunger, illness, ignorance, and pain. Lady Vashmarna might have counted it as a virtue that she listened and did not forget, except that she was bound by a secret thread to the people and the place. Her informer, that bright and talented girl, was like a piece of Lady Vashmarna's own self tucked away, out of sight, out of reach—but not out of memory—among the damned.

Thinking so, she winced as she had ten thousand times before. And as she had done as many times, she absolved herself. That child was redeemed in the only way she could have been, safely, anonymously, charitably sponsored to a place among the priests, rescued from the muck and given the chance to better herself and her kind. Given a chance to save us all was the thought that followed, but Lady Vashmarna would not place such a heavy responsibility on that young head. She would bear the weight herself, as she had borne others in her time.

She moved away from the window, restless still, and crossed to her desk. She toyed with the book of meditations, but did not open it to the marked page.

Where are you tonight? I will be obeyed!

A knock sounded at the door.

At this time of night it could be only another emergency. Lady Vashmarna glanced at the window, imagining a sudden darkness where the generating station had been, but the glass showed only herself, the steadily burning desk lamp. *Foolish,* she scolded herself as she opened the door.

Aramis Tapurnashen stood with her disapproving butler at his elbow. The young engineer looked tense and oddly shrunken with distress, but the news he brought sounded like a triumph to Lady Vashmarna.

"I have found . . . What I think I have found, Vashmarna-*jin'*, is a tap—a cable—an unsanctioned electrical cable leading from the shore-end bridge transformer into the tidal."

The connections were too obvious to require thought: the shadow cult, sabotage, the tidal. Lady Vashmarna nodded as if she had been expecting exactly this news and said, "Then our mystery is finally solved."

"Perhaps, *jinnu*. The power drain, at least. All the other effects, the—"

"Ghosts and demons," she said impatiently. "Yes. But let us take in hand the solution to the problem before us. You found this cable yourself, *andas*?"

Young Tapurnashen looked, if anything, more miserable than before. "Yes, *jinnu*. I followed . . . I noticed activity below the foot of the bridge, and I went down. . . ."

"You followed . . . ?"

"*Jinnu,* this morning you sent me with a message to . . . to the scholarium. . . ."

"And you followed . . . ?"

Tapurnashen looked at her, mute with distress, and all his pregnant pauses birthed their monsters of suspicion in Lady Vashmarna's mind. He was speaking of Moth. Moth and the illegal cable, Moth and the sabotage—*oh, gods*—Moth and the engine. Moth, who manifestly was not obeying orders tonight. What did it mean?

And what, Lady Vashmarna wondered even as she was gripped with her own horror, did it mean to this young man, who stared at her with such dread that the warm brown of his face was muddied with gray? Was he so loyal? Could anyone be so loyal as that?

Moth, she thought. *Moth!*

But whatever it meant, she had no choice, not with this so-loyal witness here to judge *her* loyalty to her own demesne. What was she cutting loose? The *mundabi,* the engine, the *rasnan*'s hope for the future? Or betrayal, sabotage, Vashmarna's ruination?

Shadows have no substance. Look past them to the Society of Doors.

Whatever that meant, it was too late. It was far too late.

Lady Vashmarna drew a swift breath and said, her voice much as usual, "What do you need to rectify the situation?"

Aramis Tapurnashen ducked his head, his whole body slumping in what Lady Vashmarna supposed must be relief. "If I could have some heavy electricians," he mumbled. "And . . . and some guardsmen . . ."

Lady Vashmarna nodded and went to ring the bell for her servants. It would take some time for messages to be sent and answered, and in the meantime the young man was soaking wet and trying not to shiver. He would have some hot tea, Lady Vashmarna thought virtuously, before he went back out into the night.

It was the least she owed such a loyal man.

THE TIDAL

Tonight there were ghosts.

Even before Moth descended the tidal stairs, she had felt haunted, as though there were watchers under every dripping eave in the bastion. She had never been more conscious of Vashmarna's guards looking out from the black cave of the fort's gate, and while the stairs offered her an escape, it seemed that her ghosts—whoever, whatever they were—came, too, unseen and unheard. Rain cascaded off the bridge in ropes and twisting strands, spinning electric lamplight into a garland: beautiful, but it made an ugly sound that echoed underneath the bridge, a sound like a hundred drunks pissing into the mud. It drowned all other sounds. The lights on the bridge's underside were weak yellow bulbs that could pick out only a stone, a join of pipes, a bracket for the massive cables that carried power from the fort to the bay; they might have been placed specifically to cast shadows, rather than to illuminate the dark.

Even so, there was light enough for Moth to slither along the platform that skirted the bridge's base. Past tides had left it slimed with weed and seething with tiny crabs, but at least it was out of the water. Moth found the lightless niche in the bridge's foot and, fighting the sense that it was already occupied, tucked herself into its shelter. There, shaking off the crabs that pinched her feet, she groped for the forbidden cable, and then she reached for the *mundab*. The vast unknown, the exiled world, the one certainty in her life. It was always there when she had need.

Dear lady: Do not be distracted by rumors of the shadow cult. . . .

As the message went, the manifestation of the working stirred, a corded illusion of stony limbs, naked sinews, spark-toothed mouth. It was only a mirage given substance by the weak lights and the misting air, but Moth was unpleasantly reminded of the Society's manifest. She could not forget the feel of the thing's false door latch in her hand. Above her, the message's manifest clambered in defiance of gravity across the groin of the bridge's high arch, and Moth, kicking the crabs off her feet with unusual violence, made her way back to the tidal stairs before she could see where the thing would go.

The rain was heavy, washing to shore on the ocean wind the way the waves washed in on the tide, and it swallowed what little light there was. Moth called, but there was no Silk, no waiting scull. For once she was early and the water was too low to float a hull. Feeling morose and hard done by, she took to the foot stones that studded the mucky streets. Rain-wet weeds glistened in the dark as the tide's first creeping fingers lifted them from the mud, a faint shimmer beneath Moth's feet like the slide of starlight off watching eyes. The eyes of the mud creatures that clustered around the foot stones for protection against the waves, the eyes of the unseen shape that crept behind her wrapped in a cloak of rain. Moth stood balanced between two foot stones and stared bravely behind her, but all she could see was the bridge curving like a lucent knife-slash into the towered bay. All else was blackness, rain, ghosts.

"I know you're there," Moth murmured. She licked the water off her lips and said it aloud: "I know you are there." She could feel it, inhuman, brooding, and mysteriously sad. The Society's manifest or hers? It troubled her that she did not know. Was the Society meeting again tonight? She did not know that either, and she had to grant Aramis his due: he kept his secrets well for such an honest man. "I know you're there," she said less certainly, but there was only the rain and the weight of its regard. She could summon it—could she?—call it to her out of the dark? She shivered as the rain trickled down beneath her clothes. The manifests had no answers; or if they did, it was an answer she already knew. The *mundab,* she thought, unconscious of the irony. The unknown.

With the tidal full of soldiers, *aras* Crab had not lit the lamps, and the fire shrine was empty but for its saints. A different kind of haunt, this emptiness. It struck Moth that Aramis was the real ghost tonight. She was haunted by the things he had said, and by the things, the one great thing, she had not. The saints smiled their brooding smiles, their untroubled foreheads glowing with the polish of a thousand prayerful touches, and Moth, nonbeliever Moth, reached out a wistful hand to brush a knee as she passed. *Morabaruun who burned in the* ramhadras *so your children could pass to safety in this world, I beseech you, bring me safely through.* But the brass knee was cold.

Despite the quiet, Hamana and a few of her crew were stationed in the stairwell. They were throwing dice, lazy and bored. Hamana asked Moth if she had seen any of the shau-dah's men outside, and Moth was briefly tempted to tell the greenguards she had been followed. But of course there was nothing there, nothing real. "You can't see anything but the rain," Moth said, and for proof she dripped on them all as she passed on her way up to the priest's rooms.

The *mundabi* did not care that she was subdued. They did notice that she was wet, at least enough to complain about the dripping. Silk was being remote, but one of the women who lived at the shrine gave Moth a cloth to dry her hair. Most of them stayed as they were, bent over Tarun's immaculate hand-drawn plans. It was a beautiful design, and Moth could under-stand Tarun's love for the elegance, the balance, the sense, but it had little to do with her. *Her* engine was what it was, and would come as it came.

"Then why," Istvan had challenged her once, "does the *mundab* not give it to us in one step, complete?"

Moth could not remember exactly what she had re-plied. Now she would have said, *Because the seed is not the plant, the quickening life is not the child, the child is not the man.* And there—admit it, Moth!—there was the real haunt: the ghost of the future she carried in her womb. *I know you're there.* She shivered, feeling the rain's chill now that she was in the lamplit warmth of the room.

"What do you think?" Tarun asked from across the cluster of mismatched tables that held the plans.

Tarun, like Moth, was a little lighter than the norm, but while Moth's skin had the polished glow of ripe bamboo, his had a dry, pockmarked look, as if he had been left to weather by the sea. He was not old, but his meticulous, self-absorbed manner made him a good companion for Istvan Soos. But while Istvan was always probing Moth, always trying to find a way to insert himself into her mind, Tarun generally let others remain peripheral to his obsession. So it was sometimes shocking when he looked at her as he did tonight, as if she were the realest thing in the room.

"What do you think?"

"It's beautiful," Moth said slightly at random. "Very fine."

"But is it right?" he said, intense.

Quiet conversations died. Moth leaned over the plans, then drew back again when the tip of her braid dripped on the fragile paper. What was right? She could see the half-made engine within the complex structure Tarun had drawn in such delicate detail. It nestled there, the wheel, the drive shafts, the joints and balances and cogs, like a key within the wards of a lock. It fit nicely, but Moth did not think that this was the answer Tarun was looking for. He knew it fit. What he did not know was whether his dream that had been laid bare by brush and ink would come true. Was it right? Was he right? Was her engine his?

"It will work," Moth said with a pang. It was not his. It was not any of theirs. But it *is,* she told herself. It is theirs; it is just not what they imagine it to be. This bit of sophistry was not as comforting as it usually was, but, "It will work," she said firmly, and a new breath of purpose came into the room.

The engine itself was the best answer for the doubts that plagued her tonight. It flowed into view as the *mundabi* carried the red-flamed lamps into the inner shrine, the lick of firelight along its curves belying its unnatural cold. It was huge, solid, yet poised on the brink of motion above the stealthy invading tide. The human building that surrounded it was as fragile and impermanent as an egg. *I am reality,* the engine said. *I alone am real.*

The midnight tide swelled around the engine's base; the

steam rose up from the cold metal; the shrine groaned under the weight of the waves. Tarun brought out the cable. Sparks arced out from the cable's bare end, snapping and spitting in the humid chill, troubling the tenuous shadows cast by the *mundabi*'s lamps, until Moth had no choice but to dive.

It is a dive, this immersion in the unknown world. Unknown purpose, unknown future, forgotten past: the *mundab*. It is as careless as the sea. Moth, if she could have divided herself from the moment, would have known herself to be both right and wrong. The *mundab* is its own Answer, but there are no answers here. But Moth is singular, her every heartbeat in the service of the invisible tide. The current is fierce tonight, not one current but many, as if raveled by a storm. For an instant Moth is as harried as the shadows that flee half-seen about the shrine. For an instant she is no more than they are, born into the lightning-riven dark, torn into a shape that the shapeless are not meant to hold.

But she has purpose, and she has desire. She is both a current braided into the whole and the wire through which the current flows, and the engine is hers and she is the engine's. Stolen power stabs down at the hissing water; it draws scorched lines across the dewy walls; it haloes the heads and upraised hands of the celebrants. Light when the stars are drowned, heat when there is more rain than air, movement when the mud threatens to rise neck-high and higher: *power*, say the *mundabi*, but Moth's silent, secret cry is *escape*, and the *mundab*, as it always has, answers her at last. *Birth*, the *mundab* says, and the engine whirs into life, a huge humming blur within the swarm of shadows, a whirling eye-deceiving gleam within the spark-wrought steam. It spins, it churns. It drones like a massive hive of metal bees, and the sound is a perfect mouth-watering counterpart to the sour-sweet tang of electricity in the air. Moth is stirred, aroused, but there is no grand release. The engine slows, its new shape becoming visible within the birth-caul of steam, but it is still all potential. The animating spark withdraws from the incomplete vessel, the *mundab* withdraws, the promised power of the living generator ebbs as life, and completion, eludes her.

It is not done.

THE BRIDGE

Moth returned as she had come, alone. It was not safe—the tidal was never safe—but it was safe enough with no shadow cult on a holy rampage. Even the soldiers were taking shelter from the rain. Moreover, tonight she walked within an orbiting escort of manifests. All around her the darkness was troubled by a flicker of bearing-jointed limbs, of wheels churning the muddy tide, of distorted mechanical reflections scattering lizardlike across tenement walls. The rain rushed and pattered and musically pinged into the withdrawing tide. Greenguards protecting the roof gardens from hungry marauders whistled their codes from roof to roof. Sluggish waves sucked at foundations like tongues lapping rotten teeth. And the manifests, the shadow gods, flitted in perfect silence, as delicate and sudden as lightning trapped in the upper reaches of the towering clouds.

They were beautiful, Moth thought, believing it; but she shook with the chill of the rain, and her feet minced with uncertain care over the slick foot stones. She was all out of balance tonight, distracted, beginning to be afraid. Was she really pregnant? Could it possibly be true? Simpler to think of it as an illness—even if it was a potentially fatal one. The more youths that, denied marriage by the shaudah's laws, poured into the shrines, the more strictly the temple elders enforced the vows of celibacy. Even laypeople took those vows, inspired to a holy desperation by the crowded isle and the shaudah's bribes, even people of high estate, like the Vashmarna, who drew enormous credibility from that solitary act. Among the ranks of the priesthood, to be caught with a lover was to be disgraced and cast down. To be caught with child—

But she was not ready to go that far. Every time she tried, she ran into memories of Aramis. Aramis! *You can't lose me, Moth. You could only cast me aside.* Is that true, Aramis? Is that still true? But she could not bear to think of him, and worse would have been to think of her lady. Cause and consequence were beyond her. The hard present wrapped her in its shell. There was only this: this rain, this haunted night, this heavy womb. *Oh,* she thought, *if only it were done*—where "it" was everything, engine and child, lies and schemes. And yet, what would that mean for her? Success, perhaps, but with what reward? *With what*—for the first time she thought it in so many words—*with what consequence? With what loss?* Thinking of Silk and Istvan, thinking of her maybe-child. Never had the towers been so distant, the bridge, on which she had been forbidden to set foot, so long. She shivered, chilled to her core, and, groping her way by the glimmer of her fitful escort, did not dare lift her eyes from her footing, and so did not recognize the darkness until she found herself almost at the tidal stairs and realized that the bridge's lights were dead.

The first blow was visceral and senseless. *Now I'll never get there,* she thought. But as Moth stared above her, the grip of an outraged conscience began to squeeze her like a fist. She had to force her head around to look along the bridge's foam-footed pilings to the towers in the bay. No, not dark, although the gusting rain made the light from the windows shift and dance. Neither was the bridge entirely dark when she looked again, but the horror did not relax its grip. Electric ghosts flowed from one lamp stanchion to the next, sparking lightbulbs only to let them die again, sketching mirror-phantoms against the curtains of rain. The manifests gathering behind Moth bore the same ephemeral electrical forms, and she was called out of herself by a kind of foreboding wonder. *Did I accomplish this?* warred with, *Am I responsible for this?* She balanced between them as she balanced on her weedy stone until she realized that some of the shifting lights were human. Engineers were out with guttering lamps and unwieldy battery torches, and some of them, Moth realized with a jolt of the heart, were under the bridge. Vashmarna's engineers, her lady's men. The cable! How—*how*—could she ever explain? Without a thought except for the new disaster looming, she started forward into the stinking cave of the bridge's first arch.

A light stabbed out from the other side of the water sheeting off the bridge deck, and a too-familiar voice said, "So there you are."

"Aramis?" Moth backed away from him into the rain. "Aramis?"

"What have you done?"

His voice was so quiet and the rain so loud that the words must have slipped directly from his mouth to her ear like a kiss. A kiss of betrayal, of grief. Perhaps it should have cut her with a blade of guilt, but it only made her want to scold, *Do not speak to me so! I am carrying your child!* She did not, but she did say accusingly, "What are you doing here? Did you *follow* me?"

"Undoing what you have done. It was you, wasn't it, Moth? Do you even begin to understand—"

"Oh, no," she said. *My cable. My engine!* "No, you can't. Aramis, you don't know!"

She started forward. He came to meet her, and caught and held her under the pounding overspill. It was a relief to Moth to feel something as hot and as uncomplicated as anger.

"Let me go! You'll destroy everything!"

"I'll destroy—Do you know what you've done?"

"*Yes*, I know what I've done. Do you? Do you know anything? Damn you, Aramis, stop this. Let me go!"

"No," he said, and he held her hard.

But he did not hold the manifests. They slipped, stilted, rolled out of the surf where they had waited unseen in the rain, and as they came in a seething crab-like scramble, they built themselves into a single thing, a muddled reflection of human and machine. It was the engine's stillborn twin, a tidal cripple, a faceless giant. Huge and gleaming with a faint rotten light, it swept past Moth and Aramis—swept around them and over them—swept *through* them, Moth thought at that sudden dreadful cold—and under the high arch of the bridge, which was not so high with the manifest of manifests beneath it.

Aramis shouted with horror and surprise. He dragged Moth away from the bridge and shouted again at his colleagues working around the *mundabi*'s cable and the transformer station above. Moth could feel the fear that shocked through him, the fear for others that made him strain toward the bridge even as he pulled her away. He shouted names she did not know—Uradin! Latisman! Peel!—and Moth said with stern authority, "Let me go."

Startled, perhaps, by the reminder of a presence he had forgotten, he let her go.

The manifest paused in its advance, but its many parts were in constant motion, changing position, changing function, changing form. The engineers were scrambling for the far side of the bridge, where deep water and a cliff would trap them—*or drown them,* Moth realized with a borrowed pang of Aramis's concern. Their lights glanced oddly through the manifest, as though the thing's own light were only the surface of a dark, translucent mass. But what use was it if it did nothing but frighten a few men? What good would that do? *My engine!* Moth thought again, and as if in answer the manifest reached—No, it had no limbs. Parts of it clambered upward, a swift oiled crawl that achieved the underside of the arch with its vulnerable cables and pipes, its catwalks and flickering lights and the bridge's stony bones. It reached, and still Moth thought, *What can it do?*

And then the electrical ghosts that had been chasing themselves up and down the bridge poured themselves onto the end where engineers still clustered around the transformer, deafened by the rain. Aramis shouted again, his voice cracking into despair. Moth just stood, strangely dislocated, a spectator where she should have been an actor. That feeling was very strong, that she surely could not just watch. Surely she should act! The manifest of electricity and rain shaped itself in shining silvery facets around the transformer, a ghostly winged jewel above the engine's dark manifest below, and Moth could bear it no longer. She touched the whirlpool of the *mundab*'s racing tide.

THE BAY

Lady Vashmarna watched from her high tower room.

The windblown water on her window made the bridge waver as if it were under the waves. What was real and what was just the rain? The lamps on their tall stanchions flared and died in a rolling pattern of light and dark: that was real. But it might have been her tired eyes that drew a pale sinuous shape along the wires where the darkness fell. *When does superstition become evidence?* Aramis murmured into memory's ear. He was out there now with a double handful of Vashmarna's men, working in the monsoon. The rain itself was tainted tonight. *Bless us, spirits of air . . .* But this wretched night asked the question of Lady Vashmarna: What if *these* are the holy spirits that I see? She rubbed her arms against a chill, and then shuddered as the voices began again. Demons in the wires, spirits in the air. The sounds were a staticky babble, words chewed by a foul mouth and spat out in sparks and hisses and jumping syllables of meaningless noise.

Is this, thought Lady Vashmarna, full of self-pity and dread—*Is this what it is like to be insane?*

Her staff was in hiding, her offices under siege. It was not the irregularity of service that terrified. It was the hostility smoldering in the air, the hostility of a material world that had become conscious of its subservience to humankind. It was as if the electricity that had run so tamely in its wires remembered tonight that it still harbored the lightning's soul. *That* is *madness,* Lady Vashmarna told herself, but still she flinched when the idiot voices buzzed, as if they were wasps that stung. She had unplugged her lamps and her fans, lit candles and incense, prayed in the humid fug of her airless suite, and felt the humiliation of being reduced to this state: she, *the* Vashmarna, the lady of the demesne of power and light.

And still the rain beat down, and still the bridge lights flared and died, and still the rain-sequined ghosts raced with the dark. And then they gathered. From Lady Vashmarna's high vantage, they piled into one another like waves cresting against the shore. They dragged all the light of the bridge with them, leaving darkness behind—and silence, for the voices receded with an ominous hiss. The wind spun the rain about the tower, drumming on the windows, and at the far end of the bridge, the spirits, the demons, built a mockery of the tower out of light and rain. *But it is beautiful!* Lady Vashmarna was astounded that she could be moved by beauty on such a terrible night, but it was a shining ephemeral castle, a tower with rain-wet wings. For a moment she felt a buoyant expansion, the breath of hope. And in that moment the bridge—

Broke.

Borne up by its wings of rain, the whole first span leapt away from the shore like an overstressed cable. Lady Vashmarna cried out, as if she could stop it, give warning—she thought of her men. She thought of herself, so high in her fragile spire. She had only a heartbeat. The bridge fell. The spirits fled. And although Lady Vashmarna would later tell herself that the generating station's fuses must have blown simultaneously, or as close to simultaneously as made no difference to the human eye, there was a still moment, a quiet pause in which she knew that she was still alive, the tower still stood, the world had not come to an end, before the fort's lights died and everything outside her candlelit room disappeared.

THE BRIDGE

Aramis pulled at Moth. Moth did not move.

The broken pieces of the bridge threw themselves through the blackness all around them. She could feel the massive stones career over her head with a tug of wind and a flying absence of rain, but she had no fear of being struck and killed. She did not assume the manifests or the *mundab* would protect her. She simply did not think to be afraid. The noise was incredible, a churning, splashing, cracking, clattering thunder that made her yell unheard into the dark. Waves of disturbed seawater swept up around them, cold and bitter with salt, and sucked away again with a foaming hiss. Still she did not move. The blackness was complete, and she was intensely grateful for the cold, the wetness, the rough and slimy feel of the rocks beneath her feet, for they meant the world had not come to an end. The bridge had fallen. For all she knew the towers had fallen, the bastion, the tidal. For all she knew she and Aramis were the only people left alive in all the world, but at least they had each other. At least they had the world.

"Gods," Aramis said as the brief, terrible thunder died. His voice was very small and thin after the tumult. "Gods," he said. "The gods. I saw them. It was the gods."

But what Moth thought was:

It was me.

THE BASTION

It was true. Even in the light of day the world had not been destroyed—not quite. Yet Lady Vashmarna, standing with her feet firmly on the *rasnan*'s shore, suffered the paradoxical illusion that the *rasnan* that she had admired and defended from her tower rooms had disappeared. Looking out from the fort's highest window all she could see was the bay, the towers, and the uncharted ocean beyond.

Her chief engineer had given her his apartment in the fort, shifting his own household into some subordinate's rooms, who had no doubt foisted his own family off on some yet more junior engineer, and so on down a long line of dispossessions that would inevitably collide with the hundreds of guards and technicians and administrators and *their* families taking refuge from the uninhabitable towers in the bay. Vashmarna's people, Vashmarna's demesne. Yet Lady Vashmarna stood gazing, her back to the necessities and impossibilities that waited for her outside her borrowed door.

The white clouds had emptied themselves last night, and drifted light and high against a backdrop of blue. It had been so long since so much sky was visible that the color was startling, a deep freshly washed blue that shone up, deeper and more vivid yet, from the water. The towers also shone, as white as the clouds, as sparkling as the waves when the sun broke against the glass, the quartz, the polished brass. The disaster of the towers, ruined by the lack of water and power, was not visible from here. The boats that plied the bay might have been a pleasure regatta dancing through the white-capped sun-jeweled waves. Beautiful the boats, beautiful the towers, beautiful the shining sea.

But the boats were full of refugees who complained over the prices charged by the gouging boatmen, who carried heirlooms instead of food, who went in terror of looters and thieves, and who were disposed to blame Vashmarna for everything. "We have power," she told them angrily in her mind. "Stop complaining and build me a new bridge!" But who was to build it? That was the question, and on some lips it meant, Who is to pay for it? Who is to design it, administer it, reap its profits? A question that sounded in the shaudah's ears as, Who is to steal the shaudah's privilege and the shaudah's tolls? Not a trivial question when the shaudah was being pressed to empty his coffers for the sake of the dispossessed, but Lady Vashmarna was troubled by the more literal interpretation. Who is to build it, when the tidal is being whipped to a bloody froth by the shaudah's men? Where are the workers to live, when even tidal tenements are being given over to the servants of the homeless rich? What are the workers to eat, when panic and hoarding have emptied the markets? What are the workers to build with, when even the quarries have been given over to the farmers in the land-starved *hadaras*?

"Stop complaining and build me a new bridge!"

The old bridge had been the shaudah's, the umbilicus between the *shadras* and the *hadaras,* the highway of information and force. But the shaudah was miserly and conservative, and Lord Ghar, whose empty demesne stood like so many tombstones in the bay, was claiming the bridge as a necessity of his demesne, and could Vashmarna afford to give over that precious and vulnerable junction to its greatest rival?

"But we can't build it ourselves!" Lady Vashmarna would have cried, if she had had someone to cry it too. Vashmarna's demesne was central to *shadras* existence, but Vashmarna, suffering under the shaudah's refusal to electrify the *hadaras,* had only its revenues from the bay, and the power fees were a pittance compared to Ghar's rents and taxes. And in any case, Vashmarna's resources were already spent on other things.

"We must create a joint fund," was what she had actually told them. "We must build a new bridge with whatever resources we have at hand, and repay the investment with future tolls."

"With interest?" the shaudah had inquired with narrow eyes.

"There is that question, *janaras,*" Lord Ghar had said deferentially, "but there is also the question of security. Who is to police the construction? Who is to police the finished structure? Who, most important, is to guarantee that the men we conscript to build the bridge are not members of the very cult that brought down the original structure?"

"Conscript?" Lady Vashmarna had said sharply. "Not hire?" But the shaudah overrode her.

"Lord Ghar is correct," he had said. "We cannot build until the threat of future sabotage has been dealt with." And he had sent his own soldiers into the tidal, leaving Lord Ghar's policemen to insinuate themselves into every corner of the bastion.

"And how," cried Lady Vashmarna to her nameless confi-

THE ENGINE'S CHILD · 111

dant, "*how* can he imagine that tearing like an invading army through the tidal will guarantee us future peace!"

But how was she to argue with such a conservative man? The shaudah was so offended by this interruption of his ordered existence that he would throw armies between himself and the threat of further change. He had always been thus, which was why Lady Vashmarna constantly struggled to defend her cause while Lord Ghar, a conservative of a different stripe, advanced his own. These were the worst possible circumstances in which to argue the shaudah around to a change of mind on any subject whatsoever, and it was a bitter frustration to Lady Vashmarna that the need for exploration and expansion should be at its most pressing, and yet be the one subject the shaudah was least willing to discuss. Too risky, too expensive, and too terrifying to be the shaudah to change a policy that had been handed down from the earliest days of government on this world. Particularly now, with the *shadras* in shambles and the shadow cult, to hear the shaudah speak of it, threatening everything from the price of rice to the sanctity of the gods.

So he sent his soldiers into the tidal as if the poor were enemies and not his own people, and so Vashmarna's greatest secret and civilization's greatest hope was threatened hourly. *Kistnu, holy mother, turn your face to your embattled children. Kistnu, absent mother, stretch out your hand.* But Lady Vashmarna's prayers rang flat in the days following the bridge's destruction, and even she could not help the fearful hostility that surged through her at every thought of the shadow cult and its blasphemous gods. If they were real, if they had destroyed the bridge, then how could she argue—should she argue?—against the shaudah's war? Even granting its terrible, perhaps irredeemable, cost.

A knock at the door recalled her to the outer world.

"Come in."

It was Aramis Tapurnashen, his light brown eyes haunted and ringed in bruises. She remembered how she had given him tea before sending him back into the rain, and somehow this deepened her sense of responsibility toward him, and toward his men—their men—who had died. Of course there were other bonds between them, the cable, the unspoken name of Moth. But she could not in all conscience make him carry the blame.

"Tapurnashen-*andas*," she said warmly, "you have news?"

"*Jinnu.*" He bowed. "Forgive the disturbance. There is a *purdar* of the bay police with a squad of men at the gate. They say they have orders from Lord Ghar to search the fort for cult members and saboteurs. And," he added ominously, "they are escorting a priest who says he is the new temple overseer, come to replace *aras* Chaiduur."

Her rage was instant, as white and clean as Shaudarand in the bay. "Have they been given leave to enter, Tapurnashen-*andas*?"

"Vashmarna-*jin'*, they have not, but the *purdar* is very pressing."

"You will come with me," she said, and swept from the room.

Even in recent generations Vashmarna had refused to allow building in the courtyards that separated the fort from its walls. Today those stone-floored yards were crowded with Vashmarna adherents, servants and junior technicians who could not secure themselves space inside. Bedrolls had been crammed into the shelter of the arcades while kitchens had been organized under the open sky. Hundreds of people squatted amid the pots and bundles and growing piles of trash. Her name spoken by too many mouths echoed against the walls, but no one accosted her, no one tugged at her robes to accuse or complain. They were hers, and she had given them shelter. Many, many people bowed to her as she made her way from the main buildings to the gate. They, along with Aramis Tapur-nashen, were a warm and solid presence at her back.

The sunshine made the shade within the gate's shelter seem even darker than usual. Only as Lady Vashmarna approached could she make out the pallor of her own guards' saffron uniforms. The Ghar's men wore dark blue, and were only visible as a mass, cutting off the light from the road.

"What is this?" she said to her own men's backs.

The ranks parted and a woman appeared, a plump, dark woman a little younger than Lady Vashmarna, with coarse black hair trailing out of its pins. Pedigan Shawm, who kept the engineers' secrets, and who had some tacit authority over the fort guards.

"*Jinnuju.*" She bowed deeply, anger in every movement.

"Shawm-*andu,*" Lady Vashmarna replied with a short nod.

Before either woman could speak further, a man in a stiff blue tunic and elaborate black turban pressed forward among the defending ranks. The fort's guards shouted and shoved him back, and for a moment it looked as if there would be bloodshed, for the Ghar *purdar*'s men pushed in behind him. Lady Vashmarna's voice rang out in the stone-walled yard.

"Stop this. Stop it at once!"

The men stopped. Her own men saluted. The *purdar* in blue drew himself up, disdaining the hands still clutching his sleeves, and bowed.

"Vashmarna-*jinnu?*" He had small black eyes and a closely trimmed beard.

"Do you have some purpose here?" she said coldly.

"*Jin',* our lord—"

"*Jinnuju!*" Shawm corrected with a scathing hiss.

The *purdar*'s black eyes glittered in the shade. "Vashmarna-*jinnu.* Our lord has given us orders, sanctioned by the shaudah himself, to search the bastion for the traitors who destroyed the bridge."

"Your lord's authority rests in the bay, *purdar*. If *aras* Baradam chooses to abjure his authority in his own demesne, that is between him and his gods. My authority comes to me through sixteen generations from the shaudah Itteran himself, and I keep it in my own hands. You have no business in my demesne."

Even as she said this, her gaze fell on the figure of a priest in loose, unbleached robes. The man was a thin dark-faced presence at the *purdar*'s shoulder, watchful but silent. It was the *purdar* who answered her.

"Ghar-*jandas* gave us our orders in the shaudah's presence."

"I police my own demesne."

"But—"

"And I answer to the shaudah. Not to you. Remove your men."

"*Jinnuju*—"

"Remove your men. I will not say it a third time!"

The *purdar*'s black eyes flickered from Lady Vashmarna, to her guards, to Aramis, to the silent crowd. He bowed and said stiffly, "*Jinnuju*, I go to report to my lord."

"Do I care? Take yourself out of my sight. Go!"

He turned with a sharp gesture to his men, who retreated into the bright sunlight of the road. The priest remained.

He gave a slight, a very slight, bow and said softly, "Vashmarna answers to more than the shaudah, as I think you know, *jinnu*."

"Vashmarna answers to *aras* Chaiduur."

"*Aras* Chaiduur is only the temple's agent, with no special authority of his own, and he has in any case been granted leave to retire to the *hadaras*. I have been chosen to replace him, and the temple requires my presence here."

Her heart was pounding. With Chaiduur gone her careful arrangements were in disorder and only one thought stood clear: she could not permit this man to enter her walls. She braced herself to attack on uncertain ground.

"The temple requires your presence here?" she said scornfully. "Or do you mean the Ghar?"

"The temple," said the priest with a tightened jaw, "and the law."

"The shaudah's law," she said, "our sainted ancestors' law, the gods' law. Not the Ghar's."

"I am a priest, *jinnu*, I claim no allegiance but to the temple."

"And to the gods?" she said pointedly. "If that is true, *aras*, you should have chosen a different escort."

"*Jinnu*—"

"No. Vashmarna does not answer to the Ghar's authority in any form."

The priest looked at her, balked and coldly angry. "There is still the law of anathema. You cannot escape it merely by closing a door."

"If the ancestors return to chastise me, if the gods themselves call me to judgment, I will answer with the truth of my soul. But I owe nothing to some nameless tool of the Ghars. Take yourself back to your masters and tell them so."

"You should think again, Vashmarna-*jin'*. You are making a grave mistake."

"Close the gate," Lady Vashmarna said to no one in particular. The fort gate had not been closed in daytime since the Lamplighters Rebellion in Lady Vashmarna's youth, but no one hesitated. Saffron uniforms vanished into recesses in the wall and the heavy gate rumbled on its rollers across the passageway, forcing the obdurate priest to step back, and back again. It closed with a soft boom, with the priest on the other side, and there was silence in the yard.

"*Jinnu*—"

"I will not hear it."

Another silence. Then,

"*Jinnu*," Pedigan Shawm said very softly. "Forgive me, but *can* we police our own?"

"The sabotage did not come from within this demesne." Lady Vashmarna spoke clearly and with confidence, but that was for the sake of the crowd. Quietly, if heatedly, she said to Shawm, Aramis, and the gate officer, "Half the people within these walls might belong to the shadow cult—or the Penalists, or the Morbidians, or the Society of Doors. Unless the Ghar has determined some mark or token that would distinguish such from the common run, what would we be looking *for*?"

No one spoke.

"Can any of you recognize a cultist when you see one?"

No one spoke. Aramis closed his eyes as if in pain. Lady Vashmarna, conscious of the watching crowd behind them, felt a chill. So many people, so many strangers who knew her name. For their sake, she made a light gesture.

"However, that does not give us a license for carelessness. Shawm-'*du, purdar* Nind. I want every person within these walls vouched for by a Vashmarna vassal. Consult with the engineers and my bay administrators. Any person who cannot be directly vouched for must go. Is that understood?"

"Yes, *jin*'."

"*Jinnuju*."

"And I want a roll of all their names, their affiliations, their origins. Be polite, if you please. Inform those who ask that the Vashmarna takes an interest in their families in the *hadaras* and the tidal. Make it seem a charitable act, if you can. But I want those names."

"*Jinnuju*."

"Very well. I must have a word with the shaudah before the Ghar's report gets too fat with fancy. Tapurnashen-'*das*, you will accompany me."

"Yes, *jin*'."

"*Jinnuju,*" said the gate officer, Nind. "May I recommend that you take an escort?"

Lady Vashmarna drew in a breath. "To go into the scholarium? In broad daylight?"

"*Jinnu,* in such a crowd of strangers it may be wise," Shawm said.

Oh, but Lady Vashmarna knew that fear. She had been eighteen the year of the Rebellion, and had learned it too well. But what was the good of the last twenty years and more if she had not schooled herself in courage?

"No," she said. "I have Aramis, and I have my name."

The sun blazed down through the ranks of cloud, conjuring steam from every ferny roof and mossy passageway. White in the sunlight and silver in the shade, as ephemeral as a prayer as it surrendered to the heat of noon. Mist was the spirit of the season, and deserved the silence of meditation, the click of bamboo chimes, a single clear voice raised in song. This was Lady Vashmarna's enduring image of the scholarium at season's turn, and it was a grief as well as a discomfort to have that peaceful evocation trampled by the bustling, complaining crowd. Displaced dedicants and priests carried their scant bundles to temporary postings in the *hadaras,* while evacuees with richer burdens shoved past them, as angry to receive the charitable refuge as the donors were to give it. There were cats and children everywhere underfoot, servants vying with novices for space on the porches, a woman scholar weeping and cursing over a broken shelf in the library, where no refugees were supposed to be.

Aramis did his best to keep Lady Vashmarna from being jostled, but people she knew—people whose hospitality she had received, people she called friends, or enemies, or fellows in her cause—spoke to her as she passed.

"Vashmarna-*jin'*, what has happened to us?"

"Vashmarna-*jinnu*, who has done this thing?"

"Vashmarna! When will we have power again? When can we return to our homes?"

The ignorant stared, the knowing called out questions, complaints, demands. Lady Vashmarna nodded, lifted a hand, kept her step even and her back straight, but it was difficult to maintain that precious balance between humility and pride when she suffered so much anger, so much fear, so much unearned shame. She was deeply grateful when she achieved the scholars' hall, where Baradam Ghar had given up his apartment to the shaudah, but she did not show that relief to the men in the shaudah's scarlet who guarded the door.

Them she icily ignored.

Aras Baradam's reception chamber had been as severe as one would expect of a scholar-priest. Wooden beams with clean ascetic lines held up the low bamboo ceiling; the worn flagstones were polished but bare. It had been a cool, spartan room, a room like the antechamber to a shrine, and it had been transformed by the shaudah's occupation. Gilded scrolls hung on the walls and from the roof beams; brilliant carpets covered the floor. The dais held so many carpets and cushions that it had doubled in height, putting the seated shaudah above the eye level of any standing petitioner, but Lady Vashmarna was glad to see—she could not help it—that even the shaudah had not managed to rescue the gaudy furniture from his tower suite.

The reception room was also full of courtiers in their fashionable dress, but the Vashmarna name was good for something here, at least. Lady Vashmarna made directly for the dais, with Aramis Tapurnashen following at a respectful distance behind her. She was still angry, but her anger had settled below the level of political strategy and civilized restraint.

The shaudah acknowledged her presence from his height.

She bowed. It would not have been correct to bow to the Ghars, who stood, father and son, in attendance near the dais, but she favored them with a look. They were very much alike, Divaram and his son, but where Divaram's face was scored by the lines of experience, Baradam's was still a smooth basalt mask. *So young!* Lady Vashmarna could not help but think.

"Already there is some commotion, *jinnu?*" the shaudah said. He affected a high, distant voice, as if he were speaking out of a dream, and he rarely looked anyone in the eye. A lean, brown, balding man with hollow temples and a delicate skull, he seemed determined to barricade himself against hurt. Lady Vashmarna's father had said once, speaking of the shaudah when he was still a youth, before he had achieved his title, "There is a young man who looks at the world with only one eye."

But the shaudah would not love her for trying to force him to stare at reality direct. Lady Vashmarna tilted her head in a demure shrug and gestured with her hand, as if to brush away a cobweb, a wisp of steam.

"*Janaras,* it is nothing, a slight misunderstanding between subordinates of two different demesnes. Ghar-*jandas*'s men, who are so assiduously aiding *aras* Baradam in ridding the scholarium of unwanted influences, thought Vashmarna might be in similar need. Vashmarna being secure, however, I have come to offer my own men to you, *janaras,* to aid your soldiers' efforts in the tidal." Meaning: I am strong. Now let me put my men between your hysteria and the expansionists' cause.

The shaudah slanted a look at the elder Ghar, who took this as permission to speak.

"*Janaras,* one trusts the Vashmarna has an accurate view of the situation. *Jinnu,* we know your wisdom and your ability. But how can you be sure that Vashmarna's demesne is free of the shadow taint? Forgive me if I malign good men, but how can you be certain that the very people who assure you of your vassals' innocence are innocent themselves?"

"Why," said Lady Vashmarna, "I am as certain of my own men as you are of yours, Ghar-*jandas,* and for as good a reason. The fort has seen no more of this cult's activities than the bay."

"What!" *Aras* Baradam must have been boiling behind that mask of a face. "*Janaras,* excuse my interruption, but how can the Vashmarna claim to be free of blasphemy when the bridge was destroyed—destroyed with forbidden and demonic powers—under her auspices?"

"Under *my* auspices?" she said in profound and chilly offense.

"The *aras* is distressed by these most unnatural and unlawful events," Divaram said smoothly. "Of course he does not mean that *jinnuju* was anything but a victim, as we all were, of the assault on the *shadras.*"

"*Janaras,*" said Baradam, "what I mean is that the Vashmarna's men were at work on the bridge—"

"And were killed there!" Aramis was fierce and, not having been recognized, ignored.

"—and so the violence occurred when Vashmarna's authority was in play, and when her engineers were on the scene."

"And were killed there," Lady Vashmarna repeated for Aramis's sake. "And may I remind the *aras,* who may be too occupied with his priestly duties to be aware of certain realities, that the bridge is, was, and always has been sovereign? No one has ever had authority over the structure but the shaudah."

"Thank you, *jinnu,*" the shaudah said with the faintest trace of irony in his voice.

Lady Vashmarna bowed. The Ghars, father and son, bowed. Lord Ghar said, "*Janaras,* no one could possibly lay claim against the sovereignty of the bridge. But if the Vashmarna will forgive me, I can only raise the still unresolved question of the several incidences of sabotage that took place in the days before the bridge's destruction."

"Sabotages," Lady Vashmarna gently interrupted, "which have been traced, thanks to the diligent work of Tapurnashen-*andas* and many others, to an illegal cable leading into the tidal. There is sound evidence, which the shaudah has seen, that the cable did not come from Vashmarna's manufactories or stores, and even sounder evidence that the shadow cult, or whoever was responsible for the sabotage, could not have been working from within my demesne. That evidence being, of course, that a saboteur with access to Vashmarna's systems would not need such a crude tap as Tapurnashen-*andas* discovered; and moreover, no such saboteur would need to take such drastic measures to protect the only tap they could hope to achieve—which in fact was not protected but destroyed along with the bridge. All this aside from the fact that, as Ghar-*jan'* knows, the only rumors of shadow cult activities have been in the tidal and the scholarium. Ghar-*jan'* and *aras* Baradam have the scholarium very much in hand, and since Vashmarna itself is, as I say, *janaras,* secure, I am happy to offer my men to the shaudah to aid in the effort to trace the saboteurs in the tidal."

She bowed. Lord Ghar bowed. The shaudah fidgeted with the tassel on a cushion.

Aras Baradam said, "But if you will forgive me—*jinnu, janaras.* If you will forgive me, there is one thread of shadow taint that has penetrated the fort's walls." His father gave him a forbidding look, but he did not seem to notice. "Although it grieves me to say this, a dedicant of this precinct has several times been seen entering the fort with no official business to take her there, and it so happens that this same dedicant has been called before me for disciplinary action in connection with spreading certain rumors—false rumors, I believed at the time—of the shadow cult within the bastion walls."

The shaudah was interested enough to look directly at the priest. "This dedicant has a name?"

"Of a sort, *janaras,*" Baradam said with distaste. "She is a tidal orphan called Moth."

Lady Vashmarna was shocked. It was a visceral shock of surprise and dismay, to hear that name spoken in this company, and a shock of anger, that her agent had been so unwise at such a precarious juncture in their joint affairs. With a resentful feeling of having been shoved off a cliff, Lady Vashmarna tried to give her thoughts wings.

"Of course I know the dedicant the *aras* is referring to," she said mildly.

The three men looked at her in surprise. She gave them a modest smile.

"What is this?" the shaudah said, almost alert. "You know her—and claim Vashmarna is secure?"

"And all the more secure because of her." Oh, this was a gamble! Lady Vashmarna was furious beneath the calm of her voice. "If you will permit me, *aras?*"

Baradam, looking at once thwarted and unsure of her meaning, bowed.

Lady Vashmarna made another of those little gestures. "It is a trifle embarrassing. I fear the *aras* will be angry with me, although of course I sponsored young Moth during his predecessor's day."

"She really—" This from Aramis, who was again ignored.

"A promising student," Lady Vashmarna said. "I forget just how she came to my attention, although my administrators do keep their eyes open for talent in unlikely places, even if"—she could not resist adding—"Vashmarna is not allowed to adopt orphans into our perilous demesne. Even as a child she showed a real talent for scholarship, particularly in the mathematical disciplines, and given that she was an orphan and therefore free from the more awkward slum connections that can cause such difficulties when one attempts to raise even a deserving youth out of the mud, I sponsored her to the scholarium—as I *am* permitted, of course, and glad to do. I was, in a small, selfish sense, disappointed when she chose to take a dedicant's vows rather than come to Vashmarna as an apprentice, but our relationship did not entirely end there. Her mystical vocation is strong, but, perhaps because she is better suited to be a scholar than a ministering priest, she never lost her interest in more practical matters, and to be brief, *janaras,* she has been helping Vashmarna with some rather esoteric experiments in the improvement—"

" 'Esoteric experiments'!" Baradam said hoarsely. " 'Mystical vocation'! *Janaras,* is the Vashmarna telling us—brazenly admitting before this company—that Vashmarna has been secretly dabbling in forbidden powers? And then claiming her demesne is free from the shadow taint? *Janaras,* I must protest!"

"When has the temple ever pronounced on electricity?" Lady Vashmarna asked stoutly. "*Janaras,* I protest in my turn. How dare the *aras* accuse Vashmarna of blasphemy!"

"The Vashmarna's reputation speaks against it," the shaudah said dryly.

"The Vashmarna's reputation was built in the days when she still permitted a temple overseer—a *tidal-born* overseer— within Vashmarna's walls. And now this"—Baradam's jaw worked—"this *seduction* of a dedicant away from her vows?"

"*Aras,*" Lord Ghar said softly, "not even the temple's vows are absolute."

Baradam shared a long look with his father, and bowed his head.

"I do not say Vashmarna is faultless," said the shaudah in his distant way. "But I would hear more of these experiments."

Oh? thought Lady Vashmarna furiously, trapped. Now *you are interested?*

"If I may speak for Vashmarna, *jinnuju?*" Aramis said into her pause.

Lady Vashmarna turned to look at him, astonished. He gave her a long, grave, steady look, and deeply bowed. She caught her breath. He knew something about Moth. What more did he know that she did not? But if she ever needed a loyal ally, it was now. She turned back to the dais and said faintly, "*Janaras,* may I make known to you Aramis Tapurnashen, electrical engineer and liaison between the chief engineer's office and my own."

The shaudah looked off into a far corner of the room and made a weary circular gesture with his hand. Lady Vashmarna waved Aramis up to stand at her side. He bowed.

"*Janaras,*" he said, and faltered.

Lady Vashmarna stood with her mild gaze fixed on her clasped hands, but she speared a thought at the young man: *Do not fail me!*

He took a breath and bowed again. "*Janaras,* before we discovered the cable into the tidal, we made several investigations into the cause of the interruptions to the power service. We had had reports of . . . of oddities beyond simple surges and losses of current, and since we had already consulted with dedicant Moth on purely mathematical questions in the past, it seemed reasonable to ask her—quietly, *janaras,* so as not to add to the rumors already disturbing the bastion—to consult with us on . . . on these peculiarities that . . ."

"You need not enumerate them, *andas,*" Lady Vashmarna said kindly. Baradam Ghar was glaring at the unfortunate engineer while his father looked stonily away, and Aramis was clearly out of countenance. "We all experienced the oddities."

Aramis bowed.

"Yes," said the shaudah vaguely. "We experienced something. So was this dedicant the same who survived with you the collapse of the bridge, engineer?"

There was a small silence of universal astonishment. Lady Vashmarna stared at her engineer. Even *she* had not heard of this!

Aramis audibly swallowed, and bowed again. "*Janaras.*"

"Yes? Is that a yes?"

"Yes, *janaras.*" Aramis's face was dewy with sweat and his voice was increasingly faint, but his words were steady. "Dedicant Moth was deeply concerned about the possibility of sabotage arising out of the tidal, and when we found the cable we asked her to join us in our investigation."

Baradam snorted, but did not speak.

"And she also saw these so-called shadow gods we have been hearing about since that night?"

"She saw something," Aramis said. "We all did, the ones who lived."

It took all of Lady Vashmarna's self-possession to say loyally, "As did I."

The shaudah blinked away from them. "And this dedicant," he said, ever more vague, "this mystical scholar who is also an electrician: Does she have an insight into this sabotage and these shadow gods?"

There was a silence. Lady Vashmarna, seeing a bitter dearth of choices, said, "As Moth's sponsor, *janaras,* I would be happy to introduce her to your service. With *aras* Baradam's permission, of course."

"Oh, do you ask my permission now, *jinnu*?" But at a hard look from his father, Baradam turned his face aside. "Of course, if the shaudah wishes the dedicant's attendance, I cannot but agree."

"Send for her," the shaudah said. "And grant her amnesty, *aras.* The shadow gods are surely a more pressing concern than these little matters of protocol."

"In your name, *janaras*," Baradam said. "But it will take some time. The dedicant in question has been sent away with all the rest to make room for the evacuees from the bay."

"Really?" The shaudah yawned. "You sent her away when you had such grave suspicions of her?"

Baradam said tightly, "Of course my suspicions were not fully aroused until after she left the bastion, *janaras*. And I only sent her as far as the tidal. I will send a messenger immediately."

"I will lend you men," Lord Ghar said, speaking for the first time in a long while. "For the dedicant's safety."

Lady Vashmarna felt a fresh shaft of unease. Why this interest in Moth on the Ghars' part? It had to be more than a nasty coincidence that her agent's name should be known to her rivals, and worse than coincidence that the shaudah had questions for Moth that she, Lady Vashmarna, did not know the answers to. Prompted by instinct, and wishing she had after all accepted an escort of guards, she said, "Aramis will also go, *janaras*. He will know the dedicant, where Ghar-*jandas's* men will not."

The shaudah made a weary gesture, his head tilting to one side in apparent exhaustion. Everyone bowed.

The audience was done.

THE TIDAL

When three hundred dedicants were dispersed to make room for refugees in the bastion, all but seven of them were sent to village shrines in the *hadaras*. Those seven were sent into the tidal, where they had been born or abandoned. They were the scholarium's orphans, tidal orphans without even an extended family in the *hadaras*, each with a name like a brand. Snake, Kelp, Moth: animal names for those who had no patronymic, no lineage, and no claim on any of the great ancestor lines. Nor any claim on the temple, nor on the temple's gods; or so *aras* Baradam seemed to be telling them.

It was *aras* Chaiduur who brought Moth the news. "It is only for a time," he concluded without meeting Moth's eyes. "Only for the duration of the emergency."

"Is it?" Moth's mouth was dry, almost too dry to shape her words.

"Well. Well . . ." Chaiduur hesitated, and then, as if some internal pressure had grown too great to bear, he threw up his hands. "Well, what can you expect? You refuse at every turn to cut your ties with the slums, you break curfew, you leave the bastion with no more permission than the dictates of your own whim—what else did you think he would do with such an excuse? You should count yourself fortunate he has not renounced you altogether."

"Do you mean me, *aras*?" Moth fought to keep the shaking out of her voice. "Or do you mean all seven of us?"

Chaiduur's gaze slipped away from hers. "I have no reason to think . . . I have heard no ill reports . . ."

Of the others being sent into exile in the slums.

"And what about you, *aras*? Are you also returning to the tidal?" With an emphasis on "returning."

"Ah. No. No. *Aras* Baradam has at last granted my request. I shall be retiring from my position here and going to the Hajim Retreat in the eastern mountains. So . . ." He looked up, as if he could see the mountaintop shrine from the heart of the scholarium. "So this is goodbye. Gods bless you and keep you, Moth. I feel certain that if you apply yourself . . . Perhaps you will find a place that suits you . . ."

In the tidal. Moth said nothing. Eventually Chaiduur went away.

Aras Baradam's order was a betrayal that cut too deep for anger. It was more like the shock of truth. *This is who you are*, the *aras* was saying. *This is where you belong.* It was hard not to agree when agreement was a defiant gesture, a slam of the door. Moth saw that defiance, that recognition, in her fellows' eyes. *Yes, this is who I am. Yes*, aras, *this is where I belong.* Kelp even said it aloud.

"Now we know," she said, looking at Moth. Moth winced at a deep stab of shame, but there was no accusation on Kelp's face, just that bleak awareness, that acknowledgment that was not resigned. "Now we know."

The seven of them gathered up their meager possessions and left the scholarium with a cool, hard show of courage that was all the more affecting for being noticed by no one but themselves. They fought their way down the tidal steps through the stream of evacuees climbing up from the docks, but when they reached the bottom of the stairs, they parted almost without a word. Old haunts, old memories, old ways of being waited like the mucky streets to swallow them down. Moth had the sense that if Baradam's messenger had found them, even in that instant of turning away, and told them that the *aras* had recanted, they were wanted, they could come home, they would have stared with incomprehension. A tidal orphan could sum it up with a shrug. What has any of that to do with me?

Too much, Moth might have told them, for she was convinced this banishment was aimed directly at her. At her, who could have been—she dared to think, *should* have been—summoned to the fort. On impulse she called out for the others to wait. Snake heard, and Eeling, and Shell. But under their eyes, buffeted by strangers and with her feet sinking into the ooze, she had too much to say, and too little.

"If you need a place, ask for *aras* Crab at Twelve Saints Shrine. He knows my name."

They shrugged. What has any of that to do with us?

When Moth was alone, her first thought was of the engine and the fire shrine. It would be as natural for her to run for shelter there as it would be for a hunted lizard to dash for its crack in the wall. But if Baradam-*tirindi* were watching to see which crack this small lizard chose—and Moth could not forget Aramis's warning that the Society of Doors knew her name—then a wise lizard would scamper as far from home as she dared. So she set herself against the flow of the crowd, heading for the docks and the Farabas Shrine.

The Farabas was the tidal's water shrine, an appellation that was ironic only to those who had seen the great temple in Sidirand's base, with its glass walls and quartz floor hovering above the shadowed waves. Old wooden Farabas was built on pilings at the lip of the deep water and was surrounded by floating docks, fish sheds, warehouses, chandlers, brothels, and sailors' dens. Moth had had many of her early lessons here, and it was reasonable that, exiled, she should return. Doubly reasonable, since the *rasnu* here knew Moth only as a name in her predecessor's rolls. In Farabas, Moth was just the name of the student who had made the most of her sponsorship.

In Farabas, the innocent Moth.

She sat alone in the mortuary chapel at an hour past noon. Cones of incense sent up their tendrils of smoke, filling the chapel with a dry holy smell. Sunlight slipped like blades of grass between the warped planks of the walls, slender leaves of light that were bent and rippled by the lazy plumes of smoke. The receding tide drew at the pilings, sending a slow chorus of complaint through the building. Voices drifted from the other rooms, a soft undercurrent of sound that was at one with the creaking wood, the sunlight, the perfumed smoke.

". . . coming back with their catch on the evening tide. The whole crew arrested and their catch left to rot in the hold."

"Someone should speak to the fishers. If they tie up here or at the Pragmass dock after dark, we can give them sanctuary until the end of curfew."

"But not their fish . . ."

Moth, sitting with one knee pulled up beneath her chin, shivered from time to time, although the shrine was stifling. The heat, despite the incense, was conjuring the stink of rot from the corpse they had found floating under the shrine that morning, and it was the smell, and the too-fresh memories of the other recent dead, that made Moth shiver.

The mud swallows everything, even the dead.

It was the tidal's bitter joke about the black muck that swarmed with vermin and in the hot season sent up gaseous bubbles of decay. Fed on sewage and offal and its own trampled weeds, the mud grew thicker and fouler with every year, but it did not in fact swallow the dead, as the whole tidal had learned. The shaudah's war was small and secretive, but it had its casualties, men and women stamped into the mud, their twisted limbs breaking the surface like the keels of shipwrecked boats. It was a shock to discover a night corpse exposed by morning's light. It was more brutal, and more degrading, to discover the dead under one's feet as one crossed a busy street in the middle of the day.

"Oh, Kardum," chanted a heartbroken voice in the shrine. "Oh, Kardum."

So at least one of the dead had been named.

There was a strange dislocation between the dead and the violence of the shaudah's occupation. The news circulated daily, another distillery smashed, another printing press ruined, another book bindery burned. "Even Heri and Quudar's," someone whispered close by. Even the tiny one-room manufactories of clockworks, fireworks, and toys came under the shaudah's undeclared edict banning any technology more advanced than a fish-oil lamp from the homes and businesses of the slum. The tidal had always been denied Vashmarna's electricity and manufactories; now even the slum dwellers' makeshift substitutions were to be declared anathema. The destruction was like a wordless sacrifice to the great towers, with their pumps and elevators and fans sitting frozen and useless in the bay.

Or was it nothing more than a petty revenge for the illegal cable and the ruined bridge? Oh, Moth! Moth, what have you done?

"Even Bramadur's," said the whisperer. "And what did they ever do but make clocks that couldn't keep time?"

But the mystery lay in the disconnection between the destruction and the deaths. It was as though there was some delayed transmutation, as though the broken press was transformed overnight into the broken pressman; as though the colored gunpowder spilled in the mud had shaped an effigy of the toy maker's wife. One heard the story of the press smashed with iron bars, the precious type cast out the window into the mud. One heard six different versions of the speech the printer made as he was arrested by the shaudah's men. One did not hear the tale of the beating, the garroting, the bullet in the skull. But then, one did not have to hear. Even the illiterate tidal could read the news in the mute remains, and there was no one in all the slum who did not know the headline. The shaudah was hunting the shadow cult, for it was the shadow gods who had destroyed the bridge.

And one heard the voices, the whispers, the maddening chants of grief.

"Oh, Kardum, Kardum, Kardum."

The waterlogged dead man soaked through his mean wrappings and dripped onto the chapel's floor. It was just one more quiet sound, one delicate tapping to add to Farabas's meditative voice.

". . . twelve years old. Who could imagine he had anything to do with . . ."

". . . but who knows anymore?"

Who knows anymore who the shadow cult is? Once Moth had said, *No one*. Now she would have had to say, *Everyone*. The bridge's destruction had begun the tidal's conversion; the first murder had finished it. It was strange to Moth that no one blamed the cult for the shaudah's reprisals, as she blamed herself. (Not that she had intended the bridge's collapse. She had wanted to save the *mundabi*'s cable, not bury it under tons of blasted stone. But it was impossible from this distance to un-tangle the threads of intention and consequence leading from that night.) As far as she could tell, the tidal had suffered the same shock of identity that the orphan dedicants had when *aras* Baradam had exiled them to their homelessness, their tidal home. *Yes, we are godless. Yes, we are scum. Yes, we are your enemy.*

Some of the morning's corpses wore the shaudah's uniform.

And some of them wore faces Moth knew.

She was still sitting with the dead man, supposedly in prayer, when *aras* Crab came gray-faced and trembling to sum-mon her to Twelve Saints Shrine.

"Tarun," he said, not a statement, another mourning cry. "Tarun."

"They asked him nothing. They asked *nothing*."

Istvan was so angry a froth of spit gathered in the corners of his mouth.

"They came, they knew where to come, they tore down the walls. They *tore* down the *walls*. We heard them coming and Tarun put the plans in the stove—we were grilling a fish, there is nothing to eat here but fish—"

Istvan growled and shook his head, a savage gesture from a self-conscious man. He was furious, crippled by his own dis-tress, and furious at that as well.

"The plans went up, you know how long the roll was. They knocked down the walls and the bamboo caught, there was smoke everywhere, everywhere there was smoke, we could not see for smoke."

Istvan was filthy, his clothing torn and striped with mud, his gray hair knotted over a crusted bandage, his voice raw and cracking into a whisper.

"People ran. All the people. *Someone* told them where we

were!" A cry of betrayal, of grief. "They knocked me down, all the shelves, those stupid toys. Tarun told them they were his, they were nothing of mine, I was no one, a visitor, nothing. I could not speak. They hit me, they knocked me down. They kicked me, a scholar, an old man! They took Tarun away."

The story stopped there, as all the stories stopped there. They took Tarun away. *Aras* Crab said, his soft voice a relief after Istvan's hoarse fury, "They found him this morning by the rafts behind Soft Ministry House. He had been beaten very badly. He . . . He was . . . He looked as though they had dropped him from the bastion wall."

"He looked like a clam on the rocks," Silk said, flat and hard.

No one laughed. A clam dropped from a *tirindi*'s toothless mouth is a shattered mess, its soft innards mixed up with its splintered shell. Moth put her hands over her mouth to catch the jump of horror in her throat. But they looked at her, the few *mundabi* who dared the fire shrine—Istvan and Crab, Hamana and Silk—and she had to speak.

"You found him this morning? He was taken yesterday? Last night?" No one spoke. "Why didn't you tell me?"

Aras Crab gently frowned, Silk drew a harsh breath, but it was Istvan who burst out with a terrible, reckless, near-senile scorn, "What would you have done? Raised up another demon and brought the roof down upon our heads? How dare you!" he raved, Istvan the scathing, Istvan the dry. "How dare you!" With the spit making a dry white foam at the edge of his mouth.

"Istvan!" the *aras* said, shocked. "Istvan, be still. This isn't like you."

Istvan gave a brutal crow of laughter. "Isn't like me. Isn't like me." He thrust a bony finger in Moth's face. "Tarun is dead. Do you hear? Tarun . . . is dead."

"Istvan. Scholar." Crab urged him down into his seat. Istvan slumped back and wiped his mouth with a shaking hand.

Moth knew Istvan would not grant her the right to weep, but she could not stop the tremble of her mouth, the tears that brimmed and spilled. Istvan, as she had anticipated, made a disgusted sound and turned away.

"It is the Lamplighters Rebellion," he muttered to Crab. "It is just the same, *just* the same."

"Is it?" said Silk staunchly. "Then why are you so angry with Moth? Be angry at your precious Mahogany we've heard so much about!"

"Mahogan!" Istvan corrected, still furious but with diminishing energy.

Silk ignored him. "He's the one who killed all your friends, got you tossed from the bastion, turned us all into outlaws for following his way. Be angry at the *mundab,* why don't you? Be angry at yourself! You're the one who taught us—"

"How dare you!"

"How dare *you,* you lousy old hypocrite! What did you teach Moth for, if not for this?"

"For *this*?"

"It's the rebellion all over again, isn't it? Isn't that what you said? Mahogany was murdered for his theory. That's what you always said. You never had the power to fight back. Now we do!"

Silk was fierce, shining with sweat in the oil-lamp gloom. She looked like one of the fire saints in the shrine below. Moth marveled at her, as heartened as she had been wounded by Istvan's words. She had not yet recognized her own shock, which had her swaying to everyone else's wind.

"To fight!" Istvan's exhaustion had brought him back to his usual self. "You irreligious little skink. The *mundab* is a philosophy of empowerment, a reconciliation between the spirits of the old world and the spirit of the new, a rapprochement between the exile and the new home."

"Then what's the engine?" Silk said, meeting scorn with scorn. "A prayer token? A talisman? A new shrine?"

"All of those things."

Silk brushed this aside with a toss of her head.

Hamana spoke for the first time, her eyes lightless between her narrowed lids. "The engine is empowerment for the tidal."

"Literality." Istvan shook his finger again at Moth. "Literality!"

"Oh, gods," Silk groaned. "Philosophy! How did you survive the Lamplighters, old man? Hiding behind your books?"

"And how do you imagine you will survive this nightmare? By fighting, little girl? By hiding behind your shadow gods?"

"By following in their bloody wake," Hamana said, silencing them all.

Moth caught her breath. "They aren't gods."

All of them moved at that, a twitch, a shrug, a flick of the hand.

"They are shadows," she said stubbornly, though still on the verge of tears. "They are shadows cast by the *mundab*'s workings. They are shadows of the mind."

"And what working destroyed the bridge?" said *aras* Crab, not gently at all. "Whose mind brought this violence down on us all?"

"Th-that . . ." Moth stammered. "That was—"

"You hold your tongue!" Silk snapped at the priest. "Did you want Vashmarna to follow the cable straight to your shrine? You'd be dead now, we all would, and Vashmarna would have our engine!"

"And that consequence would be worse than what we suffer now?"

"Yes!" Silk said. "The engine is still ours!"

Crab looked as though he wanted to be convinced. Istvan made a contemptuous grimace but did not speak. Moth, lashed by her own conscience, buried her face in her hands.

"The power will be ours," Hamana said, and then turned her head, as they all did, when footsteps rattled up the stairs from the door to the outer shrine. It was one of Hamana's bully boys.

"Policemen," he gasped. "Looking for Moth."

Moth went cold at her name.

"The shaudah's men," Silk whispered, appalled.

"No, blueboys from the bay, and a Vashmarna with them. Say they have a escort for dedicant Moth and a am'esty from the shaudah. Say the shaudah's called her to his service."

He stared. They all stared, even Silk, and in the silence Moth heard the machinery of suspicion grind into a new configuration.

"He has not," she said with the certainty of dismay. "He *can't.*"

"I'm just saying," said the bully boy, "what they says for me to say. But if you don't come, they'll come looking."

"And how," said Hamana to Moth, "did they know to look for you here?"

"I don't—"*know.* Moth remembered her fellow dedicants and closed her mouth. They might have been innocent in directing the police to the fire shrine. She, in her carelessness, was not. Her guilt must have showed. The machinery ground another notch tighter toward distrust.

"Well, go on, dedicant," Silk said coolly. "We can't let them fetch you out of here."

"I don't understand what this is," Moth said, pleading. "I don't even know . . . Amnesty for what?"

And Istvan, shockingly, laughed. "The power will be ours," he said mockingly to Hamana. "The power will be ours."

No one had mentioned, no one had needed to mention, that

if Tarun had talked, they would all be dead and the engine destroyed or taken by now.

Moth's confusion deepened when she saw Aramis standing among the saints with Lord Ghar's two men. She had seen her lover only once since the night the bridge fell, and that was at a distance, at the passage ceremony for Vashmarna's dead. He looked as stern now as he had then in the crowded temple, but there was a desperate tension around his eyes. He gave her one intense, unreadable glance, and nothing more. The shaudah, Ghar's policemen said. The Vashmarna. The Ghar. As if names were all the explanation she required. *Help me!* she thought at Aramis, but he fell in beside her between their escorting guards as if he, too, were a prisoner—if prisoner she was.

"*Andas,*" she said carefully to Aramis, "please, can you tell me why I am being recalled?"

"The shaudah," he replied shortly, "hopes that your work with Vashmarna may give you a useful insight into the present crisis."

This was bewildering, but all Moth could do was stare at Aramis's back. He had brought Vashmarna down on the *mundabi*'s cable. Could this be his doing as well?

He, like the booted policemen, was making heavy going of the foot stones. The most direct routes between the docks and the stairs had been laid with planks for the benefit of the baysiders—planks that were stolen every night, as they always had been, and replaced every morning, as they had not been for generations—but this deep in the tidal no one had bothered. Slum dwellers gave way before the uniforms, taking to the muck of the streets. No one stared, no one spat or threw fistfuls of sticky mud. The blue brass-buttoned tunics lurched and skidded and skipped down a surreal corridor of quiet, not as if they were invisible, but as if there were some fine membrane between them and the rest of the world, an eggshell of authority, a soap bubble of respect. Though gray clouds massed on the blue horizon, the sun still beat down, muffling the tidal in heat, steam, the fishy stench of rot. The oppressive silence deepened, filling not just ears, but mouths and nostrils and lungs.

Aramis! Tell me what is going on!

The policeman who led them jumped onto the porch that skirted Little Victory, one of the largest tenements. It was a sprawling building, and in the swelling heat of afternoon, the sun-filled, muck-floored bays between its wings were abandoned. The myriad windows were shuttered, curtained, screened with recycled broadsheet screens, but they were not blind. Probably no one looked out on the steaming mud. It was the building itself that watched, hostile but careless of who these particular enemies were or what their eventual fates might be. Aramis followed the first policeman onto the porch, and Moth, perforce, followed Aramis with the other bluecoat on her heels.

"Sirs," Moth said, "I think you have mistaken your turning."

The man in front did not respond. The man behind her said, with a friendly heartiness that brought her out in an icy sweat, "The *hend* knows the way, *rasnu*. There'll be a passage down this end. You'll see."

Moth stopped. "There is not."

"You'll see." The hearty policeman put a hard, hot hand against her shoulder blade. "Go on, *rasnu*."

Moth stumbled forward a step, but Aramis had stopped and was looking back at her, his dark face showing the bones of his skull. His light irises were golden in the sunlight, his pupils shrunk to dots, the whites shining at the corners of his eyes. He was disturbed, but uncomprehending. Moth, with that heavy hand at her back, knew, and she loved him profoundly in that moment, as if Aramis had become equated with life.

"Aramis," she said.

The world was so quiet, and so bright. Little Victory's walls were darkly patterned with smoke and water stains. Vines spilled from the eaves, from the boxes under every windowsill, yellow stars flowering in the rare sunshine. Lace-winged insects fluttered among them, steam wafted up from the mud, lizards pulsed their jeweled throats on the walls. The leading policeman turned at her voice.

"Aramis," he said thoughtfully. "I'll have to remember that for my report." The side of his face blossomed with red.

Moth blinked at this bloody punctuation to his statement, twitched at the report of a pistol. Aramis reacted more violently, wheeling around to stare at the *hend*'s nerveless collapse. The corpse folded in on itself and slid off the porch and into the mud. The pistol in his hand glinted briefly and disappeared.

The policeman behind Moth shouted. The near report of his gun made her duck and lean into the wall. With Aramis frozen in front of her, she had nowhere to go. But the policeman was not shooting at her. The paper screen on the window at his side burst outward, and a hurtling form drove him off the porch. He fell into the mud with a yell of outrage and did not rise. The dark form balanced on his sinking body unfolded itself to reveal Hamana's narrow, ferocious, smiling face. She looked as savage and as satisfied as a cat who has just killed its prey, and stepped delicately from her gruesome perch onto the porch just as the mud swelled up to cover the hearty policeman's form. It was not until she flicked the red blood off the knife in her hand that Moth fully understood.

"You've killed them," she said.

"So we have." Hamana was gracious.

Moth's understanding continued to lag. She had been hearing the rooftop whistles, but only with Hamana's "we" did she recognize the greenguards' code. Little Victory continued in its hateful indifference. Moth shivered with the heat.

"You saved our lives."

"Oh, were you in danger?"

Hamana lifted her brows in a very Silk-like expression of polite surprise, then grinned with a more honest cruelty before she ducked back into the ground floor window whence she had come. Heads vanished from upper windows, shadows disappeared back into the rooftop greenery, and Moth and Aramis were alone.

Aramis stared at Moth, then down at the dead men settling into the mud. He leaned against the tenement wall, scattering lizards that fled with a papery rustle of tiny feet, and raised his sweating face to the sun. Moth could see the cords in his throat above his coat collar, the sharp slide of his Adam's apple, the pulse behind his jaw. Her own throat swelled with the sense of his vulnerability. She sidled along the wall until she could rest her forehead against his shoulder and take his hand between hers.

"Who was that?" he said faintly.

"Hamana."

"Yes, but who . . ." He let it go as if he were too tired to hold on to the question. After a moment of dense silence, he said, "Do you know what they will think when we go back alive with our escort dead in the tidal?"

Moth knew. She was sure Hamana also knew, and was awed at the two-edged gift. Friendship and enmity, immediate life and distant, impersonal death. The *mundabi* were clearly leaving the question of Moth's fidelity up to the gods.

How could godless Moth fail to appreciate the irony?

"What are you?" her lover softly asked. "Who are you? How many lies have you told?"

Moth, a contrite and humble Moth, said, "Too many."

But that only angered him. He shook her off and took a long step away. "Do you even know how deep in the mire you are? I have lied to the shaudah for you! The *Vashmarna* has lied to the shaudah for you! Good gods! Why did you never tell me—"

"Because you would shout it to the rooftops where anyone could hear!"

"How dare you—"

"Keep your voice down."

Moth's intensity served to remind him of where they were. He looked first at the dead, and shuddered, before glancing about at the vine-clad and crumbling walls. No one seemed to be listening but the lizards, who posed motionless in the sun, but the memory of Hamana's abrupt appearance was much too clear. Aramis shivered and started walking with nervous haste along the walkway.

"There's no way out that way," Moth said tightly to his back. "You have to follow me."

Without their escort they received no unnatural deference from the tidal crowds. There was the usual noise, the usual skirmishes over right of way on the foot stones, the usual cool and gluey suction of the mud. Moth walked with her loose pants held up out of habit, and when they achieved the water's edge and the ruined bridge abutment, she washed in the sluggish surf, but Aramis, with his shoes and his narrow trousers, was doomed to be filthy.

No one had yet tried to move the stone blocks scattered by the *mundab,* and they were already acquiring a look of permanence, stained by *tirindi* scat and slimed by the tide. They also defended pockets of privacy from the steady traffic from the docks. Aramis hunkered down beside Moth where she perched on a weedy stone to rinse her feet.

"Vashmarna has gone very far into danger for your sake,"

he said, his voice tight with restraint. "You owe us an explanation."

"I owe *you*?" Moth said with no restraint at all. "None of this would have happened if you hadn't followed me to begin with! If you hadn't told Vashmarna about the cable, if you hadn't—"

"Friends of mine died, Moth! Two of the Ghar's men are murdered before my eyes, and you—"

"Men who would have killed you! Killed us both!"

"Don't you think I have wondered how much I am to blame? How much *you* are to blame? Yes! You owe us an explanation!"

"Which 'us'? The Society? Vashmarna? The shaudah, the Ghar—"

"I am Vashmarna's man before I am anything else, and it is Vashmarna that risks itself for your sake, even now, even in the midst of this." His voice was tight again, but his gesture at the ruined bridge was as close to violence as Moth had ever seen in him.

"Vashmarna knows what it needs to know."

Moth started to rise. Aramis caught her arm, holding her down.

"The Ghar's men are *dead,* Moth. You have to tell me—"

"Vashmarna knows what it needs to know."

Moth's voice was harsh with desperation, not anger, but she saw the sudden distance in Aramis's eyes and knew by that, and by the painful grip on her arm, that she was not dealing with her lover now. She was dealing with Vashmarna's man, a man who must wonder if he was betrayed by his lady as well as by his love. Frightened by his retreat, Moth put her hand on his shoulder.

"Aramis, your lady knows. I promise you, she knows, but I cannot speak of it."

Aramis was silent for a time, perhaps remembering the message he had carried from his lady to Moth. Finally he shrugged, heedless of Moth's touch.

"Good. She knows. What does it matter if I don't?" He was brusque, but there was a note of self-pity in his voice. "Who am I?"

"You know I love you," she said uncertainly.

He flicked her a glance, a painful look of mistrust, and then, as if he could no longer bear to be so close to her, he released her arm and stood.

Moth caught his hand. She was afraid of loss, but also afraid in a more practical sense that Aramis betrayed might become Aramis the betrayer. She loved him, knew she was dishonest and cruel, did not know what else to do. Crouched at his feet, holding on to his unresponsive hand, she said, "Aramis, forgive me. This is all wrong, the time is all wrong, but I don't know what else to do. You have to know this. I'm pregnant. I'm carrying your child."

As he stood above her, his head was against the bright sky and she could not see the expression on his face. She could not read his thoughts. Was he contemplating the gulf between their present selves and those lighthearted lovers who used to sneak blind pleasures in the heart of the fort, as if no human, no future, could possibly intrude? There was a wide, black gulf between then and now. He lifted her to her feet, held her against the stiff hot breast of his coat, pressed his face against her hair, but still she did not know. She did not know if she had lost or won.

THE BASTION

He took her to the fort, tucking her into the shadow of his authority, hiding her within the crowd of the dispossessed. Moth had never been in the administrative wing where the senior clerks and engineers dwelled. Was this really how they lived? As plain as this? The fort had been a soldiers', and was now an engineers', province, and even its highest reaches had none of the imagined luxuries of the bay. Lady Vashmarna's rooms were blocky and small, with grass mats and a scattering of lizards taking refuge from the heat. The windows were screened against the sun, and although licks of ocean breeze slipped in around the edges of the paper-and-bamboo frames, the office was stuffy and dull.

"What will you tell them?" Moth asked as Aramis turned to go.

He gave her a bleak look. "That you died in a tidal ambush

with the Ghar's men, I suppose. You can hardly present your-self to the shaudah now."

Now that she was pregnant? Now that the Ghars wanted her dead? Moth did not ask. She said, needing his acknowledg-ment, "They would have killed you too, you know."

Aramis opened the door and said without expression, "I know."

He went out, leaving her alone in Lady Vashmarna's office.

As the dull quiet seeped into the space Aramis left behind, the shock of Tarun's death, of Hamana's rescue, of the argu-ment with Aramis, receded into the past, a few more incidents in a life that was full of them. It was the oldest lesson of the tidal orphan: death was only death, something that happened to other people as long as one was still alive. Which of course Moth was, and, she gradually realized, presented with an un-precedented opportunity. In all her life she had met with her sponsor in person exactly twice, and both times they had met in the scholarium, on neutral ground. Here was the lady's own office, filled with the lady's own things. A silk shawl on the back of a chair ran like cool water through Moth's hands and sent up a faint perfume to her nose. She lifted it to her face and breathed in the scent (wood and ferns and sun-warmed hair), and only afterward was disturbed by the intimacy of her own gesture: not by her invasion of the lady's privacy, but by the in-vasion she had invited from the other side. The lady's perfume was like an extension of the lady's person, of her personality and her physical body, and Moth was shaken by the sudden re-ality of the woman who had been an invisible, intangible icon of authority for most of Moth's life. She hung the shawl back on the chair, but the scent lingered on her hands.

Or perhaps the lady's things breathed it at her, a protest, or a warning of the power of the woman who could leave this piece of her spirit to guard her things. Yet there did not seem to be much to guard. The papers on the desk read like house-keeping reports, the tea set was plain tidal work, the book with the worn once-colorful cover was all elementary meditations, not a single secret in sight. Moth wrinkled her nose at a scent that was beginning to seem unpleasant and, bold with irritation, threw open a tall cupboard door.

And then stood flat-footed with surprise before the painted icons and gilded saints, the enameled incense burners and candles melted into nubs of expensive *hadaras* wax. These were the most valuable items in the room. Moth hunched her shoulders in an angry shrug and shut the door with a slam. She was hardly able to name her own emotions. Derision? Dismay? This pious cupboard, the same cupboard that had its right of place in every household in the *rasnan*, rich or poor, should have been as dull and as expected as the tea set. So why this visceral shock? As if she had glimpsed some powerful mystery, some crucial and mostly hidden fact—not about the gods, who were what they had always been, or failed to be—but about her sponsor, who had taken another step closer to reality.

And took another step closer yet when she opened the office door with Aramis at her heels. She looked at Moth. Moth looked at her, feeling completely unprepared. Lady Vashmarna turned to Aramis.

"Tapurnashen-'*das*, I thank you. That was a more dangerous task than I ever meant to set you, but you were quite correct to bring the dedicant here. I am grateful for that, and for your silence . . . and for your survival . . . but I think you had better leave us now."

"*Jinnuju.*" Aramis bowed.

"Go, clean yourself, rest. If the Ghar or the shaudah require another interview, I promise you will not have to face them alone."

"*Jin'.*"

Aramis bowed again and went without a glance at Moth, closing the door softly behind him. Still she did not know, she did not know, and now she was alone with the woman who loomed over her life as powerful and as distant as a god. A god suddenly made flesh.

Moth bowed and whispered, *"Jinnu."*

Lady Vashmarna stood before her bright-screened window, a dark shape and a distant voice. "What is this, Moth? The Ghar's men killed and their murderers confederates of yours? Is that what I am to understand?"

Why could Moth speak to Aramis with a clear voice, and yet be strangled now? No one in the world could daunt her so. It was as if the vulnerability of her brush with death, that she had shrugged off tidal-wise, had opened up inside her like a wound. Moth swallowed and, still whispering, said, "The Ghar's men meant to kill us, *jin'.*"

"Which is itself a matter. I do not forget. But there is still the question of these killers. Confederates, truly?"

"Yes, *jin'.*" Moth tried to clear her throat, to little effect. "The engine must be guarded. We—the *mundabi*—recruited several crews among the greenguards." Trembling, she had to add, "They saved our lives."

Lady Vashmarna paced a few slow and thoughtful steps away from the window screen. Against the bare wall she gained color, texture, a face. Her short robe was silver and blue, her skin a rich russet brown, her brown hair streaked with gray. She had thin arched brows; a thin nose with arched nostrils; dark, deep-set eyes: forbidding features, though her mouth was shaped for kindness, as was her rounded body beneath her clothes. Her expression guarded her against the softer emotions. Not cold or unfeeling: guarded. It was that sense of a barricade that might somehow be breached that lured one in.

Lady Vashmarna said, "How deeply have you entangled us in the tidal's violence?"

"Do you mean the tidal's violence, *jinnu,* or the shaudah's?" Moth said, stung.

"I mean the tidal's," Lady Vashmarna coldly replied. "I mean the shadow cult's."

"When has the tidal ever begun a fight?" Moth said. The old anger freed her from her nascent awe. "You speak so blithely of the shadow cult, but it was the Society of Doors that tried to have me killed. Or don't you know yet that the Ghars are the chiefs of a society that has been outlawed for more than a hundred years?"

Lady Vashmarna, by her expression, did not know, but shock quickly gave way to offense. "Is this how they have taught you to argue? To make wild accusations about your betters, as if that is all it would take to throw me off the scent? I had thought better of the scholarium's teachers."

"The scholarium—" Moth began, about to hare off down a tangent of her own, but Lady Vashmarna interrupted her.

"Hold your tongue. It is you we speak of. You and the shadow cult. You and the sabotage of my demesne. You and the destruction of the bridge! Do you know what you have done?"

"What *I* have done?" Moth said mendaciously. Another tidal lesson: it's always better to attack than defend. "If you had left the cable in place—"

"If I—!" Lady Vashmarna drew a sharp breath. "Do you have the temerity to lay that at *my* door? I saw the shadow gods with my own eyes!"

"Gods?" Moth said scornfully. "You saw the manifests of a working, the manifestations of power. What do you know of it? Can you tell the manifests of the *mundabi* from the manifests of the Society at a glance?" By this time Moth was on fire, all her courage and all her invention roused to incandescence.

Lady Vashmarna, by contrast, was leaden with condemnation and icy with disgust.

"The Society of Doors is a fiction, a history, a harmless dream. It is the shadow cult that has raised these demons, these monsters that have plagued Vashmarna to the point of ruin. You speak to me of manifestations of power? I say it is your power! Your *mundabi.* Your cable. Your cult. Your fault. Again I ask you: Do you know what you have done?"

Even on fire, Moth could feel that cold wind. "I know what I have seen. Like you I have seen manifests where they should not be. Only a few nights before the bridge came down I saw a manifest in the scholarium that I did not raise—a manifest in the scholarium where *aras* Baradam Ghar rules in the scholars' hall—and just before the bridge fell the *mundab* was sorely troubled. I tell you, I am not the only—" She caught herself. "We, the *mundabi,* are not the only ones who are drawing on the *mundab.* We are not the danger Vashmarna should be defending itself against."

"You have seen. You have felt. But you have not touched on the small matter of the cable, of the sabotage that has put Vashmarna fatally at odds with the shaudah and the Ghars, of the betrayal Vashmarna has suffered, of the loss of Vashmarna lives. Why should I believe you? Why should I for one instant believe a word you say, when you have been lying to me from the moment I gave you my trust?"

"Trust!" Moth's heart was pounding hard enough to shake her voice. "When have you ever trusted me? You have kept as far from me as you could and still use me for your own ends—"

"The *rasnan*'s ends!"

"—and now you blame me because I haven't kept you sufficiently informed? You set me a task—a task no one else could perform—and left me to perform it without materials, without protection, without—"

"Without direction?" Lady Vashmarna's voice was arid. "If you had followed my orders that night, would the bridge still be standing? Answer me!"

"Ask the Ghars," Moth said, off-balance and sullen. "Ask your own man who followed me when he never should have."

"Oh, blame everyone but yourself! Whom will you blame for all the messages you did not send me? I would be hard-pressed to force a message into your hands, but you could speak directly to my ear whenever you chose. When did you ever tell me you needed power? When did you ever warn me of the effects of the cable? When did you ever ask me for permission or advice?"

"Advice?" Moth said, pouncing on the one question she could safely answer. "Advice from your high tower, is it? Permission, direction—what do you know about the tidal, what do you know about the *mundab*, that you think you can give me advice? The only direction you have ever given me is to stop and to go. Stop and go, build the engine and don't build it, draw on the *mundab*'s power but don't blaspheme. What do you know about the *mundab*? What do you know about the tidal? You say you're using me for the *rasnan*'s ends, but what do you know of the *rasnan*? Not the towers, not the shaudah and the Ghar, but the tidal, the *hadaras*, the poor. We are the ones who need to get off this island! We are the ones who need new land! Who are you to tell us when to stop and when to go?"

"And who are you," said Lady Vashmarna, her handsome face mean, "to force my hand? I raised you from the tidal, I gave you all the learning you have ever had, I gave you a place and a purpose in the world. The gods witness, you surely know the ways of the poor, but what do you know about the workings of power—real power—the power that shapes the future for us all? How dare you speak so scornfully, so ignorantly, of the shaudah and the Ghar? How dare you think that you can dictate to me?"

"You raised me from the tidal?" Moth was shaking with fury, a fury that only grew hotter with the start of her angry tears. "You raised me from the tidal? *You put me in the tidal to begin with*. What did you think the slums would make of your daughter, Mother? A willing slave?"

THE BASTION

While Lady Vashmarna stared in horror, the girl turned away to hide her tears. Her dark braid slipped aside to bare the thin, vulnerable neck. Her shoulders were also thin, too thin, braced against her weeping, but Lady Vashmarna could not summon any pity, any kindness, any emotion but this suffocating rage. How dare she! How dare she speak to the Vashmarna so!

Lady Vashmarna knew, in a cold rational corner of her mind, that this was a fault. Rage must give way to detachment, blame to compassion, rejection to an acceptance of responsibility. But "mother"—how she loathed that word, and the tears.

"Control yourself," she said, trying to breathe around the hard knot in her breast.

Moth was slow to respond. She turned but kept her face

averted, and it took her a moment to catch her breath, sniff, wipe her cheeks and her nose on her sleeve.

Lady Vashmarna railed at her own unfairness, but could not stop the thought: dirty habits; dirty girl. She quieted her own breathing before she spoke again.

"Very well. I left the engine and the *mundab* in your hands. I have no one to blame but myself if they have been dropped in the mud. Stop your crying!" she added, more sharply than she had meant.

Moth took a deep breath and wiped her face again before she looked up to meet Lady Vashmarna's glare. Moth's face was a mask, but her gold-ringed eyes shone with too dark and knowing an intelligence, as they always did. A wordless accusation Lady Vashmarna had seen even in the infant child she had borne in secret and given away, an accusation that she had never been able to withstand. She turned away to compose herself. When she turned back, her daughter was standing with her hands peaceably folded and her gaze on some deep infinity. *So the temple has taught you something,* Lady Vashmarna thought, and once again had to wrestle her mind into order.

"Very well," she said again. "We cannot heal the past. We must move forward with what we have. The engine is safe?"

"For now." Moth's voice was subdued. "The greenguards have been running interference with the soldiers."

Lady Vashmarna thought of the list of the shaudah's dead and said, "I do not want to know the details. Let us leave it there: the engine is safe. Is it complete? No, I remember, you said it is not. Can it still be completed without the power cable?"

"Yes, *jinnu.*"

The assurance of that distant "Yes" stung Lady Vashmarna. She could almost prefer the weeping girl to this mulish acolyte.

"How quickly can it be finished?"

"I don't know, *jinnu*. Perhaps not very long."

"Perhaps." But that scornful echo did not win her a more useful response. Lady Vashmarna took another calming breath and began to pace. "So. The engine is safe. We must keep you safe to complete the engine. The shaudah knows your name: we have told him you have been helping Vashmarna with the recent difficulties, and he has some hope . . ." She had to pause to appreciate the wretched irony. "He hopes you can provide some insight into the bridge's destruction. Of course, one cannot discount the possibility that he has had some report of your entanglements in the tidal and hopes to turn you into his spy, but that can be managed. Indeed, it might be to our advantage to have you in his household. If you can ingratiate yourself, he might be softened when we reveal the engine and the ship. If we can keep them secret long enough to let this furor die down, and if you have time to make yourself valuable—"

"There is no time," Moth interrupted, still distant, still with her gaze on some far horizon.

"What is this?" Lady Vashmarna trembled on the edge of her self-control. "Some new crisis?"

"Yes, *jin'*." Moth turned her head and looked her in the eye. "Mother." She said it without a trace of shame: "I'm pregnant."

Lady Vashmarna started to shake. "How dare you?" she whispered.

Moth looked insolent for an instant, as if she might shrug, but then she lowered her eyes and made a small, helpless gesture with her hand. "It has been at least two months, but I think closer to three. I cannot be in the shaudah's service when I begin to show."

This was self-evident. Lady Vashmarna grew bitterly calm. Some light within her guttered and died, as Vashmarna's lights had died the night the bridge fell, for her plans, her hopes, the very hope of the world collapsed in ruins all about her. "What am I to do with you?" she said in the small, blank voice of despair.

"I don't know," Moth said, her voice even smaller. "What did you do when you were carrying me?"

"When I was carrying you, my family hid me on their *hadaras* estate."

"Can you not . . . ?" Finally the girl's arrogance faltered. "*Jinnu,* can I not go away for a little time?"

"And leave the engine unfinished for six or seven months? While the shaudah's men scour the tidal and your conspirators murder them to hide what cannot be hidden? And how am I to explain your presence on the Vashmarna estate? What do I say when the shaudah asks why the dedicant who failed his summons is growing fat on Vashmarna grain?"

"I don't know."

"Nor do I." Lady Vashmarna turned away. "Go. We're done. I wash my hands of you."

And finally, finally, after twenty-two years, that wordless accusation was given voice. "Everything I have done," Moth said, "I have done for you. Do you have no kindness for me at all?"

"For you?" Lady Vashmarna turned back to meet her daughter's eyes. "For you? You, who betray your holy vows to wallow in the muck with some tidal lover when I have sworn myself to celibacy. You, who raise demons in my name to tear apart the civilization I have dedicated my life to save. You, who were got on me by some foul-breathed rebel, a child of rape! You! What have I ever given you but kindness? Ah, gods look down upon me! Bear me witness! I should have left you in the tidal where you belonged!"

THE BAY

But the tidal did not want her either.

The *mundabi* were scattered, suspicious and afraid after Tarun's death; the shadow cult had taken on a life of its own, a savage rebel army bred from a rumor and a few of the engine's ghosts, ignorant of its connection to the *mundab;* and with the shaudah and the Ghar both after Moth's head, none of the shrines was safe. She had run to Silk as if her friend's arms could shelter her against disaster, but the Red House had had no more welcome for her than anywhere else. Hamana had nearly denied her access to the roof where Silk was tending her sun-shocked plants, and it was only Silk's militant mood that had rallied her to Moth's defense. Yet even Silk could not keep her. All Silk could do was help her flee.

Leaving the *shadras*. Moth had never dreamed of such a thing. Does a nightmare count as a dream? Leaving the *shadras* with the engine unfinished, her plans in ruins—and more than that, her dream of a future that held more than a hard, dirty scrabble for survival. She should stay. She knew it in a moment of panicked certainty: she should stay, finish the engine as she had promised it to the *mundabi,* steal the real power out of her mother's hands, and . . . and . . .

"Listen!" she said to Hamana and Silk. "Listen, we can still do this, we can still beat them, we can finish the engine for ourselves!"

"We?" said Hamana. "You're right: *we* still can. *You*—"

"We still owe her," Silk said, "for the engine itself, if nothing else."

Hamana caught her breath. "We still need to get her out of the bastion's reach. Keep her out of their hands, even if we don't want her in ours. Come on."

The traffic at the docks was lessening, but there were still so many boats on the bay that one more would never be noticed. Silk and Hamana bundled Moth into a boat right under the noses of the shaudah's men, and Hamana herself took the tiller and the lines.

It was the meanest kind of boat, a *nunidal* hollowed from a log stolen from a forester's raft, with a tacked-on keel and a bamboo pole for a mast. The sail was made of thin bamboo slats with paper pasted onto the windward side, and it hissed and muttered in the wind, noisier than the ripple of water against the barnacled hull. Noisier than the three women in the boat, who traveled in silence. Hamana sat at the tiller, her narrow face drawn into a frown against the glare off the water. Silk crouched by the mast, watching the shore slowly recede, the tidal tenements disappearing against the cliff, the bastion walls and the green-clad temple roof etched against the steamy green bulk of the island. Moth, alone in the bow, was bleakly amazed that tenements and temple and all were not in ruins like the truncated bridge. The whole of the *shadras* was like the towers in the bay, gutted but still standing.

Or was that Moth, dead but for the beating of her heart?

Silent Hamana, for reasons of her own, took them in among the empty towers. From shore they were delicate spires rising above the reef, but from the water they were massive, coolly shadowed and smelling of wet stone and the salty sea. They were not pristine, as they appeared from a distance, all white and shining against the far horizon. Rain had tarnished the decorative bands of copper and brass, streaking the pale stone with black and poisonous green. The low tide of evening was near and the foundation stones were dyed a healthier green by the weeds, purple-black by the mussels, orange and meat-red by the sea stars. *Tirindi* nested in the groins of the covered bridges between the spires, and every abutment was fouled by the effluvium of their nests. And yet . . .

The hard shell of pain within Moth cracked and bled. Silenced, emptied, besmirched by the world, the towers were still astonishing, still wonderful, still somehow alive. Cold melancholy giants, they stood with their feet in the waves and their heads against the gathering clouds. They did not have the blank, spiteful hostility of the tidal's tenements. They were noble and sad as they stared, each one, out to the forbidden ocean and back on the beleaguered land. And as Hamana guided the *nunidal* in among them, daring the twisty winds that whirled through the open maze, Moth realized each one had a voice. The wind bellowed and sang among the bridges, the ocean chuckled, sobbed, and roared through the caverns beneath each tower's base. The towers spoke, and Moth, stupid with shock and slightly crazed with grief, could almost believe that if she held herself still enough, opened her heart enough, silenced her mind enough, she would begin to understand what they said.

Hamana began to name the towers as she fought the boat from one current-scoured channel to the next. Oorand and Pennimissirand. Allurand and Vhanasharand. Itteranarand and Magarand and crystal-footed Sidirand with its Temple of the Waves. Moth stared up at the vast windows, the massive slabs of gray, white, pinkish quartz, but the temple gave her nothing. The glass, dull with salt, reflected only what was all around them: the towers, the waves, the building clouds. "It's going to rain again," Silk said, subdued, and Hamana struggled to bring the boat around. They scudded recklessly under the last seaward arch of the bridge, where it joined up with Shaudarand, and the boat fled like a windblown piece of trash across the darkening waves. The sun was swallowed up by a cloud, but still burned there, sending rain-softened rays of light to touch the green water, the green slopes of the island, the green roofs of the bastion. A hundred shades of green, as vivid as a dream, as sweet as a taste, as lively as a name across the tongue. Moth had never understood the word "heartache" before now. She had always believed it was a metaphor, but now she felt that physical clutch of pain, that shaft of anguish that speared her from her throat to her womb. She turned her face from the shore and stared with wind-stung eyes out to the empty horizon, refusing to look back, as even the white towers finally disappeared beyond the western headland. The *shadras* was gone. There was only the *rasnan* and the *mundab,* only the island and the sea.

The clouds filled the sky and spat rain. The shrouded sun shone its last above the rim of the world. Soon they would have to find shelter against the shore.

Moth saw the sail first, an angle of white between the gray of sky and the gray of sea, but she did not speak. Why bother? But the sail drew closer, raising the boat's hull above the horizon, revealing a deepwater fishing boat fighting against the wind to return to the *shadras* bay for the night. Moth watched it, dull-eyed, huddled down against the wind. It was Hamana who said "A boat!" and turned her tiller to bring them near.

"What are you doing?" snapped a bad-tempered Silk. Moth could guess the regrets that must be souring Silk's mood, and knew who would get the blame. Rightly, she supposed—she supposed all the blame should be hers—but she could not cope. She pulled Silk's borrowed shawl over her face and pretended to sleep.

"I think I know that boat," said Hamana, revealing further depths of unexpected knowledge. Moth had known her only as a roof guard, a street bully, a killer. She could envy the greenguard's versatility. Without her engine and her schemes, she, Moth, was as useless as a petted baysider girl. Yes, she could envy Hamana now.

"Do we want to spread the news of our departure?" said Silk.

Hamana did not answer. Neither the fishing boat nor the *nunidal* had the wind securely behind them, and it took some tricky sailing, especially with the primitive sail, to bring the *nunidal* into the fishing boat's path. It would have been impossible if the other boat had not desired a meeting as well. After some maneuvering, the two boats dropped their sails and drifted together on the restless water. The large boat heaved, the little boat bobbed, but the steady rain flattened the waves.

"Where from?" called a hoarse voice from the fish boat.

Moth might have said, *The shadras,* but "The Red House," called Hamana.

"How come?" said the fish boat.

"On the midnight tide," said Hamana. "And you?"

Moth, recognizing the password, uncovered herself and sat up. She would never have recognized the boat, one hull being much the same as the next to her eyes, but she knew the faces peering over the side. Her battered heart gave a fresh pulse of life. This was the *Eelgrass,* missing at sea for sixty-four days.

"Out by night and home again by noon," came the counter-sign, and Moth cried out, "Sharking!"

The bigger boat, shoved by the wind, was crowding the *nunidal*. Sharking, its captain, leaned out above her. He was a sere man with weathered black skin and a shock of gray-white hair, but he had never looked old before. Sixty-four days at sea.

"Who is there?" he said.

"Dedicant Moth," Moth said. Silk ducked her head and swore.

"*Rasnu,*" he said, and stretched down his hand. She stood, reckless with hope, and clasped his fingers. Hamana clutched at the fish boat's slimy side to keep them steady.

"What did you find?" Moth should have asked after their well-being, praised their hardiness, congratulated them on their survival, but she had no courtesies left. "What did you find?"

"Nothing," Sharking said. He sounded as if he, too, had been scoured by his ordeal. "Nothing, *rasnu*. Nothing but water and wind. A lifetime of nothing but water and wind. Ah, gods! We were certain we had lost our way. What a miracle to see the island again! Gods bring us to the only shore on this accursed world!"

She should not have hoped. Surely she knew by now not to hope. Moth let go Sharking's hand and sank into the bow, pulling Silk's shawl back over her face. Let Hamana the killer give them the courtesies and the news they were owed.

Moth had nothing. Nothing.

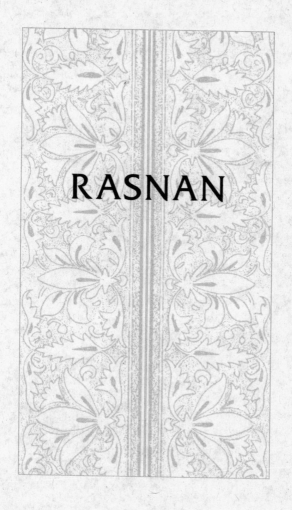

RASNAN

THE BASTION

In these crowded days Lady Vashmarna preferred to take her prayers to the temple in the hour before dawn. The bastion was quietest then, the darkness more hopeful than threatening, and the temple itself was empty save for a few quiet vigil-keepers, priests as still and rapt as the bronze figures before which they knelt. The gods' wise and secretive faces loomed up against the shadows of the roof, barely touched by the candles burning at their feet. Golden glints sketched out a brow, a cheek, the smiling curve of a mouth, but the holy eyes were fathomless; they stared at the darkness as they might meet the eyes of an equal—honest, fearless, self-contained. They did not look down, and even a grown woman could not reach higher than their hands, their knees, their prayer-polished feet. *You are all children here*, the temple said.

Every morning Lady Vashmarna came with her burden of

pain. It was a penance simply to enter the mother chapel where Kistnu sat, prayer tokens spilling out of her hands and scattered about her feet. *I am a child,* Lady Vashmarna said in her prayers. It was the only truth that gave her the courage to come here at all, into the Mother's presence. *Kistnu, absent mother, stretch out your hand. Kistnaran, mother of absence, turn your face aside.* "I am your child," said Lady Vashmarna, and she cupped her hands before her as if to catch the blood pouring from a spiritual wound. "Turn your terrible face aside," she whispered, but it was herself she prayed to, and the past was no kinder than the gods.

She suffered, did Lady Vashmarna. She suffered the loss of the child she had denied for twenty-two years, but she suffered more from the loss of her virtue. She was a good woman. She must be, for she had dedicated her life to principle, to self-sacrifice, to piety, and to the saving of her hungry world. But if she was a good woman, then whose was that hatred, that fear, that selfish cruelty that had driven her daughter away?

I am your child! Lady Vashmarna cried silently to her gods. *Have you no kindness for me at all?*

It was exhausting, this pain, this bleeding wound. She moved like an old woman to light her candle and her incense, to touch her head to Kistnu's cold foot, to rise. She might have stretched herself out on the chill floor, spent the day in abasement like the young priest lying on his face before the nameless god, but she had other burdens to bear. Now, more than ever, she had to dedicate herself to wisdom, to doing good. To doing right, she thought, and set herself as a spiritual discipline to solve the intellectual puzzle of good and right. Are they the same? A question with many answers, but no solution.

She stepped out into the lofty space of the nave, and her

sandaled feet startled a flock of echoes from the roof. The priest seemed startled as well, for he rose and, almost before he had completed his bow, turned toward her. Lady Vashmarna was surprised and warmed to see that he was *aras* Baradam, her old friend's problematical son. She chided herself for being surprised at his piety, and paused. They met in the cool rain-scented shadows before the open door.

"*Jinnu.*"

"*Aras.*"

"Do you come so early for the morning services?"

"No. I am embarrassed to say, I come for private prayer instead of services these days."

"There is no embarrassment in dedicating oneself to duty, *jinnu*. We must call upon the gods for comfort and help in these difficult times, but we must give to them our service as well as receive from them their aid. And you give more than most."

"You are kind."

"No, *jin'*," he said with a smile in his quiet voice. "I am honest."

"But you are kind." Lady Vashmarna was moved, if only by her own need for balm. "If you knew . . ."

"You are troubled."

In the darkness, in the quiet of the rain, the priestly phrase carried a depth of concern she might not have trusted at another time.

"I am troubled, *aras*. I have trespassed. I have been . . . ungenerous." Even now she shied away from the dangerous confession. "What is worse, I am afraid of being trespassed upon. I act—I am driven by fear." And it was suddenly true, in the tightness of her breath and the dampness of her palms.

"*Jinnu,* we are all afraid."

"Yes! We are all afraid. We are like vermin whose nest is threatened. We lash out without thought of the harm we might do, even to ourselves."

"Do you mean our nest, or yours?"

A penetrating question. Lady Vashmarna drew a calming breath. "Mine, yes, as well as ours. Since I left Shaudarand, I have been forced to realize how important my rooms were to me, how much I had grown into their shape like a hatchling inside its egg. Does this sound too literal? But I have hatched; I am exposed. And I cannot settle myself, I cannot protect myself, I live in a stranger's space—"

Perhaps sensing her prevarication, Baradam gently interrupted. "But, Vashmarna-*jin'*, so it is with us all, and so it has always been in this world. We are a people of exile; our ancestors cast us out of the nest long ago. Abandonment is our legacy. This is why it seems such a dreadful risk for us to put ourselves in the gods' hands, and yet therein lies the only safety we will ever find. Safety, in this world, can be nothing but an illusion. Perhaps it is not danger that frightens you, *jinnuju,* but truth."

Oh, this man! He was young, but he had his father's mind. *Abandonment is our legacy.* A terrible truth indeed. Lady Vashmarna tried to accept it with good grace, but the instinct to deflect, to defend, was too strong.

"I lost that illusion many years ago, *aras.* When you were a child sent to the *hadaras* for safety, I was here in the *shadras,* in the midst of the Lamplighters Rebellion."

"But is not memory another illusion? Do you hold those remembered fears between yourself and the reality of the now?"

"I, and everyone of an age to remember the riots—which was, I believe, my point," she said too sharply. She moderated her tone and added, "But did you not just now hold up the memory of our exile before us both? When is memory illusion, and when is it an illumination of truth?"

The *aras* was young after all. He fell back upon a priestly answer: "It is illusion when it leads us into evil, and illumination when it leads us into good."

What is right, and what is good? What is illusion, and what is truth?

Is goodness real?

The rain fell gently this morning, swathing the scholarium buildings in scarves of gray. Lady Vashmarna was conscious of human activity on the porches and in the dormitories, but she was alone within her thoughts. Her thoughts and, yes, her memories. Was this a failure, or a penance? Could one do penance through one's flaws? With the tidal gripped in escalating violence and the bastion seething with haunts and, more recently, plague, Lady Vashmarna found herself drawn again and again into the past, reliving dead pain as if it were more alive than the present. Her concern over the growing unrest was shot through with blazing flashes of the Lamplighter riots; her guilt over her lack of charity toward her daughter was like a shadow cast by her shame when she had been sent, unwillingly pregnant, into the *hadaras* by her own mother. *Abandonment is our legacy.* How dare Baradam Ghar say such a thing, with his father, his privileges, his rank! But that was unfair.

And doubly unfair to remember Moth's accusations about the Ghars and the Society of Doors.

Lady Vashmarna was haunted by her own unworthiness, as the whole world was haunted by her daughter's illicit work. Those eerie manifestations of power, that Lady Vashmarna had once derided to Aramis Tapurnashen as superstition, had become a ubiquity since the bridge had fallen. The shadow cult was loudly denounced, the shadow gods nervously whispered about, but they were both potent realities in the *shadras*. *Everything I have done, I have done for you,* her daughter had said. Had Lady Vashmarna cast her off in the hopes that Moth might take away not just her troublesome presence but Lady Vashmarna's own burden of responsibility as well? If so, she had failed. Her ignorance of what these shadows were, of what they meant, only increased her fear without diminishing her guilt.

And now there was this plague. An inevitability, the Vashmarna physicians assured her, given the crowding and the rains. The river ceaselessly battered the generating station's dam with drowned animals and drowned men, and the underground springs bled mud and mineral salts into the *shadras* water supply. It was all of a piece with the season, but the plague, of a kind no one had seen before, had become linked with the tidal's shadows, the haunts that made night dreadful. And the refugees' fears were doubled, and doubled again by their helplessness. Every day more wealthy households petitioned to be allowed to depart for the *hadaras*. Some were granted leave, those with small numbers and large estates, but the *hadaras* was also stressed by the flooding. There was no room for new structures or camps, food was in too short supply, and with the shaudah's soldiers entrenched in the tidal, there were too few reliable men to guard what stores remained. "Stay," the shaudah said, half an order, half a plea. "Have patience," he said to the dispossessed, "have faith." And to Lady Vashmarna, he said, "Give me power! Let us return to the bay!"

To which she must reply, "Give me a bridge!" But according to the shaudah the bridge had become an impossibility. It could not be built until the situation was resolved, and nothing could be resolved without the bridge. *What fools fear makes of sane men!* Lady Vashmarna thought, for she blamed Lord Ghar for this inaction. The fort, with its busy engineers and cheerful (because safe) adherents, seemed like the last refuge of productivity and good sense. Her suppliers still came through the gates, her manufactories still worked with an embarrassment of power, and with a new cable already being extruded and her long-absent engineers and workmen soon to return from the *hadaras,* sequestered materials in hand, she had a real hope of forcing the bridge's repair, Ghar or no Ghar. There would still be no water, but with the rains continuing that was not much more than an inconvenience, and new pipes would follow in due time. With power the towers could be made habitable within a matter of days. Let her give that news to the shaudah, and then see if some order could finally be imposed upon the impending chaos.

Lady Vashmarna left the scholarium in a better frame of mind than she had entered it, and, thinking these busy, hopeful thoughts, she was halfway across the inland road before she became aware of some trouble at the gate. Another household, denied the shaudah's permission to leave the bastion, was trying to force the issue with the Ghar's guards. Lady Vashmarna hesitated: the shaudah had put the bastion in Ghar's hands; let them cope. But there was something spiteful about that thought, and she knew the matriarch of the household, a woman who had been a close friend of her mother's. She made her quiet way through the press of servants and children and lookers-on.

The matriarch's son had descended into a kind of hectoring plea.

"We *have* somewhere to go. It is our family's *holding.* For nine generations the land has been ours! I myself spent a year there as a child, my mother lived there for much of her youth, my grandmother was married there! We have a *house,* we have *storehouses,* we have *plantations.* We cleared that land. We already feed ourselves!"

"I cannot act without the shaudah's orders, or the Ghar's," the gate *purdar* said. His voice had the tight monotony of too many repetitions, too much hectoring, too little courtesy. Too much rain, Lady Vashmarna thought, but the same could be said for all of them.

"The shaudah is concerned for the farmlands," the matriarch, Uludian Mahel, said condescendingly. "But we are concerned for the crowding here. It is so bad for the children, not just our children, but all the children, even the child novices who have been turned out to sleep on the porches—"

"With the haunts!" one of her daughters cried. A child started to wail, and someone from farther back in the growing crowd shouted, "And the plague! We are locked within the walls to die!"

This was shouted down as hysteria, but the same voice came back with authority: "There are two new cases in the scholars' hall, and last night one of the Ghar's own bluecoats died!"

This was the first death, and news to most of those present, including, Lady Vashmarna thought, the *purdar* and his men. Their hard faces turned to stone, painted gray by the fear and the rain.

Lady Vashmarna stepped forward and said, clearly enough to be heard through the swelling noise, "Mahel-*jinnu,* if you will permit me?"

There were bows at the front of the crowd. The Vashmarna name was passed back in whispers.

"Let us give these men a moment to consult with their superiors. Perhaps the shaudah is not adequately informed of the extent of the Mahel estate. Or perhaps, in his concern for the health of the fields, he is only being conservative in the numbers he is willing to see pass into the countryside. Perhaps you might leave some of your household behind for a time? The *hadaras* is suffering its own difficulties in this hard season—"

"Is there plague?" someone called. The question became a chorus: "Is there plague in the *hadaras,* is there death?"

"There are shadow gods haunting the western coast!" yelled another anonymous voice, and the tumult again began to grow. Pressure from behind forced the Mahel contingent forward, narrowing the space before the gate. Lady Vashmarna felt an old panic thread its way up memory's stem.

"Please!" she said sharply. "Give these good men some room!"

But they did not look like good men. Ferociously blank beneath their rain-blackened turbans, they drew their truncheons without orders, and their officer curled his hand around the butt of his pistol.

"Please!" Lady Vashmarna said again. The Mahels still looked to her for authority, but it was an authority to complain to, an authority to sway to their side.

"Our children," Uludian said. But someone behind shouted, "They were billeted in the scholars' hall! Let them go, I say! They've a child sick with the plague!"

"That is not true!" Uludian turned to shout it across the crowd. "That is not true!"

But there were more shouts of "Let them go!" mingled with "Let us go!"

"Where are we?" cried Uludian's son. "Is this the bastion or the tidal?"

"Savages!" said his wife, but to whom she referred, she did not explain. Uludian was still scolding the crowd, "We have no sickness! We are going to our land!"

"Nine generations!" her son said. "Nine generations, and they tell us we cannot go!"

Lady Vashmarna judged the crowd by her own swelling panic and knew something must be done. *She* must do something—but before she could summon more than resolution, one of the Ghar's men stepped out of line. The *purdar* growled, "Back in your place, man!" but the policeman did not seem to hear. His brown face a shocking gray, his teeth bared by clay-colored lips, he lifted his truncheon and brought it down on the air. The Mahels, fearful of attack, pressed back against the pressing-forward crowd, but the policeman ignored them. Stiff as a clockwork toy, he lifted his baton and brought it down, lifted it and brought it down, and it became clear that he was having a strangely controlled, or controlling, fit. Silence flowed backward across the crowd. Lady Vashmarna could hear the man's breath sucking in and out between his teeth. Foam began to gather in the corners of his mouth, and the foam was a deep, hideous, sulfurous yellow.

"Back in line, man!" shouted the *purdar*, visibly at his wits' end.

The afflicted man began to grunt with effort as he beat the air. His body twisted, his knees began to buckle, his chin ran with sulfur-brown drool, and still his arm rose and fell, rose and fell.

"The plague," gasped Uludian Mahel's son, and the word spread like a crack in the shell of peace. *Ghar has the plague.* Lady Vashmarna was shocked by this strange illness she had not yet seen, but she was worse frightened by the crowd. She said to the *purdar*, "Officer! Control your men!" for the other policemen were edging away from the afflicted man.

"In line!" he hoarsely yelled. "Hold your line, gods curse you!"

But he should not have shouted. The Mahel son shouted back, "We are going! Stand aside! We are leaving this accursed place!"

"Savages!" his wife said again.

"Mahel-*jinnu*." Lady Vashmarna appealed to the matriarch. "This is not the time to press the issue."

But the old woman, who had known her as a child, only said quellingly, "You do not have the authority to keep us here. And neither does the shaudah! *He* has no *hadaras* estates. Let *him* stay here with the demons and the plague! We are going! Tell them to let us through!"

The crowd was shouting now. The sick man fell, his body spasming into a more violent convulsion. Again, the other policemen drew aside. This time, the Mahels, impelled from behind, pressed forward into the gap.

Lady Vashmarna, with a clear and sudden vision of the immediate future, said swiftly to the *purdar,* "Let them go!"

But the man only glared at her from beneath his dripping shako and bellowed, "By the shaudah's authority, the gate is closed to all egress not directly authorized by the shaudah's office. Return to your appointed housing. No one may pass through!"

They may not, but they would. The gap between crowd and guards vanished with a rush. Lady Vashmarna did not see the fate of the fallen man. She was herself in danger of being crushed, until one of Ghar's policemen swept her up with a hard arm about her ribs. Her world was a chaos of shouting, gaping mouths, frightened eyes, uplifted clubs. She fought the arm that held her, kicked her feet against the force that pushed her through the crowd, for she knew how this ended: the weight, the stinking breath, the shame. She fought, and she heard and did not hear the distressed voice that said, over and over, "*Jinnu! Jinnu!* Vashmarna-*jin*'!"

But then the small-door in the fort's gate opened, her own men drew her inside, and she realized, with an even more bitter shame than the one she had relived, that she had been not abducted but rescued. The poor policeman, his turban unraveling under the weight of the rain, bowed deeply and repeatedly as the Vashmarna guard closed the door on the riot. Lady Vashmarna did not think to ask him inside. Nameless and unthanked, he was shut out with the violence, the rain, and the plague.

Oh, gods, she prayed, shaking, her robes wet and cold. *Gods, take pity on your children.*

Don't let them get inside.

THE HADARAS

Moth slipped and had to cling to the water-slick stone while pebbles dropped away from beneath her feet. The sound of them was swallowed by the voice of the waterfall that fell in ropes and sheets from the mountain's knees. Moth could not see the mountain from where she was—she could not see anything but the rock in front of her nose—but somehow the weight of it was always present, rearing over her like the towering clouds. She scrambled up onto the high ledge like a child scrambling onto a giant's lap, and found it was neither so deep nor so level as it had looked from below. With her bottom planted in wet moss she could brace her back against the cliff and her heels against the lip of the ledge and look down between her bare, scraped, and muddy feet at the water, the floating docks, the workshop, and the ship; but she was painfully conscious of the slant that wanted to slide her into the waterfall's rocky hem. It was pure stubbornness that kept her where she was. Stubbornness and the dawning recognition that going down might be worse than coming up had been.

Moth in the *hadaras*. Slum-girl Moth. What *did* she think she was doing here?

The inlet that hid the expansionists' ship was a slice in the rock of the western coast. As straight-edged as a surgeon's cut, it ran up against the bones of the island where the long thin waterfall bled from the mountain's slopes. Even in its white-foam fall the stream was stained brown by erosion, but looking up from the ship, all one could see was the green of ferns, spindly trees, and higher up, the impenetrable thickets of bamboo. Up and up, the green of growing things, the black of rock, the pearly gray of mist clinging to the forest's leaves.

Moth, perched between the waterfall and the steep mountain path that connected the ship to the rest of the world, wondered at this emptiness. Was the mountain too steep for a peasant's hut, too rocky for a terraced field? Or was there room left on the island after all? Like the long fall she could see between her feet, this thought promised a pointless end to all her striving. What if everything she had done turned out to have been unnecessary?

But while the coast here looked wild, with pale *tirindi* nesting on the cliffs and great eels snaking through the anchor chains in the water below, once there had been no inlet here at all. Once the stream had run higher than the quarried ledge where Moth sat now, following the great vein of quartz to the sea. The shipwrights had told her about the mining of the quartz that had been built into the wonderful towers of the *shadras* bay, the towers that the shipwrights, most of them, had never seen. Moth had, and gazing down the length of those twin cliffs, she fancied she could see towers outlined in the chisel marks in the glassy stone, as if the *rasnan* had been filleted like a fish. This place was no wilderness; it was the skeleton the butchers of past generations had left behind.

But it was a skeleton with an embryo within its stony womb.

Looking down, Moth was reminded of the tidal, as if the vine-clad ship with its foreshortened masts were a tenement complete with roof gardens and wind-driven pumps. The engineers' and shipwrights' barges could be raft-huts and shrines, and the gaps bridged by gangplanks could be the tidal's random streets, except that instead of mud there was green water only a little murky from the stream. Tired from the climb, Moth fell into a waking dream where water and mud became different states of the same substance, and the tidal floated on its shifting ground as the ship floated on the sea. In her dream the tidal came adrift and slipped away, the eels slid unseen through the black muck, the trampled dead swam as that young man did, diving off the roof of the smithy barge. Hamana's dead, and the manifests like the eels, circling beneath the skin of the world.

A secret touch whispered in Moth's belly, startling her awake. Her child stirring. Did every mother feel this? There was no one she could ask. Perhaps it was only Moth, *mundabi* Moth, who felt that tiny life as she felt the breath of the *mundab,* the touch of the unknown world.

The *mundab* and the child. Moth could not have named the day or even the year when she'd first felt that touch, but child-Moth had been very small, a thoughtless creature fed with a pack of others on the steps of some shrine. Moth knew she must have been sheltered by someone when she was an infant, but she remembered only a pair of hands, a tin washtub, smoke drifting toward an open window. Even wanted children might be abandoned if the only other choice were to starve, and Moth had always supposed that whoever had been paid to take her off Vashmarna's hands had found it more expedient to save the money for their own necessities, but she would never know for certain. Her childhood was one of the many things she and her mother never spoke of. For a long time she had regarded her childhood as a test her mother had set, and her survival had won her her reward. Was it possible she had once been proud of that?

The tadpole in her belly flicked its tail again.

It happened on a hot day in the dry season when the air seethed above the cracked mud and the *tirindis'* circling shadows struck like blows against her face. She was perched on a foot stone with a forked stick in her hand waiting for a mudfish to give itself away. Her head ached with hunger and the sun, her eyes stung with sweat, and she knew that the mud crawlers were either dead and rotting or sheltered by weeds, but stubbornness kept her in place. She had only recently learned how to use the crude spear—how old would she have been? five years old? six?—and the new skill made her proud. And then, like a faint impossible breeze, that whisper, that shiver, that tingling electric thread down her spine.

She had followed that thread, that current of the *mundab*, to Istvan Soos, or he had followed it to her. He had taught her from Mahogan's writings, and had sent her to the shrine for tutoring in the subjects he did not have the patience to teach. And when had Lady Vashmarna heard about her progress? There were so many mysteries between them. How had Lady Vashmarna even known her daughter's tidal-orphan name? Moth imagined some Vashmarna spy watching the child-Moth perched above the muddy street with her crude spear—so hungry she would have risked sunstroke for a meal of mudfish fed on shit and trash—and passing on his report to the bay: still alive. *How could you care enough to watch me, but not care enough to help?* A question she had never asked, but one that Lady Vashmarna had answered, in her brutal way. She had cared to know where Moth was the way she might have cared to know where an enemy was, not to have him come at her back unawares. She had cared, if hatred is a kind of love.

"Is this the mother you want me to be, little fish?" Moth asked that faint stirring in her womb. She was just as glad not to have an answer.

The ship was a soft green shape between her toes, a bit of driftwood that had rested at the tide line so long it wore a furry coat of algae. Oh yes, thought Moth sardonically, exactly that: driftwood anchored against the tide. Unfinished, mired in the *hadaras,* doubly useless without its unfinished engine—Moth felt a peculiar sense of kinship with the vessel, though it was a kinship that had little to do with the vessel's inhabitants. Just thinking about them made her restless. Reckless with the sudden reawakening of her frustration, the same frustration that had sent her up this cliff to begin with, she scrambled to her feet on the ledge and started to edge along the cliff face toward the expansionists' hidden cleft that offered an easier, if not the easiest, way back down to the water's edge.

She had barely started when the ledge arched up before her like a moss-backed cat stretching before it leapt. Moth's instinctive recoil put her heel down on a sharp rock, and her recoil from *that* nearly put her over the edge, so it was with a pounding heart that she watched the manifest part from the moss and drift like an untethered heat mirage up the cliff face toward the mountain's peak, the clouds, the hidden sun. The manifests haunted the inlet, daytime ghosts of Moth's nighttime work, as if the *mundab* were intent on shouting her secrets to the world. Silently shouting, the manifests its soundless words . . . A whimsical notion that Moth suddenly did not want to examine too closely. All the same, the question lingered in the back of her skull. *What are you saying to me? What are you trying to say?*

The ledge narrowed into nothing above the path and Moth had to slide the last little way, losing more skin in the process. The path itself was a natural tunnel, one wall and the floor of the *rasnan*'s stone, the other wall and the roof of living green, bushes and enormous ferns that filtered the rain and the light, their damp smell as musky and intimate as a creature's. Knowing where the downward path led, to the docks, the barges, the ship, to the engineers and the *hadri* and the lies, Moth was tempted to turn and climb the other way, up onto the mountain's shoulder and beyond into the heart of the *rasnan*. From here, looking up that dusky green-lit hall, it looked like a path into the unknown, as mysterious as the *mundab*'s sea, and Moth had to remind herself that it was just a path to more of the same. The same people with the same troubles, even if they were living in muddy fields instead of on floats and barges. Moth told herself that her work was here, even if "work" did take on a sarcastic twist in her mind.

She was dawdling down the trail, putting off that first glimpse of the water, when she heard a scuff of footsteps behind her. Her first senseless thought was of the manifest; her second was of intruders. Her third was an impulse of pure curiosity, and she stood and waited, and was rewarded by the sight of Hamana's road-weary form plodding into view. Moth said her name in exasperated relief—Hamana had left days ago, very much against Moth's wishes—and ignored Hamana's sharp, "What are you doing here?" Hamana was not alone on the trail, and the man who appeared at her shoulder was so familiar he took Moth's breath away.

"Aramis!" she cried in unconscious echo of Hamana, "What are you doing here?"

Aramis stopped and stared. He looked tired and strained

and—oh, what did it matter? He might have been beset by demons and gods, but Moth did not care. He was so much himself, and so thoroughly, outrageously, gloriously out of place. She laughed from sheer surprise.

"Aramis," she said, "Aramis."

"I found him on the road west of Stunnenan," Hamana said sourly, already out of patience with Moth, or so it seemed.

Moth, reminded, said, "Did you find—"

"No," Hamana said even more shortly, and started to push past Moth toward the foot of the path and the water. Moth stepped into a fern's damp embrace to let her by, and smelled the old smoke and new sweat that impregnated the other woman's clothes. The Vashmarna engineers, exiled years ago to begin the other half of the expansionists' scheme—Lady Vashmarna's scheme—had sent a messenger to the *shadras* when Moth, Hamana, and Silk had arrived at the ship, and as soon as Hamana had heard about the messenger's departure she had gone to track him down. Given what would have happened to the man had Hamana found him, Moth was not as sorry as she might have been that Hamana had failed. Though perhaps she was not as glad as she should have been either.

But then again, look at what Hamana had found!

"You!" Moth said wonderingly as Aramis started uncertainly after Hamana. Moth put out her hand and he stopped abruptly at her touch, as if he had walked into a wall. "Well? You have to say something! Why are you here?"

Aramis looked down at her—how strange to see his dear face against that backdrop of leaves!—and said, so stiffly he might not have spoken for days, "My lady sent me."

Moth forgot how to breathe. "Sent you . . ."

"To the ship," he said, "to bring the engineers home. We need them now. We need . . ." He trailed off at the stricken expression on her face, his light eyes showing a sudden warmth, a sudden concern. "Moth," he said, and touched his hand to her face.

It was like falling off a cliff: that first giddy moment of flight, so light that one could fool oneself into thinking it was nothing, and then that sudden rush as the ground approaches and the unconquerable speed makes itself known. Moth was trembling, dry in her mouth, loose and liquid in her core. She did not need to see the sudden darkness in his eyes or the ruddy stain in his dark cheeks. She could feel his answering desire shock him like a flung-open door. Had she taken this for granted? Had she actually forgotten what this was like? Or had she never really understood it for what it was until now?

"Are you coming?" Hamana snapped from below.

"No," Moth said, and for a wonder, Aramis, her cool and stubborn Aramis, said exactly the same.

Hamana shrugged and headed off alone, but Moth could feel the greenguard's attention trailing behind her like a frazzled rope. Moth knew there would be questions and arguments and accusations arising from this. She knew; she did not care.

They made a nest in a damp hollow beneath the ferns, her clothes and his, moss and sodden leaves. They shook cool water from the fronds above, the drops as sharp as pinpricks on overheated skin, and laughed as Moth had laughed before, with surprise. His mouth, his hands, his smell as strong and musky as the ferns. Moth felt as her ancestors must have felt coupling in the strange, green new world, in the jungle so thick they might have been making love at the edge of a cliff and never have realized, the future so unknowable it hardly mattered, precarious and wild. They touched each other with a luxurious freedom they had never known in their hidden meetings in the fort, more secret here than they could ever be be-

tween walls. Moth cried out, "Aramis, Aramis," and for once
he made no effort to silence her. He held her tight against the
pounding of his heart.

It was only well afterward, as the stupefaction of pleasure
gave way to an awareness of tickling insect legs and wet
ground, that he asked her, as she had asked him, just as reason-
ably but far more unanswerably, "What are you doing here?"

"What did you tell him?" Silk asked.

They were sitting on an upper deck of the ship with their
legs dangling into the well beneath the open hatch. It was
late, most of the honest ship dwellers were abed. According
to the shipwrights' grand design there were to be stairs between the decks, but the ladders that zigzagged across and
down, as rickety and makeshift as they were, had an ominous
feeling of permanence. The rain fell unimpeded into the bilge
water that drowned the bottommost hold. Silk's lantern gave
out a fuzzy yellow globe of illumination, its light caught by
the steam touched off the hot glass by the rain, but there
was nothing to see beneath their feet except for the rain spin-
dling down and a dim reflection far below. Looking up,
Moth could see the squash plants that grew on the weather
deck lean over the hatch rim like curious spectators, but if
there were any human listeners among them, they were well
disguised.

"What did you tell him?" Silk asked again.

"What do you think?" Moth said with nervous irritability.
"I told him I belong to Vashmarna same as him, and I'm here
to see the ship gets finished for his lady's sake."

"Did he believe you?"

"Seeing as how his lady sent him here to tell her engineers
to give it up and come home," Moth said bitterly, "no, he
didn't."

"So what are we going to do with him?"

Moth clenched her jaw at the "we," but she saved her strength for the arguments that mattered. "As long as he doesn't talk to the engineers, we're fine."

"*Fine?*" Silk caught herself. She seemed to have been learning restraint from Hamana, which was a chilling thought. "He's going to content himself with being our prisoner, is he? Or were you planning on sinking him when you were done having fun?"

"He doesn't know he's a prisoner." He, Aramis, was at this moment deep in an exhausted sleep in Moth's cubbyhole, and Moth hated talking about him like this. "He's not a prisoner, not unless he won't listen to reason. And nobody is sinking him."

"Oh, he'll listen to reason? What reason are you planning on offering him?"

"*Nobody is sinking him.*" This was said quietly, but so urgently that Silk leaned away.

Silk, however, was not quelled. "Then what are we going to do with him? Take turns screwing him into submission?"

"Shut up," Moth said, too nettled to placate a jealous Silk. "You just leave him alone."

"As if I want him!" Silk said scornfully. "If you think your charms are enough to blind him, by all means, keep him to yourself. I'm sure no one will notice that Vashmarna's priest has a fuck-boy in her cabin."

Silk knew better than anyone how to get under Moth's skin. Moth, too furious to reply, scrambled to her knees and took a swing at her. Silk fended her off, and for a moment they were in danger of a real fight, but their scuffling sent the lantern over the edge, and they were reminded of where they were. The candle in its glass cage kept burning a surprising distance into its fall, drawing a comet tail of half-formed manifests down the rain-shot well, but it winked out before the bottom. There was a faint splash, and a dim green afterglow against the dark.

"Damn it!" Silk said. "How many of those things do you think we have?"

"You keep your foul mouth shut, then," Moth said, still seething.

"Begging the *rasnu*'s pardon."

"Go to hell," Moth said.

"Back home, you mean? What makes you think I ever wanted to leave?"

"Well, who asked you to?"

"What? You wouldn't have got past the docks—"

"Without you? Please! I might thank Hamana for that—"

"The *rasnu* is very kind."

Moth bit her tongue. Silk hissed with surprise. Hamana sighed over them in the dark.

"They're all waiting," the greenguard said. "If you don't want an audience, you better leave it for another time."

"How much time?" Silk said as she got to her feet. "Moth should never have brought him on board. I don't know why you even brought him here. You could have solved the whole problem on the road."

Moth would probably have hit her again if the greenguard's wiry form had not been interposed.

"Having failed," Hamana said, "to solve the problem of the messenger going the other way, it didn't seem smart. I know we're going to have to deal with Vashmarna, but I'd rather put off the day until we can deal from a position of strength. And considering the problems Moth's fuck-boy could stir up with the engineers here, I would have brought him on board myself just to keep him away from them. Mucking up your priestly credibility isn't so clever, though, Moth, considering it's the only thing keeping the engineers from sinking *us*."

Thus proving that Hamana had heard the whole argument.

Who else was hiding in the dark and the rain? Silk didn't seem to care.

"Maybe it has nothing to do with being smart," she said poisonously. "Just how much do you owe him, Moth? How much do you owe Vashmarna? How many of the lies you've been telling the engineers are actually true? How many lies have you told to us all these years?"

Moth was nearly speechless with a hunted rage. She choked out, "If I were really Vashmarna's, do you think for an instant I would be here with you? That I would ever have been with you by choice?" and shoved past Hamana to the head of the nearest ladder. Bamboo creaked and gave off its warm rotten-grass smell as Moth descended.

She was two decks down before she felt the faint quiver that suggested movement on a higher rung.

It was dark below, humid and hot, and it stank of humans, chickens, and the bilge. Whether the *hadri* slept or lay wakeful and afraid in their hammocks, they were silent, but the rain drumming on the weather deck and spilling through the open hatches hummed in the ship's gut with a large, intimate, physical sound: the sea captured in a shell, the felt vibration of a lover's voice, the murmur of clouds, if clouds could have a mouth that pressed with breathy warmth against the ear. Oh, Aramis! But Silk, however hateful, was right. He was a problem here—just as Moth, it occurred to her with rare insight, had been a problem for him in the *shadras*. Did he have friends who had taken him to task even as they'd helped him hide his reckless indiscretions? Did he have friends? She didn't know. There was so much about him she still didn't know! They should have stayed in the wild, she thought, no matter how small and damaged a wild it was. There at least they had had a future, however unknowable, however brief. Here she could see nothing but the wet and stinking dark.

There was something depressingly familiar about the

flooded bowels of the ship. The wet, the smell, the vermin that were not frightened by the passage of a human: the ship was like an enclave of the tidal, an egg laid and abandoned by its parent toad. This was probably why Moth (like Hamana and Silk, she thought) was frequently confounded by how different the *hadri* were from the feisty tidal norm. Reserved to the point of secretiveness, humbly bowing to hide their eyes, they were hard for Moth to read at the best of times, and tonight, with Aramis's smell lingering dangerously on her skin and the argument with Silk still jangling along her nerves, they were more sinister than the dark. Yet these were the shadow cult, the congregation of *rasnu* Moth waiting with endless *hadaras* patience for the rites to begin.

How strange, then, that the rites themselves, transplanted out of Istvan's stranglehold by the tidal women, should be so open, so free. There was no inner shrine on the ship, no hidden engine. The ship was shrine and engine both, the vessel and the reason for the summoned *mundab*. In the tidal the cultists were co-opted decoys set to chase after their shadow gods as if the manifests were the end rather than a by-product of the means. Here the manifests escaped the ship like dreams from a sleeping head, and the peasant cultists, patient and inscrutable, waited for whatever they thought would come when the ship awoke.

Moth wished she had their faith.

The cult met between the copper-bound feet of the main- and mizzenmasts, a low-ceilinged hall beneath the level of the water as far from the weather deck as it was possible to get. This was not Moth's choice, but there was no arguing with the *hadri*'s fear of the engineers, who had not deigned to live on board the half-built ship even before it was invaded by the *hadaras*'s homeless. The shipwrights' families, dispossessed by flooding and ruined fields, had followed their men to shelter despite the secrecy of the expansionists' endeavor, and the shipwrights had acceded so quickly to the civilian conquest that they might all along have been building a floating tenement. And for that matter, how hard had the engineers fought to keep their ship, their lady's ship, inviolate? Were they so busy defending their comfortable barges that they let the ship go as the smaller loss? Moth blamed the engineers for letting the project founder, and she found the *hadri*'s trepidation laughable, given how easily they had taken over, but she had to admit, it had made life easier for her and the others when they had arrived from the *shadras,* up to their necks in Vashmarna's machinations and with nowhere else in all the *rasnan* to go.

Eyes watched her above a few trembling candle flames. She was glad of them, for they made her tamp down her anger and draw in her wandering thoughts. Silk and Hamana had joined her, playing acolytes to her priest, but she had little for them to do. Finally free of temples and shrines, Moth had shed ritual the way a lizard sheds its dead skin. Here and now there is only the *mundab* and the ship.

The *mundab* and the ship. They approach each other like a body and a soul, each shaping itself to the other like water poured into a waterproof bag. The ship sings a muted song, it purrs like a cat stroked by the hand of a god. Moth is planting the seeds of the *mundab*, laying down the threads of her intentions, no more than that. She does not dare more at this stage, although it has begun to seem as if the ship itself presses against the boundaries of her restraint. As it did with the engine, the *mundab*'s limitless flow seems to delineate a perfect ship, the *mundab*'s ideal dictating the very design it arises from, as if the human dream can be given its reality only by . . .

By what, Moth? The hand of a god?

Manifests shape themselves within the dark. Listen, Moth. The elusive forms slip among them like fish and the shadows of fish. Listen. But all she hears is the ship moaning as quiet as

Aramis's pleasure, as the one and the other of them shape themselves to her desires. This ship that the engineers and *hadri* wrangle over will be hers. This ship, this child Vashmarna begins and sets aside, will be.

So she thinks as the *mundab* drains away and she looks beyond the ring of candlelit faces to meet Aramis's stunned and accusing eyes.

THE BASTION

Every day there was another new plague victim. Every day the unrest in the bastion deepened. Every night the tidal fell more deeply under the shadow cult's sway.

The shaudah had seemed mesmerized by this steady disintegration of his demesne, but finally, from out of nowhere, he summoned the resolution to act. Would Lady Vashmarna have been so shocked if she had not been preoccupied by matters within the fort? Perhaps not, but she thought even Lord Ghar was surprised. The shaudah excoriated the Ghar for his inability to keep the bastion's peace and blamed him for the spread of the plague even as he praised Lady Vashmarna for the orderliness of her demesne, but the end result was the same for both. The shaudah's soldiers were recalled to the bastion, and Ghar and Vashmarna were charged with keeping the tidal's peace.

"The tidal is not my demesne!" said the Ghar, openly appalled by the order.

"Nor is the bastion." The shaudah may have intended to be stern, but he sounded snide. "Your men have begun to treat good people of ancient lineage as if they were tidal savages. Let us put them to work where they seem to belong."

"My men," said the Ghar with angry restraint, "have done their best to carry out *janarasan*'s orders."

"And their best is clearly not sufficient, especially now that they carry the plague," said the shaudah, perhaps revealing his true reason for wanting the Ghar's men outside the bastion walls.

Lord Ghar must have seen this as clearly as Lady Vashmarna did. His face grew shuttered. "Even if our numbers had not been reduced by this sinister illness, which I take to be an uncanny attack of our cultist enemies, as I have mentioned before—even then we would not have the strength to occupy the tidal. Does *janarasan* intend to withdraw *all* his troops from the slums?"

"Yes." This firmness seemed to exhaust the shaudah. His gaze drifted toward a more peaceful realm. "But we recognize the magnitude of the task we have set you, and furthermore, we recollect the Vashmarna's generous offer of help. Vashmarna will no doubt contribute a contingent of men to help Ghar maintain order if we ask it."

Vashmarna had nearly forgotten that offer, which had been made for reasons which no longer pertained. There was no call to defend the engine now, and the tidal was a monster-ridden abattoir. Lady Vashmarna wanted nothing to do with it. She bowed to give herself a moment for thought.

"*Janaras,*" she said, "of course Vashmarna is at your service. But at the moment our sole concern is to restore electricity to the towers, and we are employing every pair of hands to that end. Moreover, *janaras,* as you have so kindly observed, the fort has so far escaped the taint of plague, and I feel very urgently that if Vashmarna is to continue to be productive, we must guard against possible infection more stringently than ever. If there were no hope of returning to the bay, of course I would place all of my resources at the Ghar's disposal, but as it is . . ."

"You have held this hope out to us before, *jinnu*," said the shaudah in his distant voice. "Is it any closer today than it was six days ago, when you claimed the new cable was complete?"

Lady Vashmarna bowed again. "As I reported, the cable itself has been successfully extruded by our manufactory, and the new transformer, which we hope to site more securely within Shaudarand itself, is nearly assembled. However, we are having to invent a whole new means of insulation, and that process of experimentation must inevitably be slow. We must be absolutely certain before we lay the cable that it will be able to endure salt water for at least as long as it takes to build a new bridge. These tests take manpower, and time."

Later she would conclude that her mistake had been to mention experimentation and the new bridge in the same breath. The one would have offended the shaudah's conservatism, which had only grown during his exile from the bay, and the other would have been harping on old complaints. The shaudah's gaze had grown even more distant, his voice had faded to a near murmur, and he had said, "I place my own men at Vashmarna's disposal. The cable is too vital to go unguarded, and my officers will have the authority to keep both the gates and the road secure. You may feel free to lend your assistance to Ghar."

The shaudah's men in the fort, her own men in the tidal. Good merciful gods. Lady Vashmarna had shared a dark and anxious glance with Lord Ghar. Both of them had forgotten that the shaudah, for all his stubborn fears, never lost sight of his own political advantage. If the ruling powers ever did make it back to the towers in the bay, they might find that the boundaries of their demesnes had shrunk while they were gone.

This worry, as well as the practical necessities of coordinating forces, brought them together late the following day. Lady Vashmarna played host, and when Lord Ghar arrived, he crossed directly to her study window. The towers rose white as bone from the steely water, and the mist that dragged inland with the rain hid their upper stories. They looked broken, dead. Like a mourner, Lady Vashmarna was assailed by a memory of her Shaudarand study, the warm bright room full of treasures like a pleasure barge drifting among the clouds. Despite the progress being made on the new cable, the fear that she would never return was taking on the bleak chill of certainty. She drew a shawl about her shoulders as she said to Lord Ghar's back, "Will you join me in a cup of tea?"

He turned with a smile. "Thank the bountiful gods for tea. We are still civilized, however difficult it is to remember at times."

"We are still civilized," Lady Vashmarna affirmed, though with a faint emphasis on the "we."

"The tidal." He sighed. "Dear gods. What can the man be thinking?"

The Ghar sat and accepted his cup. He looked as he always did, a dear, elegant, familiar man, his dark face lined with thought and care. Lady Vashmarna felt something settle inside her, relaxing into a comfortable ritual. Tea with Divaram. *We are still civilized*, she thought.

"The tidal," she prompted. Let him take the lead for now.

"May I be frank, Vashmarna-*jin*'? If it were not for the bridge, I would suggest we burn the docks, block the stairs, and leave them to their own devices." He sounded very reasonable, a careworn lord with his saucer in one hand, his steaming cup in the other. "Once they had only themselves to feed upon, they would weaken, rather than gaining strength in their opposition as they do now."

"It seems hard, *jandas,* on those who would be law-abiding if they were not threatened or deluded by this cult." Lady Vashmarna was careful not to sound as if she disagreed. In truth, she was not certain she did disagree.

"But as long as the cult can point to the shaudah's men—or, now, to our men—and say, 'Here is an enemy,' those law-abiding few can be coerced into taking the side of their own kind."

"Yes, this is the trouble I have always had with the shaudah's policy. We make them into our enemies by the use of force. Withdraw the force and they become people again. And truly, Ghar-*jan'*, I believe there are more than a few who desire a peaceful order. Women will always want their children to be safe"—an internal blink, a hesitation that did not reach her voice—"and anyone who wishes to make an honest livelihood is bound to recognize the need for the rule of law. The poor perhaps even more than most, for they have so little they can afford to lose."

Lord Ghar nodded as he listened, and sipped his tea. "Leave them alone. Yes. It worked surprisingly well for a time. But this cult has changed things. I wish I could better understand their origins, and the origins of this dark power they seem to have tapped. I remember there were rumors at the time of the rebellion. Do you have the same feeling that I do, *jinnu,* that the Lamplighters riots were the seeds of the present turmoil? I suppose it is a function of our age. The present must always seem to grow out of the past."

"But then, it does." They shared a smile. "What rumors did you have in mind?"

"I hardly remember their content now. Blasphemy, sorcery. There was so much wild talk around the scholars' murders, and most of it was dismissed once the Lamplighters conspiracy was revealed. Too quickly dismissed, perhaps, but there are always rumors: *hadaras* witches, hauntings in the slums."

"Just as there have always been cults and secret societies, like the Lamplighters or the Society of Doors." Lady Vashmarna met her friend's peaceful gaze and confessed, "I have been meditating of late on the *ramhadras*. It is inevitable, I suppose, that we have come to think of the first world as our true home. It *was* our true home, and as such—as the place we truly once belonged—it must be remembered, and mourned. The first world is our legacy, as your son reminded me a few days ago, and so is its loss. Yet I wonder if we are in danger of forgetting that most important thing: not the fact of our ancestors' exile, which we remember perhaps too well, but the reason for it. We have come to speak of the *ramhadras* as if it were a kind of heaven, but surely, to have driven our ancestors so far, it must have become a kind of hell."

Divaram Ghar pensively nodded and sipped his tea. "I can understand how your thoughts might tend in this direction, *jinnu*. I, too, have come to wonder what kind of hell we might be facing here in this world."

"What kind of hell," Lady Vashmarna softly corrected, "we might be creating for ourselves."

Divaram cocked his head, his teacup suspended between his saucer and his mouth. "Do you equate the shadow cult with our ancestors?"

Cunning man. Was he innocent, or did he truly have some connection to the Society of Doors? When she realized she still could not guess, Lady Vashmarna felt an unanticipated thrill of anger, but she set it aside. It would not help to kill the specter her daughter had raised.

"*Jandas,* you say that you have wondered at the source of their power. I have asked myself the same bitter question. Why should these haunts, these demons, these so-named shadow gods, have so much more substance and force in the world than the good and holy gods? Why should this cult tap its loathsome power so freely, night after night, when our own priests struggle to raise a little light against the dark?"

The Ghar's cup was slowly lowered to its saucer. "And would you propose an answer, *jinnu*?"

So he would not meet her, even from hiding. Very well. She could press him from behind a camouflage of her own.

"Only another question, Ghar-*jan*'. Is it possible that the shadow cult and the Society of Doors are one and the same?"

He did not respond, did not move, perhaps did not even breathe. Lady Vashmarna's voice was soft, her gaze steady on her friend's face.

"Is it possible that the evil the cult seems to summon so freely is the same evil that our ancestors fled their world to escape? Is it possible that a door has been opened onto the *ramhadras,* as our ancestors forbade, and this is the very result they feared?"

Lord Ghar leaned forward to set his cup on the desk between them. The movement briefly shadowed his face, but when he looked up, his expression was calm, if also rueful.

"A bitter question indeed, Vashmarna-*jin*'. I wish I had an answer for you, but I fear I have only another question. If the shadow cult is the Society of Doors, why would they be so bent on destruction? As I recall my history, the Society, even if misguided and unlawful, was never evil. Their one goal was to effect the Return—a return to a heavenly, not a hellish, world. They might, I suppose, have looked in unsavory places for the power the temple priests denied them, and denied themselves, but why would they have caused this violence and misery? Why would they have summoned these demons or this plague? No, I fear the shadow cult is its own wretched thing, and we must continue searching for the roots of their sorcery in the present, not in the past."

Lady Vashmarna contemplated her empty cup. She thought that she had just heard the Society's own voice, and it was a voice of reason, a voice she was inclined to believe. The Return was all. But it occurred to Lady Vashmarna to wonder, Who was to be permitted to return to the *ramhadras*? She could understand why Lord Ghar might want to escape the *rasnan,* for this was at its core the same desire that shaped her own expansionist philosophy. And she could understand why that escape might be reserved for a chosen few. Having lived through the Lamplighters riots, having heard her men's reports on the haunted chaos of the tidal, having seen what her own daughter had become—yes, she understood.

But it was Moth's very corruption that gave her pause. Lady Vashmarna, powerful, virtuous, and Lord Ghar's personal friend, would surely be invited to pass through that apocryphal door, but never would the Ghars permit a woman like Moth, a dishonored dedicant from the slums, to accompany them back to the first, the heavenly, world. She would be cast out, left behind, abandoned once again—

And it was at this moment that Lady Vashmarna recalled, with a visceral shock and a burst of shame, that the Ghars, father and son, had tried to have her daughter killed.

Lord Ghar, meantime, had settled back into his chair. Dearest enemy, oldest friend. She hid her shaking hands beneath the rim of her desk.

"Perhaps once we have gained control of the tidal, we might discover some answers," Divaram said, still with that rueful smile. "But first we must gain control."

"Yes," Lady Vashmarna said, and cleared her throat. "Yes, *jandas,* quite so."

She made her hands steady, poured more tea. There was nothing else she could do. The meeting went on.

•   •   •

It so happened that Lord Ghar was leaving when *purdar* Nind, captain of Vashmarna's guard, arrived with Istvan Soos.

The three men met in the corridor outside Lady Vashmarna's study—or rather, the scholar and the *purdar* both bowed as the lord of the bay strode past. The Ghar spared them a glance. Did he hesitate? Lady Vashmarna, standing in her door to see her guest on his way, thought perhaps there was the slightest hitch in his stride, but she was not certain. She hoped it was only a projection of her fears, but there was no imagining the long stare the tidal scholar aimed at Lord Ghar's back.

Istvan Soos was a small man, his wiry form swallowed up in layers of worn clothes. He was barefooted and long-haired like a priest, but his hair hung loose to his shoulders, a thin, gray, greasy frame for his seamed and bony face. That sharp face turned this way and that as he snatched quick glances about the room, and that movement, along with his high narrow shoulders, reminded Lady Vashmarna unpleasantly of a *tirindi* hunched on a rainspout watching for prey.

"So," he said as he sat unbidden, "where is the girl?"

Lady Vashmarna stood behind her desk and touched her fingers to the wood as if it could lend her patience. "What girl?"

The scholar did not smile. His laugh was a bark of scorn. "What girl? Your girl, your agent, your spy. Vashmarna's little whore."

Lady Vashmarna did not flinch. She was frozen, and could feel the icy shock numbing her lips so that she was not certain she could speak.

But Nind, who had stationed himself behind the scholar, leaned on the back of the chair so heavily the tired wood creaked. "Don't scatter your insults too widely, old man. You might hit something that bites back. If you have a name to say, say it and have done."

"Why? So your lady can parade her innocence? Very well. Moth. It's a synonym for treachery, and I don't consider it any prettier than 'spy' or 'whore,' but by all means, let us spare the lady's sensibilities. Moth. I want to see her. Where is she?"

"You tell us," Nind said crudely, but Lady Vashmarna had recovered her voice and softly spoke his name. He stepped away from the scholar's chair.

"I cannot produce her," she said to the scholar. "I had supposed she was in the tidal."

"And I had supposed she was here. How else did you know to search me out?"

Lady Vashmarna glanced at Nind, who had his own sources in the tidal—sources that had found Moth for her once upon a time. Nind raised his thick brows and shook his head.

"I do not have her," Lady Vashmarna said again. "Why, if you are so bitterly set against her, do you want to see her now?"

Istvan Soos laughed the same harsh laugh. "I've been waiting fifteen years for her to betray me. After all I've done for her— That is, after such a long anticipation, I think it would amuse me to look her in the eye one last time before I die. But maybe it's even better if you don't have her. Maybe that means you're still to be betrayed in your turn. Now that would be sweet if I were only alive to see it."

"Ah," said Lady Vashmarna, her voice showing little of her anger, "now I begin to see. You believe you are under arrest, is that it? You think Moth"—she stumbled slightly on the name—"has given you up to the law. But you are not in the shaudah's courts. You are in Vashmarna's demesne."

"The shaudah. The Vashmarna. The Ghar. Oh yes, I know who's been drinking your tea." The scholar nodded at the cups on Lady Vashmarna's desk. "You're all the same to me. The Ghar was a murderer and a thief twenty years ago; why should any of you be any better today? No, I take it all back. Moth is a good, honest, loyal girl. Take her to your bosom and hold her tight. She'll drain you dry."

Oh, this hurt. It hurt so cunningly that Lady Vashmarna wondered if Moth had confided in this vicious creature before she had fled. But no, he said he did not know where she was, and Lady Vashmarna believed him. She believed him, and knew by the depth of her own disappointment that in reaching out to this man she had secretly been reaching out to Moth. And it came to her then that this betrayal he spoke of was Moth's hard-held loyalty to Lady Vashmarna and her cause.

Again, while Lady Vashmarna was mustering self-control, Nind spoke.

"What do you mean, the Ghar was a murderer and a thief?"

"Ah, the Ghar. I doubt he knew my face after so long—twenty years in the tidal changes a man—but I knew him. I knew him when he was a sulky dilettante in the scholars' hall, clutching the robes of wiser men. I knew him when Mahogan was killed and his papers stolen, what I could not save, and I knew him when I fled into the tidal to hide within the riots he helped to orchestrate. Lord Ghar. I congratulate you. You deserve your friends."

"You wretch!" said Nind. "The Ghar's men already tried to kill Moth once—and you know nothing about the lady's friendships! She—"

"Moth is indeed a danger to the Ghar," Lady Vashmarna said, feeling as though her mind were awake at last. She had not missed the flicker in the scholar's eyes when Nind had spoken of the attempt on Moth's life. That had come as no surprise to Istvan Soos. "And she is a danger to all of us if she falls into his hands. That is one commonality between us, Soos-*andas:* we would both be better off if we knew where to lay our hands on her before he does. Are you certain you cannot tell me where she is?"

Istvan Soos was scratching his chin, ignoring her stare as he studied something inside his skull. "Why should I worry about being betrayed to the Ghar when I have already been betrayed to you?"

"Why indeed?" Lady Vashmarna thought she had him now. At least she had his attention. "Did I not say we share a common ground?"

Istvan's gaze turned outward again and he met her eyes. "She betrayed me to you. I concede, it would be a fitting response to betray her to you, but I do not know where she is. There was a rumor she may have left the *shadras* by sea, but I know no more than that. If that's all the common ground between us, *jinnu*, there is precious little room for us both to stand."

He had called her *jinnu*. Lady Vashmarna smiled faintly and sat down behind her desk.

"Then let us try to expand on it, *andas*. Let us, for the sake of argument, concede that Moth was my agent among the *mundabi*. Let us even admit that I know that the *mundabi* and the shadow cult are, if not one and the same, intimately connected. Do you not find it telling, then, that *I* have not betrayed *you*? The truth is, *andas*, that Moth has been loyal to me, at least before her flight from the Ghar, and I have been loyal to you, for the sake of both our causes. Is that ground enough?"

"Both our causes? Vashmarna's cause, if I understand you rightly. You would claim the engine is yours?"

"Vashmarna has all the power it needs within these walls," Lady Vashmarna said with quiet intensity. "What use would the engine be to us when we have the turbines and the dam?"

"Ah, so you gave us Moth for the good of the tidal."

"I think if you consider her history, good *andas*, you will realize that you gave Moth to me. And yes, I gave her back again, and yes, it was for the good of the tidal. For the tidal, and the *shadras*, and the whole *rasnan*. Because if I hold the engine in one of my hands, *andas,* in the other I hold a ship. A ship to take us off this foundering isle and deliver us unto a new, fresh, unsullied land. Would *that* count in your books as common ground?"

"New land for us? New land for the tidal's scum? I don't think so, *jinnu.*"

"Why else do you think Moth would work for me? What other cause would bind her? Tell me that, who know her so well!" *Yes, tell me. Tell me that.*

Istvan scratched at his stubbled chin, the sound loud in the silence. "And now she's gone, you want me for the same cause. For your cause. You want me to serve you."

"Serve *our* cause, and serve your own. Serve the tidal, if you will. Restrain the cult. Keep the *mundabi* and the engine safe."

"Ah, the cult. Thus speaks the tidal's new tyrant. What makes you think I can do any such thing?"

"You are chief among the *mundabi,* their teacher and their leader." Yes, flatter him. Why not? "I think you must have some authority. And mind, I do not say, 'Bind the cult to Vashmarna's demesne.' I say merely, 'Protect the *mundabi*—protect yourself—' "

"And Vashmarna's engine."

"And our engine." As if it mattered now! But yes, if it would pacify the cult: "*Our* engine, yours and ours."

Istvan lowered his head between his narrow shoulders, but even though she could not see his face, Lady Vashmarna could sense the shifting gears inside him: *his* power, *his* safety, *his* advantage.

He said in a strangely defeated tone, "Promise me this ship, promise us this new land, and perhaps . . . Perhaps I will."

"Finish the engine," Lady Vashmarna said, secretly ironical and a little pitying. "Finish the engine and perhaps I will."

He smiled at that, a thin smile as humorless as his laugh. "Give us Moth, and perhaps *I* will."

Lady Vashmarna was hard-pressed to disguise her wince as a regal nod.

Once he was gone, Nind said to Lady Vashmarna, "Can he finish the engine? Can you give him the ship? Are you really going to look for Moth?"

Lady Vashmarna was not inclined to answer his presumption, but perhaps, having found Moth for her once, he had the right to ask. So she said shortly, "No, and no, and no."

THE HADARAS

"Moth," Aramis said. "Tell me again you are here with my lady's blessing."

"I am."

"Don't lie to me!"

They stood together on the upper deck among the garden beds in the rain. Remembering how Hamana had spied on her and Silk in the below-decks dark, Moth had led Aramis here, but even the water gave up little light. The faintest sheen defined the vine-clad railings and the tall leafy trees of the overgrown masts, but they were only black shapes cut against the rain.

Moth, confident of the darkness, let her face expose her pain.

"Are you sure you want the truth, Aramis? It might be easier to defend your beloved lady against my lies."

Aramis breathed. "I don't know what you mean."

"Don't you? But then, I don't know how much you already know. Here you are, after all, so it seems you know about the ship, the expansionists' plans for exploration, the search for new land."

"I only know about this ship because she sent me here to put a stop to it!"

"Then it's unfair to blame me for the secrets she kept from you. Would you love me better if I had betrayed her to you and the Society of Doors?"

"I—!" Aramis's breathing grew ragged. "I have never betrayed Vashmarna's secrets to the Society."

"While I, on the other hand, must of necessity have betrayed them to the cult? But of course I must. Who could expect a tidal slut to measure up to a baysider's honor?"

"Damn it, Moth, that's not fair! I won't let you tie me into knots. If you were here with her blessing, doing . . . whatever you are doing by her orders, then why didn't she tell me? Why would she send me here to put a stop to what she sent you here to start? It makes no sense!"

"Then you don't know your lady very well."

"And you do?" His voice cracked, and he made some abrupt movement in the dark.

The leaves all around them rustled with vermin and the rain.

"I know her better than you do, or so it seems."

"Because she's your sponsor," Aramis said heavily.

"Because I have been doing her secret bidding since I was barely more than a child! How do you think *I* know about this place? She came to me before she ever recruited her shipwrights and engineers."

"Why?"

"You saw why."

"Tell me what I saw. Tell me what I saw on the night the bridge came down."

"Oh, now you ask!" This time it was Moth who had to catch her breath. "I will make a deal with you, Aramis. If you tell me about the Society, I will tell you about the cult."

"Is that what I'm asking about? The cult? I thought I was asking about you."

"And am I not asking about you?" The pain had invaded her throat and threatened tears. "Aramis, Aramis, never think I don't love you. But can't you look for one instant beyond your own definition of 'honor'? You're like a man who spends his life gazing into a mirror; all you can see is what you want to believe about yourself. You are honest and honorable, you are good—well, you are. But you have divided your vows between the Vashmarna and the Ghar, between the expansionists and the Society of Doors. Do you imagine you aren't compromised? You have a secret lover among the dedicants, you have lied to the shaudah about a policeman's murder in the tidal, you have lied to the same lady you take me to task for betraying. Who are you that I should trust you more than you trust me? Who are you that you can condemn me when you don't even know what I've done?"

He said nothing for a long time. Beneath the susurrus of the leaves and the rain, the quiet water lapped at the hull of the ship. The air was drenched with the smell of ocean brine and the rotting greenery of the waterlogged garden.

"When I was a child," Aramis finally said, allowing Moth to breathe again. "When I was a child, my father came home one night alive with excitement. This was not long after the end of the Lamplighters riots. I remember it as a strange time. No one trusted the peace, the way we had before the uprising. If anyone had determined a cause for the murders in the scholarium or for the riots that followed, I was too young to have been told, but I think my parents did not know either. Everyone walked as if they did not quite trust the ground be-

neath their feet. But then one night my father came home."
Aramis's voice was soft and strangely impersonal, as though
he were alone, speaking to his own thoughts. "He was on
fire, striding about the room, laughing and gesturing. He was
usually such a self-contained man, but that night he seemed
huge. Proud. He was proud, as if he had taken part in something astonishing, as if he had for that one night become a
great man."

Aramis stopped, as if to contemplate a new understanding.

Moth said softly, "He had come from a meeting of the Society of Doors?"

"Yes." Aramis drew breath. "He should not have spoken so
freely, but he had to tell us. He had to tell someone, and who
else should he trust? He said that the Ghar's son had found the
way home. I became a member of the Society that night, in my
heart, though I was too young for initiation. It was my father's
pride, and his certainty in a time when nothing was certain. He
said the Ghar's son, but to me, as a child, it was he who had
found the way."

"The Ghar's son," Moth said. "Twenty years ago he would
have been speaking of Divaram Ghar."

Aramis sighed, relinquishing his memories. "Yes. Ghar-*jandas* was a lay scholar in those days. He had a place in the scholars' hall."

"Where his son now rules." Where a manifest had rolled
through the rain.

"Yes."

"And they have waited twenty-two years to open their
door?"

"I think they have been studying the Ghar's discovery. But
there is also the sense of the divine calling to the *rasnan*, calling across the worlds, so that it is not we who choose the time
but the time that chooses us. It is only because of the hunger,

the unrest, the rains, that they have dared, or needed, or felt directed, to act. To act to save us, Moth."

"To save all of us?" she asked, but so softly he did not seem to hear.

"And now this plague," he said, "but I fear the plague is theirs. Or . . ." There was defeat in the pause. "Or it is the *ramhadras*'s."

Heaven's plague. A chill moved across Moth's rain-damp skin.

"What plague? What do you mean?"

"I don't know," Aramis murmured. "I have seen such things . . . I have seen a crack in the world. I have seen the shades of the dead our ancestors left behind in their flight. I have seen a demon born of the meeting between two worlds— or between one world and the dark. And now the men of the Society are spreading this plague throughout the bastion . . ."

"The Society raises demons and plagues, and you blame the shadow cult for its gods?"

"Do you think I don't blame the Society?" Aramis said, a muffled cry. "Saints and my ancestors, Moth! They tried to have you killed!"

So. He loved her, even yet. This began to seem like a terrible thing, as if they should not love. As if they would be safer if they did not love.

"But," Aramis said bitterly, "at least the Society—at least the Ghars have been trying for an honorable goal. Can you say the same for the cult?"

"The shadow cult arose only out of Vashmarna's efforts in the expansionist cause." Moth said this absently. Somewhere beyond the emotional calamity of the night, she was still thinking. If the Society had found its new power during the Lamplighters Rebellion, how did that connect them to Mahogan, discoverer of the *mundab,* whose death touched off the riots, whose papers Istvan had tried and partly failed to save? Was it possible the Ghar was responsible for Mahogan's death? Responsible for the riots?

Responsible for Moth's conception?

But Aramis, unable to follow her thoughts, clung to the last thing she had said. "*Vashmarna's* efforts?"

"Oh, well, mine on Vashmarna's behalf. The shadow gods are only manifests of my workings. The cult was only ever meant to make the means look like the end."

"I don't know what that means."

"So if anyone outside the tidal got curious, they would find only a tidal cult worshipping shadows, not Vashmarna's engine."

"Vashmarna's engine."

"For the ship you are standing on, to take it over the horizon in search of a new land. And you can't say it didn't work."

"The engine?"

"The cult." Moth added bitterly, "The cult can take the blame for everything, can't it? Vashmarna's meddling, the Society's demons and plague. The shaudah's great enemies are the only innocents, it seems."

"Was it innocence that ruined the bridge?" Aramis said with his own weight of pain in his voice. "What about the cable, and the men who died?"

Moth wiped the rain off her face, passed her hands over her head, and wrung out her braid. She was weary to the bone, and she, who had demanded honesty, did not have an answer for him. Even at this remove she still could not say what had really happened with the manifests, the *mundab,* the bridge. For all her cavalier authority, she could not even say for certain anymore what the manifests were. *She* had not intended the destruction of the bridge. She had never even intended, in that terrible moment, to hide the cable. The engine's manifests had acted to save their parent—parent-engine? parent-*mundabi?* parent-Moth?—and she, who neither motivated nor controlled them, and who refused to acknowledge either fact, had reached for the *mundab*. . . .

Or the *mundab* had reached for her.

Whose intent, Moth? Whose shadow? Whose will?

"I don't know," she said to Aramis. "There are some things I just—don't know."

"Try, Moth. I need you to try for me. I need you to try."

"I don't know where to start," she said faintly, and then had to touch his hand to forestall his impatience. "The cult . . . We, the *mundabi,* who are at the heart of the cult and aren't really the cult at all . . . Oh, I don't know what to say! It starts with the *mundab*, and I don't know how to tell you what that means."

"The ocean? The ocean and the ship?"

"No. Yes. Yes, but so much more than that. It's the world. Listen. This island. We've made this island into our entire world: *rasnan,* we call it, the known world, and it's *nothing*, Aramis, it's a rock, a speck of land on the face of this infinite sea that we try so hard not to acknowledge. The island *isn't* the world. The world is vast, and it's alive. It's alive.

"Listen. Before I was born there was a man, a scholar, who turned his meditations away from our ancestors and their absent gods to answer the call of this world—a call the temple denies so utterly that it is not even forbidden. But it exists, it does, and Mahogan gave it a place in his soul, or found a place for his soul in the *mundab*. He said the *mundab* was more than an ocean—or rather, he said the ocean was only the embodiment, the incarnation, the avatar of the spirit of the world, a spirit that has nothing to do with the gods of the *ramhadras* or with the deliberate blindness, and powerlessness, of the *rasnan*. Mahogan said we should learn to worship the divine of this world, to find the gods of this place, to turn our faces away from the past and the absent gods and find an answer in the *mundab*. He found an answer—or at least, he was learning how to ask the question when he was killed. Twenty-two years ago, and a little more."

Rain sighed through the leaves, too quiet to drown Aramis's strained breathing. "The Lamplighters riots."

"The Lamplighters riots. Mahogan was murdered by no-one-knows-who, and the Lamplighters were blamed, like the shadow cult is blamed for everything today. Exactly like the shadow cult is blamed for everything today. One of Mahogan's students rescued some of his papers, and he always supposed the rest were destroyed. But that same year your father came home saying Divaram Ghar had found the way to open a door to the *ramhadras,* and I know that the Society has been calling on the *mundab*."

"No."

"I do know it, Aramis. I was the student of Mahogan's student, who took refuge in the tidal the same year I was born."

"No . . ."

"No? They wouldn't? The man who tried to have us killed?"

"You said no one knew who murdered that scholar."

"No one does know. I have even wondered sometimes . . ." Wondered about Istvan Soos, who clung like a miser to his scavenged, smuggled, hoarded knowledge. But she did not owe Aramis a betrayal like that. The rain sifted down, hardly more than a mist breathed by the invisible water, while he fought to take in what she had said. "Of course," she added softly to the darkness, "you know I do sometimes tell lies."

"Don't." Aramis caught his breath again, and Moth wanted to embrace him, to hold him, as if he wept. But the impulse frightened her, and the fear made her set her jaw. Why should she comfort him for the death of a few illusions? Who had ever offered to comfort her?

"So," she said, feeling cruel, "the Ghars have been hiding their secret knowledge all these years—"

"And the shadow cult has been exploiting it! Don't claim the high ground, Moth. I don't know whose it is, but it isn't yours."

"Mine? The cult's? The tidal's? It's *Vashmarna* who's been exploiting the *mundab,* Aramis. Will you grant the high ground to your own lady, your own demesne?"

"Moth. Tell me Vashmarna-*jin'* is your sponsor, and I might believe you. But part of the shadow cult? You've never understood how fine a line Vashmarna has to tread between the shaudah and the temple and the demands of the *shadras*. I just can't believe that my lady, who has devoted her whole life to earning the approbation of the temple, would throw it all away on . . . what? Fostering a tidal cult?"

"Except that what you mean to say is, throw it all away on the tidal."

"Don't lay that on me, Moth. When have I ever said there aren't good people in the tidal? Good people struggling hard and being led astray by the shadow cult—"

"Unlike all those good people in the towers being led astray by the Society of Doors."

"Yes. Unlike them, unlike *us,* who are moved—but you wouldn't understand this, would you, *rasnu* Moth? People who are moved by piety, by belief in the gods and our ancestors—"

"And a total disregard for everything the temple histories have ever told us about the *ramhadras* and the reasons our precious ancestors ever left to begin with. Don't charge me with hypocrisy! You, an engineer of Vashmarna demesne, who's a member of the Society of Doors? The Society that's using the *mundab,* the spirit of *this* world, to force a way back to the last world we despoiled?"

"At least we're trying for something good and whole! What have you ever achieved but violence and destruction?"

"The shaudah's violence! The shaudah and the Ghar!"

"Oh, so it was the shaudah that brought down the bridge? Moth, *I was there*."

Her body was clenched so hard her ribs felt like iron bars. "You were there, yes. You were there, Aramis, because your lady has never had the courage of her convictions. You were there because she was too scared to admit she had ties in the tidal. That cable was there to let us do the work she ordered us to do! She has always been too fearful, too secretive, too pious to challenge the shaudah and his policies in the open."

"So now you want to put it on my lady," Aramis said with a profound fatigue in his voice.

"It *is* on her, just as much as it is on me. Do you want me to confess, Aramis? Do you want me to shoulder the blame? It was the *mundab* itself that took down the bridge. Perhaps I was its agent—they were my manifests, or the engine's—but the engine is hers, like this ship is hers, like I was hers before she threw me away—" And that was saying far more than she had intended. The iron bars closed around her heart.

"The engine! The ship!" It was a whispered cry, all but lost in the rainfall. "What is all this? What is it for? What does it mean?"

"Expansion. Exploration and expansion. Getting off this island before it founders under the waves. What cause has your lady ever championed but that? And what cause has ever given the tidal any hope at all? Or would you tell me," she said, her voice all but strangled in her throat, "that your Society under the Ghars would ever have let the likes of me through their precious—their moral—their so pious and moral door?"

Aramis made some sudden move, a flinch away from her in the dark. "I would have taken you with me. Back when they would have taken me."

That silenced her.

"If you would have come," he added after a long quiet fall of rain.

Rain, Moth thought. *Rain, rain, rain.* "Would you have come with me?"

"On a ship," he said with surprising gentleness, "with no engine, no sails, no crew?"

"No crew?" she said wearily. "Aramis, you are so . . . so . . . so *Vashmarna*. Who do you think these people are, living here?"

"Interlopers," he said, "in Vashmarna territory."

"Ah."

"Territory that Vashmarna intends to abandon, according to my lady."

"As if discovery is worse than failure. Oh, I could live with failure, if only I were allowed to try!"

"Then you are not here by my lady's order."

"Maybe I have more courage. Or maybe it's only that I have more desperation, not having a tower home."

"Is that why you have always been so reckless?" Aramis said with that same unwonted bitterness threaded through his voice. "None of us has a tower home now."

"Oh, well." Moth wanted to say *No,* but was not sure it would be true. Instead she said sadly, and honestly, "I took some joy in it all once."

"Joy," Aramis whispered, as though it were a concept foreign to his world. Perhaps he thought it was foreign to hers. He said, "I did not know joy could be so dark."

"If you think the *mundab* is dark, then you still don't understand."

"I don't." He sounded almost humble. "I don't understand any of this. I don't even understand myself anymore."

"I wish you understood me," Moth said wistfully.

"I do, too." After an awkward pause, Aramis put his arms around Moth, both of them wet and chilled by the rain. "Do you really mean to finish the ship in spite of her?"

His lady, her sponsor. Her mother, if only he knew.

"In spite of her. Yes. If I can."

For all their honesty, she did not ask him if he would help or hinder, and he did not choose to say.

In the morning, Moth left Aramis sunk in a restless sleep to search out Silk. Transplanted roof-gardener, she hunkered in the midship vegetable beds hunting vermin in the garden mulch. There was something grotesque about this inedible harvest gleaned from under the leaves of the flowerless and waterlogged plants. Silk had a bucket half-full of twitching many-legged corpses, and she wore a scowl of distaste as she stabbed among the roots with her garden fork. It was a gruesome job, and Moth thought it could only be a point in her favor to interrupt. She knelt beside Silk and put her head on her shoulder and her arm around her neck. Silk did not stop probing the earth.

"Did you have a pleasant night?" The sarcasm was gentle, for Silk.

"No." Moth was perversely comforted by the sharp edges of her oldest friendship. It was all right to cut each other bloody as long as they could still patch up each other's wounds. "It was awful."

"What a shame." Silk lunged after a crab, but Moth's embrace hampered her and the creature scuttled into hiding under the straw rain hat around the roots of a plant farther along. Silk sat back on her heels. "People have been looking for you."

"Who?"

"Everyone."

Silk was muscular beneath Moth's arm, smelling warmly of sweat and the composted seaweed that made up the garden's earth. She might have been a peasant, but although she looked like the other gardeners working down the whole green length of the ship, she spoke the same as she ever had, with the sharp, offhand, aggressive accents of the tidal.

"What do they want?" Moth asked, her voice muffled in Silk's shirt.

"*Rasnu* Moth," Silk said in a fluting mimicry of a plaintive cry. "*Rasnu* Moth."

Moth snickered.

"You'll have to talk to them sooner or later."

"No," Moth whimpered. "I don't, I don't."

Silk stabbed at the earth with her fork. "Have you come up with a better role to play? Or does this mean we finally get to leave?"

"You can go back to the tidal anytime you like," Moth said, stung in spite of her good intentions. She had not come out here to quarrel with Silk.

Silk shrugged her off. "And leave you to do what? Make up to Vashmarna?"

"Silk. I'm not going to argue this out again."

"You're the one who could always leave before," Silk burst out. "You're the one with the sponsor and the books and the bed in the scholarium—and the lover, too, if I only knew it. You're the one who always slipped away, leaving the rest of us in the shit. And now we're here, there's no bastion, no towers, nowhere to go, and you're still—!"

The unfortunate crab chose that moment to reappear, and was skewered by Silk. She jerked the impaled creature into the air, and then dropped the fork to the deck with a choked exclamation. She and Moth both scrambled back. The crab, if it was a crab, rattled its claws on the metal tine that pierced its shell—claws so badly rounded they resembled wheels. In its warped malignancy, it reminded Moth of a tiny manifest, but it was clearly a living—or rather, a dying—animal, dripping ichor as it spasmed on the tine. Past her first startlement, Moth picked up the fork and peered at the deformed crab.

"Don't," Silk said with a shudder.

Moth smiled and tilted the nastily embellished fork in Silk's direction. "How is this any worse than a normal crab?"

"It's not natural," snapped Silk, but she responded to Moth's challenge and came closer. "What's wrong with it?"

Besides the fused claws it had too many legs and a seamlike ridge in the shell. There was something odd about the mouth parts as well, but even Moth was too squeamish to look that closely. The crab had stopped twitching and was unmistakably dead, so she scraped it off the fork into Silk's bucket; but then, puzzled and disturbed, she stirred through the other small corpses. Crabs and many-legged insects, glossy slugs and the tiny lizards that bit into flower buds in search of insect eggs. En masse the dead things were horrible, and Moth could feel her face tightening with the same expression of disgust that Silk wore. She fished the wheel-footed crab back out of the bucket and laid it on the deck with several other deformed corpses. Perhaps it was their deadness, but there was something of the inanimate about them, as if they had been made, not hatched or born. Moth was reminded of Tarun, dead Tarun, and his miniature machines that had clung like so many lizards to his walls.

"Did you do this?" Suspicion warred with awe in Silk's voice.

Moth was astonished. "What?"

"With your *mundab,* your changes. Did you do this?"

"No!" Moth said, but she was remembering a small working of Istvan's, the shadow of the *mundab* passing over Tarun's inhabited walls. Had they not spun into life in that moment? Had they not, briefly, changed?

"No," Moth said again, but inwardly she shuddered. She scooped the dead things off the deck and, rather than dropping them back into Silk's bucket, she carried them to the rail and cast them overboard for the eels. Standing there she surveyed the long garden beds, the vine-clad masts, the gardeners who knelt amidst the too-luxuriant and fruitless growth. How many—? Moth shrugged the question off as irrelevant, even as her hands covered her lower belly in an instinctive gesture of protection.

"No," she said once again, this time to herself, but she was not convinced.

She was not at all convinced, and when the ship village's elders finally cornered her in the bow of the ship, she braced herself for a repetition of Silk's accusation. But no. They had not come to accuse Moth-the-sorcerer. They had come to importune Moth-the-priest.

"*Rasnu.*" A voice with the accents of the *hadaras,* a voice with the assurance of need. "*Rasnu?*"

She had turned her back on the ship and was staring out to sea, piously meditating on lovers and vermin, power and her unborn child. These were not good thoughts, however serene her expression, and she was not sorry for the interruption. She turned after a very little pause.

It was a whole delegation: Kala Janni, the ship's headwoman, with two other elders, a middle-aged man, and a couple who were several years younger than Moth. That they were a couple was made clear by their shared expression of stubborn terror, and even clearer by the way the middle-aged man took the boy by the shoulders and stood him roughly away from the girl's side. The story was told before anyone could speak a word.

Why me? Moth thought with a small, private despair. But she said in a priest's dry tones, "Is this a wedding?" and astonished them with her powers of divination.

Although in fact Kala Janni said with a bow, "No, *rasnu,* there can be no wedding here."

"No, of course there can't," Moth said more dryly yet. She

of all people knew about the shaudah's torturous marriage laws. "Well, tell me the tale."

Do these tales ever need telling? He was the son of a farmer without land; she was the daughter of a carpenter who had died. They had no prospects of employment and no hope of achieving an independent familial establishment, and they had demonstrably failed the shaudah's first test of virtue, virginity. The law denied them marriage, and the law denied an unmarried woman the right to bear a child. Yes, the girl was pregnant, and yes, she burst into tears, and no, the orthodoxy provided no recourse for an impossible pregnancy. Abortion was anathema, though common enough in the tidal where the orthodoxy failed to thrive. In the bay, where such things mattered, a girl would be sent into the *hadaras* to birth her nameless child. In the *hadaras,* according to tidal gossip, neither child nor mother was likely to survive, a dead adult being easier to explain than a live child, but here was this girl sobbing at Moth's feet, and here was this boy shivering at his father's side, and here were these elders laying the dilemma in the *rasnu*'s lap.

Of course Moth identified with the poor girl, with her own waist beginning to thicken and her breasts starting to swell. But what did they expect her to do? *It's a test,* she thought wildly, but then the truth of that struck home: they were not just testing a priest, they were testing a shadow priest. They were testing the orthodoxy against the shadow cult.

The recognition that she did not have to play the orthodox priest, that she had an alternate role, freed her from her incipient panic. Yet a new question reared up in Moth's mind: Which did these people *want,* the orthodoxy or the shadow cult? She supposed the young couple would accept anything that let them live and raise their child in peace, but what about their elders? What did Kala Janni with her market woman's eyes want from her priest? The *hadaras* was a mystery Moth did not want to plumb, but surely the answer for these people would be the same as for anyone on this blighted island. Surely they just wanted something better than what they had.

Thoughts that took only a breath or two, nothing more than a contemplative pause. Moth folded her hands before her own inhabited waist.

"This is what the temple would say," she said in measured tones. "The boy has sinned in his actions and transgressed the law, and must pay a restitution of prayer, fasting, and a fine set by the shaudah's courts. He must be publicly named as a fornicator and a criminal in the third degree, and he will be forever barred from marriage, the ownership of property, and the swearing of any vows above the apprenticeship level. As for the girl, she bears sin within her body, as well as the sins against the gods and the law within her soul, and she must be cast out, forbidden human converse or charity for the course of her pregnancy and beyond, for as long as the child shall live. And the child must live," Moth added gently, "for the mother in her transgression has relinquished her claim on her soul. Her child carries the only soul she will ever have until the day one of them dies."

It was so quiet that Moth could hear the water beneath the hull, the patter of last night's rain falling from the bowsprit's vine. There was no shock reverberating through the air. She had not told them anything they did not already know. The girl was staring with rain-wet eyes at her despair.

"That is what the temple would say," Moth said, more softly yet. She felt the fine hairs on her neck and arms lift with the electric power of her own words. "This is what the *mundab* says. Are you listening?"

The ritualistic phrase drew bows from her supplicants. They were listening with clenched hands and downcast eyes.

"What the *mundab* tells us is that we are all outcasts. The *mundab* tells us that the old world holds no promises for us, only death, and it tells us that the time of our exile is ending, not because we are returning to the *ramhadras*, but because even the remnants of the *ramhadras* that we have nurtured in our temples, in our houses, in our hearts, are dying as the first world died. The time of the *rasnan* is at an end. The time of the *mundab* is beginning. Do we not know this better than any, we few who have cast away our former lives to make our homes on this living, growing ship? Have we not already abandoned the *rasnan* the way the gods of the *ramhadras* abandoned us? Have we not already turned our faces to the unknown? We, children of exiles, have exiled ourselves, and we are the first humans in this world to come home."

Moth let the silence build again, binding her listeners with it until they could barely breathe. And then she said it again, a whisper as fierce as a battle cry.

"We have come home. *This* is our world. This is *our* world. *We have come home.*"

They were weeping, all but the girl, who had fallen to her knees, her arms folded across her belly and her forehead touching the deck. Moth was shivering suddenly, unsure for the first time in her life if she had just spoken a terrible truth or a terrible lie. Terrible, in either case, that they believed her, as if her words—the foresworn dedicant's, slum girl's, orphan's words—could re-create the world.

"Go," she said harshly, breaking the silence with a sharp blow. "This is only a child. Life will go on. It's hardly worth all this fuss."

Yes, *rasnu*. No, *rasnu*. Shadows bless you, *rasnu*.

They went, leaving *rasnu* Moth alone to contemplate the vision of Aramis Tapurnashen, loyal Vashmarna man, speaking with the ship's engineers far down the leafy deck in the distant stern.

She might have sacrificed her priestly dignity before the

hadri, but her position with the engineers was too precarious for her to burst in upon this conference like an unschooled girl. She walked the long deck as *aras* Baradam might have walked the cloisters of the scholars' hall, serene in the certainty of ownership. But where was Silk, that the engineers had come aboard without warning? Where was Hamana, whom Moth expected to have been shadowing Aramis? Why did Moth always have to deal with these crises on her own?

She padded quietly into earshot, hoping the engineers would not notice her before she had had a chance to eavesdrop, but they were too wary. The ship that should have been theirs had become enemy territory, and they clustered near the stern ladder like an uninvited delegation, their anxious and affronted eyes watching for any approach. Their chief, a man named Hemmar Gamood, broke off what he was saying in the middle of a word.

"*Rasnu,*" he said with the shallowest imaginable bow.

"*Andas.*" Moth nodded to the same degree, then turned the same cool gaze on Aramis. "*Andas.*"

Aramis ducked his head and her gaze. "*Rasnu.*"

The amenities dealt with, a silence fell. The rising sea breeze bumped the ship against its anchors, making it thump and groan, and shaking last night's rain out of the vines that climbed the rigging and the masts. The engineers, accustomed to their floating workshops, caught their balance with unconscious ease. Aramis had to take a step, which, coincidental or not, looked as though he were distancing himself from the confrontation. That it was a confrontation Moth had no doubt. Gamood's expressions were often lost in the folds of his face, which, though not fat, had so much extra skin that it might have been intended for a larger skull. Mostly he wore a dull, creased, and sullen look, but for once his baffled anger showed through in widened eyes and loosened mouth.

"Tapurnashen-*andas* brings us startling news from the *shadras*," the engineer said.

"I expect he does," Moth said, her tone dry and her heart sinking. Indeed, there was such an abyss inside her that she thought her heart was in danger of disappearing altogether. But what had she expected? What did she have a right to expect?

"I have told Gamood-*andas* about the Vashmarna's new plans for the ship," Aramis said, as if betrayal were the last thing on his mind. But there again was the question that had always plagued them: betrayal of whom?

Almost in spite of herself, Moth spared her lover a little of the pity she had been feeling for herself.

"It is pleasing to know the Vashmarna has not forgotten us after all," Gamood said, his anger warping the irony in his voice. "Not only does she send us fresh directions, but a secret resource as well. Imagine our surprise, *rasnu*, to discover that you are more than a simple priest sent to succor us in our exile. Far more than that in degree, I gather, though I am still uncertain as to kind. Is this a priestly engineer who has been hiding her talents among the *hadri* who have sabotaged our work and our lady's goals? Or what is this?"

Aramis, to whom this last demand was made, said with a convincing display of patience, "The extent of the *rasnu*'s resources is best left for the *rasnu* to demonstrate, but as I said, *andas*, the *rasnu* was in command of the construction of the engine before events in the *shadras* forced her to relocate to the *hadaras*, and she has the knowledge, the abilities, and the commitment to bring this foundered project to completion."

Moth hid her shock with a humbly lowered head. *Imagine my surprise, Hemmar Gamood!*

"You did say that," Gamood said with heavy sarcasm. "What you did not say—what you continue to fail to say—is why the *rasnu,* the Vashmarna's secret expert and savior of our work, should have so conspicuously failed to explain herself or her presence here for all this length of time!"

"As I *did* explain," Aramis replied with a tight jaw, "Vashmarna-*jinnu* could not set her new plans in motion until affairs in the *shadras* had been tended to. Secrecy has never been more necessary, and explanations are necessarily contingent on events. Suppose it was not I who came, but the shaudah's men, or the Ghar's? The Vashmarna dares let no one of us know too much until we need that knowledge to act."

"Even so," Gamood said, "why did Vashmarna-*jinnu* not send her written authority with you, *rasnu,* or at least with the good *andas?*"

Moth met his gaze, but held her tongue as Aramis answered.

"Because, *andas,* the risk of ambush and theft was, and is, too great. Vashmarna's enemies are increasingly bold of late. Despite all the care I took on my journey here, I had reason to fear I was being followed, and it was fortunate that the *rasnu's* guard found me and gave me her protection and guidance for the last stage of the trip—thanks to the *rasnu's* foresight." Aramis gave Moth a courteous bow.

Moth nodded vaguely in return. She always admired a good lie, but she found she was a little shocked at Aramis's facility. A little shocked and a little angry. On what grounds had he ever judged her?

Gamood looked from Aramis to Moth, unconvinced but baffled. Moth knew what was in his mind. He was sure Aramis was lying, but on what count? And at least he knew Aramis, had some reason to trust him. Gamood had never trusted Moth, never wanted her and her companions on board the ship he had failed to complete or even retain for the expansionist cause, and he would trust her even less now. But what could he do? That was the crux of the problem. Which would garner him worse blame: assuming Aramis and Moth did not have the Vashmarna's authority and then, having sabotaged their efforts, finding out too late they did? Or pretending to believe them, and having to admit later on that he had been innocently duped, blinded by his own commitment to the cause? Moth could read the answer he reached in the new configuration of the seams in his face.

"Thanks to the *rasnu*," he said glumly. "Now if you can only explain what exactly the *rasnu* can do besides lend us her prayers . . ."

"Yes, *rasnu*," said a soft voice behind Moth. "What is it you can do for Vashmarna's cause?"

Moth turned to find Silk and Hamana at her back, staring at her with eyes in which suspicion had hardened into something darker and bloodier still.

THE BASTION

Lady Vashmarna dreamed she was on a small pleasure boat that scudded among the towers and out into the open bay. The towers were squat and toadlike, covered with barnacles and rotting weeds, nothing like the shining edifices of the waking world, but they were incidental. The heart of the dream was the boat, small and delicate as a shell, and the rough waves that shuddered beneath its hull. The boat was misshapen, unbalanced. It slipped, jerked, careened into the leaning wall of a wave. Lady Vashmarna fell sidelong into waking, but still the boat, the bed, jerked and shuddered beneath her. Awake, not awake, awake, Lady Vashmarna heard the chatter of loose shelves, the shattering of dishes in another room. She was awake. It was an earthquake. For an instant she was back in Shaudarand on the night the bridge fell, a Shaudarand that leaned down toward the waves, crumbling its walls, breaking its windows, scattering its inhabitants across the inner bay—for an instant Lady Vashmarna felt herself and her bed sliding helplessly across the tilting floor—but then the fort subsided, foursquare and grumbling, and as quickly as that the earthquake was over.

And the aftermath only beginning. Lady Vashmarna lay with a stillness that tried to reach down to the island's roots, to feel the *rasnan*'s heart as if it had nerves that attached to her own. Are you quiet now? Are you done? But through her windows she could hear the rising voices of shock and fear, and beyond the heavy doors of her rooms she caught the thump of agitated footsteps. She could not be found lying abed like an old woman. She sat up, swinging her bare feet to the floor, and fumbled for the lamp by the bed. Distracted, her mind working somewhere across the barricade of her pounding heart, she was slow to recognize the cool bite of glass in her sole, and slower to connect that fact to the lamp her hand still could not find in the near-dark. She caught her tongue between her teeth before the curse escaped, and bent to grope among the broken shards for her slippers. Someone began to pound on the office door.

Feeling her way across the outer room—not entirely blind, thanks to the lights that still shone up from the dam on the other side of the fort—thanks to the gods that the lights still shone!—Lady Vashmarna kicked something small and light that rang like a bell as it skittered across the floor. What was that? For some reason it nagged at her, what that small bright-sounding thing might be, but she did not stop to search it out. She fumbled for the light switch and the door handle, and found them both at the same time, flipping the one as she twisted the other, thereby dazzling herself and the woman in the hall. Pedigan Shawm, with sleep dust in her eyelashes and her coarse black hair in ropes around her face. Lady Vashmarna realized she could not look any better and stepped hastily out of sight of the hall.

"Come," she said, "come in."

"*Jinnu,*" said the trembling Shawm. "Are you well?"

"Of course," Lady Vashmarna said, snappish after her own fear. "What news do you have?"

Pedigan Shawm finally stepped into the room, allowing Lady Vashmarna to shut the door, and stared wide-eyed at the office. Lady Vashmarna followed her gaze and felt a distinct internal blow as she looked at the drifts of paper, the fallen and broken screens, the dust that made halos around the ceiling light. And her shrine. Oh, her shrine, with its doors all ajar and its empty shelves askew. Saints and gods and prayer tokens lay scattered all over the floor. That was what she had inadvertently kicked. No wonder it had nagged at her!

Dear gods, forgive me my trespass, it was not meant! (Not this time, said an inner voice. What of the engine? What of the *mundab*? What of Moth?) *Holy saints, forgive me, forgive me, it was not intended, acquit me of this much, I pray!*

"I don't know," Pedigan Shawm said. "I came directly to you."

Lady Vashmarna had to dredge up the question Shawm was answering, and the effort, as well as her own distress, made her more than sharp when she said, "I don't need comfort; I need information. Is that not what I keep you for? Where is there damage? How is the dam, the station, the manufactory, the stores? The kitchens! Dear gods, woman, how many fires were burning when the tremors began? Do you know?"

"No, *jinnu,*" Shawm said, her eyes showing white around the brown.

"Then find out! The fort could be falling down around our ears while you stand here."

Shawm bowed with a tight and unhappy mouth, and murmured "Since you are well, *jinnu*" as she opened the door. Then Lady Vashmarna felt a spasm of conscience, but too late. The other woman was gone.

There were voices outside her door, voices crying out beneath her window. The whole fort seethed like a kicked-over beehive. She was suddenly burning with impatience to get out there, to see more than this room, to know what fresh disasters had invaded her realm, but all the same she took precious moments to find the holy trinket she had kicked on her way to the door. Paper from the desk and the shelves had drifted everywhere, lists and reports and old ledgers that had burst their bindings when they had fallen. She shuffled through them, as furious with herself as she would have been with anyone who delayed her at such a time, as if suddenly she were two women, the lady of the demesne of power and light and the aging woman who dithered and sighed over the harm the other had done. *Leave it be,* the lady scolded, *there is no time!* But the woman bent like a peasant planting out rice seedlings, sifting through the drifts until she found the incense burner that, spurned by her foot, had rung like a bell. She picked it up and, as all the shelves of the shrine had fallen, set it on the corner of the desk. Then, finally, she could go and dress, and tie a scarf over her bed-tangled hair.

She acquired a tail of anxious hangers-on as soon as she stepped out her door, and led them with a few meaningless reassurances down to the receiving hall across the main yard from the gate. When the fort had still been a fort, the hall had been a ceremonial reception room, imposing even if it had never been beautiful, but now it was a storeroom for goods in transit, and even more recently a dormitory for workmen who had been displaced by clerks from the towers, and consequently it was a clutter of crates and cots and human beings. But it was central, and it could accommodate those who felt the need to crowd for comfort around the skirts of authority. Lady Vashmarna set the panicky to clearing a space in the hall and the more sensible to taking a hasty survey of her demesne. The first and most important question—did the dam and the generating station still stand?—had been answered by the turning of a switch, and truly, Lady Vashmarna thought as her own fear subsided, the other questions could safely wait until morning, but the anxious faces of her officers and the strident outcry in the yards told her it was better to give some orders and thereby reclaim some order from the shaken night. And so the reports began to trickle in.

"There are no visible cracks in the dam," said one workman with such a troubled emphasis on the word "visible" that Lady Vashmarna forgot her own growing fatigue.

"Tell me," she said.

Men had inspected the outer face of the dam by lowering themselves on ropes and "walking" back and forth across the stone curve of the wall with battery torches in their hands. This, in the dark, in the rain, above a river in flood. Lady Vashmarna found herself moved that her men should take such risks, and take them as a matter of course. The man who was reporting to her looked puzzled when she interrupted him to ask whether anyone had been injured or lost.

"No, *jinnu*," he said, "but the dam is sound. At least," he added before she could do more than draw a breath, "as much of it as we can see. The water's as high as I've ever seen it; the footings are drowned; we can't inspect them. And *jinnu*, I'm none too easy in my mind about the sluices, and you know they were never built to make a reservoir in flood times. They're wide open, but the river's nearly as high as the bottom of the gates and still rising. If it gets much higher, the water'll be backing up behind the gates. It'll be going over the top of the dam, flooding the turbines—and that's only if the added pressure doesn't force a break we can't even see."

Even as he said this, the *rasnan* shivered, sifting more dust out of the ancient ceiling, and silencing the crowd.

Bless us, spirits of air . . . But was there no prayer to the spirits of earth? To the spirits of the *ramhadras*, yes, but not to the spirits of this earth that had been scorned as alien and unworthy for so long. Perhaps Moth had such a prayer. Perhaps Istvan did, and he was in the fort tonight, trespassing on her patience for the sake of his "research," as he called it, this snooping around among the engineers' models and plans. But a prayer to the *mundab* was not a prayer to the *rasnan*. *Or have we ever known the "known" world? Is the* rasnan *a lie? Has there only ever been the* mundab, *the unknown, quivering, and deceitful beneath our feet?*

And then, into that ominous silence, came a hasty *purdar* Nind with disaster gleaming in his dark eyes even before he spoke. "*Jinnu*, forgive me. We've found . . . There is no way . . . *Jinnu*, the old scholar: he's dead."

The old scholar, meaning Istvan Soos.

"Show me," Lady Vashmarna said. She did not ask how the old man had died. If he had been killed by the earthquake, Nind would not have broken into her conference with her engineers.

Neither did she ask where he had died, and so she was surprised when the *purdar* led them into the heart of Vashmarna's territory, where lay the manufactories and the stores. Surprised, and overcome with the certainty that the death, the news of the death, would be the least of it.

Yet, despite this certainty, the old man's corpse made its own space of silence, as the recent tremor had done. Even sprawled at the threshold of the manufactory, where the new cable was being insulated and wound on its mammoth spool, a place that spoke volumes about further calamity in store for Lady Vashmarna and Vashmarna as a whole—even then, the body that was thinner and more ragged than it had been in life, demanded attention for its own sake. Istvan, dead, insisted *he* was a calamity, a subject that had come untimely to its end. *Here was a life,* his body said. *Here was a man. Notice me.*

His corpse sprawled with its head cocked against the frame

of the door. Blood, dark in the electric glare that cut the doorway out against the rainy night, soaked his shirtfront, and spots freckled his face: gunpowder, Nind said. The scholar had been shot.

"And where are the shaudah's men?" Lady Vashmarna murmured, her voice low for decency's sake.

"Still at the gate, so far," Nind murmured back, secretive rather than respectful. "And they swear they haven't left, and so say my men, but it wasn't a Vashmarna hand that killed the old man, and gods witness, no Vashmarna hand turned to the mischief within."

"Is there more to see?" she asked, knowing the answer.

"Oh, yes, *jin'*," her guard captain said with a macabre humor. "A little more."

"Move him, then," Lady Vashmarna said. Unlike her guards, she would not step over the dead man as if he were nothing but a bit of trash in the road.

Gods keep you, she thought. And then, hesitantly, Mundab *keep you, old man,* for she would make a prayer for her daughter's sake, who had been taught by Istvan, and who had betrayed him for her mother's asking. And it was true, she thought with the strange flavor of that prayer lingering in her mind. Death is as great an unknown to us as this world. Nind's men gathered Istvan Soos by his arms and legs and carried him, head hanging back so his hair brushed the muddy ground, out of the way. Lady Vashmarna stepped over the small pool of blood and walked through the manufactory door.

The smell was chokingly of hot rubber and electricity and sweat; the inaudible growl of the river and the turbines hummed upward into the bones of her feet. Unused materials and scraps lurked in every corner; empty cable spools hung like giant bobbins from the cobwebbed ceiling; broken lightbulbs overflowed several crates by the door, which was thereby rendered unclosable. The darkness of the night fell up against the dust-shrouded electric light of the overhead lamps and created a harsh confusion of sharp-edged forms.

And some of the forms drifted like unanchored boats, wavered like weeds at the turn of tide. Movement teased the edge of vision, silently shifting the clutter into new configurations every time the eye was turned the other way, and the eye had to be turned the other way, for there were full-bodied haunts clambering the walls and crossing the ceiling like spiders and flies, like lizards built of scraps and scaled with broken glass, like shell-less crabs with steel and copper wires working their silent claws. One haunt wound a path through a line of burning bulbs, capturing the light without casting a shadow, heading across the ceiling toward the door. Lady Vashmarna shrank back against Nind's arm, but the thing dodged aside with an oily change of direction—and not just direction, but of aspect, as though it built itself a new front that would take it aside, down the wall, in among the clutter, where it was so effectively camouflaged it disappeared.

Lady Vashmarna shuddered. "Are these the old man's? Did someone kill him because of these?"

She felt Nind shrug. "*Jinnu*, I have seen more and can guess at less than you."

"More . . . in there?"

"If they didn't stop us, *jin'*, they won't stir themselves for you, and it isn't haunts that shot the scholar. And no one," he added, apparently sensing his reassurance was inadequate, "is going to shoot you while I'm at hand."

Oh, to have his kind of careless courage! What would Moth do here among the haunts? Speak with them? Order them? *Play* with them? Lady Vashmarna shuddered again, and knew with painful clarity that it was pride, not courage, that moved her into the room. She would not be shamed before Nind. She would not be less than her daughter, especially given who and what her daughter was. But it was true that as she took one step and another, the haunts, the manifests, paid her no mind as they slid in their meaningless patterns about the vast manufactory room.

The new cable had a barnlike room to itself beyond the hulking machinery of the extruder. Half its length was already insulated and wound on its enormous spool, but the rest lay in loose coils across the scrubbed stone floor, its fat copper weave shining pinkly in the electric glare. There were haunts here, too, the visible aftermath of some act of power, according to Moth. As Lady Vashmarna accustomed herself to their restlessness and eerie silence, she began to ask herself, What act, and whose? Had Istvan—Istvan of the shadow cult—been raising demons, and been stopped by one of her own men?

Nind swore it was not so. "For *jin'*, if I killed him, why would I trouble to lie? Why would any of us? Stop a sorcerer raising demons in the fort—*jinnu*, it's what we're for! No, someone else stopped him, but who or why . . ."

"We don't know the demons—the haunts—are his," Lady Vashmarna said. She had trusted Istvan to hold to their agreement and was in no hurry to be proven wrong. "It is just as likely that he stumbled on a saboteur and was shot for his pains."

"He was cult, and he never loved us."

"He needed us."

Nind shrugged. "We needed him, and well he knew it."

"And well he meant to profit from it!" Lady Vashmarna said in a tone meant to stop all argument.

"Aye, well," Nind sighed. "*Jin'*, there's more you haven't seen."

"Tell us," the shaudah said.

"A man dead," Lady Vashmarna said baldly, "the cable spoiled, and a whole line of doors broken through every bar rier between the outer wall and the manufactory where the cable was made."

"Cracks from the earthquake," Lord Ghar said, for he, too, was present at the morning audience.

Inevitably present, thought Lady Vashmarna, who could not remember when she had last spoken privately with the shaudah.

"Doors," she said to the shaudah, with a certain Society all too present in her mind. "As your own men will attest."

His men, who had left the gate at the worst possible moment, far too late to do any good and nicely in time to see too much. But had they seen anything earlier in the night, before the earthquake, before that ragged portal had been carved or broken in the outer wall? No, then they had been incurious and blind. Of course Lady Vashmarna did not ask the shaudah what his men were there for. Clearly they were not there to protect her demesne.

"Can we take it, *jinnu,* that these . . . openings . . . were not achieved through the use of chisel or saw?" asked the shaudah.

"*Janaras,*" said Lady Vashmarna, "I think we must take it so. They are too clean, and were cut too silently. No one in the fort heard a thing. Except that we were checking for earthquake damage, I am not even certain they would have been noticed before morning."

"And your demesne infested with haunts, or so I am told."

"As your men have seen, *janaras.*"

"So," said Lord Ghar, portentous and grim, "Vashmarna has at last fallen under the shadow of our enemies. This is only the latest of the blows aimed at us from the tidal, more insidious than the damage to the bridge and more dramatic, perhaps, than the plague, but hardly more bitter than either if the new cable is ruined beyond repair. How can we hope for a timely return to the towers now? How can we even hope to be left in peace to make do with what we still have? They hide behind old women and children in the tidal—note I do not say 'innocents.' I doubt there are any left by now. Our men cannot winkle them out, and now it seems we cannot defend against them. How is it they have so much power, and we are powerless? *Janaras,* where is our power?"

The court was shocked into silence by the despair in Lord Ghar's voice. Lady Vashmarna was herself shocked at the old man's perfidy. With Istvan Soos the only human victim of the attack, she was certain—nearly certain—the cult was not to blame. Not that she would have gambled on their innocence, but she remembered the accusations the tidal scholar had made against the Ghar. She remembered the hitch in the Ghar's stride when the two men had passed outside her door, and then those doors . . . Those doors.

"Father," said *aras* Baradam into the silence. "Never say we are powerless while the gods hold us in their hands."

"Do you speak of *our* gods," said his father, uncomforted and as bitter as before, "or of *theirs*?"

Which, Lady Vashmarna saw, shocked even the shaudah. She herself was only curious to know what scheme the Ghar was pursuing now. She said, "I am in no hurry to make grand claims for the shadow cult's gods, *jandas,* but I do protest against the laxness of the guard on my gate. *Janaras,* whoever breached our wall did so in full sight of the gate where your soldiers were posted—"

"Did your men see who brought down the bridge?" *aras* Baradam interrupted with an odd note of spite in his voice. "They were standing on top of it when it fell. What did they see through the dark and the rain? The same as the shaudah's soldiers saw that night, the same you yourself saw: the shadow cult's demons. And no, *jandas,*" he added to his father, "I do not and will not call them gods. *Our* gods hold the making and unmaking of worlds in their hands."

"And what do their priests hold?" said the Ghar. "Incense

and books. If our gods are omnipotent, why are our priests, their vicars, helpless in the face of this blasphemous attack?"

"Because," said the *aras,* "when we escaped from the *ramhadras* we laid down our arms. If we are powerless, it is by our ancestors' choice, not by the weakness of our gods."

The Ghar looked at his son, puzzlement replacing pain on his seamed black face, and said as if he were thinking aloud, "Then can we not retrieve those arms when we are in such need today?"

"We cannot," said the *aras* with mournful and obdurate pride. "We are forbidden by laws as old as our tenancy on this world."

"There are laws older yet," murmured Lord Ghar, and Lady Vashmarna's lips parted on a silent *Aaahhh.* There it was, the conclusion of this little drama staged by the Society of Doors. She was sure of it, and saw all the confirmation she needed in the inward gazes and thoughtful frowns of the courtiers. The Ghar, abetted by his son, had just given them the first tenuous offer of hope from the treasure houses of the past, and there was no one in the audience room who looked ready to reject it out of hand. Even Lady Vashmarna felt that temptation, or at least understood it, if understanding was distinct from sharing; she was not certain it was. So the shaudah, when he spoke, sounded like a lonely voice speaking against a silent crowd.

He said, "The only law today is mine."

"And nothing more will we get from him," said the Ghar later over tea. "He holds the law, yes, and uses it to pry apart our demesnes until there is nothing left but a rubble he can claim for his own."

"We" said the Ghar. Lady Vashmarna found his tea as bitter as her thoughts and set her cup aside. Why was she here?

Had Lord Ghar believed her when she had agreed before the court that the shadow cult was to blame for Vashmarna's broken walls? He could not, not when he had himself seen Istvan Soos enter her study. Was that not half the purpose of the attack, to stop Istvan's mouth? Yet the other had been to spoil the new cable for the bay, and what sense was there to that if the Ghar, the lord of the bay, were the culprit? Perhaps the cable had after all been an accident, ruined by the sorcery that had breached Vashmarna's walls. Or perhaps the cult had struck out at Istvan, thinking him a traitor—Lady Vashmarna had to admit it was possible, despite Istvan's own assurances. Or then again, perhaps . . .

Perhaps the Ghar was losing interest in this world. Perhaps, with the towers frozen by lack of power, the *ramhadras* had come to seem like the nearer realm, the better choice. And did that answer her question? Was she here so that she, lady of a spoiled demesne, could be offered the better choice as well? Was she here because they were, in spite of everything, still equals, still friends?

Lady Vashmarna folded her hands in her lap and said, "What are we to do?"

"Do you ask me, *jin*'?" Lord Ghar pinched his nose in a rare gesture of fatigue. "We are to quell the tidal, restore the towers, give the shaudah everything that was his and everything that was ours. We are to restore the past. We are to re-create heaven in this world. Do you ask me what we are to do?"

Lady Vashmarna let this subside into a new silence before she said softly, "Do you envy your son, who answers only to distant gods?"

"The gods, the scholars, the doubting and fearful pious. No, I do not envy him. I need him; I cannot have him. Envy does not enter into it."

"Your heir."

"My . . . Ah, well. My priest, my son." The Ghar turned his

inward gaze outward once more. "We are both without heirs, Vashmarna-*jin'*. Why should we struggle to build and keep our demesnes when they will only evaporate into nothing when we are gone?"

"Because I am not Vashmarna. There is no Vashmarna without the hundreds who bear my name as well as theirs, my workers, my farmers, my engineers. They will not evaporate when I am gone. They are my heirs. The thousands who depend on the power we produce are my heirs. The *shadras* is my heir."

"Thus speaks a woman who has no children."

Lady Vashmarna felt a pure flash of rage at this, too sudden and too powerful to be entirely hidden. Lord Ghar gave her a sitting bow.

"I beg your pardon, *jinnu*. A thousand times I beg your pardon. If you only knew the admiration I feel for you, who has such a wealth of disinterested loyalty to give to us all. Even in the tidal, I know, you have reached out to the benighted. I should be asking you. What *are* we to do? We have proven— they have proven to us once and again—that we cannot fight them nor defend against them with our empty hands. Can we deal with them? Can we convince them that to pull us into the mud with them will not raise them a hand's breadth out of the mire? Is there anyone among them who is not so mad with heresy they cannot listen to reason?"

"Is heresy madness?" said Lady Vashmarna. Unwisely, she knew, but she was still quivering with a half-understood anger. "What of your own?"

He looked at her with bright eyes in a still face. "What do you mean, Vashmarna-*jin'*?"

"Today, your argument with your son in the shaudah's presence. Questioning the gods and the laws. Would you call that piety?"

"I call that desperation," he said, still watching her closely.

"But I regret offending *your* piety, which I know to be deep and strong. Still," he added with a rueful smile, "perhaps you will lend me a little of that tolerance you bestow on your benighted heirs."

Lady Vashmarna composed herself. She would have liked a sip of tea—her mouth was dry, and she could have used time—but her shaking hand would have betrayed her. "Ghar-*jan'*, I do not know what you mean. Do you think I tolerate the shadow cult, who have done us all such grievous harm? Or to whom do you refer?"

"Not the shadow cult, of course, *jin'*. I see I have been unforgivably clumsy today. I hope, nevertheless, you find it in yourself to forgive me, for I only meant your generous care for the innocents of the tidal. The question that troubles me deeply after this attack on Vashmarna is, How can we continue to protect those innocents and still hope to be effective against the cult? Can we continue—do we dare continue—as we have done in the tidal, protecting the docks and the routes to the stairs and leaving the rest to its own devices? Or is it time to take sterner measures? Or is it, gods help us, too late? Vashmarna-*jin'*, what are your views?"

A coldness settled into Lady Vashmarna's soul. The Ghar had indeed invited her here to sound her out, but he did not want to know if she would join the Society's exodus, the Society's cause. He only wanted to know how entrenched she was in the tidal, how strong her position was, if there were anyone or anything she would risk exposure to defend.

He only wanted to know how potent, and how aware, an enemy she was.

The internal chill quieted her trembling. She drank from her cooling tea and said calmly, "Whatever measures we take will depend first on the extent of our resources, will they not, Ghar-*jan'*? Have your policemen's numbers recovered from our last accounting?"

The Ghar gave her a measured look, but he allowed the conversation to turn to practical matters, the disposition and supply of their men. He preferred not to speak of the plague that continued to spread through the ranks of his policemen, which required a certain amount of tactful equivocation, and they were deep in negotiations when Baradam Ghar burst in unannounced.

"I have arrested Sirijin Naresh," he said to his father. His chin was high and his eyes were blazing, making it an unmistakable challenge, and he barely acknowledged Lady Vashmarna with a glance.

His father, in a response Lady Vashmarna had witnessed before, said aridly, "Who?"

"A blasphemer out of the tidal," *aras* Baradam said impatiently. "He has the temerity to call himself a scholar—a self-taught scholar from the slums!—and he has dared, now of all times, to demand an audience with me in which he presented claims of former occupation of the *rasnan*. It is a clear case of heresy—"

"Or lunacy. Or at the least, bad scholarship."

"—so of course I had him arrested."

"Of course." There was something faintly mocking about the acknowledgment.

Aras Baradam swung himself about and began to pace, his thick black braid twitching like a cat's tail.

"The man's scholarship is beside the point, Father, surely you can see that. He is a heretic. We have been grappling with the shadow cult for more than a hundred days without effect; it would be madness to let this man slip through our hands. We must have a show of competence, of strength. At least the temple can prove it still stands on the same solid ground where it has always stood. And in the meantime we can win some answers. This man is not wholly a lunatic. He has clearly had access to books of significant scholarship. Those books could well provide a trail that would lead us straight to—"

"The shadow cult," Lord Ghar interrupted in urgent tones of revelation.

"—the shadow cult!" *aras* Baradam finished triumphantly, then paused to give his father a puzzled look. He blinked, and looked at Lady Vashmarna, and bowed. "I beg your pardon, *jinnu*. I am too full of my own concerns. I have been rude."

"Concerns we all share, *aras*." Lady Vashmarna put her empty cup aside and rose. "You only remind me that I have business of my own to take in hand." She took her leave.

And took with her two thoughts. The first was senseless and unworthy, but inescapable: the Ghar had not deemed her worthy to return to the *ramhadras;* she had been condemned along with her daughter, whether he knew it or not, and it galled more than she was willing to admit even to herself. The second was that the shadow cult, provoked by Istvan's death and the shaudah's blame, and now by this arrest, was not likely to take kindly to a renewed assault on the tidal by Vashmarna and Ghar.

No, they were not going to take it kindly at all.

THE HADARAS

Moth sat with Aramis in the stifling room—the cabin—they had given her. It was lightless, airless, too low for her to stand erect, but a room to herself nonetheless, as her false rank as priest required. She had retreated with him here, all but taking him prisoner before he said anything else unpredictable and irrevocable to the engineers. She was so torn between gratitude and dismay at his intervention that she had found nothing to say to either. The simplest, easiest, most honest thing she could think of to do was make love to him, but it had not been simple or easy. She had always had to coax him to respond, and this time the effort, the gulf of time between her laying hands on him and his laying hands on her, had all but broken her heart, killing whatever desire she might have started with. But he had responded. He had released her hair from its priestly braid and filled his hands with its silken weight; he had brushed her face with kisses like vanishing sea foam and the falling rain. It *was* love, she thought then, and wondered how anyone survived the discovery that love is not forgiveness, is not redemption, is only what it is, as uncertain and unearned as life itself.

Oh, Aramis, Aramis, Aramis.

And now they sat, his back to the wooden bulkhead, her back against his chest, with her hair clinging to his skin and hers, and the bamboo mat on the bunk prickling their naked thighs. A lantern dangling in a wicker cage filled the cabin with a light too dull to read by, a dancing glow that only gathered the wooden walls closer in. And that was all: the light, the bunk, their scattered and ragged clothes, and them.

"Two *shadri* in the *hadaras*," Moth said. Did they have anything else in common anymore? Anything but their many lies?

"Two *shadri* in the *hadaras*," Aramis echoed, as if his thoughts had been lying as close as his body was to hers.

She touched the hand that covered her navel. A large hand, strong and smooth-skinned, dark enough to make the fingernails look pink. She fitted her hand to its shape, her fingers lying between his. "You haven't told me about your journey here."

"I followed a frog."

"What?" Moth craned her head back against his shoulder, trying to see his face. "You what?"

"A mad little frog a long way from home." He sighed. "You've forgotten. That night in the temple? Your frog with a tale?"

She had forgotten, but it came back to her: the incense, the dust, the hollow-backed gods. "Never trust a frog. They give all your secrets away."

"It's true." His free hand was gathering up her hair, pulling the sweaty strands from his throat and arms. "It wasn't so different from any of the other trips to the *hadaras* I've made on Vashmarna business. There are a lot of people on the roads, the inns are full. Did you know? There are whole villages that have been washed away by flooding and landslides, and more where people are starving because grain has rotted in the stores. None of the *hadri* care what's happening in the *shadras,* except when the priests tell them the rain is a punishment for the sins of the godless *shadri.*"

"Country priests," Moth said with a shrug.

"*Shadras* priests sent into the *hadaras* when the br—when the towers were emptied. They're full of gossip about cults and demons and . . ." He trailed off. There was no clear path through the mud that surrounded them. Moth rocked forward, and after a moment he took the hint and pulled her hair from between their bodies. She gathered it into three hanks and began to braid.

"Most of those people have never even seen the towers," she said. "You can't expect them to care."

"You've seen the towers all your life, and you don't care."

"I've seen them from the shore all my life. You know I've never set foot across the bridge."

"I knew," he said slowly. "I thought . . . You were always so involved, consumed, with the scholarium and the fort. With your studies. With . . ."

"You."

He ran his hands up her arms, and then, as if it were a new idea he wasn't sure how to express, he folded his arms around her shoulders in a tentative embrace. "Nothing stopped you from going over."

"Nothing. No. Nothing but my sponsor's orders, nothing but the temple's disapproval, nothing but the bluecoats who'll evict anyone not wearing shoes." She caught the bitter words between her teeth, dropped the finished braid to fall across her breast. "Nothing but the knowledge that when I did go there, it would be to stay."

"You want to live there?" Aramis's voice was high with surprise.

"Doesn't everyone?"

"You're always so angry about the tidal and the bay. I thought . . . Maybe I didn't think."

"I'm not angry because I think people shouldn't live the way they do there. I'm angry because *some* people live there in full view of the rest of us mucking around in the shitty dark. Of course I want to live there! Most of us do, and all of us know we can't, and some of us think that if we can't all live in shining white towers with clean water all around, then we should all be drowning together in the mud."

"Shining white towers." Aramis absently took the braid that dangled against his hand and began unweaving the strands. "They're not like that inside, you know, not for most of us. My family's apartment in Sidirand had a front room with a window looking out on Pennimissirand's base and three dark rooms buried behind it in the guts of the building. One of the bedrooms had no ventilation; our bathtub was in the kitchen—"

"You had your own bath?" Moth said wistfully. "You washed in fresh water?"

"You're making fun of me."

"We had to swim off the docks to get clean."

"Well," Aramis said after a moment, "we did that too, for fun."

And Moth had to concede that it had been fun, sometimes, splashing in the sun-jeweled waves at high tide. It came over her then, that memory, with its reminder that however grim a tidal childhood could be, it had never been unremittingly bad. She and Silk had played like fishes in the water. She and Silk had played in other ways, learning some of the pleasures a wet naked body could give—could, much to their mutual surprise, actually give away for free, with no money passing to either hand. Of course, she and Silk had also carried knives even when they left their clothes on the dock, to keep the boys at bay.

The thought of Silk, no doubt deep in scheming with Hamana even as she and Aramis lay here, made her restless. She untangled her hair from Aramis's fingers and began her braid again. "Tell me more. Tell me about the elevators."

"The . . ." Aramis caught what sounded like a stillborn laugh in his chest. "The elevators. They're like man-size cages that travel up and down in a shaft pulled by winches—"

"I know what they are! But is it true they're made of brass and gold?"

"Well . . . iron in the cage, and brass detailing in some of the passenger cars. There's only gold in the penthouse elevators, gold and quartz and frosted glass. Those are the ones the high and mighty use, like the shaudah and the Prethelmens."

"And the Vashmarnas and the Ghars."

"Them, too," he softly agreed.

"And the bridges between them are all glass."

"They have windows."

"And the towers all have windows in the ceilings and gardens growing under glass."

"Pleasure gardens. Those are for the penthouse folk, though. People like me need an invitation."

"Have you ever been?"

"Once, when the Vashmarna's father died. I was a new-made journeyman, and all the journeymen and masters were invited to witness her accession. There was a blessing ceremony in the temple, and a swearing-in ceremony in Magarand, and then a celebration in the gardens of Shaudarand. It was just gone dusk when we got up there, and there were lights shining in the trees—"

"Trees."

"Small ones, but real trees growing in pots with their branches all strung with lights, and great troughs spilling over with flowers and ferns, and lines of bamboo making corridors and rooms. There were vines growing across the windows, too, so you could only see the ocean through the leaves and blossoms and fruit. And there were laceflies with the lights showing the patterns in their wings and ruby-throated lizards hunting the flies and blue-eyed temple cats hunting the lizards and stealing food off the trays. And there was rice wine in porcelain cups so thin you could see the shadow of your hand through the bottom, and windows open so the breeze came right through the room, and the most beautiful girl in the world playing the flute on a platform high up under the dome. . . ."

In Vashmarna's gardens at the top of Shaudarand, where for all her life Moth had been forbidden to go. After a long silence, Aramis gently took her braid out of her hands and began to unweave the strands.

"I'll take you there," he said. "As soon as there's power again."

"Like you would have taken me to the *ramhadras*?" she whispered.

"Where else can we go?"

"Anywhere. Everywhere. Away."

"Where is away? There's nothing out there but sea."

"You don't know that. Nobody knows that. That's like wearing a sack over your head and then saying, 'Just because no one's ever seen the sun, it doesn't exist.' "

"Boats have gone out . . ."

Like the *Eelgrass*. Moth had forgotten. Reminded, she relived Sharking's harrowed face and his pious gratitude for finding the *rasnan* again, and she said, as much to that memory as to Aramis, "As far as they could travel, dependent on the wind and their stores. A ship with an engine, a ship large enough to support gardens and stills, a ship that can go for months rather than days . . ."

"A ship powered by what fuel? You can drive a turbine with steam, but you can't boil water with seaweed and fish bones."

"You can turn a propeller with the power of the *mundab*. You can travel to the ends of the world on the power of the *mundab*. That's what the engine is, and that's what the engine is for."

"And the ship," Aramis said slowly, "this ship. It's to go out in search of new land."

"You need to ask? What else did you think it was for? I *told* you that was what it was for!"

"I wasn't asking," he said. "I was just starting to believe. But where do you think you're going? What is this new land you're looking for going to be like? How are people going to live?"

"Like they do here," Moth said, "only better."

"I see. So they're all going to live in shining towers and no one is going to work in the fields."

"Don't be patronizing." Moth pulled away from him, skin peeling away from sweaty skin. "I sometimes wonder how you ever came to be an engineer. Don't you want to free Vashmarna from the temple's dictates? Don't you want to make all those tools and machines you are forbidden to make that would let people work the fields with something more than mud between their ears? Don't you think we can do better than we have?"

He looked into her eyes, his own gold-rimmed pupils shifting from side to side as he tried to find his way into her thoughts, and then he looked away for a longer moment yet. "Yes," he finally said, "I want those things. But I think that if we want to do better than we have done up till now, we'll need more than new machines. More than a new land. We'll need new people, too."

"It's no different for us than for the Society and their door to the *ramhadras*."

"I know." Aramis lifted his gaze to her face and then away again. "I thought we were the better people. That's what we all believed. What they believe. Don't hate them, Moth. They don't know what the Ghars have done."

"The bluecoats don't know what orders they were given? The baysiders don't know the tidal's just on the other side of the bridge? Give the *mundabi* some credit, Aramis. At least we always knew just how dirty our hands were when we did what we needed to do."

He nodded without looking at her. Swallowed, and nodded again. And then he looked up at her, a dark look that challenged with its weight of honesty. "I'll give you that, Moth. I'll say you're right. I'll admit I was wrong. But what will you give me? Will you give me anything, or do I have to make all the concessions and confess all the wrongs?"

"I have confessed," she said, stricken. "I have. You know . . . You know so much." Her voice fell to a whisper. "You know too much."

He nodded again, taking in a breath, looking away. "So that's all I get. A few of your secrets exposed."

Moth was silent for a long time. The lantern's wick, in need of trimming, trembled with a sound like her namesake's wings and cast nebulous shadows about the room. Eventually she pulled her hair back and twisted it into a knot at the nape of her neck, defying her own hurt to bare her face, her vulnerable neck and naked breasts.

"I'll give you love," she said. "I'll give you a child. That's all I have, Aramis, and I'll give it all to you. But it's all I've ever had to give, and if it hasn't been enough until now, I don't see why it should satisfy you today. Or tomorrow. Or however long we have."

His breath made a harsh sound in his throat. "That isn't . . . Moth." His face was creased with pain. "Moth."

"Well, I don't know—" She made a helpless gesture and the strength went out of her voice. "I don't know what else—"

For once, it was Aramis who put his hands on her. He gathered her up, wrapped her in the cradle of his arms and legs, pressed his face into her throat. "Just tell me you'll take me with you when you go."

"I did," she whispered. "I already did."

But then, thinking back, she realized that she hadn't, quite.

After the emotional trials of the day, the night began quietly enough. Moth, sitting a prudent distance from Aramis's side, let the engineers talk as she bit her chapped lips and watched a ghostly manifest ease like a visible draft between the window frame and the paper screen.

They held their conference on the chief engineer's barge, less a decision than an assumption on the engineers' part, and a silent acquiescence on Moth's. She was not sorry to be out from under Silk and Hamana's sullen observation, and she was curious about how the exiled engineers lived so far from the towers and the fort. Better than the *hadri,* of course, but even, oddly, better than Lady Vashmarna in her fort offices. Painted screens and fine fabrics and polished wood made Hemmar Gamood's converted barge into as pleasant a room as Moth had ever seen, a golden-brown treasure box bejeweled by the light of many lamps, and as she listened with half an ear to Gamood giving Aramis his report (no one, not even Aramis, tried too hard to maintain the fiction of Moth's importance), she was wondering if her new status as a Vashmarna expert would let her acquire such a room of her own. A private room, where she and Aramis . . . Not that they'd had much trouble on the ship . . . The manifest passing across the screen rippled the painted mountain like the heat of a summer afternoon and then, like a fish that changes direction with the flick of a fin, moved on to wind a pattern around the lamps hanging from the gleaming roof beams. No one but Moth seemed to notice. Gamood was complaining about the changes to the ship's design.

". . . and even the access ports to the masts have been built over."

"Oh," said an innocent Moth, "is that what those gaps in the decking were?"

Gamood's dark face grew a few more seams. "Of course we planned to emplace ladders," he said, his emphasis on "planned" making it clear where he thought the blame should be laid: not with him.

"I see," Moth said wisely. "Ladders where the gaps are, and stairs where the ladders . . . ah . . . where the ladders and the other gaps are."

"The 'gaps,' as I said, are access ports for the inspection and maintenance of the masts—"

"Do you know," said Moth, "I've never quite understood why the ship needs masts at all."

"For the sails," said one of the other engineers with cloying patience. "The wind blows on the sails, the ship moves through the water . . ."

An undercurrent of amusement, not quite audible, moved around the table, much like the manifest still twined about the lamps. Another manifest was oozing around the screen like sauce around the lid of a pot, a jellyfish that borrowed the colors and textures of the bamboo frame. Still no one noticed but Moth, who let a smile crimp the side of her mouth.

"Yes, sails are very nice, I'm sure. But did you forget about the engine? Engines are nice, too, and you've left such a lovely big space for it at the back of the ship that I wondered if the masts were perhaps an accidental addition. A very big, heavy, expensive, time-consuming addition. Or rather, *three* very big, heavy, time-consuming additions."

"Redundant systems—" began one of the engineers—not the patient one, who was sulking at Moth's tone—but Hemmar Gamood overrode him.

"Engine! What engine? Speaking as Vashmarna's assistant chief engineer, I know, as I have always known, the disposition of *all* Vashmarna's engineers, here and in the *shadras*, and I can tell you that no one—no one!—is now nor has ever been assigned to design or build such an engine. So of whose engine do you speak, *rasnu*? The gods'?"

"Mine," Moth said mildly. "I speak of my engine, *andas*, and so yes, in a sense, you may also speak of it as the gods' if you choose."

Gamood rubbed his hand across his face, massaging the loose skin on his jaw and hiding his expression. "You will forgive me, *rasnu*, if I'd rather rely on wind than a prayer."

"Yes, well, thank you, *andas*, for your views. I myself would prefer to rely on an engine rather than the wind, since it is the only thing that makes a very long journey feasible. And it would be even more feasible—and please, *andas*, please do correct me if my mathematics are at fault—but it does seem to me that a long journey would be even more feasible if the ship was not weighed down, and the holds were not filled up, by masts and sails that we do not need."

"Where is this engine, then?"

"Waiting for you to finish the ship!"

"And is that not what you are here to help us do?"

Moth caught her first response between her teeth—and caught, too, a sidelong look from Aramis. She folded her hands carefully on the table before her. "Yes. And now that I have, at last and with great difficulty, convinced the *hadri* on board to cooperate, we should be discussing our priorities. I gather the propeller is actually in place? But there is, I think, the matter of the wiring?"

"I think," said Hemmar Gamood, deliberately mimicking her pose, "there is also the matter of what the *rasnu* has been doing on board the ship at night. There is the matter of changes effected without consultation. And there is the matter—or does the *rasnu* think we are all blind and deaf?—of the spirits, or worse, that have been haunting the inlet since the *rasnu* arrived."

"By no means," said Moth with a laugh trembling at the edge of her voice, "by no means do I think you are blind," while the manifests shifted like folding ghosts across the ceiling and the engineers sat scowling and unaware.

"Or ignorant, perhaps, of the recent events in the tidal? Tapurnashen-*andas,*" Gamood added with a snide look at Aramis, "is not our only source of news from the *shadras.*"

"As Vashmarna demesne is not *my* only source," Moth said, and then shifted abruptly in her chair: she had just realized how much like her mother she sounded. She changed her tone. "Look, *andas,* I have no doubt that you've heard news of recent events, not to mention a whole lot of gossip, rumor, and speculation. We could sit here for the rest of the night trying to untangle all the threads—but it's not going to get us any closer to finishing the ship and giving the *rasnan,* and Vashmarna, the hope of progress we so desperately need."

"But I'm not asking you about the *shadras.* I'm asking you about *shadri* ghosts right here in the inlet. I'm asking you about *hadri* cults and unauthorized construction on the very ship you say we have to finish!"

Well, there was clearly no dodging this. What a pity Tarun could not be here for this! Moth mustered her half-truths and outright lies, and then, practiced liar that she was, she dropped all persuasiveness from her manner. *I don't care if you believe me,* she said with her flat tone and impatient mien. *I tell the truth only because it is true.*

She said, "As for the ship *hadri,* I will say nothing beyond the fact that their presence predates my arrival. I work with what there is to hand. As to changes to the ship's design, I can only direct you to ask the *hadri* who are responsible—though I will say this, that if they have been making it easier to live on board, then it's quite possible that they have been improving a faulty design, considering the length of voyages we are antici- pating for the eventual crew. And as for the 'ghosts,' which are utterly harmless, I will tell you plainly that they are no more than the spirits of this place made momentarily incarnate by the work I do here to draw the blessing and the power of the divine into the fabric of the ship itself."

There was a silence about the table, the kind of silence that could happen only in the *hadaras,* full of wind clattering the bamboo chimes under the eaves, the chuckle of water under the hull, the *thunk* of the barge tugging on its mooring chains, but empty of any more human noise than that. So Moth thought, and then it occurred to her to wonder, in that part of her mind that held itself aloof from her lies, what the silence would be like without chimes, without hull, without the an- chor chain. A truly inhuman silence. The silence of the *mundab.* A silence no one would ever hear.

"Forgive me, *rasnu,*" said an engineer who had not spoken to her before. "I don't understand what that means." And an- other said, so swiftly he must have had the thought before the first response, "That sounds like heresy."

To which Hemmar Gamood said, "That sounds like more trouble than Vashmarna can afford."

"More trouble than a ship and an engine?" Moth said sharply. "We're already far beyond the bounds of permitted technology, *andasi,* already treading on forbidden ground. I assure you, neither the temple nor the shaudah will make the slightest distinction between a trespass beyond the limits of your permitted territory and a trespass beyond the borders of mine."

Hemmar Gamood absorbed this in silence, while the first engineer said again, and more urgently, "Yes, but what does it *mean*?"

"It means a ship strong enough to carry a crew into the farthest reaches of the *mundab*." Moth felt the resonance of the double meaning in her bones, and some of it must have reached her voice, for the silence deepened, shaded by thought. "It means a ship that does not have to fear spirits of the ocean untamed by the *rasnan*'s shores. It means a ship that can ride out the *mundab*'s storms. It means a ship that will know and keep safe its own anointed crew. It means a ship blessed by the gods' own divine hands."

And did it really mean any of those things? Moth wondered. She drew, by the most delicate of touches, the *mundab* closer to the ship, or the ship closer to the *mundab,* with some ill-defined notion of transforming this clumsy, too-human vessel into a cradle for the living engine, a body for the *mundab*'s beating heart. But what, as the engineer said, did that *mean*? What would it mean for the ship's human crew? If the *mundab* were truly what Mahogan had claimed—the spirit of the world, soul, if not consciousness, of sea and sky and land—then what would a ship infused with that spirit need with a human crew? How, in point of fact, was a human crew to sail a living ship? Moth was presented with a rare and uncomfortable glimpse of her own ignorance, vast as the sea, threatening to engulf the tiny crumb of understanding she balanced upon—and again she had to wonder (each time more forcefully, as though realization were a rising tide that sent wave after wave against her shore) how much of what she did was driven not by her own needs, ambitions, desires, but by the *mundab*'s.

But it's too late, she thought, trying to counter her quickening pulse. Too late to change direction, far too late to stop.

And it is—it is—isn't it?—still better than any of the alternatives.

"These are temple matters," Aramis said into the lengthening pause. "The *rasnu* acts with the Vashmarna's blessing, and blesses our endeavor with her actions. Our concern must be with the earliest completion of the Vashmarna's design."

"Easily said," said Hemmar Gamood, "if we accept the orders you carry."

"If?" Aramis said with a degree of stern authority that seemed to surprise no one but Moth.

"Not so easily done," the chief engineer forged on, "without a complete survey of what damage the *hadri* have inflicted on our previous work. And for that—Chessuriman, I think you had an itemized report . . ."

Papers were shuffled, throats were cleared; it looked as though the engineers might actually be about to get down to work, in their own fussy and methodical fashion. Aramis even uncapped an inkwell and smoothed the tip of a brush between his fingers, ready to take notes, and as if this were a signal to some part of Moth her mind could not reach, her heart closed like a fist, skipping one beat and then two, opening an extraordinary hollow in her chest and prompting a quiver in her womb where the tiny fish-child thrashed in protest.

Which was when the screen clattered to the floor, thrust aside by a more substantial manifest shaped a little like a sea urchin, a little like a jumble of ropes and spars. Men leapt up with cries of fear and disgust, scattering from the table, everyone except for Moth, and except for Aramis, who was watching Moth. Moth was watching the manifest roll weightlessly across the wall, sending the engineers scurrying from one end of the room to the other. They ducked as someone noticed the ghostly shape of air drifting by the ceiling and tried to find an unoccupied corner, a comedy of panic that would have had Moth laughing in other circumstances, but she was too busy querying the *mundab*. What? What is this? What do you want? She touched that limitless, troubled flow, and it was then that the ship began to scream.

Everyone froze. A dying god might sound like this, or the end of the world. The shrieking agony of iron and wood echoed up and down the nighttime inlet until it seemed that unseen monsters bellowed from the cliffs, imagined creatures the size of buildings that clung to the quartz with their black claws and teeth and spiny tails, the dreadful children birthed from a broken vessel. Broken, breaking, the ship screamed aloud.

"Hamana," Moth said as she rose from the table at last. "You little shit."

No one but Aramis could have heard.

The night was dark after the lighted room, dark after the rain. A blustering wind, warm and soft with mist, rolled up the inlet from the open sea. Moth could hear nothing but the wailing ship, but she could feel Gamood's barge tug at its anchors, restless with wind and tide. The ship rose above his barge's deck like another cliff, black and ill-defined against the streaming clouds. Glints of momentary stars touched its viny masts, its naked yards. Its cries were as varied as a human's, drawn out by wind instead of breath but rising and falling as if some sense might be buried within the sound. Moth strained to hear, to understand—then realized that the words she was groping for were the terrified shrieks of the *hadri* trapped on board. Pity moved her as much as anger, and curiosity as much as either of those. What exactly did that tidal skink think she was doing?

"Hamana!" Moth yelled. The ship howled. The cliffs howled back. Moth was almost convinced she could see the monsters there, glimpsed as the clouds tore under the weight of wind and stars.

The gangplanks between the barges and the ship had been heaved overboard. Moth scrambled from deck to deck, ignoring the thump of Aramis's feet behind her, until she reached the low dock slung beneath the ship's stern. As she had hoped, Hamana had left an escape route open: the rope ladder still hung from the ship's rail. Moth scrambled up, swaying and barking her knuckles on the hull, and barely paused at the top when a knife-blade was flourished before her eyes.

"Stand back, gods curse you!" Moth shrieked through the noise. "Do you think these demons are mine?"

"*Rasnu!*" She barely heard the voice, but the knife fell away as she vaulted over the rail. "They said no one—"

She lost the words, but not the sense, and took a moment to slap the knife hand back down as Aramis came into view. Then all three of them had to leap aside as the afterdeck was split open at their feet. A tusk of ice-cold *mundab*-matter reared up and up, arching toward the bow. It gleamed in the starlight as if wet with birth fluids or blood. Even Moth gaped, until the deck grew cold and slick beneath her bare feet and she skipped aside. Aramis grabbed her arm and hauled her back toward the rail.

"What in Prosepurn's name is going on?" he shouted in her ear.

"Hamana!" she shouted back. It was all she had breath for. Hamana and Silk were growing the seeds she had planted in the ship's fabric, trying to force its completion, trying to make it their own. *But it's mine,* she thought with an anger as stubborn and cold as the stuff of the *mundab* beneath her hand. Almost without noticing she had shaken off Aramis and gone to lay herself against that new-made tusk or spine. What did

Hamana think she was making? Or did Hamana even know? She had never been more than a body and a voice in Istvan's needless ceremonies, a novice with no vocation, a land crab tiptoeing in the foam at the edge of the boundless sea. No one, not even Istvan, knew the *mundab* as well as Moth, and Hamana would have been powerless to raise more than a ghost of a manifest if Moth had not already planted her seeds, sending down her taproots into the *mundab*'s reservoir of power. Moth felt her icy anger meet the *mundab*'s chill and poured herself inside.

And still the ship sings. Its voice is loud to human ears, ringing from the glassy cliffs, but to the night, the wind, the star-edged clouds, it is only one more mortal voice among the millions. It is a spark, as the *rasnan* is only an island, and barely that: a grain of sand in the vast encircling sea. The wind sweeps through the heavens, the waves roll from horizon to infinite horizon, the *mundab* pours itself through it all. Pours itself into what? What is this bit of rock, this shell, this moth who tests her wings against the rising gale? What vessel is this?

The ship pulls against her anchors. It is the wind and waves against her hull, but it feels like an animal motion, as if she yearns to be free. Yet if she slipped her chains, she would be dashed against the mountain's rocky foot, for the wind blows straight down the inlet's throat. It would break this shell, silence her voice, drown the bird that batters her ribs with its invisible wings. *Set me free!*

Not yet, says Moth, mistaking that voice for the flutter inside her belly's cave. *It's not time.* But the ship, the bird, cries out—a manifest lifts itself into the wind-ravaged dark, a scrap of cloud, a broken wing—the bird, the *mundab*, cries out, *Yes, now, set me free!* as though the ship were not a trap, a prison, an unbreakable egg, but freedom. Freedom. *Set me free!*

Moth hears the ship's screams and the faint human cries that are nearly drowned by the dreadful noise. She feels the *mundab*'s spirit-bird beating its wings within this eggshell ship, and like another echo, she can feel the delicate flutter of her child.

Mother! says the one, while the other cries *Let me out!* until Moth again confuses the two. "Not yet," she gasps. But she is in the grip of the *mundab*'s demand: the ship, the bird, the buried reality that must be released. The *mundab* thunders through her until her body aches, until it seems she is gestating the child and the ship and the ocean they sail upon.

The ship shudders and more spines erupt, the unholy flowering of the seeds of her exile.

What has she been planting? Did she ever know? The floats and barges jerk at their anchor chains in sympathy with their tormented queen. Moth does not know any longer what changes she wreaks. The ship is merely a channel down which the *mundab* flows, and although she is peripherally aware of another will, another channel for the power, it, too, hardly registers. The current is hers, and soon so are all the open channels, whosesoever they once might have been.

But the bird still beats its wings, frantic as a pounding heart. *Let me out!* And Moth, as the *mundab* recedes and the froglet jumps again in her womb, is bewildered. She is trying. The ship is nearly done. What more can she do?

Stars glitter above the crystal cliffs. One star blooms into a beacon of red, and then another, and then the whole limb of the eastern cliff bursts like a night-blooming vine into flower. The ship sings; the red and gold blossoms drift down. They sink through the *mundab,* and as they fall, they are transformed, blossoms into flames. The ship's echoing cries drown the shouts of alarm from the lesser platforms that clutter her anchorage, but can't drown the smash of a glass bomb bursting on the smithy roof. Some bombs splash harmlessly into the waves, but more hit home. Smash! on the wood decks and wicker roofs of the barges, the workshops and offices and dorms. Crash! on the ship's glossy deck and green-bannered masts. There are racing feet, shouts and screams, the pop of pistols too far off to do harm. There are tongues of flame licking through the gardens, a rigging of smoke twined through the burning shrouds. There is a hard hand on Moth's arm.

"We can't reach them. We have no guns. Do something!"

The balance is all. Moth leans into the *mundab*, away from the gripping hand. "What?"

The hand bruises. The hand shakes her arm. "Wake up, damn you! Do something! Raise the monster that took down the bridge!"

Monsters and manifests, they are only bubbles in the stream.

There are other voices, other hands. There are black shapes against the fire, men scrambling over the rails, women with buckets, and gouts of steam, and more fire flowers floating down.

"How many bottles can they have?"

"Enough."

"*Rasnu!*"

"Who is it?"

"The Society, the shaudah—the gods know."

"You don't, Vashmarna's man? Who was it that brought them here if it wasn't—"

"Do you blame me if they followed me? It was you who showed me the way here, Hamana!"

"*Rasnu!*"

"What's wrong with her?"

"I don't know!"

"She's in a trance."

"She's been cursed!"

"*Rasnu!*"

"Leave her. We don't need her. Aren't we *mundabi*, too?"

"I don't know what she did to the bridge."

"It doesn't matter. Leave her, Silk! We started this. We can finish it ourselves."

The hand lets her go. Another manifest is spoken. It rises, a plea for release, and a pebble is dropped into the stream. One gossamer thread of a current, but it runs counter to the main force of the flow. It lances toward the manifest, stirring ripples that mount into waves, and the manifest bubble bursts, leaving a void. The void is filled by a beak, a talon, the feather of a wing. The burning ship screams. The tiny fish in her womb leaps and wriggles toward escape.

"No!"

"She spoke."

"Moth! Dear gods! Wake up!"

"*Rasnu!*"

The inlet is ablaze. The glassy cliffs reflect the flames, echo the shouts, the shots, the fire's roar. Even the water burns, slicked with spilled oil and drifting wood. Fire climbs the vines on the masts, drops from the wooden yards. Children are bundled below, where they will roast beneath the burning deck or suffocate in the fire-starved air. Freed by Hamana, the *mundab*'s bird springs into the air, a solid ghost of smoke and iron, of leaping flames and glassy stone. It sweeps its wings across the night above the ship, the dead ship as lifeless as a broken shell, and there is a human silence of bewilderment, dread, awe, that cuts through the roar of flames.

"My god!" cries a voice into that silence.

My child! cries Moth into the silence of her mind. She gives herself up to the current, she is the current, she will brook no turbulence now. The child is her child, the god is her god, the ship is entirely hers. The thrown pebble drowns, the cross-current dies: this is what Moth knows. But her eyes are open and she sees what they all see as the glassy fire-winged bird tears itself into three. Three gods perch on the ship's three masts, and the burning yards add their flames to the burning wings, and the burning wings become sails of fire. The wind is against them, but the *mundab* is behind them, and the *mundab* is hers. Though she cannot think, cannot breathe, cannot any longer even see, she knows when the anchor cables are cut, and she knows when the ship, the living, the miraculous, the gods-haunted ship, noses its way through the burning wreckage of the shipyard and slips, utterly contrary to the wind and the tide, out into the open sea.

My ship. Not a word, not a thought, but an absolute claim—*mine*—and the fire-sailed ship answers to the movement of her will.

But there is no answering movement in her womb.

THE BASTION

Boats plied the sparkling waters of the bay. The sun pierced through low swags of cloud to draw a blaze from the white towers. A busy hum filled the air.

Lady Vashmarna, turning away from her office window, felt a queasy sense of dislocation. It was the exodus from the towers again; it was the return to the towers; it was the shaudah's latest folly. The shaudah's final folly, Lady Vashmarna found herself thinking, as distant shouts spiraled up beyond the fort's walls. The shaudah, driven beyond some boundary of sense by the attack on Vashmarna, had declared a quarantine for the plague victims. A sensible procedure in itself, and Lady Vashmarna had found herself nodding in relief through the first part of the shaudah's proclamation. But she, like every other courtier, had fallen still, silenced by shock, as he had explained where the quarantine was to be established. Not in the temple, not in the scholars' hall that already housed so many victims, not even in one of the commandeered buildings in the perennially disease-ridden tidal. No, none of these. It was the towers he gave to the dying—the beautiful, empty, unlivable towers with their waterless pipes and unclimbable stairs, the white spires that stood in the shining bay like monuments to the people's exile.

Like monuments, thought Lady Vashmarna as she left her office, to the people's dead. She ignored the bow of the red-coated guard outside her room. The shaudah's men were everywhere now; Vashmarna had precious few secrets left, but she would preserve them as long as she could. She took a circuitous route through the fort to one of the cramped storerooms near the generating station, a dusty corner the shaudah's men had not, so far, seen fit to guard. *Guard it from what?* she asked herself again, knowing the answer. Guard it from her, the lady of this demesne.

Pedigan Shawm, her mistress of secrets, was already there, along with the mistress of stores, the section chiefs, the chief engineer. *Purdar* Nind, his watchful mind hidden behind mustache and belly, bowed.

"*Jinnu*. We are all here."

Lady Vashmarna closed the heavy door on the station's roar, dulling it to a throb. Cobwebbed shapes—shapes that in another, braver age might have been electric motors and steam engines and counting machines—gathered the dim light into their convolutions, leaving only a dusty pall to fall from the bare ceiling bulbs. Her people's faces looked drawn and old in the gloom. They looked poor, Lady Vashmarna thought. They had that defeated, desperate look. Glancing aside from their dark eyes, she saw that someone had brought paper, brushes, and ink, and had laid them on a shelf ready for use. There was a virtue to clinging to the habits of honest officialdom, but Lady Vashmarna doubted she would be writing any messages or taking any notes. This was not the sort of meeting that required a record.

Lady Vashmarna looked up again and met each pair of eyes in turn.

"So. We have come to this." Should she apologize, take the blame? No, they would decide for themselves where the blame belonged. With the shaudah's men in control of the fort and their own homes given up to the dying, they would surely know. She took a breath. "We have always been a divided people. Before this present crisis it was too easy to overlook the cracks in our society, the barriers and tensions between *shadras* and *hadaras,* between bastion and tidal, bay and tidal, bastion and bay—all those cracks that have become deadly chasms in recent days. We were fortunate, perhaps, that for so long we could say 'rasnan,' the known world, and include everyone, all the pieces of our jigsaw society fitted into a whole. We were fortunate. Or perhaps we were deluded." Eyes glanced away from hers. She smiled faintly. "Forgive me my oratory. I know this is no place for it, but I will come to the point soon enough.

"We have been divided by wealth, education, experience. We have also been divided by faith. The harder the orthodoxy has held on to the ways of the past, the more people have been squeezed through the temple's fingers. I think it is important to remember that, though the shadow cult is the most visible example we have before us now, there have been many other cults, societies, fads to illuminate the inadequacy of the orthodox tradition."

There was a stir of surprise, a soundless protest in the air.

"Oh, yes." Lady Vashmarna's gaze traveled once again across the array of faces. Her people, Vashmarna's own. "Yes, I say inadequacy, and I have given my heart to the temple for half my life. If the temple gives us all we need, would the Lamplighters ever have spun their web throughout the scholarium? Would the shadow cult have taken root in every soul in the tidal? Would the Society of Doors still be active today, more than a century since it was outlawed? No, the temple, like the shaudah, demands absolute adherence to its laws, and, like the shaudah, its laws do not offer absolute justice in return. And therefore, like the shaudah, it invites rebellion." Lady Vashmarna softened her voice, until the *purdar* in the back of the room had to lean forward to hear her next words over the turbines' throb. "Like the shaudah, it invites alternatives."

The silence was deep. Outside, unseen, beyond the fort's walls, the transportation of the sick and dying carried on with its accompaniment of shouted orders, protests, cries. Outside, clouds shifted, casting light and shade across the window screens. Outside, *tirindi* sang their monotonous song. Here there was nothing but the dust, the forbidden dreams, the growl of Vashmarna's power—almost the only power Vashmarna had left.

Almost.

"We are a divided people. Even Vashmarna is divided. Some of you are old enough to remember the Lamplighters, and may well do more than remember. There are Society members within the fort, and perhaps within this room. By the sheer logic of numbers, we must shelter Penalists and Morbidians, and almost certainly shadow cultists as well. Vashmarna must be a jigsaw of faith and doubt, of willingness and anger, of hope and despair, just as the *shadras* is, just as the *rasnan* has been for so very long."

"*Jinnu,*" said Pedigan Shawm, as if she could not contain herself any longer. "*Jinnu,* you cannot doubt our loyalty. Please, you cannot doubt *my* loyalty."

Other voices sounded. Lady Vashmarna waited for silence.

"No," she said finally. "Shawm-*andu,* all of you, I do not doubt your loyalty. If I did I would not have gathered you here today. It is because I have such faith in you that I can dare to speak of faith, of these divisions that lie even between those of us in this room. It is because of your loyalty—No, I misspeak. It is because *we can be loyal,* however our faith speaks to us. We can be loyal to the demesne, and to the *rasnan.* We can be loyal to the future of our people—not of our cult, our society, our shrine—but the future of our world *regardless* of these divisions of experience and belief. Together, we can hold fast to the greater good.

"And that is why I have called you here. It is clear to me, as it must be to all of us, that the shaudah's latest actions can act only as another wedge in the gaps that—"

A knock at the door broke into her speech. She hesitated, angry at her own burst of fear. Everyone froze. The shaudah's men. Who else? The door bumped against her back.

"Forgive me, *jinnuju.*" It was one of the *purdar*'s aides. "*Purdar* Nind said that if there was something urgent . . ."

Purdar Nind pressed forward through the others. "I'm sorry, *jinnu.* I'll go—"

"No." Lady Vashmarna's hands had gone cold; she clasped them together at her waist. "I will hear his report."

The saffron-coated subaltern entered and, after a startled glance at his audience, bowed as best he could in the cramped space.

"Go on, man," said Nind. He gave no indication of either impatience or nerves, and Lady Vashmarna found herself admiring his fortitude.

"*Purdar. Jinnuju.* I'm sorry to intrude, but *aras* Baradam has just ordered the execution of Sirijin Naresh, and I thought, sir, we might need to change the disposition of the men before the news reaches the slums."

"Who is Sirijin Naresh?" asked a bewildered section chief.

"A tidal heretic," said *purdar* Nind.

"A poor mad scholar the *aras* wishes to kill in order to

prove the temple's moral authority," Lady Vashmarna said dryly. "Is the subaltern correct, *purdar*? Will there be trouble in the tidal because of this?"

"*Jin'*, I do not see how there can fail to be."

"Nor do I. What do you suggest?"

"If we are still permitted?"

Lady Vashmarna acknowledged the point. Nind shrugged.

"If the shaudah means to go on with the quarantine, the Ghar's men are going to need reinforcement on the corridor to the docks. Too many of them," Nind added, "will be making the trip out to the towers. The corridor is undermanned as it is."

"Cannot the shaudah's men . . . ?" asked the chief engineer.

"The shaudah's men have their hands full," Nind said dryly.

"Is it as bad as that?" asked the mistress of stores.

"It is not as bad as it will get if the sick are killed before they can reach the docks," said the *purdar*.

A shocked silence followed his words. A silence that was broken by another thump on the door. This time Nind cracked it open, his broad body filling the gap. Nevertheless, Lady Vashmarna could hear what the messenger said. A *purdar* of the shaudah's private guard had come with a squadron to escort Lady Vashmarna to the shaudah's presence.

"There is a ship," the young man said, his voice breaking in wonder. "There is a great ship on the bay!"

The ship. Blessed gods. Lady Vashmarna thought of Aramis, first, whom she had sent to the *hadaras* to bring home the engineers and their badly needed supplies. But she had sent him with orders to abandon the ship—the unfinished ship—not bring it here! Which was when, inevitably, she thought of Moth.

Moth. Is that where she had gone? Had she responded to Lady Vashmarna's dismissal, to her mother's refusal of shelter, by dedicating her talents to the hidden ship? Lady Vashmarna felt strangely, bitterly diminished. Had her corrupt daughter triumphed where she herself had failed? Did she have to bow before a superior virtue that could rise above the wrong she had inflicted when she'd stumbled under the weight of the present and the past? She felt ill, physically ill, bathed in a sweat of shame.

"*Jinnu?*"

Lady Vashmarna had to look up to meet Nind's troubled gaze. "Leave the corridor to the Ghars. Send half our men to the Twelve Saints Shrine—they are to keep it safe at all costs. Make sure they understand: *at all costs*—and recall the rest to the fort."

"Begging your pardon, *jin'*, but—"

"No. This ship is ours. Do you understand me? This ship is ours, and the Twelve Saints Shrine protects its heart. The ship is nothing without it. And, *purdar* . . ."

"*Jinnu?*"

"If I don't return from the shaudah's audience, I want you to turn his men out of the fort. Vashmarna will hold its own. Do you understand me?"

"Yes, *jinnu.*" Nind seemed to be the only one of her people capable of speech.

"Once you have taken the fort, I want it made absolutely clear that if Vashmarna must make a full withdrawal from the tidal, my men *will* be coming through that gate, and they will have full support from the demesne if they meet any opposition in the bastion. I want men with guns in the galleries. I want guards on the stores. I want all the men in the fort given some kind of weapon and put under the authority of at least one trained guard. I want them formed into squads, I want them disciplined and drilled, and I want them ready to defend this fort against any and all attackers. Is that clear?"

"*Jinnuju.*"

"And sirs and ladies, whatever your other allegiances, I want—I *expect*—you all to give Vashmarna your loyalty. The entire *rasnan* may be about to fall to pieces, but Vashmarna will stand. Is *that* clear?"

Yes, *jinnu. Jinnuju.* Yes.

"Gods keep you all."

THE BAY

Like the sun wending its way through the clouds, the *Firebird* crept into the *shadras* bay, towed by an ignominious flotilla of rowboats recruited from fishing villages along the way. Moth was not insensible to the embarrassment, but she was exhausted, her soul scoured by the *mundab* and the *Firebird*'s flaming wings. Those wings were quiescent now, reduced to black rags of vines on the masts and a smoldering flutter within the ship's fire-blackened hull—and a smoldering flutter in Moth's womb.

Oh, little mothlet! What have we done to you? What have we done?

The surviving engineers had been scathing on the subject of sails, for the ship's store had been burned with the workshops and barges, but Moth, driven to panic for her child's sake long after the rest of the crew had relaxed into their survival, their escape, even their burning new god, had let the *Firebird*'s wings burn out, her heart beating as fast as those other wings fluttering in her belly. She could not, would not, explain— could not even summon the wits to exaggerate her fatigue. She had simply said, arbitrary as any priest, "Enough," and let the ship wallow on the sun-jeweled waves. Now, captain of a crippled miracle, she stood alone in the stern, while Hamana and Silk leaned, eager as figureheads, over the bow, watching the *shadras* come slowly into view, and Aramis pulled an oar in a boat at the other end of a creaking hawser as far from Moth as he could physically get.

Which said everything, Moth thought, that Aramis could not bring himself to say.

Oh, little bird, what have we done?

The *shadras* had not changed. The towers were white and shining, the bastion a handsome patchwork inside its wall, the tidal a negligible jumble of green-topped stone between the cliff and the creamy surf. Moth felt too much emotion as the *Firebird* slipped behind its weary rowers into the bay. Pleasure and dismay, the fiery heat of the challenge and the cool, ashy bitterness of defeat, relief and trepidation and pride. But they were only facets arrayed around the core of . . . what? What was it that struck her with such a visceral blow? Recognition. That the *shadras* was there, that it was itself. That it was hers, and yet had a wholly separate existence derived from its physical buildings, the lives of its inhabitants, its future and its past. The *shadras* belonged to her; she belonged to it. She might change the course of its history, change its very face; and yet it was indifferent, separate, whole, and wholly its own.

Moth fell into a sulk. She had come through her trial of fire with fire in her belly, a fiery ruin behind her, the *Firebird* her fire-hardened shell. The *shadras* should have burst into flame at her return, or abased itself with orange-embered ruins. There should have been smoke to darken the sun, coughing sparks and roaring tongues of flame to shout out a greeting. The ordinary peace of the sun-splashed afternoon offended her, not because she was arrogant but because it seemed to her like a lie, a blatant denial of the undeniable approach of doom. Moth did not believe she was the *shadras*'s doom. Moth believed she had been swallowed up by doom, as if it were a towering monster wading through the ocean waves toward her home. Moth believed she returned in doom's dark and smoldering gut, at once eaten and conceived by the end of the known world.

Moth had not slept in a very long time.

The boats towed the *Firebird* past the towers on their reef, close beneath their still-shining windows and gold-capped walls, the ship a charred sacrifice laid at the feet of tall white indifferent gods. They dropped anchors in the shallow water near the remains of the bridge, and the small boats nestled close to the curving hull, their weary crews scrambling up rope ladders, trading places with others waiting by the rail. Moth watched Aramis come aboard. She saw the droop of his shoulders, the way he wiped his filthy shirtsleeve across his face, the gold painted by the sun across his dark face as he frowned at the blisters on his palms. Her heart broke again, like a mended egg that is more glue than shell, and it was an afterthought that noticed how Hamana, striding from the bow, waved him peremptorily away from the rail. And how he, startled at first, and then grim, obeyed.

Walking as though she carried a glass child beneath her skin, Moth met him in the barred shade of the superstructure's bony wing.

"What was that about?"

Aramis, watching the commotion by the ladders, said flatly, "She trusts Vashmarna enough to pull her ship, but not enough to take us with her onto shore. We're to stay here, under guard."

"We?" Moth's heart started up its troubled thumping.

"Vashmarna's men. The engineers." Still without looking at Moth, he added, flippant and hard, "I doubt she'll leave you behind."

"*She* will leave *me*?"

"I said she won't."

"She," Moth said, and then realized she was arguing with the wrong person. She did not want to argue with Aramis at all.

The new crews, Hamana's choices, were dropping down the ladders into the small boats, while the others milled around, excited, confused, a few, like Aramis, resentful. Moth dodged through them to Hamana's side. "*Andu,*" she said like a humble supplicant, "a word, if you will."

Hamana gave her a dismissive glance, and then looked again. "*Rasnu,*" she said, conscious, as Moth was, of listeners at every hand. She even bowed. "We are nearly ready. If you have any final preparations to make before we go ashore, there is not much time, but enough."

"What I would like," Moth said distinctly, "is to talk to you. If you will?" She indicated the far rail with a priest's gesture, gracious but expecting to be obeyed.

Hamana's face tightened, but she led the way across the busy deck, weaving through the crews, the lean uprights of the *mundab*'s additions, the glossy black plants that had rooted themselves into the sleek deck. Moth's eyes kept snagging on the new strangenesses of the ship, as if her organs had more time and attention to spare for them than her mind.

"Well?" Hamana said when they had achieved a minimal privacy.

"Tell me," Moth said with mustered patience, "what you think you are doing."

"What I *think* . . . ?" Hamana's brows lifted into an arch. "I'm readying the crews to go into the tidal."

"And?"

Hamana studied Moth, thoughts turning over behind her eyes. She was squinting against the sun glare on the water, a brightness that the glassy towers doubled as they caught the wave-rippled sunlight, and the expression lent her an unwonted uncertainty. Silk wandered up to them as Hamana spoke, and was not acknowledged—did not need to be acknowledged—by either of them.

Hamana said, "Best I can figure without knowing what's been happening on shore. Whatever's been going on, I'm hoping that when people see the *Firebird,* there'll be enough interest to stir out the greenguards, if there are any still alive, and the cult. I've formed the landing party into crews, and given them the best maps of the tidal that I could make, and the whistle codes, as well as whatever weapons we could fake up with what we saved from the fire. I'm assuming there'll still be the shaudah's guard on the docks, and at first I thought we'd make one hard push to get through to Twelve Saints. But even if we made it into the tidal, they'd just follow us straight to the shrine, so I reckon the best thing is to send the crews by separate landings and different routes, and hope there's enough confusion that the shaudah's guards won't come down straight on us."

"We're going to the shrine for the engine," Moth said, half a question.

"You, me, Silk. The engineers are staying on board; they'd go straight up to the fort otherwise. We'll have the biggest party, and we *have* to make it through to the shrine, so you need to keep your wits about you."

"What, to walk from the docks to the shrine? I think I can manage."

Hamana did not dignify that with a response. She also did not bother to explain why she was so certain the shaudah's soldiers would greet their landing parties with hostility, but then, she did not need to. At the very, very best the soldiers would want to escort them to the shaudah's court for questioning.

There was something bracing, something wonderfully simple and clear, about the certainties of the human world.

Moth said, "Are you forgetting that as far as the Vashmarna is concerned, this is her ship? Just as the engine is, nominally, her engine. Wouldn't it make sense to use the engineers to contact Vashmarna and let them help us finish the ship before we take it for ourselves?"

"Why?" said Hamana. "We've already taken it for ourselves, haven't we? Or have we?"

Silk stirred uncomfortably, but said nothing.

Moth reached out to touch the rail, felt a leaf as furry as ash beneath her fingers. "What do you mean?"

"Are you smarter than everyone else? Really? Because it's not like we didn't notice you fucking Vashmarna's messenger. Your scam with the engineers wasn't a scam, not like the scam you ran on us about the engine. You lied to us, but you told them the plain truth, didn't you? You're Vashmarna's vassal. You always have been, and you are right now while we're standing here. So no, I'm not going to help you call in Vashmarna's engineers and Vashmarna's guards, just so's to have the honor of handing over the ship and the engine to Vashmarna's whore when they're all done."

Silk turned her fascinated gaze from one to the other.

"I am not Vashmarna's whore," Moth said, her voice thin with rage.

"What I'm going to do," Hamana said, dangerously soft, "is take you to the shrine, where you're going to finish the engine for us, for the tidal, for the people you've been betraying since you were old enough to read, and then after that, I don't give a shit. You can go to Vashmarna or the shaudah or to hell. Just so we're clear."

Moth could not punch Hamana the way she had Silk:

Hamana would kill her. But that was almost the last thought of self-preservation she had left. "I'm not Vashmarna's whore; I'm Vashmarna's daughter. And I didn't go to the ship because she sent me there; I went to the ship because she sent me away, and she sent me away because she's afraid of the cult and the tidal and everything I am. She sent me away because she wishes I had never been born. And no, the ship isn't Vashmarna's, and neither is the engine. They are mine. And I will do exactly what the hell I choose to do, when and how and for whom I choose to do it, because you cannot make me do a damn thing that I do not choose to do. Just so we're clear."

Hamana did not look taken aback. She looked furious and deadly, but she caught the first thing she would have said, and the second, between her teeth. Finally she swallowed and said thinly, "Then, begging the *rasnu*'s pardon, what does the *rasnu* intend?"

Did the *rasnu* know? Moth opened her hand and let the crushed leaf spin away into the waters of the bay. "We'll go to the shrine," she said. "With Vashmarna's engineers."

And Silk, typically, laughed.

THE BASTION

Lady Vashmarna walked between her guards, regretting everything she had not done. Her first impulse had been to climb to her study, where she could look out on the bay, but with the escort waiting and other messengers racing to the Ghar, she had not dared take the time. She could see that had been a mistake, now that she stood at the shaudah's door. She had come to bare her expansionist schemes on what felt like little more than a rumor. She should have seen the ship with her own eyes. Truly, she should have gone down to the docks to greet her daughter, to praise her, to beg her forgiveness, but that was impossible. Even if his guards had permitted it, the shaudah himself would never have forgiven her. If she were to convince him that the ship had been built for his good, or at least for the good of his demesne, she had to come and lay it at his feet—especially as Vashmarna no longer had a cable, nor anything else, to offer.

But if Lady Vashmarna felt an urgency, it seemed that the shaudah felt none. He did not keep her waiting in his anteroom long, but any delay felt like an eternity, and in the fly-buzzing quiet, under the gaze of the guards, her certainties began to erode. It was as if the shock of the ship's arrival—of Moth's arrival, for surely, surely, her daughter must be on board—were not a single fact, a single blow, but a succession of waves that struck again and again, each wave a question. Had she done right? What must she do now? The carefully plotted course of her plans was reduced to a single line scratched in the sand, and the tide was coming in. She should have known where to go from here.

The door opened onto the shaudah's private office. Lady Vashmarna supposed that it would have been too much to hope that the court might have convened to hear the news. The shaudah had been wary of gatherings since the quarantine had heated tempers to the boiling point, but Vashmarna would have benefited from a few expansionist allies. The next best thing would have been a private interview, with no third party for the shaudah to play off against her, but there, too, the shaudah had not obliged her. The commander of his army was there with several of his officers, the shaudah's chamberlain, his chief of ministers, and, inevitably, Lord Ghar. There were the usual greetings, the usual bows.

"We are honored that Vashmarna attends us in her person and not by proxy," said the shaudah with a voice so flat it was nearly sarcastic. "I assume you have heard about this monstrous totem these mad villagers seem to have dragged up to our door."

Totem? "I have heard about the ship, yes, *janaras*."

"The ship." The shaudah tasted the word, as if it were a strange choice of word. "We have sent a boat out to investigate. You are welcome to remain here and wait with us for the crew's report."

Was the man toying with her? Lady Vashmarna bowed, but she could not see any way but straight ahead. "Thank you, *janaras*, I have come not to beg for news but to give it."

The shaudah watched the lazy movements of a lizard across the far wall. Sunlight slipped through slatted blinds to stripe the room with dust-spangled gold. The lizard found a band of heat and stopped, its emerald throat pulsing in time with its quick heart. "Have you?" said the shaudah in his distant voice, and Lady Vashmarna had to tear herself free from his spell.

"I have." She felt strangely, absurdly young before the shaudah's servants, under the Ghar's black, intelligent gaze. "*Janaras*, the ship is mine."

She had not thought to shock them. She had thought, rather, that she was confessing to a crime barely before she could be accused, and yet her accusers seemed surprised. Stunned, even, as the silence deepened. But Vashmarna was the heart of the expansionist movement! To whom did they imagine the ship belonged? Lady Vashmarna was abruptly impatient with them all.

"It has become all too obvious that this island we call our world is not sufficient to sustain our numbers, or our way of life. With the greatest respect, *janaras*, the conservatism of the shaudah's office has trapped us on a shrinking isle, and it is clear to me, at least, that the present crisis would not have brought us to the brink of irredeemable disaster if the pressures of crowding, poverty, and imminent starvation had not turned the tidal into a boiler without a safety valve. Indeed, it was obvious to Vashmarna more than twenty years ago, when the Lamplighters Rebellion nearly swept the *shadras* into the sea. It was then that my father conceived of the idea of a ship— of a whole fleet of ships—that might carry colonists across the ocean to other lands. When I inherited command of the demesne, I devoted Vashmarna's resources to realizing that idea. Which is why I can offer you, *janaras*, this ship as a means of relieving the pressures that threaten the *shadras,* and the *rasnan.*"

She bowed. The silence persisted. The chief of ministers, a fat old man from the shaudah's father's time, stirred.

"With deference, *jinnu,*" he said spitefully, "Vashmarna's repeated requests for exemption from the Artifacts and Inventions Law have been denied. Repeatedly. This 'ship' is clearly in contravention—"

The shaudah raised a finger from the arm of his chair. "Not long ago, Vashmarna-*jin',* you promised me a power cable to the towers."

"I did," Lady Vashmarna said weakly, disconcerted by this change of subject. She collected herself, and bowed. "*Janaras,* I assure you, Vashmarna's mandate to provide power to the *shadras* has always been my first priority."

"Yet instead of a cable, I get a ship."

"My men are repairing the cable even as we speak, *janaras.* But the ship is done." Except, gods be her witness, it was not. Was it? The magnitude of her gamble swept over Lady Vashmarna, leaving her queasy and sweating under her robes.

"Repairing a cable that is not even complete."

Damn the man! Was he obsessed? "We continue to be plagued, as has the entire bastion, with these so-called demons—"

" 'So-called'!" blurted the shaudah's commander.

Again, the shaudah raised his finger. "One does not wish to question Vashmarna's intentions, or Vashmarna's loyalties. But when I ask for a cable and am given a ship, a ship that must be towed by rowboats into the bay, I have no choice but to wonder. Is there a cable? My men have been frustrated in every attempt they have made to investigate the matter. Was there ever meant to be a cable? Perhaps the Vashmarna can enlighten us on the matter. Are we intended to accept this ship as our only alternative to catastrophe?"

The way the shaudah pronounced the word "ship" was

abrading Lady Vashmarna's sorely tested nerves. He curled his tongue around the "sh," bared his teeth on the "i," made an exaggerated popping sound out of the "p." He made a mockery out of the greatest risk of her life, and she had the dreadful sense that he would make the same mockery out of her death. She bowed.

"If I may remind *janarasan,* the shaudah's soldiers have in fact seen the cable in its various stages, and they have seen, too, the effects of the contact with the shadow gods that—"

"Shadow gods."

The Ghar's voice was so quiet that Lady Vashmarna was not certain he had intended to interrupt. It was the fact of his speaking at all that startled her. So focused had she been on the shaudah, she had almost forgotten her old enemy was present. He gathered himself, as if surprised by the silent attention of the room.

" 'Shadow gods,' you say, *jinnu.* 'These so-called demons.' These are your words, when everyone else in this room— everyone else, I'll wager, in the bastion—calls them monsters, demons, plague carriers. The evils of the night. These *so-called* demons."

The Ghar's musing voice trailed into a silence that buzzed like carrion flies in Lady Vashmarna's ears. When she spoke, her voice was harsh.

"Is 'shadow god' somehow more fearful or superstitious than 'demon,' Ghar-*jan*'? I fail to grasp your point."

"I have not reached my point. *Janaras,* I must beg your forgiveness in advance of my offense. Your own suspicions, suspicions that I would never have entertained, have engendered yet more dreadful questions in my mind. Questions, I say only, Vashmarna-*jinnu,* but questions that must be asked. This ship the Vashmarna advances as our only hope—though what kind of hope carries a few dozen, perhaps a few hundred, people away from the million that must remain behind? This ship that is offered in the place of the cable that was promised and never delivered. This ship, as the shaudah has said, offered as our only alternative to catastrophe. Oh, it is a dreadful question! But does it not force us to wonder about not just the ship, but the catastrophe that drives us to accept it out of sheer terrified necessity? Vashmarna-*jinnu* . . ."

He looked into her eyes. His own were black with grief, his face deeply scored with lines of pain.

"Vashmarna-*jin'*, you are my friend of twenty years. I cannot ask for your forgiveness. I can only ask why did Vashmarna play host to a disgraced tidal scholar with ties to the shadow cult? Why does Vashmarna continue to escape the plague when the bastion is decimated? Why has Vashmarna never applied for exemption for the inventions that crowd the fort's workshops? Why does the Vashmarna speak of so-called demons and shadow gods? *Why was the bridge destroyed?*"

Her friend of twenty years. Lady Vashmarna stared into his eyes, until the beam of their twinned gaze was like another black bar drawn across the blind-shaded room. *This is the man,* she thought. This *is the man who tried to have my daughter killed.* The Ghar's crepey lids shaded his eyes. He bowed his head.

"Do you lay the plague at my door?" she whispered. "O Master of Doors?"

His gaze flicked back up to meet hers.

"*Janaras,*" she said, "I am loyal, as Vashmarna has always been loyal, to the shaudah, to the *rasnan,* and to the greater good. I have always acted in good faith, and unless the Ghar wishes to advance some *evidence*"—she bore down heavily on the word—"that I have ever done otherwise, I will not dignify his wholly unfounded accusations with a response. But I will ask him a question in return. One question, Ghar-*jandas*. How can you dare—how can you *dare*—to put Vashmarna to such a righteous inquisition when you are yourself the master of the outlawed and heretical Society of Doors? How can you slander me with implications about Vashmarna's freedom from plague when the undeniable fact that your men have been hit first and hardest only proves that it is your Society that raised the plague in the first place? How can you accuse Vashmarna of impropriety in building our ship and offering it up for the greater good when your illicit and dreadful door to the *ramhadras* has already proved itself a part of the impending catastrophe, and not its solution? How can you even speak to me of the shadow cult within my walls when my workmen are still repairing the *doors* broken through those same walls in the attack that ruined our cable? How can you dare?"

"That is more questions than one," said the shaudah in his arid voice. "Let us start with the first. What of this Society of Doors, Ghar-*jan'*? Will you deny the *jinnu's* accusation?"

Finally Lord Ghar looked aside. "No, *janaras,* I do not deny it. But with your leave, I will defend it."

"And without my leave?" But having said this, the shaudah waved Lord Ghar on.

"*Janarasan.*" Lord Ghar bowed. "I will not argue against the law, or the heresy, since both are founded on the fear of our ancestors, and it is difficult to argue against the fears of the dead. I will say only this: that while Vashmarna's expansionists offer only a ship, a long voyage for a very few, and no promise of success, the Return offers a whole world—"

"A ruined world," Lady Vashmarna said. "A hell."

"So we have always been told. A ruined world our ancestors escaped from with their lives, a hell we dare not seek for fear of losing ours. Thus speak the priests. These priests who cripple our understanding and our will; these priests who direct any search for freedom or knowledge or power into the hands of powerless gods."

Even now such a thing could strike at Lady Vashmarna's

heart. "These priests who oppose the Society—*and* the shadow cult!"

"Yet do these priests never lie? Must I believe men who have their own authority to protect before I believe the words left to me by my own ancestors? And not only mine. How many of our grandfathers told the same tale? Not the priests' story of a hell narrowly escaped, but a heaven from which we were unjustly exiled, and to which we have both a right and a duty to return."

"Your own son is a priest!"

"And does he not therefore know, as well as his fathers' truth, his predecessors' lies? I tell you, we have our hands on the very door to heaven!"

He might have been speaking to her alone. What did he want of her? To believe? To submit?

"Would the door to heaven release a plague, or a plague of demons, upon the world?"

"And again I say," said the Ghar with his first flash of temper, "give me your proof that these things are the work of the Society and not an attack of the shadow cult!"

"It seems we are somewhat short of proof at either hand," said the shaudah.

"It was not the Society that brought down the bridge," said Lord Ghar, still hot.

"Nor was it Vashmarna! Why would we abrogate our duty and the people's trust? Why would we kill our own? We had no cause!"

"No cause? How else could you hope to stampede the shaudah into accepting your hopeless gamble?"

"Our gamble. Vashmarna's gamble. What does the shaudah risk but Vashmarna's ship, Vashmarna's resources, Vashmarna's crew?"

"Vashmarna's lease on whatever new land might be found."

"Better that than Ghar's lease on hell!"

"And better either of those than the shaudah's lease on the land we can this moment call our own?" said the shaudah in a voice as thin as a knife.

Lady Vashmarna felt the cut of that, the harsh edge of the shaudah's intelligence unsheathed.

"Where are Vashmarna's resources when we must shelter the homeless and shore up our fields?" the shaudah continued. "Where is Ghar's secret power when these demons, *whosesoever they are,* have us under siege? How can our fate be anything but disaster when the powers of the *rasnan* have their gazes fixed everywhere but on the *rasnan* as we teeter on the brink of the foundering waves?"

Lady Vashmarna felt as if, turning from the argument with the Ghar, she had come up against an unlooked-for wall. Her heart stuttered, her breath caught in her throat. But—*No,* she thought. *No. Everything I have done—No, I was not wrong.*

But did she see the same shock and the same denial in Lord Ghar's eyes?

"I will tell you the truth," the shaudah said as the lizard crept from a bar of shadow to a bar of sun. "A ruler's truth. My truth. These demons and plagues, this shadow cult, *whosesoever they are,* have done me a greater service than the two of you combined, simply by reducing the number of hungry mouths in the *shadras.* What good has either of you done for the *rasnan?* Not in the maybe future, not in the dreams of the past, but now?"

His silence was a heavy weight. Lady Vashmarna struggled like an unjustly scolded child to speak with a reasonable calm.

"I have always—"

But the shaudah stopped her with his raised hand. "No, *jinnu,* we have all heard our respective truths. Let us contemplate what we have each of us been offered before we speak again."

Lady Vashmarna bowed. Lord Ghar bowed.

"And in order to ensure you a fruitful peace for your contemplation, Commander Shimmadan will take you both into a guarded seclusion."

"Both?" said an incredulous Lord Ghar.

"Both?" said an outraged Lady Vashmarna.

But the shaudah had exhausted his store of patience, and he waved to his guard commander without deigning to respond.

The green-throated lizard snapped, toothless and deadly, at a fly.

THE BAY

The curious boats that circled around the anchored ship were a boon to Hamana's crews. Once they had pushed off from the *Firebird* with their rag-wrapped weapons concealed beneath the gunwales, they were indistinguishable from the other boats. They circled and scattered and, freshly anonymous, headed shoreward to the long guarded line of the tidal docks.

Moth watched the *Firebird* dwindle against the sparkling blue of the bay. The *mundab*'s restless bird did not come with her, but its echo did, its twin cradled in Moth's body. The child was more than a reminder. It was a chain looped around her ankle even as she was free to move away. Free to let the paired oars pull the boat in long, hard strokes toward the shore. Free to taste the salt spray on her lips and raise her face to the rare touch of the sun. The clouds were fraying on the wind, and above the southern horizon they rolled up a ragged hem to show the unplumbed blue of a summer sky. A promise, Moth thought, of heat, flowers, and food. The promise of stinking mud, tainted water, and flies.

The oars swept together, and it was as if a hand gripped the boat's hull and dragged them a giant's step closer to shore: a surge, the hiss of droplets cast from the oars' blades onto the smooth-backed waves, a rhythmic surge. The boat was a cradle; the lilting ripple of water against the hull was a lullaby that soothed even the terrified tadpole in Moth's womb.

Moth opened her eyes and saw that the ship, a black shape against the white spires on their foam-limned reef, was a terrible thing. A prison, a witch's cauldron, a crucible of ungodly change. Or godly change, where the god was a tormented exile, torn from its true being in the *mundab* and twisting everything it touched out of true. And she, Moth, was the witch, the warden, the surgeon who had excised the *Firebird*'s soul from its parent world. And why? For a ship, an engine, a dream of that blue horizon. Nothing was saved, too much was harmed.

The oars swept, the giant pulled, the boat strode toward the shore. Moth folded her hands over her belly and rocked to the movement of the waves.

THE BAY

They tumbled her like a bundle of laundry into the bottom of the shaudah's boat and thrust the craft away from the shore. There was shouting. There would be fighting. Lady Vashmarna wondered if the shaudah had anticipated violence when he had ordered their arrest. Perhaps he had. Perhaps he had only been awaiting an opportunity to set his troops against Vashmarna and Ghar. He had the advantage of numbers, and a greater advantage against the Ghar, who had lost his tower stronghold and too many men to the plague. Vashmarna at least had its fort, but there it was hunger that would be fighting on the shaudah's side. Even as the boat's ribs dug into her hip and bilge water soaked her robe, Lady Vashmarna's mind scudded between storeroom accounts, guard schedules, rationing, the list of essential personnel.

Like a woman, she realized, who snatches at tufts of grass

on her way over the edge of the cliff. It would be more grace-
ful to fall with empty hands. Unaccustomed to the small boat's
movement, she untangled her robes from around her legs and
tried to reclaim her loosened hair from the wind. A hand
around her upper arm urged her onto the narrow seat that
pressed against her back. When she was seated, her breath and
some kind of order regained, she realized that the hand belonged to Divaram Ghar.

"One gambles," he said, philosophical and wry. "One occasionally loses."

She understood that he, too, was trying to fall with empty
hands. But why, then, clutch at their old friendship? It was
grotesque.

The shouting from the docks carried clearly across the
water, but Lady Vashmarna's back was to the shore. Before her
she could see the paired faces of the shaudah's grim oarsmen,
and between their ranks, the plague-haunted towers, the dia-
mond-cast waves.

And the ship. Her ship.

It might have been an alien thing, not a vessel built to pierce
the unknown but a vessel of the unknown come to pierce their
insular world. That was the first shock, the first wonder, the
first dismay. She quickly reassured herself that this must be
Vashmarna's ship, of course it was, but still it was not the ship
that had been designed under her aegis. It did not look as if it
had been designed at all. It looked as if it had been grown, or
hatched from some enormous egg. She was reminded of the
shadow gods that crept through the fort and left everything
they touched a little changed, and she was thereby reminded of
her daughter.

Not the wronged and loyal saint she had invented, an idol
at which to lay the burden of her guilt, but the real Moth, the
independent, erratic, secretive Moth who had raised the
shadow cult and its harrowing gods without Lady Vashmarna's

knowledge or permission, the Moth who had destroyed the bridge and set catastrophe marching across the *shadras* and beyond. The Ghar was right to scorn the ship as inadequate to the *rasnan*'s present need, but Lady Vashmarna knew that it had never been intended to answer such a wholesale disaster as the island now faced. It had been intended to stave off disaster— No, not even that. It had been intended to open a door, to pave a route of escape from a disaster that only distantly threatened. The ship was meant to be a beginning, not an end.

But now she feared they were facing the end, and the ship was all she had.

THE TIDAL

At first it was the busyness of the docks that struck Moth, the hurried crowd making room for itself against a backdrop of Vashmarna uniforms, saffron tunics as bright as the sunshine against the splintery bamboo of net lofts and drying huts. The *Firebird*'s longboat was jostled by smaller craft as the oarsmen pried a space for them at the float's end, and the *Firebird*'s crew was jostled as they climbed out onto the warm, waterlogged planks that swayed low on the receding tide. The *hadaras* firebirds (the crew had been christened in the same instant as the ship) gawked at the crowd, the warehouses, the green roofs of the tidal rising beyond them, and the wall of the bastion rising beyond even that, just as they had gawked at the towers and the gap-ended bridge from the ship's deck, as if the *shadras* were all equally wondrous in their eyes. They were, from Hamana's point of view, temporarily useless, which was a problem because the instant the firebirds had climbed out of the boat, a large segment of the crowd had claimed it for their own needs. The firebirds were sightseeing, Hamana was shouting, and Hemmar Gamood, his burned arm wrapped in someone's shirt and his hair gray with ash, cut a path as efficient as one of his rulers through the crowd toward the Vashmarna uniforms that hung like a line of laundry against the back side of the dock.

Hamana noticed. Of course Hamana noticed, and judging by her face and the strident cracks in her voice, she was about to combust from the heat of her temper. Moth, inwardly delighted, made a point of being earnest and reassuring as she said, "Don't worry, I'll fetch him. Them," she corrected herself, because the half dozen engineers who had survived the attack on the inlet, including Aramis, were trailing Gamood as if pulled by a string. Moth skipped after them, dodging the crowd with a happy feeling that she had had a surfeit of disasters. Whatever happened next could only be outrageous, and therefore fun. Certainly more fun than the smoldering *mundab* ghost trapped inside the dreadful ship and whispering secrets to the little bird inside her womb. Even in this slightly crazed state, however, she could not help but notice the people she pushed past: most of them too well dressed to be tidal folk, yet seeming too desperate to be baysiders going home. Moth looked with more attention and saw how many of them were obviously sick, gray-faced and wooden-limbed, some so ill they were lying on homemade stretchers, a mother or a child kneeling over them with damp cloths and wild eyes. There was a potent wrongness at the heart of this busy dockside scene, and Moth had to concede that even she, doomful Moth, could not find any entertainment in it. She caught up to Aramis and tugged at his elbow.

"Is this the plague? The Society's plague?"

Aramis gave her a queasy look, his face nearly as gray as the afflicted, but did not answer—did not have to answer—in words.

"So many!" Moth said in shock. The whole dockside was full of them. "Where are they going? Where is there for them to go?"

Aramis had no reply, and Moth suffered the bizarre but unshakeable notion that the sick were setting out for the *Firebird*, or maybe even for the far horizon without any ship at all.

Meanwhile, Hemmar Gamood, either not noticing or not caring about the ill, had reached the Vashmarna platoon and was demanding to speak to the man in charge. Fortunately for Moth, the engineer was so angry, and so anxious to gain an ally, he was all but incoherent.

"I demand your immediate— These people have stolen Vashmarna property and taken—and destroyed! Destroyed Vashmarna property, and killed us, they've killed us and taken us prisoner— *Hend* Parradu! You know me! I demand your immediate assistance! Listen to me!" This last was a shriek of frustration, for the turbaned *hend* seemed to care only about the muster of his troops and had yet to give Gamood more than half his attention.

"*Andas,*" said a soothing Moth, "please calm yourself. You are distressed," which so infuriated the engineer that, as Moth had hoped, he was effectively silenced, choked on his own spleen.

That did not stop the other engineers from clamoring for the *hend*'s attention. "We are Vashmarna men!" the loudest of them cried.

"So are we," snapped an exasperated *hend*. "And we have orders from the lady that have nothing to do with some *hadaras* theft. Talk to the Ghars if you can't wait. The docks are theirs now!"

"Par, wait." Aramis put out a staying hand. "It's the lady's orders that have brought us back with the ship. Can't you tell us—"

"You came with the ship?" Apparently they now had *hend* Parradu's full attention.

"The lady's ship. Vashmarna's ship."

"Yes," blurted Hemmar Gamood, "and these people have stolen it right from under our feet!"

The *hend* gave them a puzzled look. "Stolen? I thought you said you brought it here?"

"We did." Aramis put a hand on Gamood's shoulder, restraining or soothing, Moth could not tell. "But it seems matters have changed since I left with the lady's orders. Par, what's happening here? Are the towers . . . ?"

Parradu explained about the quarantine, which silenced even Gamood. "And now this ship has put a shark in among them up in the bastion," the *hend* went on. "The gods alone know what's happening up there. We've orders to divide forces between the fort and some shrine in the thick of the slum, and I drew the short stick, gods help me—and gods tell me what for. No one else will." He turned to Gamood and added in a more conciliatory tone, "I'd send an escort to get you up to the fort, *andas,* but I have my orders, and our numbers are too thin as it is."

"A shrine?" Gamood said as if he could not believe his ears. "You would abandon us to protect a *tidal* shrine?"

"Of course," Moth said happily. "Twelve Saints Shrine. We caught you just in time then, *hend.* What a piece of good fortune. Thank the gods!"

Everyone stared at her, including Hamana, who had finally given up on saving the boat and came storming up with Silk and the chastened firebirds in tow.

"Par," said Aramis with a suspicious wobble in his voice,

"may I introduce *rasnu* Moth? It so happens that the *rasnu* has urgent business—urgent Vashmarna business—at the shrine."

The *hend* was a small beady-eyed rooster of a man, and the look he turned on Moth was not the look he had given Aramis, being more like the look he would bestow on a bug than on a friend, but he bowed. "*Rasnu,*" he said, and turned back to Aramis. "Do you mean to tell me Twelve Saints is Vashmarna's?"

Moth, seeing Hamana take on that sleek and joyful aspect that spoke of killing, said hastily, "Not precisely Vashmarna's, but it is allied, *hend* Parradu. It is allied. The shrine holds something of equal value to Vashmarna and the tidal—and indeed, to the whole of the *rasnan*—and we of the ship have as great a stake in protecting it as your lady. Surely the obvious thing to do is to join forces at the outset?" She flicked a glance at Hamana to make sure the greenguard grasped her point.

"And put ourselves in the same sights as the yellowcoats?" hissed a scandalized Hamana, who did not seem inclined to be reasonable.

"And afford them the same degree of protection they will afford us," said Moth, her voice still bracingly cheerful and her eyes promising mayhem. She gave her hands a brisk rub. "Well! That's settled then. Shall we get under way?"

"You—" said Hamana.

"But—" said Gamood.

"*Rasnu,*" said the *hend,* and he turned to give orders to his men.

"Why were you so helpful?" Moth muttered to Aramis as they left the chaos of the docks behind.

"Do you think I'd be welcome at the fort?" he said, and twitched his arm out of her grasp.

"And whose fault is that?" she demanded, squeaking with the effort of keeping her outrage quiet.

"Mine," he said shortly, and after a moment laid his hand on her arm.

Moth was beginning to lose track of everything that was wrong between them. Why had he been angry? Why had she? She touched his hand and then, feeling Hamana's eyes on them, stepped out of reach. By this time Hamana needed no more reasons for enmity. Moth just did not want to set her off.

On a sunny afternoon, with the heat rising and the water too shallow to carry even a tidal scull over the mud, Moth would not have expected crowds, but there should have been someone in the streets. There were always errands to run, deals to make, assignations to keep—and *hadri* wandering, lost, from the flooded countryside—but not today. The quiet after the noisy docks was menacing; every tenement glared down at them with a hundred blank eyes. The only sound besides the whining of the *tirindi* and the receding hiss of the tide was the whistling of the greenguards signaling from roof to roof. There could be no doubt that the signals had to do with Moth's group; even the Vashmarna men knew it and balanced on the foot stones with their pistols primed and in their hands. Moth knew from a lifetime of dodging tidal feuds that the street was the worst possible position to hold. One was either lined up on the foot stones like hooked fish on a string, or one was bogged down in the mud, a sitting target for marksmen on the roofs.

Hamana surely knew it as well as Moth did. She could have led her crew to the shrine, and shut out Moth and the Vashmarnas. She could have turned on the Vashmarnas with her untried *hadaras* crew and risked losing an unequal fight toe to toe. But as Moth knew, she was too dogged to do the one and too smart to do the other. Instead, with a look of rare desperation in her eyes, she stuck two fingers between her teeth and shrilled a quavering burst of code.

The whistlers on the roofs were silent.

"What does that mean?" asked one of the firebirds.

"Nothing good," Silk said dryly.

Moth looked at her and saw that Silk's mood had turned much as her own had. *What the hell,* her crooked grin said, *since we're there already.* Moth grinned back, and then made her face saintly as she pressed her hands together and cast her gaze up to heaven. *Only the gods can help us now.* Silk snickered, and earned one of Hamana's ferocious glares.

They wound on, deeper into the tidal.

Wave-rippled mud began to show above the water's gleam, and so did other, stranger things. Moth might not even have noticed them, her gaze being mostly on the rooftops, where the whistles had started up again. But the *tirindi* that drifted down to scavenge in the muck on pale bone-shadowed wings drew her eyes to those other bone shadows beneath the dwindling tide, and she saw the dead that the tidal mud held in its embrace. Half-rotten and half-consumed, they had been left in the street like trash for the vermin and the tide. Crabs dashed about in glistening colonies, sending up a fine spatter as they fled the *tirindi*'s omnivorous hunger.

"Is it the plague?" Moth asked *hend* Parradu.

"*Rasnu,* I've been on the docks or in the fort since the bridge fell. All I can tell you is the night shift hears things back here that no one bothers to explain. Plague or demons or *them.*" His eyes turned up toward the green roofs. "Likely it's all the same to the dead."

"Even in the tidal we . . ." Moth hesitated, but the man already knew her name. "Even in the tidal we burn our dead."

The *hend* looked at her, not without compassion. "Likely you did, *rasnu,*" he said. "But there's only the cult here now."

What did that mean? Something as dreadful as the stink of the steaming mud.

There were other changes in the tidal, things she saw only when her wounded eyes flinched away from a naked rib cage too small to be a man's. The tenement called Rohanil's Promise

had a great black shadow painted across its four-story front—
a shadow Moth might have taken for a smoke stain from some
extinguished fire except for the two splashes of red that made
eyes high on the blackened wall. Windows were blinded by
the paint. Who lived in that darkness? Surely people she
knew? Coming around the corner of Green Remembrance, she
stopped, as they all stopped—too suddenly. They teetered on
the foot stones, and several of the *hadaras* firebirds fell off into
the watery mud, but they stared even as they scrambled away
from the eager crabs—shocked by a line of corpses hung like
drying fish from the eaves of the neighboring building's porch.
Moth felt a peculiar grief rising inside her, a feeling of betrayal
that had nothing to do with trust or with schemes, but before
she could make sense of it, the first shot was fired from Remembrance's roof. Their shock had made such good targets of
them that someone could not resist.

The pistol made a harmless-sounding *pop!* and one of the
Vashmarna guardsmen fell into the mud. Two more men
dropped down after him to haul him out before he drowned—
he was still alive, his breath an ominous hiss, his blood spreading like a scarlet badge across his chest. Such was the tidal's
quiet that all the sounds rang out as bright and distinct as the
clean sunlit bones in the street.

The man's wheezing curses.

The heavy breathing of his helpers.

The obscene sucking of the mud that did not want to let
him go.

Hamana whistled and shouted "Red House! We're Red
House!" her voice ringing up toward the scattering clouds.
Hend Parradu said, his voice dark and rough beneath
Hamana's cry, "The porch. It's the only cover," and everyone
scrambled for the gruesome shelter, feet slapping stones or
churning mud into a slurry. Moth's own breath was loud in her

ears. The next shots—*pop! pop! pop!*—were scattered like peppercorns across the stew of the group's flight. Someone struck Moth from behind, a check that sent her into the street. The hand she threw out to save herself plunged into the mud up to the shoulder. Her legs floated on what remained of the tide. The rest of her began to sink.

Mud like a hand around her throat, mud against her mouth, mud in her nostrils, mud in her eyes, mud in her ears. Her heart threatened to burst with terror. She flailed, knowing it was stupid—yet the mud was not that deep. If she stood, it would only reach her thighs! But she could not stand. She was tipped forward on her face, her feet kicking the sunlight. A sudden force tore her free and sent her plunging through the air, clawing at her face even before her feet found the soft wood of the porch, alive enough not to want to taste the mud that she wore like a mask. Finally, desperate for a breath, she hauled her shirt off over her head and used the clean back of it to scrub her face and her hands. Then she could breathe, and see, and hear. Aramis stood beside her, the whites showing all around the golden lights of his eyes.

"I love you," she gasped, while tears washed clean her eyes. "I love you, I love you, I love you."

"You're mad," he said, and he wrenched at the buttons of his coat so he could pull it off and give it to her to wear.

Pop! pop! said the rooftop pistols. *Pak! pak! pak!* said the pistols of Vashmarna's men. To shoot, the men took cover behind the sun-blackened corpses, and looking at those dangling shapes, Moth realized they were not actual dead men but effigies made of sacks and rags sewn with fish skeletons and *tirindi* bones.

"What are they?" Aramis said with muted horror when he followed her gaze.

"I don't know," Moth said, but she did. *Bless us, spirits of air, against the dark-shrouded evils of night*. That was what the chimes in the scholarium said, rattling from every eave. What did these charms say?

Bless us, spirits of darkness, against the light-shrouded evils of day.

The saffron-coated guardsmen ducked beneath the scant shelter of the porch railing to fumble with powder and shot, then crouched to fire again at the roof across the way. The smell of burnt gunpowder was an antidote to the stinking mud.

Pak! pak! pak!

Moth realized that the roof across the way belonged to Twelve Saints Shrine at about the same time that she noticed the hot pain growing in her hip and side and the warm trickle running down the inside of her mud-caked pants. She fumbled to fasten the buttons of Aramis's coat. It, like her muddy pants, was dark enough not to show the blood, which seemed terribly important just then.

"Hamana," she said. "Tell them who we are."

Hamana rounded on her, a pistol in her hand. "They know who we are," she snarled, as if it were Moth's fault. It probably was. "They think we've gone over to the other side!"

"Which other side?" said Aramis through clenched teeth.

Hamana leveled her pistol at him, but did not fire, probably because of the Vashmarna pistol nuzzling her ear. Suddenly even the bewildered firebirds could grasp the situation. Knives and gaffs appeared from nowhere. Vashmarna guns turned from the shrine to the porch.

"Well," said Moth, distracted by the warmth of her own blood finding new routes around her waist and into her groin, "now they know otherwise." And fearing she might soon lose her grasp on the situation for the worst, or best, of reasons, she bolted off the porch and into the mud of the street.

"Nindi!" she yelled, with only a hope that the *mundabi* pirate was in earshot. "Nindi, it's me!" A lead ball whizzed past her ear. She did not duck so much as drop to her knees with af-fronted surprise.

"Moth!" Aramis shouted. Actually, there was a lot of shouting going on behind her. Looking back the way they had come, Moth could see why: a contingent of blue-coated police-men, Ghar men, had followed them from the docks.

Moth, inspired by the sight, shrieked, "You want to give up the engine to the Ghars, you go ahead and kill us, Nindi! But we have the ship, and our crew won't give it up to you if we're dead. They'll sink it first and you won't have a damn thing!" Shots from up the street were kicking up dull spatters of mud. Moth wailed, "Nin-di-i-i! Together we can have the ship and engine both!"

The greenery along the edge of the fire shrine's roof was in-expressive, but the voice that came from behind it was laden with skepticism. "Who is we, little Moth?"

"Us!" Moth shrieked, as Aramis dropped down the porch stairs to grab her and lift her bodily back onto the porch. The bluecoats' shots *thunked* like axes against the tenement's cor-ner and sent up bursts of stone dust.

Nindi on the roof said nothing, but the shrine door swung open and *aras* Crab, gentlest *mundabi,* still in command of his own shrine, beckoned from the darkness. Silk ran for it, Hamana behind her and the firebirds on Hamana's heels. Moth did not run so much as direct Aramis in that direction: Aramis, for some reason, was determined to be her transport. The Vashmarnas followed after him, Hemmar Gamood argu-ing against it all the way. The shrine door swung shut behind them, and was hammered by a brief barrage of shots. After the bright daylight the shrine was dark, starred rather than lit by the lamps guttering at the feet of the saints, so Aramis could only be guessing what that wetness on his hands meant. Guess or no, he blurted it out into the panting silence.

"Moth! You've been shot!"

"I know," she sighed, and slithered down to sit on the weed-slimed stone of the step. Silk threw herself down beside her, and Moth had to fend off her anxious hands even as Aramis crouched down on her other side.

Not that everyone cared. Out of the darkness by the door a man's voice gasped out, "*Hend* Parradu! Are you there?"

"Who speaks?" demanded a testy *hend*.

"Majun, sir."

"Where the hell did you come from?

"The *purdar* sent me . . ." The man had to stop for air. "I've been behind you the whole way. *Hend,* the shaudah arrested Vashmarna-*jin'*. She's in Shaudarand . . . with the Ghar . . . and the fort and the scholarium are both under siege."

"What do you mean, under siege?" said the *hend* in profound offense.

"The shaudah," said the messenger. "He's taking Ghar and Vashmarna both."

"Then what the hell," said the *hend,* "are we doing *in* here?"

THE BAY

As if they had been partners in crime, Lady Vashmarna and Lord Ghar were lodged together in the foot of Shaudarand. They were not badly kept. Lady Vashmarna had a bedroom with a cot and an unlocked door; a servant served a meager supper in a sitting room she shared with her fellow prisoner. But the pale stone walls wept condensation, the windows were slits, the guards spoke harshly outside the door. Lady Vashmarna had seldom spared a thought for the soldiers' demesne when she was in her gracious rooms high in the tower's crown. Now she felt painfully balanced between her former eminence and the lower, darker wave-haunted cells below.

"He behaves no differently now than he has ever done," said Lord Ghar. He had been trying to engage her in conversation throughout the long afternoon, and his voice had acquired the same nerve-scratching buzz as the flies bumping against the cloudy window glass. Once again, he was speaking of the shaudah. "Like a man in a boat, he sits still and hopes the situation will find its own equilibrium. But without us he has lost his balance. He will discover this soon enough."

Lady Vashmarna stood with her back to the room and her face pressed against the edges of the narrow window frame. She could not see her ship. From this low vantage she could see the heavy, complex, and useless structure of the bridge's near end, a slice of shadowed water, and in the distance a prettily framed sketch of the scholarium wall, the road, the fort's seaward face, and the foaming river's mouth. The westering sun cast the bridge's shadow across the sluggish waves, and the water was a deep, unfriendly blue. The bridge's footing was shaggy with algae and glistened obscenely with gaping mussels and fleshy sea stars in liver and orange. Even through the glass she could hear the gassy suck of the waves. Time and again she tore her gaze away and lifted it up to the still-sunny bastion, but nothing happened there that she could see. It was a static scene, pretty and uninformative, and her eyes drifted down again into the shade of the bridge, where at least the crabs picked their delicate way through the weeds.

"He will have to act," the Ghar said. "Soon he will have no choice but to choose."

He has acted, Lady Vashmarna thought. *He has already chosen.* But Lord Ghar did not need to hear her arguments. He was not even arguing with himself. He was just casting up a veil of reason as if he hoped to hide himself again.

But I have seen you, Lady Vashmarna thought, and she raised her eyes to the bastion once more, to the fort where her people were fighting, or surrendering, or dead, and where the shadows were growing long.

THE TIDAL

Aramis insisted on carrying her across the mossy floor of the shrine and up the inner stairs. Moth would rather have walked; the way he held her pulled at her hip and side and wrung yet more blood out of her flesh to wet her clothes; but she was feeling sick and shivery and in no mood for an argument. Which wasn't to say she would not get one. Crowded into the priest's room with her and Aramis were Hamana and Silk and *aras* Crab, Nindi and *hend* Parradu and Hemmar Gamood, plus assorted greenguards and yellowcoats and firebirds. *Aras* Crab started to slide a screen aside from the small window to give them some light and was dissuaded by a Ghar round thumping into the window frame. Everyone in the room ducked except Moth, who was too sore, but the greenguards on the roofs of Panajil and the shrine sent down a volley in reprimand, and there were no more shots from below. *Aras* Crab, leaning against the wall as if it were all that kept him upright, carefully twitched the screen back into place. The coarse paper backed by sunlight gave a dull shadowless illumination. The room was airless and hot, and stank of the mud tracked in by Moth and the rest of her crew.

Hemmar Gamood broke the silence that followed the shots.

"Where is the engine? I insist that you show me the engine before we go any farther."

Any farther in which direction? Moth wondered, but she did not ask. No one responded, and Gamood did not insist again. Moth broke the next silence.

"Where is Istvan?"

"Dead," Nindi said. "The Vashmarna had him up to the fort and he died there."

"Killed by intruders," *hend* Parradu said. His voice was as matter-of-fact as the greenguard's, but there was no doubt these men were enemies who had entered into a very tentative and temporary truce.

Istvan? Dead? How was Moth supposed to cope with this? She was too sick, too sore, too weary, too afraid. She also doubted she had a choice. She passed a shaking hand over her face and said to Crab, "*Aras,* is there clean water for washing? And maybe something to drink?"

"And bandages," added Silk.

"It can wait," said Moth, though her voice had developed an unprecedented wobble.

"Moth."

"Oh, leave me be!"

Silk huffed an exaggerated sigh and said to Crab, "And bandages, please, *aras.*" An unwonted courtesy designed to show Moth up for the ungrateful child Silk had clearly decided she was. Crab sidled like his namesake along the wall and slipped out of the room.

"How bad is it?" asked a grudging Nindi.

"It's just a crease," Moth said, though she knew it wasn't. The lead ball had torn a chunk out of her hip after it had scored her side. "If it were going to kill me, it would have done it by now."

Another lie, of course, given the mud that fouled the wound. Blood poisoning killed more people in the tidal than old age. Moth could not stop the tears that wet her eyes and trembled her mouth, but no one questioned them. Apparently, even someone suffering from a mere flesh wound was allowed to cry. She scrubbed her face with a filthy hand, and then Crab returned with a tray. She took the wet rag he offered her and wiped her face. Silk, with rough care and a pointed indifference to Moth's modesty, folded down the waist of Moth's trousers and began to clean the wound, scrubbing hard enough to make it bleed freely and wash out the poisonous muck. Moth bit a clean corner of the rag and lost track of the conversation for a while. Once the worst of it was done, she became aware of a hand on her head, stroking her hair. She knew at once it was not Aramis, and only after that did she recognize the hesitant care of the Twelve Saints priest.

"Thank you, *aras*," she whispered.

" '*Aras*,' is it now?" Crab said with friendly irony. "O *rasnu* Moth?"

Moth gave him a weak smile and traded the cloth for a cup. There was silence while she drank. Moth did not mistake this for respect for her or her authority. They were simply men on a badly built raft: no one wanted to be the first to move, in case that movement drowned them all.

Someone on the roof fired a single shot, presumably at an incautious bluecoat down below.

"Are they just going to squat outside the door?" said Nindi to *hend* Parradu.

"I don't know," said the *hend*.

"Well, what do they want? You?"

"All I know is that my orders are to protect this shrine—" The *hend* broke off when Nindi laughed.

"Protect it! Be my guest. We're damn near out of powder and shot. We'll be throwing stones by dark."

"Then why the hell were you shooting at us?" demanded Hamana.

"Why d'you think?" said Nindi, his black gaze flicking over the Vashmarna faces.

"We're here to protect the shrine on our lady's orders," *hend* Parradu said heavily.

"So you said," said Nindi. "Protect it from what, is what I want to know. Them as wants to take the engine out of tidal hands, is it, Vashmarna? You going to protect us from them . . . *Vashmarna*?"

"I don't know anything about an engine," the *hend* said doggedly. "All I have are my orders."

"From a woman in jail," said Hamana scathingly.

Aramis stirred at Moth's side. "What about that, Par? Do we know why?"

The *hend* shared a glance with him. "Majun? You brought the news."

One of the yellowcoats stepped forward. "All I know is the order went out to recall the men from the docks, and then the news came from the scholarium that the lady'd been taken to Shaudarand. It was *purdar* Nind who sent me over the fort wall when the shaudah's men laid siege. He said to fetch you back before they blew the gate."

All the yellowcoats leaned forward. "*Hend* . . ."

"But those weren't the lady's orders," Aramis said. His face was lean and damp with tension. "*Her* last orders were to protect the shrine."

"Protect the shrine?" Hamana said scathingly. "Protect the engine? Sure, protect it from them who built it, from them who own it! Don't you see?" She appealed to Nindi first, then the other greenguards in the room. "Without the ship the engine was worthless to her. But we finished the ship, we brought it right into the *shadras* bay, and then—oh, yes!—*then* the engine meant something to her all right. *Then* she wanted to take them both. They're no allies, Nindi, they're just thieves. Let the bluecoats take them, I say. It's all they're good for!"

Nindi was a hard man to impress. "What ship?" he said.

"I don't know anything about a ship," *hend* Parradu said, looking at Nindi with a puzzled frown.

" 'What ship?' " Silk said, laughing. She nudged Moth's good side. " 'What ship?' "

Moth put her head in her hands.

"Listen," Aramis said urgently. "The ship and the engine are the only way off this island—for anyone! We *all* have a reason to protect them both."

"Protect them for Vashmarna," Hamana said.

"The only way?" *hend* Parradu said with a meaningful glance at Aramis.

Aramis took on a hunted look.

Hemmar Gamood said pedantically, "There will be no Vashmarna if the shaudah takes the fort."

"And," Moth said, inspired, "if the shaudah takes Vashmarna and Ghar, then what's left to keep him out of the tidal? With no more opposition he'll have the ship, the engine, and us laid out like fish on a slab."

"No opposition?" Hamana said softly. "What makes you think we can't muster an opposition? Or do you mean you won't?"

"I . . ." Moth closed her mouth.

"Of course she'll fight," Silk said, as if there could be no argument.

But Hamana said more softly yet, "For us, or for the engine?"

"Which 'us'?" Moth asked Hamana abruptly. "Do you

mean you and Silk, or the tidal, or the cult? Hamana, would you still burn your dead?"

"What?" Hamana rocked back on her heels. "What?"

Nindi understood what. He gave Moth a long black stare.

"Our dead burned," Hemmar Gamood said. He leveled a finger at Moth. "The dead you left to burn."

"*Andas,*" Aramis said in a rough voice, "that is unfair. None of us would have gotten out alive if not for Moth."

"Aramis," said *hend* Parradu, "I don't know anything about a ship, and I don't know anything about an engine. What I know is that these people don't want us to protect them. They don't—gods witness!—*need* us to protect them, and the *andas* is right: with the Vashmarna in prison, there's nothing left for us if the shaudah takes the fort. There will be no Vashmarna—and we'll be either dead or down here with the rest of the . . ." He took a quick glance around the room. "With them, whether they want us or not."

"Oh, probably not," murmured Silk.

"So what are you saying?" said Aramis. "We ignore the Vashmarna's orders?"

"Yes!" said Hemmar Gamood. *Hend* Parradu chewed his lip.

Aramis scrubbed his mud-streaked hands through his hair. He was sweating through his shirt. "You say that without the fort there is no Vashmarna. I say that without the ship and the engine there is no *point* to Vashmarna. Don't you see that without the bridge and the towers Vashmarna barely has a reason to exist? What's the use of the generating station if there's no need for the power? What's the use of the manufactories if everyone's too sick and poor, or too dead, to buy the goods?"

"But you're talking like this ship is already ours!" The *hend* sounded angry at his own confusion.

"It is," said Aramis.

"It is," said Hemmar Gamood.

"*It is not,*" said Hamana. "The ship is ours, the engine has always been ours, and I don't care if the shaudah throws the whole lot of you to the sharks, and the Ghar, too. They will always be ours."

"Moth," said Aramis, turning to her with desperate eyes.

Hamana turned to Moth with a challenging stare.

Everyone turned to Moth. Moth who hurt with a raw, sickening pain. Moth who was still painfully thirsty, and hating the smell of mud, and tired to death of the argument, all arguments, forever, but especially arguments that no side could win.

And because they can't win, they'll go on fighting, won't they? said Moth's pain to Moth. In another moment the greenguards and the yellowcoats would be killing one another in this very room, killing one another over a ship none of them could sail, and an engine none of them could use.

Moth looked up and saw Aramis's death in Hamana's eyes. How very clear it all was!

"One of these days," she said to Hamana, "you will learn to listen to me. As I have been saying all along, the engine is ours. The ship is ours. And you're perfectly right, *hend,* we neither need nor want your help in protecting either of them from the bluecoats or the shaudah or anyone else."

"Moth," said Aramis.

"We may, however, be willing to deal with Vashmarna, if there is a Vashmarna when it comes time to supply and crew the ship—because after all, *andas,*" she said with a sweet smile to Hemmar Gamood, "it would be a shame not to make use of your expertise. So I suggest that you take yourselves off to the fort—or better yet, why not make a try at rescuing the Vashmarna? I'm sure she'd be grateful, and it would take a hostage out of the shaudah's hands. Or what were you planning on doing when the shaudah tells you to surrender or watch your lady die? Yes, that's the best idea. Rescue Vashmarna-*jin'.*"

Moth gave Aramis an impish grin. "If you have a hard time getting her into the fort, you can always bring her here."

But Aramis was blind to Moth's intentions. He was looking at her as if she had shot him through the heart.

Only live, Moth thought at him as hard as she could, *only live and I will explain. You don't even have to listen. Only live!* But he did not seem to hear.

It was Hamana who heard at least some of Moth's hidden intentions. She said, showing her teeth, "Oh, by all means. Rescue your lady and bring her home to her little Moth. Her good little, obedient little Moth. Where will you live with your mother, Moth? A pretty little tower built in the mud?"

"Mo-ther," Aramis said, breaking the word over two breaths. Hemmar Gamood stared with an open mouth. *Hend* Parradu let his eyes glaze over, leaving them to get on without him.

"Think what you want," Moth said to Hamana with a weary shrug. "If you think we can take on the shaudah and the Society *and* the Ghar without an ally, then by all means . . ."

"You are my ally," Hamana said with a menacing weight to her words.

Moth put a hand to her side, where the bandages already hung wet and loose, and then held her hand up bloody for Hamana to see. "You can hope," she said weakly, and let herself sag against the back of the chair.

Aramis dropped to his knees at her side. His shirt, too, was blotted with her drying blood. "Moth," he said, and put out his hands to touch her.

What the hell did she have to do to send him away? "Leave me be!"

His hands hovered, clenched to fists. "But the child," he whispered, not for secrecy—they could all hear him—but for pain. "The child."

Moth closed her eyes. Was it possible? Her heart hurt more

than her torn hip. She looked at Aramis, challenging him to read the truth—all the truths—in her eyes, and said, "The child is already doomed, Aramis. It was drowned by the *mundab*, burned by the *Firebird*'s soul. I promise you, you have nothing left to keep you here."

He believed her. It was enough to break her heart all over again, but he believed her.

And Hamana let him go.

THE BAY

When night fell, the lights of the fort blazed out against the black bulk of the land, and Lady Vashmarna was comforted. At least that much of Vashmarna still stood. All she had for herself, however, was a single candle, and even that was a kindness of her guards. The meagerness of that kindness, the bitter inadequacy of the gift, only served to illuminate the poverty of her resources, and of theirs. There was so little to distinguish between them, Lady Vashmarna and her guards, that it was both offensive and absurd that she should be in their custody. Why were they not in hers? They were all prisoners in Shaudarand, all exiles in the dark.

She recognized that if she had been truly resigned to her powerlessness, she would not be thinking this way.

I am still lord of my demesne, she thought. *They can take me away from my demesne, but they cannot take my demesne from me.*

Sophistry and bluster. She was no better than Divaram Ghar.

She had retreated to her bedroom to escape his attempts at conversation. She had found herself on the verge of shouting at him *What do you want of me? Haven't you already taken all you can get?* but she would not give him the satisfaction and took herself away. Now, with the flies buzzing around her candle and the lights of the fort as far out of her reach as the stars, she wondered why she should hold herself aloof. Why not have it out with him? Why not throw her accusations in his face, why not demand his justifications, why not hear what he had to say? What frightened her more, that he might be justified or that he would prove that he was not?

Or was it that he would demand her own justifications, and would sit in judgment upon them?

Disgusted with herself, and sick of the flies that buzzed like her thoughts, Lady Vashmarna took her candle across the hall, across the narrow range of her liberty, and opened the door to the sitting room. Divaram Ghar was still there, but he sat with his head bowed and his face in his hands, deep in prayer.

THE TIDAL

Moth's buttock and leg had seized up on the injured side, protecting her torn hip by making it impossible to walk. She had to haul herself along on the backs of the chairs, and even so felt another trickle of fresh blood seep through the bandages and down her thigh. It felt clean as it tracked through the drying mud on her leg. She propped herself against the jamb of the inner door and with a shaking hand fumbled it open onto the secret shrine. It was dark here, the windows long ago bricked up and no lamps lit, but the engine stole its own light from somewhere else, a dim, warm, brassy gleam. Like a manifest it illuminated nothing but itself, its curves and its long straight shafts, the smooth upper limb of its wheel like the lid of a half-open eye. Moth dragged her useless leg across the gallery and propped herself against the rail, though it was not much sturdier than she. As the pain of movement subsided and her other senses awoke, she could feel the engine's cold breath, smell the briny stink of the low-tide basement, hear the groan of the fire-scorched balcony under her feet. The shrine was very quiet with everyone but Moth and *aras* Crab gone. And Istvan dead. Istvan dead.

"All right," Hamana had said to her with a hateful satisfaction, "I let your lover go. Now. What are you going to do for me?"

"For you, Hamana?" Nindi had said. His voice had been quiet, his black eyes almost—almost—amused.

Hamana had stared at him, recognizing the threat but refusing to give in. Still, she did not speak. It was Silk who said, "Finish the engine. Until it's done, we don't have anything but a bluff."

"And when it is done?" Crab asked. "Then what do we have? Can we put everyone in the tidal on board? Is there land waiting for us all out beyond the rim of the world?"

"The *aras* is right," Nindi said. "I don't know anything about this ship, and I don't care. While you've been off doing whatever you think is so important, we've been fighting a war. And now, with Vashmarna and Ghar killing the other side for a change, we have a chance to make some real gains."

"Take the towers!" said one of his crew. The stir of enthusiasm among the rest suggested this was not the first time the suggestion had been raised.

Nindi shot it down with a sneer. "Full of the plague? Let the baysiders have them! No, we don't want the towers, but we can take the docks. With the bridge out, holding the docks is the same as holding the towers, and we'd be holding their sick as well."

"And the Vashmarna and the Ghar," someone said, "if what that yellowcoat said is true."

"So we'd have hostages—the towers themselves'd be hostages—and we'd have the ship, for what it's worth. If we take the docks and hold 'em, we can finish the engine when and how we like, and use it how we like, too. Why trouble ourselves over a ship if we can hold the whole *rasnan*?"

This was well received by everyone except for *aras* Crab, who looked glum; Hamana, who still quivered with indignation; and Silk, who was hovering over Moth.

"Well, whatever you're going to do," said Silk, "you're going to have to do it without Moth. She's out cold."

She was huddled in her chair with her eyes mostly closed, and bless Silk for falling for her ruse. The quantity of blood on Crab's cushions probably helped. Faking unconsciousness, Moth could not look up to see the expression on Hamana's face, nor the sudden move the greenguard must have made. She did feel Silk leap to her feet, and she heard a scuffle and Hamana saying furiously, "She's the one who started the whole thing! This whole cursed thing! *Are you just going to let her lie there?*"

"Talk to the man who shot her," said Silk, just as angry. "Huh, Nindi?"

"No one meant to hurt Moth," Nindi said irritably. "We didn't even know she was with . . ."

"Us?" finished Silk. "You knew Hamana was with us right enough. You might have guessed!"

"What we might have guessed," Nindi said with thinning patience, "is that you were prisoners being forced to betray the shrine. I might accept the blame for bad aim, Silk, but I won't take your shit for anything else. Not unless someone who's been here all along wants to make a complaint. Anyone? No, I didn't think so. So. We don't have Moth. Do we need her? Have we needed her all this time?"

Aras Crab said, "Istvan might have needed her. He surely needed someone. And the Society of Doors is still—"

"The Society! Gods and demons, Crab, let it be. Where is the Society in all of this? Who fucking cares about the Society and their holy door? We have the shaudah's soldiers cutting Vashmarna and Ghar down to size, and with a bit of luck they're repaying the compliment, and I say we make the most of it while we can!"

So they left. Not without more argument, but they left, leaving only two guards on the roof since the contingent of blue-coated Ghars had chased after the Vashmarna men. Crab might have rebandaged Moth's wound then, he had certainly had enough practice, but she had fended him off as feebly as she could and still make her point. She did not think he would run after Nindi to tell him Moth was faking, and neither did she think he would seriously disapprove of her ducking the greenguards' plans, but it was wisest for her to keep her head down. The more they discounted her, the freer she would be to act.

When and if she figured out what she should do. Oh, Istvan! He would have known. He would have been wrong, but he would have known.

What Crab had apparently decided to do was to pray to the scorned and forgotten saints in the cult's borrowed shrine. And who was Moth to judge him? She hung against the gallery railing for a long time, watching the slide of light down the engine's curves. In the windowless room it was like a faint sketch against the darkness, the merest outline of the complexity and power hidden within the shrine's permanent night. Tracing its lines with her gaze, Moth ran her mind just as lightly over the bitter iron-hard tangle of her life. Her life, which was somehow the same as the calamity of her world. Istvan dead, Lady Vashmarna imprisoned, Aramis cut loose from every loyalty he had tried to serve, Silk caught up in a fight for plague-ridden towers and flood-ruined fields. Moth herself shot and abandoned by her own kind.

Self-pity bent Moth against the gallery railing, and the railing threatened to give way. She lurched back, cracking the new scab at her waist, and swore at the breaking of her mood as much as at the breaking of the scab. Now she couldn't even feel sorry for herself! Exasperated, sullen, and stubborn, she dragged her leg across the gallery to the wall, groped for the sulfur matches in their box by the door, and, limping and sweating with pain, lit fish-oil lamps in sconces all around the room. Each match struck with a *rutch* and a *pop* of flame; each wick caught with a sigh. Outside, the sun would be sinking below the western headland. Within the shrine, the lamps, one after the other, conjured shadows out of the dark. They circled with Moth, keeping the engine's bulk between her and them, justifiably wary of their creator. The light lay oddly on the engine itself, refusing to mingle with the thing's own stolen glow, so that it looked permanently askew from the rest of the shrine, impossible to see clearly, in motion even when it was still.

Or was it still?

Moth took a lamp from its bracket and leaned gingerly over the gallery rail to bring her light as close to the engine as she could. On the floor below, tidal slime shimmered as tiny crabs fled the light. Their claws made the same breathy patter as the lamp flame behind its chimney of rippled glass. How many of them scuttled on too many claws, or too few? Looking more closely at the engine, she could see the effects of the *mundabi*'s tampering, their efforts to finish it in her absence. Despite all of Istvan's disapproval of Moth's own modifications, there was nothing left of Tarun's rational design. No longer an engine to power the tidal or the ship, it had become an abstract, a machine with no purpose, a concrete prayer. And to what? To whom? None of the *mundabi* really understood the *mundab*. They prayed, they infected the *mundab* with their dreams of god, and the *mundab* looked at the world with brief wonder— Is this what I am?—until it forgot what it was. These were the words the manifests spoke, the words the manifests were: Is this what I am? And receiving no answer, the engine, that was and was not a half-born god, warped a little further out of true.

Gods, thought Moth, who had never expected an answer to a single prayer. What would you be without our ceaseless demands? The engine stood tall enough to look her in the eye, cold, strange, powerful, deformed. It was not aware, but it began to stir, woken by her awareness. Slowly, slowly, the wheel turned, blinking the imagined eye. Slowly, slowly, the drive shafts groped for a propeller that was not there. Gears and armature turned deep within, a complex dance so ponderous that Moth felt the shrine tilt into dizziness around her, as if it were the world that tried to turn around too many axes, and the engine that stood still.

As if it were the engine that could turn the world.

"Not that," Moth said, "not so much as that." But she was not arguing, not even protesting, she was merely voicing her awe, and her doubt. She, in her ignorance, could not have made such a thing. Could she? She stood in the icy draft of the engine's slow movement with the lamp held high in one hand and her womb hidden behind the other, while half-born manifests rolled on their ghostly wheels, stalked on their steam-ripple armature legs, until the gallery was filled with the restless half-visible crowd and their electric tension, their silent demand to be heard. Moth, as always, was slow to understand, but eventually, dipping one mental toe into the *mundab,* she got the hint.

The engine was not stirring because of her. It stirred, it had been prodded into motion, because the *mundab* itself was in flood.

The *mundab* is a current with no direction, a river with no banks, an ocean without a shore. Moth, slipping warily into its depths, is a boulder that spins up eddies, little whirlpools that turn the world a little, just a little, her way. So what is this? What is this gaping maw, this dreadful void that gulps the *mundab* down?

Moth surfaces almost before she dives, and gasps for air as the *mundab* rushes on without her, rushes on to nowhere, rushes on beyond the shores of the world.

"The Society is opening its door," she says, and knows—as though the voice of a god has told her—that this is true.

And here she is, crippled and alone, with nothing she can do about it, and no one she can tell.

THE BAY

It was a crime in Lady Vashmarna's code to interrupt someone
at his prayers. She hesitated, but she had had her fill of the prisoner's solitude of her room, so without speaking to Lord Ghar,
she set her candle down and returned to her post at the narrow
window. If it were not for the lights of the fort, the water of the
bay would have been as dark as the land, and the dead line of
the bridge would have been invisible. But the generating station sent its proud glare skyward and the bay shimmered with
its false stars. There was no rain, and Lady Vashmarna allowed
herself the luxury of hoping for the end of the monsoon. The
floods would subside, the fields would be planted, the plague
would end. The cable would be repaired and the towers
brought back to life—but that they had not already been resur-
rected was not the fault of the rains, and by this route Lady
Vashmarna's thoughts were brought back to the realities of the

day. The rebellion and the shadow gods, the Society's sorcery and the source of the plague. The shaudah's opportunistic power-grabbing stubbornness and the ship that rested on the water somewhere outside of Lady Vashmarna's sight. Spurred by restlessness, she turned away from the unchanging view. Divaram Ghar still hid his face like a theatrical child who wishes to prove—what?—fear, repentance, shame.

I don't believe you, she thought at him, but it struck her that there was something sinister in his stillness. It was as if not just the gesture but his whole body was the lie, as if he had escaped their prison, leaving her behind with a husk. It was not reasonable for her to feel angry and afraid, but her nerves had been scraped to live wires by this dreadful season, and speaking at random she said aloud, "I wonder how much will change with the change of seasons."

Lord Ghar did not by so much as a breath reveal that he had heard her speak. Now Lady Vashmarna was offended as well as frightened.

"I have put all Vashmarna's resources into the ship and the new cable. I have offered them to the shaudah, and he has rejected them both. I have nothing left to give but Vashmarna itself, and he must know that I will never offer him that. But if he means to take it, why bother with this incarceration? Why not kill me, after all? What do you think, Ghar-*jan'*, does he mean to save us for some pretense of a trial, or does he truly only mean to scare us into subservience and thereby avoid a civil war?"

Still the Ghar did not respond. Was this punishment for her earlier rejection of his conversation? That would be childish, and the Ghar had never been that. But the sound of her own carping voice reminded Lady Vashmarna that she was breaking a cardinal rule, and she turned back to the window. For a moment all was as it had been, and then the tremor struck, shivering the windows in the fort an instant before it shivered

Shaudarand's windows, half a heartbeat before it shook Shaudarand's floor.

"Bless spirits of air, save from dark-shroud evils of night!"

The rote prayer came out in a frightened gabble, and Lady Vashmarna, embarrassed, turned again toward her companion. But Lord Ghar did not stir, did not even seem to breathe, and Lady Vashmarna, closer to the edge of her self-control than she had realized, wanted to shout at him. She turned back to the window and gripped the stony frame in her hands, pressed her face into the narrow space before the glass. Were there lights out in the fort across the way? The huge lamps that burned atop the dam were untouched—she counted them at a glance—but some of the windows were dark. Lamps knocked off desks, or turned off in sudden fear? A second tremor hit, stronger than the first, and Lady Vashmarna saw a terrible thing. The lights in three, four, five windows did not go out, they *fled,* streaks of light whipping away through the darkness beyond the bulk of the bridge abutment past which she could not see. *Spirits of air,* she thought, and she remembered the night the bridge fell. Moth! Feeling a strangely happy exasperation, an illogical relief, she turned yet again to Lord Ghar, as if she could share her daughter's accomplishments, though the gods alone knew what those accomplishments were.

But still he had not moved, and finally Lady Vashmarna could not endure another second of this absence, if absence this was. "Ghar-*jan'*," she said sharply. *"Jandas!"* And when he did not move, she strode over to his chair and gripped his arm.

For a terrifying instant she is in another place; as if she has clutched a sinking man, she falls, she drowns.

She let him go with a gasp and sidled away from him until her back touched the door. The floor was also sidling, but then it dropped and beat back up so suddenly that she fell to her knees. Her candle was overturned, and snuffed itself harmlessly in its own wax. Lord Ghar's candle was knocked out of its holder and rolled across the bare floor, spilling shadows that wrestled one another across the ceiling. Lady Vashmarna scrambled after the rolling candle, frightened by this threat of darkness, but when she had it in her hand and the flame was only trembling, the shadows still leapt about the room. Lady Vashmarna, with the last of her dignity and all of her courage, pulled herself to her feet and walked out of the room and down the hall to the corner where their guards stood braced against another tremor.

"Please help me," she said with an honestly shaking voice. "The Ghar is summoning demons in our room."

THE TIDAL

The door, the door, the Society's door. Moth shivered with cold, with pain, with jealous rage. In that moment, if she could have claimed absolute ownership of the *mundab,* she would have. How dared they? How *dared* they touch the *mundab*—touch her engine? They might as well have put their aristocratic hands on the nascent child in her womb. The bloody Ghars, laying claim to the most intimate, the most crucial, the only certain element of her life. She had despised them for their contempt for the tidal, she had felt a hot and salty anger for their attacks on her and Aramis, but this, this was cause for hatred, bleak and bitter in her mouth.

The engine itself was silent, but it roiled the air like an oar pulled through still water, and the cold eddies ripped at the lamp flames and hissed in Moth's ears. She imagined all her enemies walking through the door to heaven and leaving the *mundab,* this unknown, unwanted world, to those who would call it home, but she knew how childish that was. Even if Aramis had not told her about the darkness and the plague, it would have been childish, simply because nothing was ever so easy. But thinking about Aramis made her sad. Aramis, whom she had driven away. *Oh, love! Never believe me, you know how I lie!* But some lies could not be forgiven, even if they were not believed. How could Aramis forgive her? He had betrayed the Society so thoroughly for Moth's sake that they would never allow him through the door, any more than they would allow her. Not even Lady Vashmarna, she thought, could pass through that or any other door so long as she was the shaudah's prisoner. In spite of everything it was slightly cheering to think of herself and her sponsor, her mother, as finally the same: friendless and trapped, going nowhere, stuck in the mud while even the ship slipped from their grasp. All they had—all Moth had, she corrected herself—was the engine. The engine, churning like a waterwheel in the *mundab*'s stream, and the child, turning tiny circles in her womb.

Never believe me, when even I don't know what's true.

Moth shivered again and dragged her useless leg over to the door, where she could put the heavy lamp on its shelf. Yes, the engine was hers as much as the child was, which was to say— witness Lady Vashmarna!—not hers at all. Not really. Hers to birth, maybe, but not hers to keep. Not hers any more than she had been her mother's. That was the painful truth. Even if Lady Vashmarna had kept her, she could not have *kept* her, not from the *mundab,* not from the trials of the world. If she had, if she had even tried, Moth would have been her prisoner. At least Lady Vashmarna had spared her that.

Oh, yes, she thought grimly, *there* was a reason for love.

But what did that mean for the engine? Forget the child. (Moth's mouth took on an ironical twist.) The child would come in its own time, but the only time the engine had was

Moth's. The engine was even more dependent on her than her child. Think of that! This little piece of the *mundab* that wanted to be bound into the world, this god-in-waiting that wanted to be set free, looking to no one else but her. Moth had opened the door to the priest's room, wanting to get out of the chill wind, needing at the very least to sit and rest her throbbing hip, but she hesitated, looking back. The wheel spun out its chorus of reflections, its sentences and paragraphs of ghosts. Is this what I am? Is this? Is this? It demanded, it desperately needed an answer, and Moth—

Moth was distracted by the sounds rising up from the shrine. A splintering crash that had to be the broken door. A cry of dismay that had to be *aras* Crab. A pistol shot— "*No!*"—that also had to be *aras* Crab. The thump of booted feet on the stairs and more thumps overhead, where the greenguards made their escape to the neighboring roof, firing their pistols only to cover their retreat. Discretion in the face of an invasion. The shaudah's troops? Vashmarna's? Ghar's? Or did it even matter any longer?

Moth, her teeth bared at the sheer bloody-mindedness of the world, lurched back into the inner shrine, through the manifests that parted around her like shapes painted on gauze, and to the ladder that led down to the floor below. Dropping down to ease herself onto the ladder's top rung, she saw the red gleam of her footprints on the bare boards. She laid her face against the floor. It was such a relief to be lying down, her weight off her hip and cramping leg, that she suffered a momentary temptation just to lie there and wait for Crab's murderers to come and shoot her, too. Her and the child. Ah, well, there was that. The door to the priest's room cracked open, revealing a hand holding a pistol and a dark blue sleeve, and she let herself slide down the ladder into the darkness of the engine's well, most of her weight on her hands.

The bluecoats weren't talking. She had no idea how many

there were, but she heard the gallery groan and pop as they stepped through the door.

"What in Prosepurn's name—" one of them said, but he was hushed by someone else. Moth imagined them pointing out her bloody footsteps to one another, finding the splotch of blood she had left at the gallery's rim, and she dropped belly-down on the basement's slimy floor. The pain was bad enough to steal her breath. She felt the crabs pinching at her pant leg, drawn by the scent of blood, and in a convulsive motion she rolled away from them. Her good knee hit something hard. The tall bamboo ladder, after a quiet and leisurely fall, dropped with a bouncing, bonging clatter to the lower floor.

Moth kept on rolling until she was under the gallery and against the barred door to the outer shrine, stupid with pain and covered with slime, but out of sight to the men leaning over the gallery rail.

The engine pumped and churned and spun. From this low angle it was as huge and wild as a tidal wave galloping up to the shore. Overhead someone said "Find another ladder," and Moth saw the shadows of men moving through the shadows of manifests along the gallery's far side. Of course. These were the Ghar's men, Society men, not to be put off by a few demons. They couldn't shoot her through the engine, they couldn't even see her in the gallery's shade, but they knew she was there. It was peculiar to hear them talking about her as they moved around.

"He's already injured."

"Not much of a threat."

"One of the Vashmarnas, shot and left behind?"

"They would." This was spoken with contempt, but in fact was not true. *Hend* Parradu had taken the injured yellowcoat with the rest of his platoon.

Incompetent bastards, Moth thought of the Vashmarna guards. Couldn't they even make a decent job of drawing the

Ghars off? How did they think they were going to get Lady Vashmarna out of the tower and into the fort with that kind of effort? They might just as well have stayed.

How she wished they had stayed!

"No ladder," said a voice that gulped for air. "But there's a door down below. Barred or bolted from the other side, but we still have powder enough for another charge."

Moth was *lying* against the door down below. She pulled herself onto her elbows and began to slither toward the corner, crabs scattering around her as she moved.

"No," said the voice in charge. "We'll save the powder for the abomination. If him down below was a threat, he would have made his move by now."

More groaning footsteps, some muttered gunpowder-pouring conversation. Moth crawled, and seethed. So now she was an abomination? Those plague carriers should talk! But then she remembered that they thought she was the wounded Vashmarna guard. The abomination was the engine.

They were going to blow up her engine!

She touched the *mundab,* ready to do she knew not what, and for an instant she thought it was the pure force of her fury that shook the earth. But as the men overhead cried out— "Don't drop the keg! Watch the lamps! *Don't drop the keg!*"— she realized the earthquake was none of hers. The *mundab* poured away, away, away, and the Society's door made a crack in the shuddering world.

Or so Moth thought, as the world, or at any rate the shrine, fell down around her ears.

What kind of counterstroke was that?

THE BAY

The shaudah's guards failed Lady Vashmarna. They took one look at the shadows clambering around the Ghar's still form, and they ran. She should not have blamed them. Here was everything dreadful in the world. But she did blame them, she blamed them bitterly.

"Cowards," she said, a cold judgment spat at their backs. One looked back, but she saw hatred on his face, not guilt. She regretted having said it only when she was alone, and then only because, having said it, she could not now run herself. She stood in the doorway to the sitting room, her candle the only light, and watched the shadows build themselves into fantastic shapes only to tear themselves apart. It was as if they meant to form themselves into a room inside the room, but could not bear the weight, the discipline, the pain. They fled, grappled with one another, fled again. Lady Vashmarna, seeing a gargoyle arch take shape for a heartbeat before it dissolved into chaos, was illuminated.

"You are summoning your door," she said to the unresponsive Lord Ghar. Her voice jumped and flickered like her small yellow flame, but the shadows took no more notice of her words than they did of the candle. "You are wrestling with the world to force it to take the shape of your escape. Is your son joined in the same struggle? Is that why it resists you, because you are apart? Is that why the earth protests?"

Pillars formed like plumes of inky smoke and fell away again into a headless tangle of shifting limbs. The shadows were less shadowlike as they peeled free from the ceiling, walls, and floor. They loomed larger when they stood on their own, giants bent by the confines of the room. Lord Ghar's hands shone with the sweat that trickled through his masking fingers, the only sign that he was not a statue but a living man. Lady Vashmarna's voice gained in strength.

"But no, poor Baradam, he has always fought you, hasn't he? He has always resisted your rule, even as he struggled to serve you with all his being. You never saw that, did you? You thought he demanded equal power to yours—equal or greater, that was your fear—but he never has. He does not want to rule you any more than he wants to be ruled. Your poor son, I do pity him, for the only relationship he has ever wanted with you is one of love. Not power, not politics: love."

Her voice caught. The frantic shadows seemed to be stirring up a ghostly breeze, odorless and cold, and she had to wonder, Was the Ghar conjuring a door to his son, or a door to the *ramhadras*? Heaven or hell: at this moment there was little to choose between them. Lady Vashmarna stooped to put her candle on the floor and then clasped her hands before her mouth as if in prayer.

"Shall I tell you a secret, Divaram? I also have a child. Yes," she said, although he had not moved, "I'm glad that surprises you. I would hate to think all this desperate secrecy had been in vain. But it's quite true, I have a child, and like your child, she would have done anything for me for one honest moment of love. Yes, I think that's true. Love has been so scarce between us that it would have seemed like a treasure to her. One honest moment of love."

Pillars, a roof beam, a trembling arch. The shadows were solid enough to cast their own shadows now. Was there to be another door, an infinite regression of doors? The arch collapsed. The shadows lingered, struggling in their turn to hold—or escape?—the desired shape. Lady Vashmarna, with too many things to watch and all of them frightening, fixed her eyes on her old friend as she stepped inside the room.

"We are so alike, you and I. Perhaps we should have married after your wife died. But no," she corrected herself, "that would have been terrible, though it's difficult to say exactly why. Perhaps only because that would have made this moment too grievous to contemplate. And if we were such wretched parents apart, what would we have been together? Fighting for power on every hand. But I can't help but wonder what you would have made of my daughter. I mean what you would have thought of her—or, no, perhaps I did mean 'made.' For you know, Divaram, I have not made anything of her at all. She has made herself. She is out of my hands, and always has been. But you." She laid her hands on the back of the other chair. "You have never let poor Baradam go, have you? Even now you cannot let him go."

Lord Ghar took his hands away from his face and looked up at her. She knew even before he did that the door had finally taken shape, for she could feel the draft of it on her neck, and the cold airless breeze was replaced by the sweet familiar perfume of the temple's incense. But the real, dreadful shock was the realization that he had heard every word.

"Who knew such a thing was even possible?" Lady Vashmarna said, gripping the chair back with all her strength.

"Not even I," said Lord Ghar with a restrained triumph, "until this very hour."

"And now you will open the other door."

"It is already opening. Vashmarna-*jin'*, Kalind, it is not too late. You, at least, can still come with us. You can still come home."

"Now you ask me? You ask me *now*? My dear friend," she said, her voice shaking with the force of her scorn, "I do thank you, but no."

"So," said the Ghar as he prepared to rise. "We were friends once."

"When I was worthy, do you mean? But I never was. No, truly, we never were."

"You dishonor the past," he said with a stern, patriarchal scowl. He was scolding her.

He was scolding her.

This was more than she could bear. Before he could gain his feet, she lifted the chair and swung it with all her strength at his head. Contact jarred the chair out of her hands. It tumbled into a dark-haunted corner. Lord Ghar fell in a heap, and having felt the chair strike and having heard the brittle snap of the old man's neck, she had no doubt that he was dead. She had meant to stop him; she had killed him. It would take a lifetime to reconcile intention with action, and action with result, and she did not have that time just now. There were footsteps pounding down the hall, a gasp of horror at the door. She turned and saw not the shaudah's men but Aramis Tapurnashen, staring as if it were he who had struck, or been struck by, the blow.

Her rescuer, come far too late to do her any good at all.

"Gods forgive me," she said formally, and stepped between the black pillars of the Ghar's restless and unwilling door.

THE TIDAL

The tide was on the rise. Moth came to herself when she began to drown.

The whole shrine might not have fallen on her, but the gallery certainly had. She was enmeshed in a crosshatch of timbers and planks, splintered boards, broken lamps, starting nails. More than her hip was injured, but she did not know how badly. The salt water seared her throat, and for a time there was nothing to life but coughing and coughing and trying to pull herself free. She spent a small eternity trapped there with fire in her lungs, but in the world's time it probably was not long before she was standing up in the ankle-deep water. Standing and bleeding—she had been ruthless with herself in the struggle—but she could wipe the hair out of her eyes and take stock.

The lamps were all out, dashed to oily pieces in the earthquake, but one limb of the gallery that still clung to the high wall was burning. The fire leapt in the cold wind, for the engine was still alive. It reared above Moth, terrible and huge, threatening her with death with every lunge of its armature, every turn of its hissing spark-stung wheel. Stupid to be afraid of it, but it was fearsome, thrashing the smoky air with its cold limbs, its every motion magnified by the darkness, the firelight, the glittering tide. Manifests swarmed the walls, man-size incarnations of Tarun's lost toys, as if they borrowed substance from the dark. Blue-white sparks rained down all around her to kiss the water with pinpricks of steam. It was pure bravado that carried Moth through the water to the engine's base.

Someone was shouting in the orphaned door high in the wall where the gallery had used to be.

"Lashman! Lashman, is that you?"

Moth had forgotten the bluecoats. She looked up, and the two of them stared at each other in mutual shock.

"Who the hell are you?" the bluecoat said at last.

Moth considered what she must look like, battered and thin, an orphan girl in ragged clothes. She did not have to fake a shiver. It came quite naturally, wet and injured as she was.

"Please, sir!" she cried. "I only wanted shelter for the night!"

For a moment she thought it might work, but the bluecoat was obviously a man with a logical mind. He said skeptically "Down there?" and drew his pistol out of his sash. While he was checking that its pan was primed, Moth dropped to her hands and knees and scrambled around the corner of the engine's base.

The lead shot hit one of the drive shafts and whined off into the dark.

"Lashman!" the bluecoat shouted, his voice hoarse from the smoke of the growing fire. It dawned on Moth that he was calling for a fallen companion at just about the time a dark shape too clumsy for a manifest separated itself from the darkness.

"I'm here, sir! I'm busted up some."

"Watch yourself," warned the voice from above. "You've got one of them down there with you."

"I know. I see it."

Not for long. Moth turned one more corner of the base and scuttled like a wounded crab into the lightless heap of the gallery's wreckage.

The officer called down from the door. "Can you get it?"

"Don't see it now, sir."

"Well, if that's what was bleeding up here before, I doubt it's much of a threat. Can you get to the door down there and throw the bolts?"

"I think so."

"Do it, then. I've sent the rest of the men down below. As soon as you're through I'll light the charge. I want you men to head straight for the street, you hear me? And shut the door behind you. I've got a short fuse on this thing and I don't want to bring the roof down on your heads."

"What about you, sir?"

"I'll be there before you. That's what windows are for. Have you got that door open?"

"I just have to move . . ." The bluecoat's voice faded as he bent to haul at a chunk of floor.

Meanwhile, Moth was arranging the pieces of the bluecoats' plan in her rattled mind. She did not like what she saw. Armed men behind the door, a fused charge big enough to bring the roof down . . . Never mind the engine. Once Lashman had the lower door open, they were going to blow *her* up.

A manifest rolled by, paired wheels propelled by long spindly machine arms reaching out from its axle. It had fingers like spider legs, too delicate for its size. Moth drew up a thread of the *mundab*, touched the manifest as it passed. This was no

Firebird, no flaming god. Its own faint gleam reddened slightly as its new substance caught the light of the burning gallery, but the only real change was the fine spray it sent up from its wheels and grasping hands as it rolled around the engine toward the bluecoat at the door. Moth could not see what happened in the shadows there. She reached for another manifest, a bouquet of stilt legs like a sharp handful of calipers, and sent it snick-snacking after the first.

The bluecoat at the door started to scream.

"Lashman!" The officer leaned out of the door to look down. He held a heavy globe in one hand, a gunpowder bomb with an unlit fuse dangling over his wrist, and Moth had to admire his presence of mind as he ducked inside the priest's room to set it carefully down. Moth herself was shuddering at the sounds that had replaced the screaming. The officer leaned out the door again and discharged his pistol. The muzzle flash was bright through the wind-torn smoke. The worst of the noises stopped. Squinting through the dazzle in her eyes, Moth saw the officer straighten and look about the shrine even as he groped in his sash for his powder and shot.

"Hey, tidal! Do you think your monsters can frighten a real man?" he said, his voice thick with smoke or rage.

"I don't care if they frighten you," Moth said honestly, "as long as they can kill you."

As calm as if he were leaning in the doorway of his own home, apparently oblivious to the manifests that glided across the ceiling and down the wall at his side, he tapped a measured amount of powder into his pistol's muzzle and tamped down a ball and wad.

"I've seen worse," he said. "Worse than you can imagine."

"When your lord first tried to open his door?" Moth was shivering badly. She could hear the newly corporeal manifests snicking and splashing as they explored their limited realm, but she was curious to know what the bluecoat would say.

He tapped priming powder into the pan and lowered the hammer into place. "The demons that guard the way are terrible, but the righteous have nothing to fear."

"Like you have nothing to fear from the plague?" Moth no longer had to shout. The engine was running quietly as the last of the earthquake dust sifted down into the rising tide.

"The plague was the cult's!" He fired the pistol at her voice. "We always knew that, whatever the Vashmarna said."

Moth ducked, far too late, at the sound of the lead ball thunking into wood. "It wasn't, you know. If you think it was, you're just believing your own lies."

"Better ours than yours." He tapped more priming powder into the pan without loading the pistol, cocked the hammer, and picked up the bomb in his free hand.

Moth touched another manifest that wandered by, a lizard-like affair of broken beams and nails and glass. It fought gravity and its own newfound mass to clamber up the rough stone wall. The bluecoat held the end of the fuse over the primed pan.

"What about your lord's lies?" Moth said desperately, trying to buy her manifest some time. "Did he tell you when he sent you here he was going to open the door before you returned?"

The bluecoat froze. "He did not send us. We followed the traitor off the ship on our own."

"The traitor . . ." He must have meant Aramis. *Dear man,* Moth thought, *not again!* She had to grope after her next line. "Do you know the door is open, right now, even as we speak? Do you know they're about to leave you behind?"

The bluecoat visibly shook off her words. "More lies," he said, and pulled the trigger. The pan flashed, the fuse caught— Moth could have told him where to find Crab's matches—and just as her manifest reached the threshold of the door, he threw the bomb into the engine.

The engine tossed the bomb right back at him, only much, much harder, and bowled him through the door.

Moth was still staring, wide-eyed and openmouthed with surprise, when the explosion filled the upper door with fire. The shrine shuddered. More debris fell from the ceiling to scream in the engine's sparking wheel. It sounded like a howl of triumph, and Moth shuddered with superstitious dread even as sense caught up with what she had seen. When the bluecoat threw the bomb—Did he flinch, after all his brave talk, when the manifest touched his feet? He had aimed at the engine's heart, but he had hit the racing wheel, which had returned his throw as naturally as spit in the wind hits the eye. Not godly retribution, just bad aim.

Moth would have laughed if the blast had not caught her splintery manifest and knocked it burning merrily into the wreckage piled against the lower door.

THE BASTION

Lord Ghar's door collapsed as Lady Vashmarna stepped through, its shadows fleeing like leaves on a racing stream. Dizzy, as lost to herself as if she and not Lord Ghar had died on the other side of that chasm, she had one slow breath of time to encompass where she was and what she saw. Heaven or hell?

A meditation hall in the scholarium. A low ceiling with long, dark beams, paneled walls, a polished floor. Lamps on sconces and the warm ghost of incense on the air.

A crowd. Dark blue tunics, a clutch of unbleached scholars' robes. Shadows pressed in among them like a second crowd, so that human faces were etched against darkness, frightened faces drawn in the hard lines of mortal strain.

The shadows built themselves into shapes of anguish and then fell away as if the room were a torn net and some fast-moving current dragged them through the tears. Perhaps Lady Vashmarna slipped in the same way? There were always more shadows, the ghosts of cornice and arch, of lintel and jamb, of the memories of buildings twisted into nearly human form. Aramis had spoken of the haunted door.

Aramis, who stood breathing hard at her side, having followed her through. Divaram's son was also there. He and all his people stood extraordinarily still, as if they were the fixed points in an otherwise rushing universe, frozen and timeless as the shadows were flung up out of nothing to mime their brief agonies before being swept into the nothing of the door.

The door that was not a constructed shape like Divaram's invention, a door that was a lightless wound in the air.

In that one slow breath, Lady Vashmarna had time to think, despite the flight of the shadows and the beating of her heart, that she had stepped outside of time. But then it was made clear that all those frozen people were merely struck dumb by the surprise of her arrival. Soldiers groped for their pistols, a woman among the scholars bit off a cry. *Aras* Baradam, his dark face stiff and his voice thick in his mouth, shouted, "Where is my father?" And Lady Vashmarna told him, "He is dead."

THE TIDAL

Moth perched on the engine's base, a jointed arm as thick as her waist beating the air above her head. Her ears throbbed with the silent concussions, and she shivered in the wind, though it summoned an occasional current of heat from the fire against the wall. The fire would probably spread farther before the tide rose high enough to put it out. The upper door also gave cheerful glimpses of flames between the gusts of smoke from below, but Moth doubted she was going to burn to death. The shrine was mostly stone. She was far more likely to be flattened when the walls came down.

Her and the engine, crushed together, mingled into one. Her and the little froglet inside her womb.

A manifest swam by, a thing of smoke and fish bones and cogs, and she touched it into reality. It floundered for a moment, then found its bearings and slithered off to join the others at the lower door. They scattered burning planks into the water, threw sparks into the air. Some of them caught fire—or perhaps they wore the fire as Moth wore blood and mud and algae slime. It was hard to tell if they were consumed. She hoped they might clear the wreckage from the door, or even batter the charred door down for her, but they were ungainly things, not shaped for work.

The *mundab* nagged at her every time she pulled a manifest into the world, its flood tide tugging at her the way it dragged at the engine, spinning it into life. Where did it go when it spilled away through the Society's door? With her own wound throbbing and blood caking her clothes, Moth had a dreadful sense that the *mundab,* the world's spirit, the world itself, was bleeding away, as if the limitless ocean that cradled the island were being drained through a hole in the sky. As if the *rasnan* were a stone plug shaped to fit a gap, and the plug was jolted loose by the earthquake that still shivered the ground from time to time. More dirt filtered down from the weakened ceiling, making the engine scream and throw off electric sparks, blue-white stars against the fire's sullen red. Moth dropped her head to her one raised knee to rest her smoke-stung eyes.

What would this world be without the *mundab*? The same as it always had been, she supposed, for almost everyone besides Moth. People would still yearn for the *ramhadras*'s silent gods, never knowing they had lost the hope of an answer closer to home. And perhaps the Society was right. Perhaps they would all go through the door, back to the *ramhadras,* where the gods waited to welcome them to the first home, the one true home where they belonged.

All except for Moth, who would be left behind in a world drained dry. Moth, and Lady Vashmarna, and Aramis the traitor. Silk. All the tidal folk, all the *hadri* who at this very moment had no idea anything was happening beyond the collapse of their homes and the ruin of their fields. If they were ever to achieve heaven, it would be the hard way. And in any case, Moth did not believe in heaven. She believed in this world. She believed in the *mundab,* bleeding away into the Society's door.

As if her thoughts drove them, the manifests broke through the lower door. There was a loud groan, a rending crash, a gust of air and a leap of flames. The refreshed fire shone like sunlight on the water covering the floor, making a gorgeous carpet above the slime. The manifests rolled and trundled and floundered out into the shrine, mobile torches that burned bright as they circled among the peaceful saints. The wreckage they left behind them made a flimsy barrier before the doorway, hissing as the rising water doused the embers. Moth rested her chin on her knee and looked out past the smoke and the manifests and the saints to the shrine's outer door hanging on its blasted hinges. Out there was night, Nindi's army, the shaudah's war. Out there, somewhere, was the Society and their wretched door. Moth had to face the fact that even if the roof held off collapsing long enough for her to make it through the door, she would never find them, not with one working leg and a battered head and too much blood on the wrong side of her skin. Just the thought of trying to negotiate the mud of the streets in rising water made her want to lie down by the fires and go to sleep.

But still the engine pounded away, like a vast heart that refused to die. Could she save something from the flood? Could she give herself and her world one god before all the *mundab* was gone? A strange, voiceless god it would be, a small god tucked away in a ship's hold, a seafarer's god. A seafarer's god. Moth liked the sound of that.

When she calls, *mundab* listens, *mundab* comes. It is everywhere, it is nowhere, there is no place to come from and no place to come to, but it comes. *Mundab* has always come for Moth. That moment of hunger when the heat lay heavy on the cracked mud, this moment of pain when salt-stung wounds bleed through her ragged clothes, they are the same moment. They are this moment, and this moment is the *mundab*'s time. It turns away from the nothing of the door to the something of the engine, the something that is a place in time and space, a mold that gives the everything that is the *mundab* the specificity, the individuality, of function and form. Why does the limitless divine want to confine itself within the skin of a god?

How does the ocean know itself without the contrast of the shore?

But this is Moth clutching at a breath of reason. Moth is simply trying not to drown. The *mundab* has already discovered the Society's *away*, and the Society's *away* is infinite and absolute. Moth has to offer an equally absolute *here*.

Here.

The engine struggles within its caul of smoke, growing new limbs, wheels, cogs, cylinders and shafts, and spinning rods. There is no reason, no design, no logic to the form. It grows and changes and grows. The burning scrap of the gallery that still clings to the wall is struck and falls into the tidewater with a silver gout of steam. Battered walls ring out with a terrible noise and a rain of sparks, the ceiling subsides a little more, the wheels scream an untuned chorus of burning dust. Leaves of fallen plants cascade through a gap in the roof and are torn to green shreds, confetti mingled with the sparks. The engine has grown beyond its stone platform now. Moth is inside it, surrounded by a cage of moving parts, huge, deadly, and cold. Soon the engine will grow beyond the confines of the shrine, and the building will come down around her ears.

"Moth! Moth! Are you here?"

THE BASTION

"You can stop now," Aramis said to Baradam Ghar, ignoring the guns leveled at him from across the room. "You can stop this now."

"How did he die?" *aras* Baradam said to Lady Vashmarna.

"We're losing it!" one of the scholars gasped. "It's failing! *Aras!*"

"Baradam," Lady Vashmarna said to Divaram's son, "where is your heaven? Your father is dead. You are tearing the *rasnan* in two. Where would you have us go?"

The earth shook again, as if to punctuate her words. The wound of the door was drifting, ever so slowly, moved by a current entirely different from the one that swept the shadows away. Where it moved, a crack formed in the floor, and the earth groaned with a deep, quiet, impossible sound that silenced them all for a breath.

Baradam looked as though he, too, were being torn apart. Lady Vashmarna, having seen the effort his father had needed to construct his lesser door, his momentary bridge from there to here, could not imagine what strength Baradam must spend to keep his door and the situation both in hand. His narrow, handsome face was the unnatural grey-black of weathered basalt, and rather than sweating, as Aramis was with the tension, his skin looked dry enough to crack.

"*Aras,*" a scholar whispered.

"Here," Baradam said. The word was like a stone dropped into the fearful silence, meaningless in its isolation. But then he turned his black gaze on Lady Vashmarna, and the weight of what he carried struck her like a blow. "Here? What does this place matter? It is there. It is there."

"Where is the good of it?" Aramis said, speaking like a man in pain. "Don't you see this is the only world we will ever have? *Aras,* there is *nothing there.*"

"This is the way. It is on the other side." Baradam spoke as if he and not his words were stone. "He will show us the way. You will see it," he said to Aramis, finally moving his stare from Lady Vashmarna's face. "You will see it first, and you will see what welcome heaven has for a traitor. Put him through."

His father's policemen understood him sooner than the rest of them. Two of them darted forward, shoved Lady Vashmarna aside, pulled Aramis toward the door. They dragged him as the shadows were dragged by nothing visible, and even Aramis needed a step or two before he grasped what was happening. He braced his feet against the floor and threw his weight against the policemen's grip.

"Vashmarna!" he shouted like a war cry.

"Aramis!" Lady Vashmarna cried out, freed by his voice from her shock. "Baradam, *aras,* you cannot go so far."

But the *aras* said nothing, watching the struggle with fixed and staring eyes.

Lady Vashmarna started forward, unarmed, without so much as a chair. One of the blue-coated policemen caught her back, effortlessly strong. She snarled with outrage. Another man pressed his weight against Aramis's back.

"Vashmarna!" Aramis was hoarse, but he sounded more furious than afraid. "Vashmarna!"

At which point, to everyone's surprise, the door behind *aras* Baradam burst open and men in the scarlet coats of the shaudah's livery crowded into the room, pistols in hand. The Ghar's men moved to defend the room, and they were the obvious targets for the shaudah's guards. Lady Vashmarna, shoved aside by the policeman who held her, was horrified to see both sides firing without compunction. What had these men learned in the tidal? Yet they were saving her. How ironic, that the shaudah should be saving her! For a dreadful moment there was nothing in the room but the crack of gunfire, the flare of muzzle fire and bursts of acrid smoke, the shouts of wounded men and the screams of the noncombatants. But every pistol could only manage a single shot, and when they were empty, there was no recourse but gun butts, batons, knives, and fists. A grunting, cursing masculine mayhem that was too familiar to Lady Vashmarna, who with the scholars scrambled to keep herself at the edges of the battle. There were other doors to the hall, but even then it did not occur to her to try to escape. She knew that this room was where the future of the *rasnan* would be decided.

The door still hovered like a black flame of nothing in the air.

THE TIDAL

"Moth! Are you here?"

Silk. Moth lifted her head, dizzy, her soul still streaming with the *mundab* even as her body was clenched in the engine's midst. She did not dare lift her head very far, and could not in any case see Silk past the engine's trashing limbs.

"Silk," she croaked, trying to shout through the smoke and the screaming dust. "What are you doing here?"

"Where are you?"

Moth had never heard that note in Silk's voice, a fearful desperation, a foretaste of grief.

"I'm in here."

"In . . . there?" Silk's voice went ragged. "Moth, are you still alive?"

"What?" Moth was jolted further into the tangible world.

"Of course I'm still alive! But you won't be if you stick around. Can't you see the building's about to fall down?"

"Can't you see . . . ?" Silk gulped. "Gods, Moth. Get the hell out of there!"

"I don't think I can," Moth said with perfect honesty. The engine surrounded her like a convulsing cage. "You get out."

"I knew you weren't that badly hurt," Silk said, though the accusation did not fit very well with her presence. "You come out of there right now!"

"I can't," Moth said. "I have to finish this."

"Finish *what*?" Silk shrieked.

It was too much to explain in the here and now, especially with the ceiling about to fall on Silk's head. "I'll tell you later," Moth said.

Silence beyond the engine's throbbing scream. Then Silk yelled, "You better!"

"Are you going now?"

Silk said something, but her voice was stretched too thin.

"Silk? Are you there?"

No answer. Moth was momentarily desolate, yet still warmed by the knowledge that Silk had come back for her. Silk had come back.

But the *mundab* is still pouring away.

She begins to drown. The *mundab* is absolute, but she is not. She is Moth, dedicant Moth, *rasnu* Moth, pregnant and lonely slum-girl Moth, and she cannot become the perfection of here. The engine must be that, the pole that balances the pole of the door, but it grows and grows and she fears it will never be large enough. The shrine's stone walls are battered out of true, the roof beams begin to fall, and the engine, a thrashing monster of ghost-lit limbs, tosses them aside like straws. The tide-washed floor shakes, another earthquake or the engine's pounding, and waves foam around the engine's lower limbs. It grows and grows, an embryo that will shatter its egg and still not be born, and Moth knows that she has got it wrong. Ignorant Moth, arrogant Moth. She sits inside her mad and useless child, her half-born god, and beats her fists against her head, trying to shake loose a single idea. She is cold to her bones, deaf from the screaming wheels and the pounding of the beaten air, breathing through the harsh pain of smoke and the salt of the swallowed sea, and still she does not know what to do. Let the *mundab* go, let the engine die unborn, let the door suck them all into heaven or hell.

But she can't, she won't. Stubborn Moth. She has been taught by scholars and engineers. Can she do no better than this? "Think," she says aloud, her voice no more audible than her child's. Poor froglet, are you even human anymore? "Think!"

The *mundab,* that ocean without shores, has discovered the concepts of here and away, of come and go. Moth needs to strike that balance, to stop this earth-tearing current from seething back and forth, to fix the *mundab* in place.

Oh.

Stupid Moth! This engine was conceived as the heart of a ship. It was designed to move, to travel, to pass between here and there. And why should the *mundab*'s ocean not move? Does the world's ocean not have its twice-daily tides, high at noon and midnight, low at sunset and dawn? Here and there, to come and to go, to have left and to arrive: these are not separate poles, they are two faces of the same thing. And Moth laughs aloud, unheard by anyone including herself, because she has already had that same thought, and had not realized what it meant. The Vashmarna and the Ghar and their plans for escape were always the same. Her engine and the Society's door are the same thing!

Brilliant Moth, whom the *mundab* loves. It will give her everything.

THE BASTION

The fighting was ugly. There were dead men on the floor.

Lady Vashmarna was in less danger now than during that first fusillade, but she was more frightened. Pistols are anonymous; men trying to kill one another with their hands have faces, blazing eyes, contorted mouths. The hatred among these men had been growing throughout the crisis, and now it was palpable, harsh as gun smoke in the air. Many of the scholars had fled, swept away by the violence as the shadows had been by the force of the door.

But the shadows, too, were fighting now, resisting the current that would suck them out of the world. It was hard for Lady Vashmarna to make sense of these apparitions. They were more like shadows than ever, the shadows of the fighting men that had torn themselves free from lamp flame and wall.

They were part of the chaos, like the wavering flame of nothingness that was the collapsing door.

Yes, it was collapsing. Lady Vashmarna felt a faint, distant triumph at that, or perhaps that was a lick of regret, but the forefront of her mind was occupied by fear. Fear for her own skin, and fear that the shaudah's men could not capitalize on their initial surprise. The Ghar's policemen were well trained and fighting for their lives. Instead of isolated knots of individual combat, there were groups forming, tactics being deployed. The shaudah—here in person! it must be the end of the world—was shouting orders from his corner, and Lady Vashmarna had a dreadful feeling that she should be doing the same, but "Stop!" was the only word in her mind. She pressed herself against a wall in panic when she heard her name in the shaudah's exasperated voice. A firm hand took her arm, and for an instant she was grateful.

"Come. Come with me. I'll show you the way."

But it was not Aramis, not even one of the shaudah's men. It was Baradam, stony, thick-voiced Baradam whose father she had killed (*Did I mean to?* she thought again. *Was it accident or murder?*), and his grip on her arm pressed the muscle against the bone.

"Come."

It was the Lamplighters riots again. It was the tyranny of animal strength over everything that makes a woman a person, her thoughts and feelings, her wit, her experience, her will, all of it rendered meaningless by the strength of an arm. Lady Vashmarna did not lose her head, but even so, what could she do? It had taken three men to force Aramis toward the door. Baradam towed her behind him with one hand. She was as helpless and as furious as a child about the unfairness of this, but she was too proud to scream.

But then, as if her need conjured him out of the midst of

battle, Aramis was there. He was bleeding from a red-lipped wound in his forehead, his mouth was split and swelling, he stumbled over the crack in the floor left by the door's slow drift, but he was there.

"*Jinnu,*" he said, putting himself in Baradam's path. "May I be of assistance?"

Oh, she loved this man! Tears of gratitude came into her eyes. "Please!"

"She goes," Baradam said. "We all go."

"*Aras,*" Aramis said gently. "You have the plague."

"We all go," Baradam said, and the door that wavered so close at hand trembled like a flame in a sudden breeze. "No!" Baradam cried, and stared, his concentration in tatters. The door continued to fail, while the tremors of plague shuddered through his limbs. Lady Vashmarna twisted free of his grasp, but this may have been a mistake, for she had regained his attention. He struck her in the face, and as she fell, he cried, "Ghars! To me, to me!"

"No!" Aramis shouted, and he grappled with Baradam.

Lady Vashmarna scrambled from under their feet, but there wasn't anywhere to go. The shadows crowded closely here, fighting to keep from the door, and they darkened this end of the room. Lady Vashmarna was afraid to touch them, and so were the men who tried to answer the *aras*'s call. They could not reach the three at the threshold of the door in any case; the shaudah's men had renewed their assault. The shaudah was shouting. There was nothing Lady Vashmarna could do. She turned back to the door as the floor began to shake again. A subtle shifting slide that mounted into a violent quake. Lady Vashmarna fell to her knees, most of the men fell, the lamps began to spill from their sconces on the walls. What she saw, she saw through a shaking, haunted darkness, a confusion of shadow and smoke and oil-fed flames.

Yet she saw it so clearly.

She saw Baradam and Aramis locked in a wrestlers' hold before the dwindling door. There could be no doubt that the door was closing. It was eating itself as it had eaten the shadows, as it would have eaten her. The shadows were thick now, their numbers growing as they were summoned and could not leave. In their midst, Baradam struggled with Aramis. To get away? To force Aramis through the door? To throw himself through the door? Lady Vashmarna could not guess, but she felt horror and pity at his plague-maddened face, the yellow foam that stained his gasping mouth. But the plague seemed to give him strength. Aramis was losing ground. Whether Baradam was trying to force him through the door or whether he was simply between the door and Baradam, Aramis's feet could not gain purchase on the polished floor. The door was failing, thin as shadows, nearly closed. Someone among the shaudah's men had kept his head better than the rest. He had primed his pistol and now, with Aramis's heels sliding, sliding, he shot Baradam in the back. Baradam's hands flew up, away from his enemy's shoulders, and he fell to his knees.

Aramis, deprived of Baradam's opposing force, overbalanced and fell into the closing door.

THE TIDAL

All Moth has to do is remind the *mundab* that it has always been one.

There is a paradox here, in that the engine's god, like the ship's, will be separate and distinct from the whole, but as a god it, too, will be whole. It will be the god of journeys, the god of departure and return. A kinder god than the *Firebird,* a more impartial presence to balance the exclusiveness, the fierce protectiveness, of the ship's partisan soul. Moth can feel that balance come into play as if a door has opened between two rooms, or a valve between two chambers of a heart. The engine, her new god's manifestation, slows its mad proliferation of cogs and pumping arms. It has filled the shrine, broken holes in the walls, and torn leaf-edged gaps in the roof. The stars are brighter even than the sparks that still lightly spangle the engine's form. Moth can see the constellations through the huge working parts that, running with condensation and brassy with the *mundab*'s reflected glow, mesh into a single dynamic pattern above her head.

As the Society's door closes into a singularity that becomes half of the god's twinned heart, the engine folds itself into a new configuration. The flailing armature withdraws from the crumbling walls; the grinding cogwheels tame themselves into a sleek and quiet whir. The whole churning mechanism settles peaceably into itself, and for one instant, as the *mundab* slips quietly past its new shore and the engine contracts in one elegant motion like a heart that beats for the first time, Moth—flesh-and-blood Moth with the torn skin and the burning lungs and the growing mystery in her womb—suffers a moment of salty terror that she is about to be crushed by a folding metal arm. But no. The engine settles itself around her as kindly as a lover, and she is haunted by a sudden powerful memory of Aramis's kiss.

And then it is done.

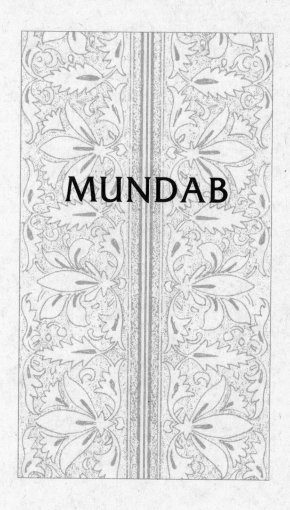

MUNDAB

THE ISLAND

Summer's heat had followed swiftly on the heels of the rain, but the shaudah had made a promise to herself, and she counted it a virtue that she always kept her promises, even those made in the privacy of her skull. She had led her staff on a tour of assessment through the towers, and now, while they immured themselves in Shaudarand's cool bottom story to write up their notes, she began the long climb up the stairs to her old apartment on the topmost floor. The tower's dead architects had put few windows in the stairwell, but the outer wall was made of milky quartz and she did not need to carry a candle. On this cloudless noon, the shaudah climbed through a light that was as soft and as hot as steam. Red-throated lizards fled her approach like glass beads spilled from a broken necklace. Their sticky toes were silent. The shaudah's feet tapping on the white stone steps made the only sound.

At first her mind was occupied with what she had most recently seen. The end of the plague had emptied the towers again, but the quarantine had left its mark. The public spaces that footed most of the towers were filthy, and so were many of the private apartments on the lowest floors. Toilets and bathrooms had become cesspits in the absence of running water and were overrun with flies. The shaudah had seen one room that had been blanketed with flies, every surface seething with a glossy, iridescent black before the startled insects had taken to the air, and the memory was all the more distinct against this white stairwell and its shy jewel-like inhabitants. But what did the lizards eat, if not this rare bounty of flies? The shaudah paused on a landing to catch her breath and contemplate this thought, but she drew no special meaning from it. What was, was.

A bad attitude for a ruler. The shaudah blotted her face on her sleeve and started up the next flight.

Her reign would be haunted by flies. The flies of the towers, the flies of the *hadaras,* where the receding floodwaters had left behind ruined terraces and muddy fields. "But the silt is very rich," a farmer had assured her. "The crops will be very fast, very good." A bad sign when the *hadri* felt the need to reassure their rulers, but what she remembered most clearly was the red mud drying on his calves, the black flies that crawled across his sweating neck. After having seen such extraordinary and terrible things, her eyes were obsessed with the ordinary. The flies of the *hadaras,* the flies of the tidal, where the dead still lay beneath the haphazard cairns of fallen walls. The slum dwellers seemed to assume that the tenements destroyed by the earthquake were permanent graves, for they had transplanted their roof gardens into earthy pockets among the rubble, wherever the tide could not reach. The shaudah had been offended by this—the dead were unclaimed, unnamed, seemingly unmourned—but she bit back her first comments until she had swallowed the lesson those rubble gardens offered her. "This is how hungry we are," those green-patched monuments said. "This is how little faith we have that you will rebuild our homes."

"Whose people are they?" the shaudah's daughter had said before she left. Or, no, she had put it more compellingly than that: "Remember whose people they are."

The shaudah decided she would stop to rest every five flights. In the months following the earthquake she had toured half the island and walked down every street and alleyway in the *shadras,* but the stairs were something else. With no one here to see, she slipped off her outer robe and hung it over the end of a handrail on the twentieth landing, to be collected on her way back down.

Remember whose people they are.

"They are your people." The startled lizards moved like a visible echo up and down the stairwell, a colorful shiver of the stone. The shaudah stopped on the stairs, forgetting herself. She was trying to remember if she had given Moth that answer at the time. Probably not. It was a subtle answer, and the circumstances had been wrong to try to speak to each other as equals. "They are your people" meant "therefore you should be the one to rule." It meant, "If I govern, it will be only as your predecessor." It meant, "You are my heir." But they were still strangers to each other, and Moth would probably have heard only "They are not mine."

Are you making excuses, Kalind?

The shaudah's conscience had taken on the voice of Divaram Ghar. It was the voice of a courteous ghost, unforgiving and dry.

You would have understood that subtlety, the shaudah told that voice. *She is too angry, and too young.*

Why be subtle? She would have understood if you had made it clear, Kalind. You were only afraid that she would see how little need any of them have for you, including her.

But they did need her, all the factions of the new *rasnan*. (The shaudah was puffing slightly, frowning, treading the stairs as if they, too, argued with her.) That was never so clear as in the hour after the earthquake, after Aramis's disappearance and Baradam's death. The tidal's rabble army had stormed the bastion; there was looting and senseless pockets of violence, arson, murderous confusion. If she had not taken command of the soldierly remnants of Ghar, if she had not summoned reinforcements from the fort, if she had not opened negotiations with the shadow cult's leaders, the whole of the *shadras* would have looked like the tidal by now.

If you had not traded your predecessor's life for your own, said Divaram's voice.

Yes, thought the shaudah with humility, *that too. But you see, while my daughter had the power to conquer the whole of the* rasnan, *she would have had to conquer it. The wealthy, the scholars, the craftsmen and* hadri *and engineers, all those people who had not dedicated themselves to the shadow gods as their only hope of salvation: those people would never have accepted her. They accept me, as the tidal accepts me for Moth's sake, and for the ship's, and so I can hold us together for a time.*

Until Moth returns with news of the new world, said the ghost, his voice as dry as the lost deserts of hell.

Until then.

It was perhaps her only remaining article of faith.

The shaudah remembered to stop. She was running with sweat and used her damp undersleeve to blot her face. The truth was, if Moth had stayed, the shadow cult would have been unmanageable and the good people of the bastion, the towers, the fort, would have risen up in their turn. Let Moth take herself and that haunted ship out of sight for a while. Let tempers subside and rumors wear themselves down into legend. Let the shaudah impose some order on their small world before her heir returned with her child and her gods in tow.

If you can, Kalind, said that dead, wry, knowing voice. *If you can.*

The shaudah climbed the last few flights of stairs and let herself into the upper corridor. It was black and airless and smelled dismally of mold. There were only two apartments on this floor, hers and the Chettenjis's. She groped her way to her door and fumbled the key into the lock.

The heat in the apartment with its big windows was intense. Like a weight, it squeezed a distinct odor out of every one of her things. The sweet smells of honey and aging wood out of her polished desk, the acidic smell of bleached rice straw out of her books and ledgers and scrolls, the bitter smell of dye out of the drapes, and the more homely smell of feet out of the rug. The familiarity of everything was painful. She had shaped these rooms to fit her, and the shape they made was a lonely one. Unbearably lonely. How had she never recognized that fact before? Loneliness furnished these rooms, loneliness chose these prayer tokens and artists' scrolls, loneliness wore this threadbare patch in the carpet before the study window. Loneliness stared through this glass for twenty years and never admitted to itself what it was looking for.

Today the shaudah knew. She stood in the heat of the fanless room and took stock of her demesne. The river spilled like a blue-green scarf down into the bay, barely touched by the lace of foam: the dam with its sluices was gone. She had known that, of course, but its absence was still a shock, even from this distance. "We will rebuild," the shaudah said over and over. "We will rebuild." But she had yet to determine where the labor and supplies would come from. They needed housing. They needed cesspools and gardens even more, and it was only the fact of the towers that kept a new generating station on anyone's agenda. Here was housing begging to be filled, but impossible to live in without power, without water, without a dam and a bridge.

Though "impossible" was a word whose definition changed daily. The shaudah's gaze took in the fort that threatened to slump into the river as the current eroded the dam's footings; the scholarium with its blackened and missing roofs; the bridge whose landward gap had become ordinary over time. And then she took in the tidal. Once, standing here, she had seen it as a singular entity, its details as meaningless to her as the pattern of scales on a lizard's back. But now she knew which tenements had fallen, and she knew the names of those that still stood. She knew which raw ruin under the hem of the bastion cliff was the broken shrine where the ship's engine had been born, and she could trace the path it had taken on its barge, floated out on the noon tide to the bay only three days after the night of the earthquake.

How had they managed? Cultists and Vashmarna engineers and the *Firebird*'s peasant crew had ignored the devastation around them, had made use of what they could, and had worked their way around the rest, as if it were the most ordinary task, as if they had been working in their natural state. It had been part work party, part circus, part funeral cortege— full of the emotions that might yet blow the *shadras* apart like a powder keg, but the shaudah gave its memory only half her mind. Mostly she was thinking about the towers, about the tenement wind pumps that she could see spinning on rooftops even from here, and about the ferocious will and ingenuity the slum dwellers brought to the fight for survival. Seawater could be used to flush pipes, and it could be distilled for potable water. Strong legs could manage the stairs. Fans and pumps could be driven by the wind. The shaudah nodded in unconscious confirmation of her decision. Her staffers were already plotting out the logistics, but it was she who would have to carry the new policy into the *shadras*. The former baysiders who had not already retreated to the *hadaras* and who could or would manage the new circumstances could have their old residences back, but all empty apartments and public spaces would be given over to the tidal's homeless. Let them bark.

Because their bark is so much less daunting than the prospect of your daughter's bite, murmured Divaram's ghost.

The shaudah left her old apartment empty-handed. In the black hallway she groped for the door across the hall. She had Shaudarand's master keys, and the Chettenjis' lock was no obstacle. She was not very interested in the apartment, although she did notice it was cluttered with useless things: she was developing an eye for the practical. She also noticed the heat, which, on the south side of the tower, was immense, but that, too, was irrelevant. It was only the window that mattered, the window that looked out past the towers, past the white stone and shining glass, the green-streaked copper and blackening bronze, past the domes and peaks and still-brilliant crowns, past the invisible boundary of the bay to the ocean, the wide horizon, and the deep impenetrable blue of the sky.

When she comes home.

THE SEA

"Are you asleep?"

Moth blinked. She was not asleep, but she had been somewhere very far away. "No," she said, and cleared her throat, summoning voice and expression and her waking self.

Silk climbed the rest of the way into the bower and sat at the end of Moth's sleeping mat. Moth pulled up her knees to make room, curling around her taut belly, and Silk settled comfortably on one arm, a very casual first mate. She seemed in no hurry to make her report, but the bower had that effect on people. High in the superstructure above the main deck, it was a room of dark leaves and scarlet flowers, smelling equally of honey and brine. The constant wind parted the leaves, opening windows onto the infinite blue of sea and sky, the golden shafts of the sun. The *Firebird* was a quiet ship, and up here Moth could hear the rustle of leaves, the claw-scratching of the emerald- and ruby-carapaced crabs in the vines, the mild voices of the crew on deck, the song of the lookout high above. Of the quiet engine she could hear nothing, but she felt it, as she felt it everywhere on the ship, the heart that beat softly against her own. She laid her hand against the smooth surface of the bower's floor, an unconscious gesture that she became aware of only when Silk echoed it with a touch of her own.

"The ship is well," she said. This was a ritual. Moth did not need to be told.

"And the crew?"

"Oh, the same." Silk rolled onto her stomach with her knees bent and her feet in the air, a position Moth had seen her take a thousand times, and pulled a vine aside for a clear view of the deck. "We fall into a trance of going and going and going, and then someone wakes up and there's a flurry."

"What this time?" Moth suddenly yawned. She had been closer to sleep than she had realized. She wondered sometimes how much of the crew's mood was really hers, transmitted by some quiet dreaming of the ship, but she usually scolded herself for the thought. Arrogant Moth.

"The stars again."

This had happened twice before: someone sleeping on deck would wake to see strange stars overhead, the constellations of an alien sky. Moth had never seen it, and doubted the ship could slip into other seas without her knowing, but she was never entirely certain. The *Firebird* knew her own mind, and the engine was half the Society's door.

"Well," Moth said now, "if there are other seas, they are as wide and empty as our own."

"I hope you don't talk like that in front of the crew," Silk said without heat. She had her chin propped on her hands. "Believe me, with that timepiece of yours always in front of them, they know how long it's been since we last saw land."

"Timepiece!" Moth was mildly offended. "What am I, a clockwork womb?"

Silk grinned, and after a moment's silence—the leaves, the lookout's song, the deep watery hiss of the bow cutting through the swells—she crawled over to press her ear against the warm bare skin of Moth's belly.

"Tick, tick, tick," she said.

Moth pulled Silk's hair, and shifted to accommodate her rangy form.

"I'll bet you haven't heard that story yet," Silk said.

"What story?"

Their voices did not change, but Moth was aware that this was what Silk had climbed up here to say.

"That that's the ship's child, or the engine's." Silk made a small sound, a fragment of a laugh caught in her throat. "It depends on whether you're talking to a crewman or an engineer. The engine or the ship."

"That old division persists?" said Moth, but Silk was not to be diverted.

"They say that you never lay with a man—mark you, that you're too innocent, or too holy, or too strange to have lain with a man—" Silk laughed.

"Thank you."

"They say it was conceived when the ship was, or the engine, or when they were wedded in the *shadras* bay. That's the best story. There'll be a song about that, about the ship and the engine being wedded and bedded and leaving you to carry the consequences."

"The timing's all wrong," Moth said, still mild. "I'd hardly be showing if that were true."

"Well, and that's part of the argument. Oh," said the *Firebird*'s mate with an irresponsible glee, "there'll be blood spilled over this, you wait and see. But there's some who say that as it's an unnatural child, there's no expecting it to keep to the natural term. And there's some among them who say that the term of the child is the term of the journey, and the larger your belly gets the closer we come to the new shore—and there's some among *them* who're laying down bets about the day."

"What odds did you get?"

Silk gave a sly, involuntary grin, but then she sobered. "But it's in the dark that the dark tales are told, about what's going to be born, and what kind of shore we'll reach come the day. They'll love it, mind you." Silk laid a gentle hand over Moth's prominent navel. "Whatever it is, they'll love it, the ship's child. But they're afraid. Afraid of what they'll become, and afraid of what new land they'll have to live in, if they must change to live in it."

The new land. That was all any of them thought about these days: the new land, not the old. The future, not the past. Now *there* was a change worth fostering, thought a Moth who carried almost too much past to bear. Children were playing in the vines, climbing through the ship's folded wings, the vine-clad bones and secret bowers of the superstructure, risking worse than broken necks if they disturbed some lovers in a tryst, but none of them dared the narrow section above the bow. That was Moth's, and the children never risked disturbing her.

Moth sat up, oppressed by Silk's proximity. Sunlight danced through the shivering leaves, casting bright patterns across her skin.

"You knew him," Moth said at last. "Aramis. He was a good man. A good and loyal and entirely human man. There is nothing strange about the seed the child grows from."

"So, well." Silk picked at a frayed edge of the mat. "The Vashmarna men talk about how he died."

"He's gone, not—" But Moth bit off her protest. He wasn't, and yet he was, if she believed her mother's tale.

"He's a hero." Silk broke off a straw end and flicked it

over the bower's side. With rare diffidence, she said, "But even those who were there when he spoke of your child don't really believe it was ever his. If you'd let me put that story about, just to balance the shadow tales—"

"No."

"But it's a good story. It makes you more human. It'd reassure the crew."

"No," Moth said again. "Let them believe it's the engine's child. Better they be surprised by a human infant than by the other."

Silk ducked her head so Moth could not see her face. "Is it . . . ?"

"I don't know."

The lookout had begun a new song, this one as sad as the last, a peasant's song about hunger and rain. The wind blew through the dark leaves, a small crab bright as gemstones clung to a nodding vine, the sun painted the red flowers with a pollen of gold. The ship powered on, the engine driving as steady as a living heart. Silk straightened and tucked her hair behind her ears.

"How long before it's born?" she asked practically.

"Soon," Moth said, feeling again the slow tightening in her lower back, the hard pressure at the floor of her womb.

"My money's on a few days more. You won't make me lose my bet, will you?"

Moth grinned in spite of herself. "I'll try," she said. "But you'll have to cut me in."

Silk opened her mouth to respond, but did not speak.

The lookout had broken off his song.

Moth could feel him thinking. She could feel his hands tighten on the crow's nest rail, she could feel the sweat start out all over his wind-cooled skin, she could feel the strain of the muscles around his eyes. She knew he was testing himself against all the false hopes they had already seen: the fog banks, the rafts of weed, the clouds that all looked like the rim of the new land breasting the horizon. In a moment he would relax, clear his throat and spit, take up his song. Moth could feel the air move in his lungs.

And then she felt the tension of the moment give in a rush of clear water from her womb. Silk, feeling the sudden dampness soaking the mat, looked down at Moth's belly, and then up into her eyes.

"You've cost me five ripe *dayendis*," she said.

GLOSSARY

andas: A secular term of respect for a common man. **Andu** is the feminine form. **'das** and **'du** are the abbreviations.

aras: The priests' and scholars' honorific. The feminine form is **rasnu.**

bastion: Built on a shelf of land defined by low seaward cliffs to the south, the Anamas River to the east, and hills to the north and west, it contains some of the oldest buildings in the *rasnan*. The **fort,** a stone fortress of classic design, was the first permanent dwelling place of the ancestors after their arrival in this world; the **scholarium** is a more organic community of buildings built and amended through the generations.

bay or **towers:** The grandest precinct of the *shadras* and the demesne of the Ghar family. The towers were the solution of the shaudah Itteran to the increasingly dire problem of crowding in the bastion. This visionary ruler ordered construction of immense towers on the rocky reefs that protected the *shadras* bay from the worst of the ocean storms, and in doing so he completely changed the face of the *rasnan*.

dedicant: A scholar-in-training who has passed through a priest's novitiate but who has not yet taken priestly vows.

demesne: *Hadaras* demesnes are typically identified with their physical territories, but in fact a demesne is more accurately defined by its governing family or lord, membership, and occupation; this is especially true for Vashmarna. With the sole exception of Ghar, all the demesnes are bound together by a complex web of leased territories and "lent" personnel, traveling buyers and pack trains, village agents and *shadras* godowns or warehouses. "The **temple**" is the popular shorthand for the demesne of scholars and priests.

hadaras: Literally, "countryside." The vast majority of the *rasnan* is rural and divided into demesnes typically governed by a single family, although in the western mountains there are a handful of collectives. Villages are densely populated in order to preserve the maximum amount of arable land. Literacy is low, and the orthodoxy flourishes. **Hadri** means "of or from the countryside" and is used as both an adjective and a noun.

hend: A noncommissioned officer.

janaras: A term of respect reserved for the shaudah, derived from the same root as *aras*. **Janarasan** is the objective form, as one might say "His Majesty."

jandas: A secular term of respect for the lord of a demesne. **Jandasan** is the objective form, equivalent to "his lordship," and **jan'** is a familiar abbreviation. The feminine forms are **jinnu, jinnuju,** and **jin',** respectively. Please note that the objective form is occasionally used to denote particular respect in direct address.

manifest: Moth's word for the visible, and occasionally tangible, "manifestation" of the act of drawing power from the *mundab,* or possibly the manifestation of the intersection between the mystical and the physical realms. Called **"shadow gods"** by the tidal folk and **"demons"** by the orthodoxy. No one knows manifests' substance, their genesis, or their purpose.

mundab: Literally, "the great outside" or "the great beyond." The ancestors' word for the ocean surrounding the *rasnan,* which was regarded as a wilderness devoid of human meaning and absent of the *ramhadras*'s gods. In modern times, the martyred scholar Mahogan conceived the idea that the *mundab* was home to, and even the embodiment of, the divine force native to this world—a force more responsive than, and perhaps superior to, the lost gods of the *ramhadras.* The **mundabi** are followers of Mahogan's teachings, heretics and rebels against the temple's orthodox rule.

purdar: An officer in a regular military or paramilitary force holding a field command.

ramhadras: Literally, "birth country." According to orthodox belief, *ramhadras* is the world of human origin, also called the "first world." Tradition holds that the first world was destroyed or rendered uninhabitable (interpretations vary) by a combination of technological and magical excess.

rasnan: Loosely, "second country"; more literally, "foster-land." It refers to the land the ancestors discovered when they escaped the destruction of the *ramhadras*. Popular usage now defines *rasnan* as "the known world" because it is in fact the only land ever discovered on the face of the ocean. As far as anyone knows, the *rasnan* supports the only human population in the world.

shadras: Literally, "not countryside." The *shadras* is the only large population center in the *rasnan*. Divided into several distinct precincts, it is densely populated and characterized by the most advanced technology in the *rasnan*. Each of the precincts is ruled by a different demesne, owing allegiance directly to the highest governing power, the shaudah, except for the tidal slum, which is claimed by no one. **Shadri** means "of or from the *shadras*," and its usage is equivalent to that of *hadri*.

shaudah: The ultimate legal authority of the *rasnan*. Originally, the shaudah was a kind of chief justice, but in modern times, the shaudah rules all demesnes through an uneasy combination of social contract and implied force.

tidal: The *shadras* slum, built on the tidal flats below the bastion's seaward wall during the generations it took to build the towers; the first tenements were the "temporary" living quarters of construction workers conscripted from *hadaras* farms. Those born in the modern tidal still retain the fierce pride of their ancestors, and remember with great bitterness the sudden loss of employment once the towers were completed. Tidal-dwellers also remember the lack of welcome from extended families who had remained in the *hadaras,* and the wealth, both material and technological— that the towers represented and that the tidal-dwellers were denied.

ABOUT THE AUTHOR

HOLLY PHILLIPS' poetry and short fiction has appeared in magazines as diverse as *Asimov's Science Fiction* and *The New Quarterly*. Her first book-length publication, a collection titled *In the Palace of Repose*, received widespread critical acclaim, won the 2006 Sunburst Award for Canadian Literature of the Fantastic, and was nominated for two World Fantasy Awards. She lives with her cat in Victoria, British Columbia, Canada.